Susan Salli of the most
successful v Her novels
include the d by Angels,
*Choices, Co Garden, The
Apple Barrel ydia Fielding*
and *Five Farthings*. She lives in Clevedon, Somerset.

THE PUMPKIN COACH

Susan Sallis

CORGI BOOKS

THE PUMPKIN COACH
A CORGI BOOK : 9780552151443

Originally published in Great Britain by Bantam Press,
a division of Transworld Publishers

PRINTING HISTORY
Bantam Press edition published 2004
Corgi edition published 2004

3 5 7 9 10 8 6 4

Copyright © Susan Sallis 2004

Set in 11/12pt New Baskerville by
Falcon Oast Graphic Art Ltd.

Corgi Books are published by Transworld Publishers,
61–63 Uxbridge Road, London W5 5SA,
A Random House Group Company.

Addresses for Random House Group Ltd companies outside the UK
can be found at: www.randomhouse.co.uk
The Random House Group Ltd Reg. No. 954009.

Printed and bound in Great Britain by
Cox & Wyman Ltd, Reading, Berkshire.

The Random House Group Limited supports The Forest Stewardship
Council (FSC), the leading international forest certification organisation.
All our titles that are printed on Greenpeace approved FSC certified paper
carry the FSC logo. Our paper procurement policy can be found at:
www.rbooks.co.uk/environment.

Mixed Sources
Product group from well-managed
forests and other controlled sources
www.fsc.org Cert no. TT-COC-2139
© 1996 Forest Stewardship Council

For my grandparents

Prologue

Early in June 1910, the Honourable Richard Bracewell of the Great Western Railway came to visit the Forest of Dean network of private lines – bought by them piecemeal and often closed down immediately – with a view to housing an arsenal in the forest; an arsenal easily accessed by the myriad lines snaking through the trees. It wasn't a very serious investigation; after all, no one believed there would be a war – not when all the royal families of Europe were blood relations. But it was a day out riding trains, and the other members of the Board had had a wonderful time in Wales and Cornwall. Now he was going to do likewise.

The Honourable – as he was known – was not disappointed. Two of the local station masters accompanied him and at one point he actually rode in the cab and blew the whistle. He was not without imagination, and could see how these small fingers of iron must have connected families as well as coal mines. The wood – English oak, no less – which, over millions of years, turned into coal, had been on hand for the sleepers, and there had been plenty of ballast dug out of the family-owned mines. The foresters could not have continued to lay railway lines wherever it suited them: the danger was appalling. But he could see in his mind's eye how convenient these meandering iron roads must have been. Mothers visiting daughters in service, neighbours exchanging a basket of eggs for a sack of turnips . . . And now the massive Great Western was going to swallow it all up. Not that he cared; not really. He was trapped in a marriage made for him by his father, and for the first time in his dilettante life he had fallen in love. He couldn't think clearly of anything else. Rosalind . . . his beautiful Rosalind. Modest and high principled, too. She would need – and deserved – a very special seduction.

They could not investigate all the redundant lines; he saw it would take days and he rapidly lost interest in the project. In a way, he wished there would be a war so that he could do something splendid, and she would adore him as he adored her. But because he wanted a war, he was pretty certain there would not be one. That was how things worked.

However, the Honourable saw enough that day to give him a wonderful idea. This was an idyllic place; there were clearings in the forest like enormous cathedrals, where light filtered through the leaves as if through stained glass. Some of the overworked pits were filled with water and lined with ferns; he could imagine swimming there . . . being dried by tender hands . . . frying bacon over a camp fire.

He spoke in a low tone to one of the station masters by his side. 'I might send a spare coach along one of these sidings.' He frowned, recalling the latest rolling stock in the Swindon workshops.

'Yes, I think I could manage that. I suppose I could buy a piece of land around the siding, sufficiently large to give me some privacy.'

The station master, who knew exactly what he meant, said cautiously, 'The forest is owned by the freeholders, sir. There are meetings when certain rights are discussed.'

'You can arrange it for me then, can you? The siding by that pool would be excellent,' he beamed. 'Good man! I knew I could rely on you. I certainly won't forget this.'

Hoping for promotion, the station master did his best with the stubborn forest freeholders. With great difficulty, he got some kind of lease cobbled together and sent it off to the address given to him so privately. In due course, a brand-new coach arrived from Lydney and was shunted into the siding. The station master's wife made curtains for the windows and provided her best linen. When the Honourable arrived with his companion, she brought food and pails of water. The station master arranged for milk to be left by the ganger. The lady – the station master's wife soon discovered her name was Miss Rosalind Chatterton – wore a veil, through which she gazed dotingly at her companion. Everyone was happy.

The station master smiled sentimentally. 'They looked happy as pigs in clover, missus. I reckon they'll be here again within the month.'

'Not if she tells him she's expecting, they won't.' The station master's wife pursed her lips. 'He don't want no trouble. Not in his job. Honourable, indeed – he's a married man. His wife might stand for a weekend now and then, but if there's a baby she'll make a fuss.'

9

'Surely there won't be a baby! Not after one weekend.'

His wife stared at him pityingly. 'There will be a baby, I can tell. Next May or beginning of June, I reckon,' she said, working it out as she spoke. She closed her eyes for a moment. 'It'll be a girl.'

The station master looked sharply at his wife, because she had a reputation for spotting a pregnancy during its first week. 'I hope not. She wouldn't say boo to a goose.'

'That's why he chose her,' she said scornfully. 'But she's a Chatterton. Crest on her case. She'll be all right. The family will rally round.'

They never found out what happened to Miss Rosalind Chatterton; but the station master heard that the Honourable Richard Bracewell had taken a commission in the Guards, or, as his missus put it succinctly, 'Someone told his wife and she kicked him out.'

'Told you, didn't I?' she said, several times.

'We don't know that's how it was,' he protested, because he was a fair man. 'It might have nothing to do with . . . all that.'

His wife did not bother to reply, and he sighed regretfully. 'Anyway, there goes my promotion. Wouldn't have minded a bigger station. Or a nice warm job in the office.'

But his wife was forest-bred. 'Couldn't leave here. Not now.'

When the War started, the Honourable Richard Bracewell was amongst the first casualties. There were some mild enquiries about the ownership of the coach and its site, but there were more important things to think about during those four years. The coach stayed where it was, ignored by the freeholders and railway officials alike. Paint flaked from it and the curtains were eaten by moths; but it had been well made and would remain there for many years to come. The station master's daughter liked to swim there in the summer, and used it for changing into her bathing dress. A few local lads would hide behind the bushes to watch her. She never discouraged them. Other couples used the coach as well and for a time it almost became a house of ill-repute. No decent girl would be seen dead anywhere near it.

Then came the second great war – the one to end all wars. This time the Forest of Dean was used by the Ministry of Defence, whose rolls of barbed wire made the area inaccessible. The pools were requisitioned as a water supply for possible fires and a huge camouflage net was draped over the coach – though no one could understand why, as it would have been invisible from the air anyway.

A woman and child came that way during the War. She was still young, not yet thirty, and the boy was eleven, still in knee-length trousers and gartered socks. He helped his mother avoid the barbed wire and was obviously anxious for her.

'Why have you brought us here, Ma? You're going to rip your skirt or something. And we're probably not supposed to be this side of the wire.'

His mother was puzzled. 'Your grandmother brought me here when I was expecting you. I wanted to show you . . . it must have gone. It doesn't matter.' She let herself be led back the way they had come and on to the main footpath.

'Anyway dear, boys aren't supposed to mind a bit of barbed wire! If the War lasts much longer, you'll have worse than that to contend with!'

'Thanks, Ma!' He smiled at her encouragingly, because when she spoke like that he knew she was thinking of his father and the way he had died, and was likely to become melancholy.

But after a moment, she grinned back. 'Sorry, love. It's just that it seems awful it's vanished . . . Mamma always was a bit of a dreamer, if you recall. She showed me this place in the same way as I have taken you to Kent and shown you that little naval house where Pa and I lived when he was stationed—' Her voice broke slightly and the boy hugged her arm. She laughed apologetically. 'Sorry, love. I take after your grandmother, don't I? On the sentimental side.'

'A bit, yes.'

'It's just that . . . I thought it sounded rather romantic.'

'What did?'

'The coach where she spent her honeymoon. A railway coach. Next to a deep lake. She and my father used to bathe there in the moonlight. And cook by a camp fire.' She laughed again. 'I thought, as we were here, I might be able to find it again. But it must have rotted away.'

The boy looked doubtful. 'There's no railway here, Ma.' He glanced sideways at her. She had not been herself since his father had been killed in action. He hugged her arm to his side. 'Let's go back to the digs and have some tea, shall we?'

'Why not?' She glanced behind her and then said, 'She called it the Pumpkin Coach. Like Cinderella's. You remember?'

'I remember. Watch you don't walk in that mud, Ma.'

'All right, my dear.' She smiled. 'This little holiday was such a good idea. We can go home soon and make a fresh start.'

'Yes.' The boy nodded. 'Let's do that.'

And they wandered back through the canopied trees to their digs, which their parish priest had recommended to them as offering a complete change.

One

The real reason Alice Pettiford left school when she was sixteen was because she did not have a hope of getting a State scholarship to go to University. So what was the point in hanging on? She had just finished her first term in the Lower Sixth, doing English, History and German, and backing them up with a secretarial course which took place once a week in one of the school attics – which just went to show how seriously shorthand and typing were taken by Dr Grey, the headmistress. Alice could now take shorthand at 100 words per minute and type at sixty, so she could apply for any of the jobs advertised nightly in the *Citizen*. And though she would miss her teachers, especially English scholar Miss Plant, Miss Stone (known as the Ancient Brit) and Fräulein Schmidt, whom Alice would cheerfully die for, most of the jobs listed in the Situations Vacant columns paid thirty shillings a week, which seemed like a fortune at the start of 1946.

Alice's mother and father never stayed up to see in the New Year – it had gone right out of fashion during the War – but Alice woke when the tugs in the docks blew their hooters, and sat up in bed to rub a peephole in the window. She looked out at the stars above Farmer Davis's field and made a resolution.

'You see, God,' she began – she had bargained with Him all through the War to keep her friends and family safe, and He had done just that, so she was on good terms with Him – 'there are just two scholarships, and one is for a boy, so as far as I'm concerned that means just one scholarship. And we both know who'll get it, don't we?' She tugged emphatically at her fair hair to make her point.

God sighed and said He supposed so. He didn't agree with competition among His children, but that was the way they wanted it.

'So I might just as well leave, mightn't I?'

God sighed again but said nothing, which meant He had a lot of reservations.

Alice tried for compromise. 'Tell you what.' She humped one of her pillows round to the front and hugged it. The space she had cleared in the window rime had frozen over already. 'I won't say anything to Mum for a bit. Till you send me a sign. Will that be all right?'

God tried to explain yet again about free will and Alice said hurriedly, 'I know, I know. But I'll still make up my own mind.'

God said nothing, which Alice guessed meant she'd gone too far. She closed her eyes, then opened them quickly in case she could get a glimpse of a comet through the iced windows. That at least would be a sign that He had heard. There were no flashes, not even one firework. It was her turn to sigh. But just as she had returned her pillow to the bedhead and snuggled down again, expecting that sleep would come instantly now that there were no doodlebugs, V2s, or broken-engine sounds as the Nazi planes made for Birmingham and Coventry, someone let off a detonator down at the marshalling yard. She opened her eyes wide for a moment, wondering whether that was the sign. But her father was a railwayman and she knew that the shunters who were already assembling goods trains down at the yard were choosing their own way of heralding in 1946.

She smiled, closed her eyes and was instantly asleep.

That was the real reason for 'throwing her grammar-school education on to the back of the fire', as her mother would doubtless put it. But then, after the snow finished falling, for two weeks making a landscape of such exquisite beauty it 'fair took your breath from your body' – that was from Gran – and then changed into grey slush that was utterly depressing, something happened which appeared to make Alice's decision inevitable. It could have been a sign sent by God, though it was against His usual policy. His penchant for non–interference had extended to refusing to stop the War on the grounds that He had not started it. So He was hardly likely to have engineered a little war within the Pettiford family. But a war there was.

Alice had been aware since she was twelve that her mother and father were not the ideal pair, even if they looked it. Dad was rather ordinary, brown hair and moustache, deeply grey eyes; but he looked all right, sometimes almost handsome. But Mum was special; her hair was deep gold, her eyes intensely blue. Alice took after her, but Alice was just fair; Doffie was vivid. However, Dad was not like the men portrayed in Mum's magazines, who would produce flowers and chocolates, black-market or otherwise, walk on the outside of the pavement and protect their beloved from the faintest of chill winds. Dad hadn't been around much during the War, because he had been involved in the troop movements up and down the country and had had to work all hours. So Doffie and Alice between them had got in the coal when there was any, and when there wasn't they'd taken the old pram and walked the three miles to the coal sidings to buy their own and walk back home again. More often than not, Doffie emptied the grate. Alice would have done it but the ashes were usually still hot and her mother was frightened she might burn herself. There were lots of other things: whenever her father forgot to wipe his feet or change into his slippers, Doffie would stare pointedly at the muddy footmarks on the linoleum. Ted had to keep his strength up for work of national importance, so his wife and daughter would halve their cheese and butter rations and give the rest to him. He didn't know, of course. He was amazed when – after he'd told Doffie smilingly that Gran used her own rations to make him 'proper butter sandwiches' whenever he called in – she erupted.

'We've been giving up our own food for you! And all the time . . . my God, never again! Alice is a growing girl and needs every bit of sustenance. I am appalled that you could take your mother's food from her mouth, your daughter's food from hers—'

Ted, bewildered, was unable to argue with his

fiery wife. He stared at her and his slate-grey eyes turned cold. Alice knew what would happen next; so did Doffie. Whenever there was a row, Ted had only one method of defence. He clammed up. He hardly spoke to Alice and he did not speak to his wife at all. He sent them to Coventry.

Alice's heart sank. If only he would shout back, all would be well and Mum would forgive him in about two hours. But this . . . Silence drained her mother of her lifeblood. She would swear he was not going to get the better of her this time. But he would.

Alice tried to mediate. 'Dad, we don't mind. Honestly. You have to keep the trains going—'

Doffie interjected bitterly, 'Single-handedly, of course.'

'And we know that the only way we can help is to support you.'

Ted looked coldly at her and said briefly, 'Keep out of this. You don't know what you're talking about.'

That did it. Doffie went into a purple rage. 'How dare you speak to your daughter in that way! She's being utterly reasonable and you tell her to shut her mouth! I simply won't stand aside and see her insulted—'

Ted raised a placatory hand, and Doffie screamed, 'You touch her and we leave. I've warned you, Ted! Put a hand on Alice, and we're finished!'

He made a sound of disgust and turned away.

That night, Doffie slept next to the embers of the fire, on the camp bed they had used under the stairs for Alice in the War. Alice had thoroughly enjoyed it, until she realized that if her parents were both killed and she was left alive under the stairs, she would probably have to live with Gran. She did not sleep there again.

Doffie was warm next to the grate but, as she confided to Alice the next morning when they were washing up the breakfast things, it should have been her father sleeping there.

'He had a very poor education,' she said, glancing meaningfully at Alice. 'He probably does not know the meaning of the word "chivalry".'

'He wasn't going to hit me, Mum,' Alice mentioned unwisely.

Doffie took her hands out of the water and looked round like a wounded tigress. 'Whose side are you on?' she asked.

'Yours, of course. But you know how it gets you. Not speaking and everything.'

'It won't this time. I shall simply ignore him, as he is ignoring me. And next time I go to see Gran, I shall tell *her* a thing or two.'

Alice made no comment. Gran had never considered Doffie to be a suitable wife for her son, and tended to give her a great deal of unwanted advice unless Ted or Alice were there to jolly things along.

At first Alice did not see this as a sign from God at all. All she was concerned about was trying to get Dad to talk to Mum. When he fluffed open the newspaper at mealtimes and held it as a screen in front of his face, she would say cheerfully, 'Anything interesting, Dad? Fräulein Schmidt says she is going to work for the Red Cross in the Displaced Persons camps. She says there are millions of people trying to find their families. She says—'

Dad rustled the paper like a firecracker. 'Nothing about that here. That woman knows a sight too much for her own good, I reckon.'

Alice bit her lip; she had forgotten that her father had always maintained that Fräulein Schmidt was a Fifth Columnist and should be interned.

She said as mildly as possible, 'She's married to a German Jew. That's all, Dad. She had to call herself Fräulein because the school does not admit married teachers.'

'He knows all that, Alice.' Mum spoke wearily. 'We've told him often enough. Don't bother. Ask him whether he wants any bread and butter pudding.'

'Do you want any bread and butter pudding, Dad?' Alice asked obediently.

'No. You have it, Alice. You need building up.'

Mum did not wait for Alice's message. She piled the pudding on to Alice's dish and passed it to her with a smile.

'Did he say no thank you?'

Alice swallowed. 'I didn't hear.'

'I bet you didn't.'

Alice could almost hear Mum's mainspring being wound up. She shivered.

Two days later the spring broke.

It was Sunday, so they were having afternoon tea. Mum had made a caraway seed cake, which Dad always liked, and had put it on the cake stand with a paper doily underneath and the cake slice at the ready.

'Will you ask your father if he would like a slice

of cake, Alice dear?' she asked with a slight tremor in her voice.

Ted did not wait. 'No, thank you.' He could have been speaking directly to her, so he added quickly, 'Alice.'

Doffie said almost pleadingly, 'It's seedy cake.' That was what he called it. He had said on many an occasion, 'No one makes seedy cake like you do, our Doffie.'

Alice knew, of course, that Doffie was concertina'd from Dorothy, but she had asked Dad once why he always prefaced it so possessively. He had been flummoxed. 'Don't know, Chick. Family, you know. We've always done it.'

That was true. Gran always called him 'our Ted'. She even called Mum 'our Dorothy'. And another thing, Dad often called Alice 'Chick'. And Gran called her 'Duck', even though they were railway people, not poultry farmers.

Alice looked at the back of her father's newspaper and willed him to put it down and accept a slice of seedy cake. But the paper remained in place and not a word was spoken.

Doffie poured the tea. Her hand was definitely shaking now. She passed Alice a cup and then held another one in front of the newspaper. Alice could see her gathering herself together to slam through the barriers.

She said, her voice high, 'Your tea, Ted.'

Nothing happened. Nothing at all. The cup began to shake in its saucer but the paper did not move and Ted did not speak.

Doffie stood up and looked over the top of the back page. She held the saucer in one hand, the teacup in the other. 'Can't manage it all by yourself, Ted? Here you are, then.' And she flung the contents – and the cup itself – right at him.

She fled the room and hurried upstairs, while Ted spluttered and threw down the paper, up-setting the milk jug in an attempt to beat the scalding tea from his chin and his shirt front. The bedroom door closed with an almighty crash and two or three flakes of whitewash floated gently from the ceiling, adding to the general disarray of the tea table.

Still, incredibly, Ted said nothing. He made noises – of pain and disgust – but there were no words. Alice, tight against the back of her chair, watched in horror and knew that this was it. Just when they should be getting back to normal after the War, everything was smashed. What Hitler couldn't do, the Pettifords had managed very well for themselves. She started to cry. And at last her father spoke.

'Stop that, our Alice! Get me a cloth and some cold water.'

She ran for a clean tea towel, discovered the enamel washing-up bowl full of dinner pots soak-ing, scrabbled them on to the soggy wooden draining board and took the dripping bowl into the front room.

Ted had taken his shirt off and was holding his vest away from his body. 'You took your time,' he said. He soaked the tea towel and applied it to his chest. 'What's that floating on the water?'

'Burnt bits from the bread and butter pudding,' Alice sobbed.

'Oh Christ.' Ted closed his eyes. He never swore, so Alice knew he must be in considerable pain. 'What's the matter with the woman?'

Alice's heart sank. Her father had never before referred to her mother as 'the woman'. She was sure it must be the end.

She gave a great cry and cast herself at him.

'What the—?' His question was smothered by Alice's sobbing, but eventually her voice emerged almost clearly. Much later, she was to marvel at how her brain had continued to work through such distress. It confirmed her belief that God worked in mysterious ways.

'Don't leave her! Don't leave her, Dad! I love you! I can't bear it if you go!' she cried.

He swore again, but took her hand in his and held it very tightly. She eased herself away from him slightly but did not get up. 'Listen – listen, Dad. I'm going to leave school at the end of next term. Let me come and work with you in the office. I can do shorthand and typing and filing and – and—'

He was trying to look into her eyes, but her hair was everywhere. He said slowly, 'You and your Mum, you've never been interested in what I do. Why this sudden change?'

'I want to be interested! Then I can tell Mum and—'

'She's bored stiff when I tell her about work.'

'That's because you go on and on about wagons and rolling stocks stuck in depots somewhere when they're wanted somewhere else.'

'Wagons *are* rolling stock, our Alice.'

'Are they?'

'What did you think they were?'

'Stocks on rollers.'

'Stocks? Stocks of something?'

'No. Stocks like in villages. When you're

locked into them and people throw stuff at you.'

'Oh, Alice. And you a grammar-school girl!'

But he was smiling. He was actually smiling. She tried to smile back, but her mouth was still trembling.

'There aren't any jobs in the office, our Alice. And I don't know whether you'd like it there. And I know damned well your mum would hate you working there.'

'I can talk her round, Dad. I can, really. I'll go to Tech and do evening classes. Then maybe one day . . . you never know.'

He looked doubtful. 'Well, you can certainly talk to your mother, I'll say that. If a job comes up, I'll let you know. Will that do?'

'Yes. But only if you promise not to leave us. You must stay till I can make it better.'

He looked surprised. 'What's all this about me going?'

Alice waved her hands. 'Well, the rows and all. Mum can't take it.'

'Then surely it would be Mum who would leave?' He wasn't taking her seriously, there was a little smile under his moustache.

She sighed. 'We've got nowhere to go, Dad.'

'My God. Would you go with her then?'

'I'd have to. I'd have to get a job so that we could live.'

He stared at her for a long time. Then he lowered his knee so that she had to stand up. 'You don't know what you're on about, our Alice. But . . . all right, I won't go. And neither will you and Mum. And we'll see about a job on the railway.'

She stood in front of him uncertainly, then began to clear up the mess. Ted took his shirt into the kitchen and put it in a bucket of water. When he came back, Alice was eating some seedy cake. He had a slice too. Then he took a slice up to Doffie.

That night Alice said, 'Dear God, it was a big sign but it was a good one. I'm quite scared about working for Dad. You'll have to help me. Then I can explain properly to Mum about what Dad does.'

God smiled. He liked his children to talk to each other.

Alice looked out of her window at the rain trying futilely to wash the dark away. She thought of something and beamed happily. 'I must tell Dad that in the beginning was the word. It might stop him sending us to Coventry.'

Two

Gran stirred the teapot with one hand, holding on to the table edge with the other, and surveyed Alice from beneath the brim of the hat she put on at six each morning and took off at nine each night.

'Thought you said you had two years still to go?'

'Yes ... Well.' Alice had not anticipated even the slightest criticism from Gran regarding her decision to leave school at Easter. It had been Gran who had told her she should be earning her living at fourteen, not swanning around living off her dad. It had been Gran who had reminded her – for the millionth time – that she herself had been in service at the age of twelve, sending home five shillings a week and relieving the family of the burden of her food and 'keep'. Whatever that was.

Gran said, 'What's the good of a well without water?' She poured the tea. It was as thick as treacle.

Alice said hastily, 'What I meant was, things change. And you have to make new decisions.' Gran said nothing and Alice filled the gap. 'Take new directions. In life. And everything.'

'Oh.' Gran pushed across a bone-china teacup

in an earthenware saucer and held up a spoon. 'Real sugar. Want some?'

Alice nodded eagerly, then said, 'Where did you get it?'

'Last summer's bee sugar.'

Gran did not have bees, but she had applied for bee sugar every summer of the War on the pretext that her bees were helping the War effort. So far she had not been found out. Ted said that Gran's mythical bees must be arthritic, because they could never find any nectar whether it was a good year or a bad year. He suggested issuing them with miniature crutches. Gran had watched Alice laughing and suggested tartly that if they did not want her bee sugar they need not have it. They laughed no more.

Gran also had a mythical dog, and her butcher saved bones for him every week. So there was usually a pot of stew on Gran's range. This week it was pork bones and Alice thought they smelled a bit iffy. Even Gran had wondered aloud whether she should add some more onions.

Gran sat down with her own cup. 'It's Reggie Ryecroft's girl, ennit?' she asked.

Alice almost gasped. Gran wasn't supposed to know a thing. She lived in the past. She used her best china cups with old saucers she shared with her cats. Yet she could get sugar and meat and butter and eggs, and she knew about Hester Ryecroft. She was an amazing woman. Dad often said so and he was right.

She managed a shrug. 'There's only one scholarship for girls, Gran. Hester is brilliant. I haven't got a chance.'

Gran shrugged too. 'Well, then, you're doing

27

the best thing, our Alice. The very best thing. Getting on with it. Why wait till Easter?'

'Term's started. I can't really leave till the end.'

'Started yesterday. So you'd made up your mind before.'

Gran would never understand that Alice needed time to say goodbye to her teachers. 'Well . . .'

'Come on, out with it. No well without water, remember.'

'Oh, Gran. It's just that . . . Dad's going to try to get me a job in the office.'

She'd thought that Gran would be delighted. They were a railway family, and for the baby to be folded into the warmth of the GWR should have been Gran's dream. But Gran tightened her mouth in disapproval.

Alice said helplessly, 'What? I thought you'd be pleased.'

'Does your mother know?'

'Not yet.'

'She won't like it.'

Alice knew that. And she knew too that her mother would be even less pleased if she heard that Gran had been told before her.

She said defensively, 'Mum will understand. Eventually.'

'Yes. Eventually.' Gran looked thoughtfully into the coals. They were sitting on either side of the range where it was warm. On the other side of the table, between the two doors, it was bitterly cold.

Alice frowned, trying to make sense of Gran's reaction. She said tentatively, 'I thought it would be a good idea to try to learn about the railways. We're doing transport in History and railways are such a tradition with our family. So . . .'

Gran said heavily, 'Your grandfather. Your father. And now you.'

Alice repeated, 'And now me.'

'And Reggie Ryecroft.' The words seemed to drop from Gran's mouth syllable by syllable.

Alice frowned again. 'Uncle Reggie, yes. And don't forget Uncle Duggie and that big fat man – Inspector Jones. And there's—'

'Yes, yes, yes. You know most of them, of course. But what's the betting you'll end up in Reggie's office?'

'Well, that would be all right, Gran. He was always nice to me when I played with Hester. He pretended to be W.C. Fields and called me his little chickadee and told me I look like Mum.'

Gran looked across at Alice with heavy eyes. 'You know he lived with us when he joined the Great Western as a lad?'

'I think so. Didn't Dad go and live with his parents?'

'Yes. 'Tisn't railway policy for young clerks to start work at their home stations. So Reggie came to Leadon Markham and lodged with us, and your dad went to Crabbington on the Golden Valley Line and lived with Reggie's people. They kept a pub.'

Alice smiled mistily, remembering Gramps and Leadon Markham. Gramps had looked so important in his station master's hat with the gilt sphere on the top.

Gran had gone quiet, like she did whenever she thought of Gramps. So Alice said, 'I can remember playing with Hester when we were little. I was really frightened of Uncle Reggie, but Aunt Dorothy was nice to me. And there was Valentine, too.'

Gran snorted like a horse. 'Valentine, indeed! Fancy calling a boy Valentine!'

'It's after St Valentine, Gran,' Alice protested. 'He was a saint and a martyr. He lived in Rome in the third century.'

'How do you know all that, my girl?'

'I looked it up.' In spite of herself, she blushed slightly. Valentine Ryecroft intimidated her, but he also held a strange fascination too. 'Anyway, Hester usually calls him Val. So does Aunt Dorothy. It's only Uncle Reggie who calls him Valentine.'

'That's another thing. You won't be able to call him Uncle Reggie if you're going to work in the office.'

'Oh Gran, he won't mind that. He'll probably call me Miss Chickadee!' But nevertheless, she felt a qualm. She had long since lost her fear of Uncle Reggie, mainly because she hardly ever saw him. But Hester had told her of his 'displeasures'. Hester had once said cagily, 'He never loses his temper.' And Alice had nodded understandingly. 'Neither does my father.' She could never have told Hester that it was her mother who lost her temper; that was the kind of friend Hester had always been – there were well-defined limits. After all, it was familiarity that bred contempt, and the one thing Alice dreaded about the Ryecrofts was their contempt. One of Hester's favourite put-downs was, 'You are absolutely beneath contempt.' Alice thought it was a horrible word; like spitting.

She said, 'Anyway, Gran, I think I'll probably go into the Staff Office with Uncle Duggie.'

'Is he the one whose feet smell?'

'Well . . .' Alice thought she would have to stop saying 'well' and giving Gran the chance to come up with the waterless one. 'Yes, he is actually. But you get used to it.'

Gran cackled, then leaned back in her chair and stared into the fire, fingering her apron. That meant she wanted to pull it up and over her head and have forty winks. Time to go.

Alice pecked her on the cheek and assured her she did not need the outside throne – though in the summer she loved sitting there with the door open, looking down the garden. In the winter, the long bench seat lost its attraction. 'See you next week then, Gran,' she said.

'Once a week,' Gran mumbled. 'Wonder you can spare that much.'

Alice was determined not to leave the cottage steeped in guilt as she usually did. She kissed Gran again and said firmly, 'You know I love you.'

Gran smiled sleepily and then was suddenly awake. 'Luvaduck! Nearly forgot to tell you! Our Hattie's coming home next week! After all this time. She's coming home!'

Alice stopped with her hand on the doorknob. This was news indeed. Hattie's mother, the unknown Aunt Mitzie, who was Dad's older and very naughty sister, had handed her daughter to Gran and Gramps at birth; the only clue to the baby's identity was Mitzie's insistence that she should be christened Harriet. They had done their best for the child; she had boarded at a good school in Ross-on-Wye until she was fourteen. And then Gramps had died and Hattie had come home to live with Gran and work in the bank. Until the War. The War had been her salvation. All she had ever really wanted to do was dance and sing, and that became her War effort. At eighteen, she joined together with a like-minded group and they slid gently into what was known as the Camp Circuit. She had sung and danced at practically every Army and Air Force camp in the country. She had a wonderful time, and her rare letters and visits were a delight to everyone. Gran often said sadly, 'Just like her mother. All she ever wanted was fun. And look where it landed her.'

Alice had heard this before, and thought that if only there had been a war when Aunt Mitzie had produced her little Hattie, it would not have been so bad. Illegitimate babies these days could always be blamed on the War. No one just disappeared off the face of the earth any more. Alice half smiled, thinking of Hattie with her smouldering dark good looks, and wondered what tales she would have to tell this time. She said, 'What about the others? The musicians?'

'Don't know.' Gran fiddled with her apron again. 'We shall hear all about it, I expect.' She flipped her apron over her hat. Alice left.

She wheeled her bike down the long garden path to the gate. It was cold and raw, and getting foggy. On the other side of the road, the fields sloped steeply down to the river, which was swollen and swift-moving. Ten years ago, when Gramps had died, Gran had threatened to 'put herself' in it. But she never had. Instead, six-year-old Alice had gone to stay with her and give her a reason for living. Every day for almost a month they had walked all the way to the cemetery, and Alice had played by the brook while Gran sat by Gramps's grave and wept. Doffie had often arrived on her bike from the other side of the city to sit anxiously with her. Alice had known even then that it was for her sake, not Gran's, that Mum made that long trip. And then Hattie had left the little school back in Ross-on-Wye and had taken over from Alice, who, much relieved, had gone home.

And now her much-loved cousin Hattie was coming home to tell of her adventures – and, Alice hoped, to advise her on office life: what to wear, how to speak . . . everything.

Alice smiled and swerved to avoid a puddle as she emerged from the lane into Bristol Road. Hattie would be pleased she was leaving school; she would sweep away all her doubts and make the future sound so exciting. Yes, Dad had once called Hattie the family's loose cannon. You never knew what she would do next.

Gloucester's Bristol Road became Southgate Street after what seemed hours of pedalling. Alice avoided getting stuck in the old tramlines and sailed over the Cross and past the Bon Marché; then, on an impulse, turned left into St John's Lane and the maze of streets around the cathedral. For some reason she couldn't fathom, she wanted to see Hester Ryecroft.

Deanery Close was a dead-end street of narrow terraced houses, built a hundred years ago to house the many servants needed by the cathedral clergy. The dwellings all sported a downstairs bay window next to the narrow front door, which was surmounted by a stained-glass transom. Like all the other houses, the Ryecrofts' had two upstairs windows, side by side, which made the big bedroom seem palatial. Behind that were two tiny rooms for Hester and Valentine. Hester's would have been bigger, but a slice had been taken off several years ago and made into a bathroom, the door of which also boasted stained-glass panels. Until last summer, what with the stained glass and the blackouts, the house had been as dark as the nearby crypt. It was slightly better now, without the thick black curtains at every window.

Alice propped her bike against the kerb, sniffed the vinegar-laden winter air from the nearby pickle factory, and walked the two yards to the front door. Hester opened it before she could lift the knocker. Her long dark plait swung over one shoulder as she peered past Alice.

'Have you seen him?' she asked.

'Valentine? No. I've just come from Gran's.'

'Oh.' Hester stood there for a moment, working out Alice's route. 'He probably went down Westgate Street.' She bit her lip and stood aside for Alice to come in. 'It's so cold. He ought not to walk for so long in this weather.' Her translucent brown eyes were anxious.

Alice, brotherless, had never understood Hester's concern for Valentine. He was so obviously well able to look after himself. She felt a certain relief that he was not at home and walked more confidently into the dark hall with its patterned quarry tiles and muted light filtering through the transom. Without Valentine, there was no menace. She said, 'I've got something to tell you.'

Hester made a sound of acknowledgement, but

then went outside again and stared fruitlessly up and down the foggy street. Alice scrubbed her feet loudly on the doormat for Aunt Dorothy's and Uncle Reggie's benefit, then waited.

Hester came in reluctantly. 'Mother and Father are in the kitchen,' she said.

They always were. It seemed strange to Alice that on a late Saturday afternoon in January they would be sitting in the kitchen. Her parents would be in the living room with a good fire going and the papers all over the floor. They were officially speaking again, but it would be silent in the back room except for the fire falling in on itself now and then. If Mum were reading the newspaper, she might share bits of it aloud to Dad; it was more likely that she had her book and Dad the newspaper. Dad never read aloud.

'Well?' said Hester. 'Do you want to tell them the news as well?'

Alice bit her lip. 'I don't think so. Not at this stage. Just you.'

'Upstairs then,' Hester said impatiently. She was not interested in gossip.

Alice trudged up the stairs, which were almost as familiar as her own at home. Perhaps the colourless stair carpet was slightly more threadbare here; it so happened that Mum and Dad had replaced theirs in 1939 and the Ryecrofts had not. After six years of war and Heaven knew how long before that, the Deanery Close carpet was definitely the worse for wear.

Hester's bedroom was like an icebox and as neat and empty as a nun's. The only mark Hester put on it was her choice of reading. At present this consisted of Latin texts. Hester was desperate to go to Oxford, where Valentine was in his final year, and by some terrible oversight she had only recently learned that Latin was a must for Oxford. Like Alice, she had spent the last six years learning German. Alice had done so because Mum had hedged her bets about the outcome of the War and thought there was a distinct possibility they would need someone to talk to the local Gauleiter. But Hester chose German because she wanted to learn a language Valentine did not know. They had all had the option of learning Latin: when Hester discovered her ghastly mistake, she had wept for a whole night. Valentine had found her in the morning, almost drowned, and had said sternly, 'You can still do it. Come and look at my texts.'

As Alice sat on the edge of the bed, the springs groaned loudly. She said, 'I wanted to tell you, because our families are linked – you know.'

Hester went to the window and moved the net. The fog pressed against the glass. She said, 'Oh, just look at it. His chest . . .'

Alice joined her; it was getting worse. 'It's only down here, by the river. It's much better on Southgate and Northgate. Don't worry.'

'But he'll be by the river, with the gypsies. He likes to see them going about their business.'

'Won't he be in the cathedral? Doesn't Mr Makin play the organ on Saturday afternoons?'

Hester turned and stared at Alice, then dropped the curtain and smiled. 'Oh Alice! I'd forgotten that! Of course, he practises for the Sunday services and Valentine loves to hear him! Oh, thank you!' She laughed, and moved to the chest of drawers to adjust the pile of books there, which were already straight. 'Oh, I'm sorry not to pay attention. It's really good to see you. Such a nasty afternoon, and Father has switched off the oven, so it's cold in the kitchen.'

That was why they sat in the kitchen. They lit the gas in the oven and sat around that. They'd started in the War when there was no coal, but they still did it. And Uncle Reggie got hot so quickly . . .

Alice went back to the bed and smiled. 'You know what I mean about our families, don't you? Our mothers having the same name, and our fathers changing places when they joined the railway.'

'Yes, of course. Though your mother never uses her proper name, does she?'

'No.' Alice heard the disapproval and agreed with it. What sort of a name was Doffie for someone as vibrant as Mum? And when you put it with her surname, it became ludicrous. Doffie Pettiford. Oh dear.

Hester regretted the implied criticism and said briskly, 'Well, come on then!'

Alice smiled. 'Gran would ask, "What's the use of a well without water?"' She saw Hester's lips tighten and added quickly, 'But I won't, it's all right.' She straightened the smile and blurted out, 'I'm going to leave school at Easter.'

Hester stared at her in disbelief. Then she said slowly, 'You absolute idiot!'

Alice tried to laugh. 'You too? That's what Mum will say. And Gran wasn't terribly thrilled, either.'

Hester said nothing, which Alice knew was a ploy she used to make people say more than they wanted. But it was irresistible, and the next minute Alice was gabbling her reason for leaving. But not the real reason, only the one about not standing a chance of a State scholarship.

Hester said slowly, 'Are you blaming me for your decision to leave school at sixteen?'

Alice was horrified. 'No! Of course not! I'm blaming myself!' She laughed and hit her head with the heel of her hand. ' 'Cos I'm so thick!'

Hester sat on the spindly-legged kitchen chair which had graduated to her room quite recently. She said slowly, 'You've got a decent brain, Alice. And there are other openings besides University. What about Fishponds?' Aunt Dorothy had trained at Fishponds and had taught for ten years before she met Uncle Reggie and got married. You weren't allowed to teach when you were married.

'I don't fancy teaching.'

'You'd be good at it. Funny – Val said that once. That you'd be a good teacher.'

Alice blinked. 'What on earth made him say that?'

'Can't remember. Oh yes. D'you remember that game we used to play, where he played a few notes on the piano and we had to guess what the piece was? And you didn't say anything for ages—'

'Because I hadn't got a clue,' Alice interpolated, suddenly remembering.

'And then he played something staccato and you said it was from Chopsticks!'

Alice blushed with shame at the reminiscence.

Hester said, 'It was ages ago now, when Val started at Oxford. He said it didn't matter that you weren't intellectual, because you had a sensitivity that could feel what you could not understand. Which I thought was very perceptive, because I've

38

always said you feel your way through any problem!' Hester smiled fondly. 'It was then Val said what a jolly good teacher you'd make.'

'Gosh.' Alice was only too aware of what an honour this was. And that Hester should actually tell her about it . . . It was a reward, of course – for pointing out that Val was safely in the cathedral and not hanging about the gypsy caravans on the Barton.

She said impulsively, 'That's not all I wanted to tell you, actually. Dad's going to get me a job in the office!'

Hester was flabbergasted. Alice did not want to risk further condemnation and gabbled on, 'Don't you see, Hester? We're meant to be close – the Ryecrofts and the Pettifords – and this will be another link between us.'

Hester said slowly, 'You might be in my father's office.'

'That's what I mean! We're like the Montagues and the Capulets—'

'They hated each other!'

'Well, apart from that, I mean. We – we're . . . *meant*!'

Hester was silent. She sat upright on the insubstantial chair, her feet neatly side by side in their brown Oxfords. Alice could say no more; she could not explain about her parents. She too was silent.

At last, Hester said, 'Well, I still think you're mad. Surely you can see where this closeness has led? Two men supporting families on the pittance paid to railway clerks. Promotion only possible when someone dies or retires. No real prospects. And it's worse for women.'

39

'But railway people are always so *nice.*'

'Yes.' Hester considered for a moment. 'Yes. And that is important to you.'

'Isn't it to everybody?'

'Oh, no. Not at all. Stimulation, that's what I look for in a person.'

'But they can be nice *and* stimulating, surely?'

'I haven't met anyone who is both.'

Suddenly Alice felt sorry for Hester. She stood up and smiled gently. 'You will, one day.' She sighed. 'I'd better go. It's getting dark and with this fog . . . You're wearing your outdoor shoes.'

'I was going to look for Val.' Hester smiled. 'Perhaps you're doing the best thing, Alice. But if you change your mind, come and talk to Mother about Fishponds. She'd like that.'

Alice was touched. As she was leaving, for a fleeting moment she considered kissing Hester goodbye. But instead she grabbed her bike and pedalled back up Deanery Close towards the gas lamps of St John's Lane, wishing she had put her cycle lamps in her bike basket. It was only four o'clock but was already getting dark, even though the nights were supposed to get shorter in January. She grinned into the fog and said aloud, 'Obviously no one has told you that fact.' She liked the way her voice came straight back into her mouth at each word. She added as a tribute to Hester, 'That *incontrovertible* fact!'

And that was her downfall, literally. As she lifted her head to let the wonderful multi-syllabled word float into the fog, her bicycle mounted the kerb and she fell over her handlebars.

Luckily, she missed a lamp-post by a hair's breadth. She lay there, tangled in her bicycle, stunned for a moment. Then a voice spoke through the fog. 'Good gracious! It's Alice Pettiford, I do believe!'

She recognized the slightly supercilious voice immediately. It belonged to Valentine Ryecroft. There was no helping hand, no concern. The voice went on, definitely amused now, 'Yes, that is an *incontrovertible* fact. Alice Pettiford. Herself in person. No less.'

He might have gone on in that vein, except that Alice groaned, and then said, 'Anyone less *sensitive* than Alice Pettiford might imagine that Valentine Ryecroft, himself in person no less, cares nothing for the hapless maid who lies injured at his feet!'

There was a moment's pause, and then he burst out laughing. And so did Alice. She hauled herself to her feet, retrieved her bicycle and spluttered, 'You, on the other hand, are the most insensitive person I know!'

He offered no help. In the lamp-light she could see he was smiling broadly.

'And why do you say that, hapless maid?'

'Not only did you leave said hapless maid to fend for herself; you caused great anxiety to your sister by loitering with intent among the gypsies by the river!'

The smile disappeared. 'You've visited Hester. What did she say?'

'Only that the fog is bad for your chest.'

'What makes you think I was with the gypsies, then?'

'Oh, she might have mentioned the gypsies. I can't remember.'

'Just Hester? Not the parents?'

41

'Just Hester.'

'Is she out looking for me?'

'No. I told her you would have gone to hear Mr Makin practise.'

'Did you, by God?' He laughed again. 'Well done, little Alice.' He stared at her through the fog, then decided enough was enough. 'All right. Off you go.'

She got on her bicycle and pedalled away. He hadn't offered to walk her up to Northgate Street; he didn't care tuppence. And she was the only one who knew what he had been doing that afternoon. It had come to her quite suddenly on seeing his white glowing face, his light-blue glittering eyes and his fringe of pale hair beneath the peak of his cap. He had been kissing the gypsy girls down by the river in the dense fog where no one would recognize him.

Alice giggled and pedalled hard up the hill to the church. He knew that she knew. It gave her a slight edge. Not that it mattered; she wasn't likely to see him again, once he went back to Oxford.

Alice free-wheeled down the other side of the hill, out towards the open country. Mum had pikelets for tea. She would toast them on the fork that Dad had made when he was at school. She would tell them about Gran and about Hattie coming home. And perhaps – just perhaps – she would also tell Mum about leaving school at Easter. She reached out her left hand so that her gloved fingers flipped the blackthorn looming out of the mist. 'I'm going to need some help there,' she said aloud. The hedge snagged a finger of her glove and whipped it away. She did not stop. Throughout the War, Mum had knitted enough gloves to last two lifetimes. And this was probably a sign from God, anyway. Unfortunately, she did not know what kind of sign. That was the trouble with God. He worked in such mysterious ways.

Three

Sunday-morning breakfast was difficult at the narrow house in Deanery Close. Dorothy laid it out in the dining room and lit the fire before she went to the eight o'clock service at the cathedral, and Hester warmed up the porridge in the kitchen and brought it to the table in the big brown casserole normally used for stews. The Sunday after Alice's visit, the fog persisted and the dining room, hemmed in as it was by what Reggie called the East Wing, but was actually the narrow kitchen, was dark and marine-like. The fog seemed to have slipped under the sash windows somehow, so that the neatly laid table and the flickering fire swam around insubstantially.

Reggie looked up as Hester came in with the steaming pot of porridge. He approved of her Sunday dress – the cream blouse beneath a ribbed blue sweater, the pleated skirt and the shining lisle stockings. He became pretentiously jovial.

'Well done, my little housewife! Nothing like a bowl of good hot porridge to start the day properly. Serve your brother first, Hester. If he gets much thinner he will disappear altogether! I don't think your mother has managed to put much meat on your bones over Christmas, son.'

Valentine looked at his father for four unnerving seconds, then thanked Hester and picked up his spoon.

'Wait for it! Wait for it!' Reggie mimicked one of the comedians on the wireless, then smiled at his own joke. 'Your mother might not be honouring us with her presence, but I believe your sister is a shining example of the opposite sex. Am I not right, Valentine? Hey? Am I not right?'

Valentine transferred his steely gaze to Hester and waited until she picked up her spoon. Her face was red. She hated it when her father was like this, and she feared that Val was now going to be excruciatingly sarcastic. But you never knew what Val would say or do next.

Disconcertingly, he smiled, a proper smile which lit up his face, so that he no longer looked like his father but took on some of his mother's sweetness.

'You're right, Father. Hester is a shining example of femininity.'

He would have said more, but Reggie cut in quickly. 'Now, now. None of your banter, young fella-me-lad!' He lowered his head and began to eat, so he did not see Valentine lift his spoon as if toasting his sister. Hester turned redder still and lowered her own head over her bowl.

Reggie paused long enough to complain. 'It doesn't seem to matter how often your mother scrubs out this pot, the porridge always tastes of onions from our last stew!'

Valentine laughed. 'Something a bit different, anyway,' he commented.

'It's not funny, son. Just because your mother has decided to go to the eight o'clock Eucharist instead of the seven o'clock as she always used to—'

Hester protested. 'Father! You know that she hates walking through the Close in the darkness! It's just about light by the time she leaves for the eight o'clock.'

Reggie's eyebrows drew together and she wished she had not spoken.

Valentine said languidly, 'Anyway, what's that got to do with the taste of the porridge?'

Reggie sighed heavily. 'You obviously haven't noticed that as a general rule we eat our breakfast in the kitchen, and your mother dishes up the porridge straight from the saucepan. *Ergo*, no taste residues from the casserole.'

'And is there any reason why that could not happen on a Sunday?'

'Not one!' Reggie sounded triumphant, thinking he had won the argument. 'Except that your mother has decided – no, decreed – that on Sundays we use the dining room. Which means the extravagance of an extra fire in the grate during winter. And, of course, having to imbibe onion-flavoured porridge.'

Hester wished heartily that her father had not used the word 'imbibe'. She knew it would make Valentine laugh.

He laughed. She cringed, waiting for the inevitable riposte. She was so tuned in to Valentine's way of thinking that she could anticipate it. *'Oh dear. We try so hard to get away from our working-class roots, and then a word like "imbibe" slips in unawares and we fall on our faces.'*

But, incredibly, Valentine turned his laughing face towards his father. 'Oh, Dad. Sometimes I love you so much it hurts.'

Hester couldn't believe it. There was no mistaking the sincerity in the words; the fact that Valentine had actually called their father 'Dad' was astonishing enough. That he should then speak of love was absolutely unbelievable.

Reggie was startled enough to put down his spoon. But Valentine gave no time for reaction. He went on easily, 'That still doesn't account for the fact that we could so easily bring in the saucepan instead of the casserole.' He turned to Hester. 'Wouldn't that be a viable possibility, Sis?'

Hester said weakly, 'Mother doesn't like pans on the dining-room table.'

Reggie said robustly, 'And neither do I, son.' He was truly happy; his long, lugubrious face was alight with happiness. 'So we're just going to have to put up with onion-flavoured porridge!'

'Makes a nice change,' Valentine reiterated in a comic cockney voice.

Hester, who couldn't taste anything except porridge, said eagerly, 'I don't mind.'

'Neither do I,' Reggie said magnanimously. He scraped his bowl, put it to one side and reached for bread and butter and the marmalade dish. 'Your dear mother. Even the marmalade goes into a special dish.' He looked around sentimentally. 'It's good to eat in here. To do things properly. She has standards, has your mother. We must honour them.'

Valentine glanced at Hester and closed one eye. She flushed instantly.

Reggie said, 'And while she's not here – because

I know this sort of thing upsets her – where were you yesterday afternoon, Valentine? She didn't say a word, but I know she was very anxious about you. And that's not on. To worry Mother is definitely not on.'

Valentine reached for the marmalade. Hester could see his blue eyes become cold again. The lovely few minutes of happiness were over.

'When would that have been, Father?' He frowned, as if casting his mind back. 'I was at the library from nine until eleven. Then I believe I went straight to the museum—'

'We know all about that, my son. Then we expect you to join us for an hour or so in the afternoon. Your sister was with us until Alice Pettiford called at four o'clock. You were still conspicuous by your absence.'

'I'm sorry, Father.' Valentine spooned marmalade on to the side of his plate and looked up innocently. 'I did not realize that at twenty-one I had to ask permission to go out of the house.'

Reggie's neck brightened. 'Age has nothing to do with it. Courtesy has. And while you are under my roof I expect courtesy.'

Valentine took a deep breath and Hester burst out, 'Val! Surely you remember! You went to hear Mr Makin practise in the cathedral. Alice saw you there!' She wished she hadn't added that bit, but it certainly gave her statement credence. Valentine stared at her, saying nothing.

Reggie puffed a laugh. 'Well, of course. Why didn't we think of that?' He turned to Hester. 'I know you were just as worried as your mother, my girl. I saw you'd put your outdoor shoes on. You were about to go out in the fog to look for your brother, weren't you?'

Hester forced a laugh.

'Were you, Sis?'

'I was. Then I opened the door to Alice and saw the fog. And changed my mind.'

'It was lucky that she'd seen me in the cathedral then, wasn't it?'

'Yes.'

Val smiled at her. 'Listen, when you've cleared the dishes and re-laid the table for Mother, d'you want some help with the Latin?'

'Oh, Val, would you?'

'You've only got to ask, you know.'

That was not true. She had asked – begged – before now and he had told her to get on with it.

Reggie went out for the Sunday papers. Dorothy came in looking pale and drawn. Hester sat her down, kissed her cheek, fetched tea and more bread and butter, while Valentine sat with her and talked about Oxford before Reggie came back. Dorothy loved that. It reminded her of her days at the teacher-training college, when she had been given the greatest gift of all: time to read. She ruffled her dark hair, flattened by her Sunday hat; her clear brown eyes, so like Hester's, sparkled. Reggie was always reminding her that she was seven years his senior; now, in front of the fire with Valentine, she did not look it.

Val said with enthusiasm, 'Have you heard of Nietzsche, Ma? I've got one of his books upstairs. Helps you to understand the Nazis, in a way.' He spread marmalade on some bread for her, in spite of his mother's upraised hand. 'He's got something. Man needs power more than anything else.

To disempower a human being is worse than killing him.'

'What rubbish, Val!' Dorothy laughed. 'It's fun to discuss ideas – any ideas – but don't fall into the trap of believing any of them!'

'Ma, you are so cynical!' Valentine cut the bread and marmalade into squares. 'Come on, I'm reversing roles now. I'm going to feed you.'

'You are ridiculous sometimes.' But Dorothy smiled and opened her mouth. They went on talking while Hester cleared the table and her mother ate her way through a slice of bread and butter and marmalade. And then Reggie came back, took the chair by the fire and opened the paper.

'Can't think why everyone thinks this new United Nations lark will work. League of Nations certainly didn't!'

Valentine got up and went upstairs ahead of Hester.

At twelve-thirty, Reggie called up the stairs that someone was desperately needed to lay the dinner table. The extravagant adverb meant that he was still in a jovial mood. Hester called that she would be down as soon as she had put her books away. She knocked on Valentine's door and waited for his permission to go in. Then she presented the exercise he had set her. He glanced over it, looked at her, then read it more carefully. She could scarcely breathe.

He said, 'You've got a photographic memory, Sis. It will serve you in good stead for the examination.'

She let her breath go in a gasp of relief. 'I thought for a moment . . .'

'Everything I told you is here. Verbatim.'

'Thank you, Val. Thank you so much.' She took back the paper and held it like a trophy in front of her.

He said slowly, 'You know, even without Latin you will get into a good university. London, for instance.'

'I want to go to Oxford.'

'I'm thinking . . . with the demob entry, it could be crowded. And more women will want places now.'

She said slowly, 'Isn't this any good?' She held up the paper.

'It's perfect. As I said, you've got a photographic memory.' He smiled suddenly. 'You know when I shocked you to the core and told Dad I loved him?'

She blinked at the sudden change of subject, then nodded.

'I meant you as well. Ma. This house. All the narrow-minded nonsense we've had to put up with. But especially you.' He looked down at the book he was reading. With shock she saw it was the Bible. He said quietly, 'Sometimes I wish you were like Alice Pettiford. I wish you could get married quickly, stay here in the city, close to the cathedral, have children and bring them up and just . . . be happy.'

'I could never be happy, doing that,' she said.

'No. I know that.' He looked up and grinned. 'So, what did Alice come to tell you? It certainly wasn't that she'd seen me in the cathedral!'

'No. But she suggested that was where you might be. And I knew instantly that she was right.'

He opened his eyes wide, then sighed and said,

51

'Yes. All right. I thought she might have something interesting to – to – *impart*!' They both laughed.

'Actually, I suppose it was interesting. To her. She's leaving school at Easter. Not bothering to sit the Highers.'

Val showed no surprise. 'There, what did I tell you? She will meet a similar male creature from the Cathedral School, struggling to make ends meet as a clerk somewhere, she will think she is in love, she will marry, and because she is supposed to live happily ever after, she will live happily ever after. Poor little Alice. So predictable.'

Hester nodded wisely, then said, 'Why do you call her "little Alice"? She and I are the tallest girls in the school.'

'Yes, but you have carriage and are beautiful. She has no dignity whatsoever, and is merely pretty.'

Hester felt as if she were a flower bursting into bloom – this, coming from Valentine, was an enormous compliment.

'She is so funny, Val! She thinks our families are linked, like the Capulets and Montagues! Can you believe it?'

Val smiled. 'Is that why she came to tell you her news?'

'Yes. But there's more – she wants to get a job in the office. Become a railway woman. She thinks she might be able to work for Father!'

He was startled by this, and did not seem pleased.

Hester said, 'I'd better go.' She waved the paper. 'Thank you again for this, Val. I'm going to do it, you know!'

She walked down the stairs very carefully, head held high, toes pointing downwards for each tread. She must remember her carriage. And that she was beautiful. Because she was walking with such care, she moved silently, and she entered the kitchen to discover her father with his arm around her mother's waist, bending her right back and kissing her.

She was so amazed that she did not realize until later that she was also quite appalled.

Four

Sunday morning in the Pettifords' modern detached house in Lypiatt Bottom was so different from at Deanery Close that it could have taken place in another country. The Pettifords had moved from Gloucester back in 1936, when four box-like houses had been built by an ambitious developer between Tewkesbury and Cheltenham. Unfortunately for him, Lypiatt Bottom, though boasting a village green with a pond and ducks, an ancient church and two or three run-down farms with their accompanying cottages, did not attract buyers and the houses did not sell. Eventually the prices began to come down, and one by one the houses were bought by people who, like the Pettifords, wanted to get out of the city. One house remained. Ted Pettiford, goaded by Doffie, put in a ridiculously low offer and was nudged up to four hundred and fifty pounds.

The couple, with their six-year-old daughter, were moved by the railway coal wagon drawn by two shire horses. It rained, so all their belongings were soaked. The plaster in the house had not dried out either; the cesspit shared by all four houses was very smelly; and there was no gas, so

Doffie had to learn to cook on an electric cooker, which sparked alarmingly and smelled of burning wood.

They had not been happy there for that first winter: Ted hated the long bike ride into the office; Doffie was lonely; and Alice missed watching for the lamp-lighter to come round with his long pole, missed going to the shops, which were just at the bottom of their old street, missed the stepping stones across the little river, missed the municipal park and her school and her dancing class, missed all the people clustered around the butcher's shop on a Saturday evening, buying cheap meat for the next day, missed the covered market that smelled of fish and rotting fruit . . . there was so much to miss she couldn't name everything.

But then spring arrived, and Lypiatt Bottom came into its own. There were no street lights, but the daylight seemed to linger longer than in the city, and the flowers filled the air with their scent, and people appeared in ones and twos, so that you got to know them. They had names that told you what they did for a living: Ditcher Harris and Roadman Perkins, Eeler Jenkins and Topper Morgan. Alice thought that Topper made spinning tops, until he explained to her one day that he took the tops off apple trees so that the sun could get down into them and ripen the apples. He cut hedges and scythed long grass as well, though that could also be Ditcher's job so he had to be careful. She often wondered what Eeler Jenkins did when the eels were 'lying fallow', as he put it. But there was never a lack of work in the country. At harvest time it was all hands on deck: Mum wore a hanky over her head and a pair of Dad's old trousers, and could pitch and toss hay expertly – she had learned down at Leadon Markham when she and Dad were courting. Dad was a dab hand with the reeds, and when he was on lates he would get up at dawn to labour for Thatcher Williams. Alice went with the other children to pick and bunch snowdrops, then daffs, then bluebells. They would sell them for a halfpenny a bunch to the gypsies, who piled them in their baskets and walked into the city to offer them up and down Westgate Street. When Hester came for the day she would keep hers and take them back for her mother. Aunt Dorothy would write little notes in her beautiful copperplate, thanking Doffie for giving Hester such a good time.

Alice once heard her mother grumbling to her father about her friendship with Hester.

'I did hope that when we moved out here we might be able to shake off the Rollicking Ryecrofts. But no such luck.'

Ted said, 'Rollicking Ryecrofts?'

'I was being funny.'

'Oh, I know he's a bit po-faced, but Dorothy is really nice and the kids—'

'Never let him hear you call his children "the kids"!'

'I know what you mean. He was so delighted when Dorothy accepted him, wasn't he? Going up in the world – despite her age.' Ted laughed. 'All right, he's pretty awful. But he's almost family. Him and me swapping homes like we did, then him going after my sister. Poor beggar didn't realize what Mitzie was like.'

Mum laughed. 'Before my time. But I can imagine.' She sobered. 'He's not a very nice person, all the same, Ted. I wish Alice wasn't so keen on Hester.'

'It will wear off, never fear. Once winter comes . . .'

Dad was right. It did wear off that second winter. And when spring came again, Hester did not seem quite the friend she had been. She refused to pick cowslips in case she stood on a pat. She would not even pull the delicate blossoms to suck out the nectar. And she always had an excuse for cycling back home early. 'Mother isn't very well . . . Val's singing at the cathedral . . . Val is coaching me for my scholarship.'

No one was surprised when Hester got a place at the grammar school. They were very surprised, however, when Alice did too. Hester informed her that country girls were accepted at a much lower level because it was well known that they did not have fully developed brains. Perhaps Hester was right; Alice did not tell her that Mum had developed Alice's brain until it could easily have burst. During the long winter evenings she had coached Alice in mental arithmetic and problems, she had got Ted to bring home a typewriter from the office and had typed up stories as Alice dictated them. Alice herself was so impressed by the neatly typed, wildly exciting pages that she began to write things herself. One of the governors called her a highly imaginative girl. Hester said that that was another way of saying she was a liar. Alice hit her quite hard with her brand-new satchel. And then she and Hester became friends again.

While Dorothy Ryecroft attended the eight
o'clock service at the cathedral and left her family
to eat their breakfast alone and with unusual
formality, Doffie Pettiford slid aside the modern
serving hatch between her kitchen and dining
room, and pushed through three boiled eggs in
eggcups that looked like malformed hens and a
plate piled high with buttered toast. Alice had
already poured three cups of tea. The fire was
roaring, Ted Pettiford had spread the Sunday
paper over the cruet, and the atmosphere was
now one of sweetness and light.

As Doffie came in from the kitchen, Ted dis-
carded the paper, got up and hugged her soundly.
Doffie pushed him away self-consciously. 'Stop it,
Ted. There's a time and a place.'

'Can't help it, sweetheart.' He turned to Alice.
'D'you know, Alice, this mother of yours hasn't
changed a day since we got married.'

Alice smiled cautiously. She loved this – the
whole thing. The only snag was, when she told
Mum she was leaving school, things might
change. Sometimes she had the sense of living on
the edge of a volcano.

She said, 'Miss Plant thought she was my sister.'
She had already told her mother that. It had been
after the Carol Concert in the hall. Dad hadn't
been able to come. Miss Plant had said, 'Do you
live with your sister, Alice?' Of course, if Dad had
been there she might not have jumped to the
wrong conclusion.

Dad laughed and sat down to slice off the top of
his egg. 'Perfect,' he said as the yolk ran over the
side.

Mum said, 'How was Gran, poppet? Did she give you some tea?'

'Yes.' Alice exchanged humorous glances with her mother. Gran kept her teapot stewing on the range from one Saturday till the next. 'She had some really good news. Hattie is coming home.'

Doffie was delighted. She and Hattie got on like a house on fire. When Gran and Ted had thrown up their hands at Hattie going off with her 'dance-hall' friends, Doffie had said robustly, 'Either it will work or it won't. If it doesn't she will come home and go back to work, and if it does she will be having a wonderful time.'

Gran had nodded at this, but Dad had said gloomily, 'If she throws up her position at the bank, they certainly won't take her back.'

'Then she'll find something else. Hattie is a survivor, Ted.'

'She is that.' Gran was still agreeing with Mum. It rarely happened.

Now Mum said, 'She'll have some stories to tell! When is she coming, Alice?'

'Gran didn't actually say.'

Dad finished his egg and put the empty shell upside-down in the eggcup. 'Now the War is well and truly over, they'll be short of work. Nearly all the camps have demobbed now and that's where they got their engagements.'

Doffie smiled nostalgically. She and Mrs Mearment next door had helped the vicar's wife with many a dance in the church hall for the local RAF. They had taken on local bands: a piano, a double bass, a crooner . . . She had nearly danced her legs off. She knew that Hattie would have had a wonderful time. The Spitfire Fund, Queen

Alexandra's Nurses, the Stalingrad Siege Fund . . .
they'd all received their thirty-pound cheques and
sent back letters of thanks, which were kept in the
vestry.

Dad passed Alice his up-ended eggshell and
went through the usual joke. 'Have another egg,
Alice?'

Alice loved everyone so much that morning
that she went along with it. 'Gee,' she said in an
exaggerated American accent, 'that's mighty good
of you, Pa!' She cracked the hollow egg, said 'Gee'
again and then laughed. So did Dad. Mum
frowned as she began to gather up the plates and
put them on the hatch.

Later, when she and Alice were washing up,
Doffie said, 'Did you talk to Dad on Friday, after
I'd gone upstairs?'

Alice did not at first identify her own frantic
tears and her mother's dramatic departure as
'talking to Dad' and 'going upstairs'. Then she
recognized Doffie's rationalization of their awful
row and nodded reluctantly.

'Not exactly talked,' she said. 'Just sort of . . .
said things.'

Mum smiled and said no more. Alice dried the
eggcups and said, 'Let's go to Matins, shall we?'

Mum wiped her hands doubtfully. 'I've got
quite a decent shoulder of lamb. And you know
what this oven is like.'

'Let's put it on really low, then crisp it up when
we get home. We can skip the last hymn. I'll
pretend I've got stomach ache—'

'In the house of the Lord!' Mum mocked.

'God will understand. He wouldn't want us to
spoil our dinner.'

So they left Ted to the fire and the Sunday paper, wrapped themselves up in the pixie hoods, scarves and gloves they had knitted, and the coats Mrs Mearment had made from car rugs – everyone in Lypiatt Bottom had one – and trudged over the icy ridged mud of the lane down to the thirteenth-century church, with its Victorian lychgate and leaning gravestones. Alice's heart beat slow and hard. She had told Hester about leaving school and joining the railway, but what was much worse, she had told Gran. She must tell Mum today. She must.

They said good morning to the sidesman, took their prayer books and sat at the side, where they had a good view of the pulpit. The church was beautiful in its plainness. The grey stone was scoured with age, the flags undulated from the pressure of thousands of feet, the pews were carved from Dean Forest oak – the same oak that had made Nelson's ships. Alice slid on to the kneeler, closed her eyes and made one of her divine bargains.

'I don't want to make Mum unhappy. And I know you don't either. So can you help me with this? Just make her understand that it's for the best. Please, God. Please.'

She opened her eyes and glanced around so that she could take in a wide angle of the nave and any sign that God might send. All she saw was Topper Morgan changing the hymn numbers. She closed her eyes again, in case there was a message on her eyelids. The number 360 had been imprinted there from the hymn board, which had to mean something, because that was one of her favourites. She had sung it in her head whenever she heard the German bombers going over. *'Thou whose almighty word, chaos and darkness heard, and took their flight.'* She loved that. And the final pronouncement, *'Let there be Light.'* It had to mean something.

She inhaled the eau de cologne Mum always put on her handkerchief; she was deeply thankful that no one else was her mother. Aunt Dorothy was very nice, and made Alice feel like a grown person instead of a child; in fact, all her friends had nice mums. But not like Doffie Pettiford. Not pretty and blonde and fashionable. Not fun. Mum could make anything fun – washing up, chopping wood for the fire, or cleaning the wick on the oil stove. When Dad was on nights and they slept together, they would make up stories. One sentence each. Until the whole thing became ridiculous or ran out of steam. And then they would go to sleep, smiling into the darkness. She couldn't hurt Mum. She must never, ever hurt Mum.

The sermon finally ended. The Reverend Geoffrey Hyde often said jovially, 'I like my parishioners to get their money's worth.' When Doffie had told Ted this, he had suggested putting a button in the plate and hoping that the sermon would then be non-existent. The Reverend spent at least half an hour that particular morning on the solace of forgiveness – the offerings must have been more generous than usual – and Alice clutched her stomach as soon as the hymn began and tugged at her mother's arm.

Doffie put her mouth to Alice's ear. 'It's all right, darling. Let the meat take care of itself.'

But Alice wouldn't give up. She had spotted Mrs

Mearment in the front pew and knew that she would want to walk home with them. She grimaced and bent right over until Doffie, alarmed, almost carried her down the aisle to the door, where they slipped quietly out.

Outside the porch, everything had changed. It was magic. Snow fell slowly and quietly, huge flakes, settling instantly on the gravestones and already capping the holly trees. Alice had thought the snow was over for the winter, and here it was again; a direct and unmistakable sign from God. 'Oh, Mum . . .' she breathed.

'Alice, are you all right?' said Doffie. 'Is it serious?'

'No.' Alice decided on complete frankness. 'I wanted to talk to you. And now . . . to walk through the snow.'

'So long as you're all right. Oh, it is so *pretty*! What did you want to talk about?'

They hung on to each other as they went down the path, and then stood under the lych-gate roof looking back at their footprints. As they walked on, Alice told her mother of her plan to leave school. She was relieved to find that Doffie understood.

'I know what you mean about Hester, of course. And I suppose . . . We must look in the paper for a job. Something interesting with possibilities. How about the library?'

Alice felt a pang. It would have been grand to work there, amongst all those books. She said, 'Mum, don't faint with shock. I've asked Dad if he will find me something in the office. It – it sort of feels right. In the family.'

Mum said nothing as they scuffed through the

snow. As they turned down the unmade lane, a robin hopped before them and then up on to a twig, making his own little shower of snow.

As they came to the house, which looked cosy and welcoming, Mum finally said, 'I don't know what to think.'

Alice replied eagerly, 'Listen, Mum. If I don't like it after – say, six months – I can always look for something else.'

'You won't, though.' Mum turned the key and they went into the hall. It was filled with white light from the snow. Alice thought of the long dark passage in the Deanery Close house and hugged her mother suddenly.

Doffie laughed. 'I'm eating your snow as well as my own now!' She took off her pixie hood and shook it. Then she said quietly, 'I know why you're doing this, Alice.'

Alice took off her gloves first and began to unwind her scarf; she did not look at her mother.

Doffie sighed. 'Well, at least I'll know you're safe.'

They went through to the kitchen to look at the lamb. Ted had adjusted the temperature and it smelt delicious. Alice made onion sauce, while Doffie did the vegetables. Ted came out and asked how church had been, and then whether either of them had heard of a man called Trygve Lie. They had not. Ted informed them that he was the first Secretary-General of the United Nations, so they'd better remember him. Then he paused and looked at his wife.

'Doff? You're not crying, are you?'

Doffie said, 'It's the snow and the onions. You haven't even noticed, have you?'

Ted peered through the kitchen window. 'Good God. It's snowing!' Then the onion smell hit him and he blinked. 'And now I'm bloody well crying!'

Doffie didn't tell him off about swearing. In fact, she started to laugh. Ted put his arms around her and rocked her to and fro.

Alice scooped the chopped onions into the milk and went to rinse her hands, repeating silently, 'Thank you, God. Thank you, thank you, thank you.'

Lunch was really late because they all wrapped up again and went into the garden to roll a giant snowball and start carving it into a man. Ted never usually did that sort of thing. Alice was busy shaping feet for the snowman when a snowball hit her squarely on the back of her hood and soaked into her neck. In one smooth movement she scooped snow, squeezed it into a ball and threw it at her father. He fielded it so that it spattered all over him, then doubled over, laughing.

Alice looked around. Mrs Mearment was waving from her kitchen window; Mum was rolling snow, her breath puffing around her like steam from one of Dad's engines; Dad was laughing and stamping his feet. The garden was fairyland and the snow was keeping them close and safe. Alice took a mental photograph and leaned down to finish the snowman's feet. She whispered again, 'Thank you, God.'

Five

Alice's last term at school was filled with nostalgia. The one bright spot was when Hattie turned up, blown in by a blizzard during the third week of term, wearing a fur hat like a Russian, a fur coat almost down to the ground and, typically unsuitable, high-heeled court shoes.

Ted was on nights so he was at home, and Alice had just got back, frozen to the marrow after standing next to Milkman Jenner in his float from just outside the school. She had been glad enough to see him; it would have taken her well over an hour to walk home in the snow, but poor old Dobbin had not dared break into a trot, what with his hooves being wrapped in sacking and snow clogging his blinkers.

'Darling!' Hattie was all concern, hugging Alice into her snow-speckled coat and chilling her all over again. 'If only I'd known! I've driven out from Gran's – yes, sweetie, I've got a car! Can you believe it? Oh Ted, darling, of course I was careful. Percy had chains fitted as soon as the snow began. He'd wrap me in cotton wool if he could!' She laughed. 'It's absolutely marvellous, Doffie darling. That's what I've come to talk about.'

Doffie was more concerned about her shoes. 'Hattie, your feet are soaking. Take off those stockings and you can borrow my slippers.'

'They're nylons, Doff. They'll dry on my legs. And don't put the shoes too close to the fire, sweetie. The leather will go all funny. Alice, darling, can you tear up that *Citizen* and stuff it into the toes for your poor old cousin Hattie?'

She pouted adorably and everyone laughed, even Ted, whose heart had sunk when she arrived as he knew that his quiet two hours before work were wrecked. 'Lovely to see you, Hattie,' he said belatedly.

Hattie slid out of her fur coat and cast herself over him, before hugging Doffie. Then Alice had a second turn. 'I've missed you so much, darlings. But it's been such fun! I can't tell you just how much fun it has been!'

She proceeded to tell them.

Doffie groaned. 'All we've done is scramble through each day—'

'Rubbish!' Hattie removed her hat and ran her fingers through her hair. It tumbled everywhere, as black as night and wavy, without the frizz which typified the perms everyone had these days. 'Alice has done wonders at school. You've all been working on the land . . . Gran tells me things, you know.' Her face was alight, her full lips parted. Alice thought she looked like a gypsy one minute, an Indian princess the next. She was adorable.

'How is she, with the snow and everything?'

'I got home yesterday in the light. Someone had swept a path. They're pretty good round there. They remember Gramps.'

Everyone was silent for a moment. Anyone

who had known Gramps remembered him.

Hattie went on talking about Gran and the unsuitability of her cottage next to the river. Doffie got up and made tea. Alice finished stuffing the court shoes and put them to one side of the grate, then leaned against Hattie's nyloned legs. Ted glanced at the clock on the mantelpiece and called through the open hatch to Doffie, 'Are my sandwiches ready?'

Hattie said, 'Oh, don't tell me you're on nights!'

'All right,' Ted said, in an attempt to be humorous.

'Darling, I can take you in the car. What fun! I can come into the office and give them all a bit of a thrill!'

'No, you can't. If you've got anything to tell us, you'd better do it now.'

'You can't *want* to cycle three miles in this weather!'

'I don't want to go anywhere in this weather, but I need the bike. I might be called out.'

'Darling Ted, the War is *over.*'

'We're still seeing a lot of troop movements.' Ted grinned. 'Come on, Hattie. Just who is –' He went into a mincing falsetto. 'Who is *Percy*?'

Doffie materialized with the tea and a sandwich tin dating from Gramps's days. Alice met her gaze and winked. She was almost sure she knew what the news was.

Hattie simpered. 'He works in the Goods, actually, Teddy boy.'

Ted frowned. 'There's Percy Westbrook . . .' He looked at her face and his frown deepened. 'What have you got to do with Percy Westbrook?'

'Everything, darling. We're engaged. We're going to be married in August and I want . . .' She took Alice's head gently between her two hands and massaged it. 'And I want you to be my bridesmaid, Alice. Will you do it?'

Alice hadn't anticipated such dramatic news. Usually Hattie would describe a new man friend as 'someone rather special'. She was thrilled.

'Oh, Hattie! How marvellous. I've never been a bridesmaid. What shall I wear? And you . . . married. It's amazing!'

'You thought I might stay an old maid for ever?'

'Not an old maid! But to tie yourself down to someone . . .'

Doffie was twittering too, patting Hattie's shoulder and asking what he was like, until Ted's voice cut through them all.

'You can't marry Percy Westbrook, Hattie. If this is another of your dramas, just forget it!'

Doffie said, 'Ted! It's Hattie's life, remember!'

Hattie said, 'Darling Ted, I knew you'd be like this. You've always tried to be a big brother to me. And I enjoy it! But you've got to let me go some time, sweetie. And Percy Westbrook is so – so – *suitable*!' She took her hands off Alice's head and held them out, ticking off Percy's attributes one by one. 'He's so mature compared with all my other men friends – I mean, I can utterly rely on him. Thick and thin. He wants to look after me, Ted. And isn't that what you all want – for someone to look after me? Anyone, so long as it's not you?' She did not wait for a reply. 'Secondly, he's a railwayman. GWR, Ted. One of our own. He's respectable. He's got a lovely house in Cheltenham. Four bedrooms, so you can come and stay with me whenever you want to. I can have Gran to live with me. I can *entertain*. Evening parties, afternoon teas – there's a tennis court there, Doffie.' She turned and took Mum's hand. 'You used to play tennis, darling. We can all play doubles. It will be such fun, Doffie. Won't it, Ted?' She turned to him again, almost pleadingly.

'Percy Westbrook is in his fifties, Hattie,' replied Ted. 'He lives with his mother and sister in that house in Leckhampton. He's right under his mother's thumb – she holds the purse strings.'

'Darling, she adores me! Look, she bought me this –' She pushed up the sleeve of her woollen dress to reveal a tiny cocktail watch. 'She can't wait for us to get married and for me to move in there!'

'She thinks you'll be her maid!' Ted gave a shout of laughter. 'My God, she's got a shock coming to her, hasn't she?'

'Ted!' Hattie's eyes filled. 'How could you be so heartless? And you haven't asked me the most important question of all. Has he, Alice?'

Alice whispered, 'Do you love him?'

'Thank you, darling. Yes, I do. Last June we did a VE concert at Fairford. He asked me to dance.' Suddenly her face flamed. 'I – I fell for him. Right then and there on the dance floor. And believe me, I've danced with a lot of men in the last two years. But this was ... different. Passionate, terribly passionate.'

Ted turned away and gazed into the fire. Doffie said cautiously, 'There's more to marriage than passion, Hattie.'

'Oh, I know. But it's such a good beginning, isn't it? He sets me on fire, Doffie! He really sets me on fire!'

'Not in front of Alice, please.'

But Ted was past such niceties. He looked steadily at the fire as he spoke. 'Are you pregnant, Hattie?'

'Ted!' protested Doffie.

Hattie was not indignant. 'That's the thing, Ted darling. He doesn't want children! And you know I've never ever wanted a baby. Being fat and ungainly and miserable all the time . . . not that you were, Doffie. I didn't mean—'

'Never mind that.' Doffie was worried now. 'A lot of women feel like that about babies before marriage. But later you will want his child, darling.'

'No fear! I'd much prefer the tennis parties!'

Doffie was forced to laugh at that, and after an anxious look at her father, Alice joined in. Ted sighed deeply, but said no more.

After another hour of chit-chat, Ted tied his bike on to the lid of the car boot and let Hattie drive him to work. Doffie and Alice waved them goodbye, then hurried back to the fire.

'He wants time to talk her out of it,' said Doffie.

'But Mum, why? I know everyone worries about Hattie, but like you said, she survives everything. And if this man looks after her, it will make it easier for Dad.'

'Perhaps. Perhaps not.' Doffie gave Alice the same cryptic sideways glance she'd used not long ago, when Alice had told her about leaving school and going to work for the GWR.

Alice said, 'I know he's a lot older than Hattie, but perhaps that will be a good thing.' She wrinkled her forehead. 'Is he older than Dad?'

Doffie nodded, and lifted the fire gently with

the poker. 'She never knew her father. It could be that she sees this Percy as a father figure.'

'Perhaps. Perhaps not.' Alice grinned, and her mother threw a cushion at her.

Alice pictured Percy Westbrook as a kind of Mr Rochester, although by no stretch of the imagination could she cast Hattie as Jane Eyre. But Percy – they'd simply *have* to call him something else – would probably be tall and dark, with broad shoulders on which to weep or laugh or just lean, and a general air of substantial authority.

In the event, he was a terrible disappointment. He was not very tall; he only just topped Hattie when she wore her high heels. He had a paunch, and rather narrow shoulders. He was dark with no trace of grey, but he used too much Brylcreem. But the worst thing of all – the absolutely worst thing of all – was that his eyes, though black, were small behind thick glasses, and he actually had a squint. Alice tried to be fair: he couldn't help his appearance, except for the Brylcreem and perhaps the paunch. He must be charming, polite and dynamic in order to attract anyone as vivid as Hattie. Obviously he couldn't display these attributes at the tea party in late February given by a very nervous Doffie, but they must be there somewhere.

Doffie was nervous because Ted's disapproval, which had escalated over the past four weeks, was so obvious to her that she thought it must be clear to everyone else. However, his towering silence was hardly noticeable alongside Percy's gruff taciturnity. Luckily, Hattie, Doffie and Alice filled the void without any difficulty at all. Gran grunted and snuffled her peculiar laugh at everything her

Hattie said, and then everybody laughed. Except Ted and Percy, of course.

Hattie had developed a technique for dealing with her silent partner which Alice thought Mum could emulate very well. She quoted him in every sentence.

'Darling Percy was only saying to me yesterday, if we'd hung on to Mr Churchill for another three or four years, we would have found our footing. Percy always says people need to find their footing, feel secure . . . What is it you say, Percy darling? Rock-steady. That's the word. Rock-steady. Then they know which way to jump.' She hugged Percy's arm and rubbed her cheek against his shoulder. 'Percy is so wise, you know.'

Gran said, 'That's quite enough of that, Hattie.' But Percy did not respond in any way.

Alice said, 'Dad always says we should have hung on to Winnie. Don't you, Dad?'

Ted was ominously silent and Mum said quickly, 'Yes, Alice.' She took Ted's arm but forbore to rub her cheek on his shoulder. 'You often say that, Ted darling.'

Percy cleared his throat alarmingly and they all waited for him to speak. Just when the wait was becoming embarrassing, the door knocker clacked.

'Who can that be?' Doffie asked, disentangling herself from her husband and the low tea trolley.

'Must be something important, Doff,' said Gran. 'Coming down that lane in all this mud . . . must be important.' She scented an emergency, and Gran loved emergencies.

But Doffie brought in another visitor from the city. It was Valentine Ryecroft.

He stood bare-headed in the doorway, rain-drops glistening on his pale hair and eyebrows, twisting one of his father's old caps between his hands. 'I'm interrupting your family party. I'll leave.'

Doffie had to push him into the room so that she could get in herself. She smiled at him welcomingly. She was still beautiful, and in her best dress, with her fair hair waved around her heart-shaped face, she looked quite stunning. 'Come on, Val. You know all of us. And you have obviously come with some news. Sit down and have a cup of tea and tell us what it is.'

Val was used to having control of situations; Alice had never seen him in a position like this before. He was almost pushed into a chair, a cup was fetched and tea was poured. Scones were offered. Hattie, looking like a Spanish señorita, leaned over him and adjusted a cushion.

'Let's be cosy,' she said. 'This is my fiancé, Percival Westbrook. Another railwayman. You see, Val, you cannot really get away from the railway. You went to Oxford, I went on the road as a wartime entertainer, but in the end . . .'

Val was surprised by Hattie. He had not seen her since he was a schoolboy, when she had been dismissed as 'fast'. Now she was a mature woman, engaged to be married, and she had contributed wonderfully to the War effort.

He said, 'How right you are, Miss Pettiford.'

She screamed with laughter. 'Hattie, *please*, Valentine darling!'

Her name reminded him of his cap, which he turned to hang on the back of his chair. Alice took it and put it on the hearth to dry. She was secretly

agog at his arrival. He must have come to see her
. . . with a message from Hester? He wouldn't be
likely to say anything in front of the family, so after
he'd sipped his tea she would see him out and
then he would be able to tell her. She wished he
would hurry and pick up his cup.

Gran said, 'Your sister has taken after your
mother's side, then?'

Val looked bewildered, and it was left to Doffie
to say, 'Yes, Hester is dark.' She smiled at Alice.
'The two girls look rather striking side by side.'
She turned the smile on Val again. 'Don't you
agree, Val?'

Hattie put the scones under his nose and he
took one. Alice could have screamed with
impatience.

'Yes, I suppose so. I've never really thought . . .'

Gran said grimly, 'And you're like your father.
Just like him.'

'I always felt that Uncle Reggie had a kind of
charm,' said Hattie enthusiastically. 'Quiet, you
know. And of course Valentine is the spitting
image of Leslie Howard.' Val flushed as everyone
looked at him; then he bit into his scone and
coughed crumbs. Doffie beat him on the back.

Ted sat back with the air of a man who had had
enough nonsense. 'Well? Your father sent you
with a message. Shall we hear it?'

Val stopped coughing and breathed carefully
and deeply. Then he said, 'The message is for
Alice, actually. Not of much interest to anyone
else.' He glanced at Ted. 'Nothing to do with my
father . . . er . . . Uncle Ted. In fact he doesn't
know yet.' His colour was receding all the time
and he suddenly looked very ill. 'I've decided not

to continue at Oxford. It's not . . . real life, you know. Not for me, anyway. So I came home this weekend to think about it.'

There was a stunned silence. Hattie might have been away from home for the past few years, but she had known that Valentine had won his scholarship and had been well aware of the honour that was. Ted had not been so impressed; he tended to think that higher education of any sort was a waste of time. Probably Gran thought the same. But Doffie and Alice were all too aware of the enormity of Val's announcement.

Alice was appalled. 'You *can't!*'

'Val – think. What are you doing? Nothing is worth such a terrible sacrifice,' said Doffie.

'It's no sacrifice. It's an escape.' Val had been looking at Hattie; now he turned to face Doffie and spoke earnestly. 'Aunt Doffie, it's all so false. I've met probably just two or three others who are interested in what they are reading. The others – it's just a waste of time for them.'

Unexpectedly Ted said, 'What about the deferred men? The demobs who are taking up their places since the War?'

Val turned again. 'Yes. They're the ones who matter. They know what it's like to – to live.'

Ted jerked his head impatiently. '*Live.* What do you mean by that?'

Hattie said, 'I know what he means, Ted darling. To read about things is to see them in a mirror. Val wants to stop reading and do things himself.'

'See them in a mirror.' Val smiled. 'Yes, that's it. Reflections. In a dark glass.' He looked around the room appreciatively. 'This is living. Hattie back home – and engaged!' He looked at Percy. 'Congratulations!' His gaze swept on. 'Food on the table and a fire in the grate and everyone together.'

Alice felt her heart clutch. She tried to picture Sunday tea in Deanery Close: the dark kitchen, the cold dining room. She felt a sudden rush of love for everyone here and now. Even Val. She listened to the teatime conversation until Percy at last contributed something.

'Time we were going, Harriet.'

'Oh, darling Percy!' Hattie looked around. 'Don't you absolutely adore him? *Harriet!* He thinks I'm such a lady, you know!' She stood up and curtsied deeply, then perched on his knee and put her arms around his neck. Alice realized that love really was blind.

Percy did not seem in the least embarrassed by all this attention, though behind his pebble glasses his eyes became smaller still, and one of them looked right ahead while the other seemed about to fall into the front of Hattie's blouse. Hattie looked around at Val. 'We can drop you off, darling. And maybe come and say hello to Uncle Reggie and Aunty Dorothy.'

Val turned bright red again and started to make excuses. Alice gave him his cap and went into the hall with him.

She said in a low voice, 'You can't do this.'

'*You've* done it.'

'I've got proper reasons. And I'm just at school, not at Oxford on a State scholarship.'

'You've chosen to start living, Alice. You can't deny it.'

'I'm going to get a job on the railway. Dad will fix it nearer the time. What will you do?'

His narrow sombre face split into a grin. He pulled her towards the kitchen as the dining-room door opened to let Percy and Hattie through. He closed the kitchen door and leaned against it.

'I'll go on the railway too! Your father might be able to wangle something. Hattie's right, we all end up there eventually. And I'll marry you, Alice. And we'll settle down and be normal. Have children who won't ever have to go to school because I'll teach them. Oh, Alice, it will be wonderful!'

Alice was flabbergasted. 'I'm only sixteen!' she said.

'There's no hurry.'

The serving hatch slid open and Doffie pushed through the teapot. 'Aren't you going with Hattie, Val?' she asked. 'They're just getting Gran into the car.'

'Yes. I'd be grateful. This rain . . .' He moved from the door and opened it.

'And Val – don't say anything to your father just yet. You might change your mind,' said Doffie.

He paused. 'All right, I won't tell them yet. But I won't – change my mind, I mean.' He grinned at her. 'It's all Alice's fault, Aunt Doff. If she can do it, so can I!'

And he was gone.

For some unknown reason, Ted blamed Doffie for everything and wasn't speaking again. Alice went to bed before her mother could throw any tea at him. She wondered whether her head might explode. Was this what Val meant when he talked about living?

Six

Miss Plant's hair looked like George Eliot's, folded back from a centre parting like curtains, covering her ears and looping up from the neck into a loose knot. Her nose was long and bony too and her eyes were intense. In fact, the very image of George Eliot as pictured on the back cover of *Silas Marner*.

That distilled greyness was now beaming in on Alice and Hester as she discussed their latest essays, which had been about Ophelia's character in *Hamlet*. As Miss Plant congratulated Hester on her analysis of a girl on the edge of madness, Alice thought with a sinking heart of how she had dealt with the subject. It didn't matter any more, of course. As Mum had pointed out when she had asked for her opinion, 'It's interesting, Alice. Adventurous, too. And if it offends – well, there are no more exams, are there?' She had then looked intently at her daughter with her sharp blue eyes and asked, 'Any regrets?'

Alice had none. She was certain of that. The agonizing drag inside her chest at the thought of never being a pupil to Miss Plant again had nothing to do with leaving school. After all, she would have to do that at some time.

Miss Plant turned to her, smiling gently. 'Now, Alice,' she said, shifting the files so that Alice's was now on top of Hester's. Alice's heart plummeted further.

'Alice,' Miss Plant's smile widened and her eyes twinkled, 'You have entertained me royally with your essay on Ophelia.'

Alice remembered that Keats spoke of his heart 'leaping up'. She knew what he meant.

'I thought my mind was wide open, Alice. But I find that is not true. I have never considered the possibility of Ophelia being a designing woman. Or, as you put it succinctly, "a little minx".'

Hester turned to stare at Alice, who blushed from neck to hairline.

'You carry through the argument excellently. I can find no flaw with it – until the moment of death. Your explanation that this was a dramatic gesture that went wrong does not quite hold water.' Miss Plant paused and waited for the girls to laugh at her pun. Hester did so. 'It would be hard for someone so calculating as your Ophelia to stay underwater too long.'

She paused again and looked at Alice, who immediately said, 'Yes, you're right. I should have made her slip as she steps into the water . . . hit her head or something.'

'Ye–es. Perhaps. But there is a risk of making the whole play farcical . . .'

Alice interrupted eagerly. 'Don't forget Polonius – he is comical. She could carry that through . . .'

Miss Plant laughed delightedly. 'Oh, Alice. Your imagination is limitless. And as an essay, this production of *Hamlet* is superb. I only hope you have no ambition to see it performed! I know that this is your opportunity to let rip. And you have seized it. All I can say is – well done.'

'Thank you, Miss Plant.'

'You are due up in the attic now, I believe? A Pitman speed test?'

'In half an hour, Miss Plant.'

'Very well. Hester, I will meet you in the library in fifteen minutes. Alice, stay here. I would like to discuss your reading for the summer term.'

Alice's heart began its downward journey again. Mum had had to give a term's notice of her leaving school; she imagined Dr Grey would have mentioned it to her teachers by now. Obviously she had not.

Hester slid her file neatly into her satchel and thanked Miss Plant for her A grade. She had already seen that Alice had a B plus.

It was March and an early spring. Hester fetched her coat and wandered through the front garden of the school towards the library. Primroses were embedded in the grass beyond the drive. Dr Grey's Morris sported a small flower-holder next to the steering wheel, which contained a rose. Hester stood and looked at it in amazement. Had Dr Grey put it there herself, or was there a Mr Dr Grey? Nobody knew anything about anyone in school; she and Alice probably knew more about each other than anyone else. But though Hester thought she knew everything about Alice and her family, Alice knew very little about Hester. Not the reality. The wires of tension that tightened and loosened in the narrow house in the shadow of the cathedral were unknown to anyone except those at the end of them. Mother and Father. Valentine and Hester.

Hester smiled slightly at the thought of connecting wires. It was a strain; yes. But it was also a comfort. The wires could never be broken or disconnected. They would be there until death and maybe beyond. She and Valentine.

She stopped by one of the flower beds at the corner of the school. Daffodils, tulips, narcissi and hyacinths were pushing their leaves up for the sun. She had never seen this part of the garden at this time of year before. Last year, in the Upper Fifth, and before then, since they had arrived as eleven-year-olds, they had been forbidden the front garden. The recreation area lay at the back of the school: tennis courts, hockey and netball pitches were all there. The front garden was for visitors, staff and the Sixth Form. Hester smiled to herself at that. There were five of them in the Lower Sixth this year, and once Alice had gone there would be four. At the end of the summer term there might be three; even two. She would be Head Girl, that was certain. There was no one else. In a way, she would miss Alice; but only in a way. Alice was the nearest she had to a rival; she wasn't as clever as Hester or as hard-working or as well-organized, but she was ... different. If Dr Grey wanted someone different, then it could well have been Alice who was chosen as Head Girl.

Hester reached the front gate and was just about to swing round to the back of the building when someone who had been standing outside stepped forward. It was Valentine.

She rushed to the gate. 'Val! What brings you

here? Hilary hasn't finished, has it?' Hester liked using the proper names for the Oxford terms.

'No.' He smiled. 'It's good to see you, Hester.'

'Oh, you too!' If only they were the kind of brother and sister who hugged. She touched his hand briefly; it was like ice. 'Val, you're frozen. Is anything wrong?'

'No. Everything is surprisingly right. I came to see you first. Just got off the train.'

She flushed with sheer happiness. 'Oh Val, how nice.'

'Nice? Nice to see your only brother?' They both laughed.

'Wonderful, then. Great. Marvellous. Terrific . . .' The joke ran out of steam and she stood looking at him, registering that he was thinner, even paler than usual and obviously chilled to the bone. As he returned her gaze, his pale eyes betrayed that something was wrong, whatever he said.

She whispered, 'Is Mother . . . has something happened to Mother?'

'No. But there's going to be an almighty row tonight, Hester. I wondered whether you should go and have tea with Alice. In fact, spend the night with her.'

She was completely bewildered. 'A row? Alice? Why?'

He blinked. 'She hasn't told you, has she?'

'Told me what? Who? Alice?' It sounded so ridiculous that she smiled. And then stopped. 'What does Alice know?'

'I told her – told her family – last month. D'you remember when her cousin Hattie got engaged to some God-awful chap called Percy Westbrook?

They brought me home in their car. D'you remember?'

Of course she remembered. She had had terrible difficulty in hiding her jealousy on that awful late-afternoon in February, when Valentine had used up some of his precious time at home to trek out to Lypiatt Bottom in the teeming rain. Valentine was looking impatient, so she nodded.

He spoke in staccato bursts. 'It was then. Three weeks ago. I thought girls couldn't keep secrets, but obviously I was wrong. And Uncle Ted couldn't have told Father, either. I respect the Pettifords, Hester.' He pursed his mouth. 'I've packed in Oxford, Sis. It's finished.'

'I – I – oh God, I don't understand, Val.'

He said nothing, and she continued sharply, 'You're not making sense, Val. You've only got another term to go. You can't just walk away from it.'

'I've done it, actually.' He smiled. 'Last night. Saw my prof. Told him. Packed. Caught train. *Fait accompli*, Hester.'

'But – but – you *can't*! The scholarship! Mother . . . you cannot do this, Val. It's not just about you, you know. It's all of us. Especially Mother. And Father – oh Val . . . you cannot do this thing!'

'Darling,' he never usually used endearments and covered himself with an awkward laugh, 'I told you, it's done. I'm free, Hester! I can live like a normal human being! I'll have an ordinary job and get a room somewhere. I'm not looking forward to the interview with the aged p's, but that will soon be done too.' He stopped laughing. 'But it will be unpleasant, I grant you that. So you go home with Alice—'

'She knew. She *knew*. You told her before me.'
There was no holding back the jealousy any
longer. 'I wouldn't go back home with her if she
was the last person on earth. Why did you tell
her?'

He was astonished. 'Because she'd already done
it. I knew she'd understand. And if they'd
accepted her decision, I knew her parents would
understand too. I needed someone to understand, Sis.'

'You could have talked it over with me!'

'You simply wouldn't have believed me, Hester.
Look at you now.'

She was silent, sobbing drily, swallowing on a
sandpaper throat. The jealousy was like gall.

Val began to turn away. 'I'm going now. Mother
will be alone until this afternoon. I want to talk to
her properly, before the fireworks start.'

Hester said desperately, 'I'm not going to
Lypiatt Bottom. I can't bear it that they know.'

Val glanced back; it seemed to her it was a care-
less look. 'Stop behaving like a child, Sis.' He
disappeared behind the hedge, and she went on
standing there for a long time.

In the end Hester went home with Alice, exactly as
Val had wanted.

Miss Plant had arrived late at the library, which
meant that she had given Alice more time than
she was allowing for Hester; another black mark
for Alice. But Miss Plant was so interested, so concerned, that very soon Hester was absorbed in the
list of books that would be helpful with the
Shakespeare, the Chaucer, the George Eliot. With
the expertise of long practice, Miss Plant found

references and marked them with her personal straw bookmarks.

'I don't like this narrow approach, Hester,' she said. 'But I trust you to read around your subject anyway. There's a new George Eliot biography out – no, published before the War, of course, but the most recent. It's excellent. Ties in with the other women writers of the day. Brings you right up to Woolf.' She glanced at Hester. 'Have you heard of her? You should read *Mrs Dalloway*. Unfortunately she drowned herself at the beginning of the War.'

'Was she influenced by George Eliot?' Hester asked. It would be a useful sentence in an essay.

'Perhaps. But she was an innovator. Unique, I would say.'

Hester immediately discounted her. The State scholarship was a light at the end of a tunnel; nothing else on either side.

It was as if she had spoken aloud, and Miss Plant sighed audibly. 'English Literature has not always been a recognized degree subject, Hester. It's up to each one of us to show that it broadens the mind as much as Philosophy, Classics . . . Time spent reading is never wasted.'

'Of course not, Miss Plant.'

'All right, Hester. I'll leave you with those books.' She turned to leave and then came back. 'Hester, I think Alice is feeling rather lost at the moment. Perhaps you could keep an eye on her.'

Hester's eyes widened with surprise. Perhaps, if she could help to cheer up Alice, it was her duty to go home with her.

Alice, however, did not seem depressed; just the opposite, she was positively euphoric.

'Oh, Hessie!' She occasionally shortened Hester's name when she was feeling particularly affectionate. 'Miss Plant is so special, isn't she? I've been reading a book called *Mrs Dalloway* and she'd read it too! She said my essay was influenced by the author.'

'Virginia Woolf,' Hester said tonelessly.

'That's it! You've read her, too! Oh, Hessie . . .' The euphoria escalated into tears. 'We're so close. Miss Plant, too. We mustn't lose that. You and I won't, of course. But Miss Plant . . . how can I keep in touch with her? She said I must, but I don't see how.'

'Oh, stop crying, Alice!'

'I can't help it. Things coming to an end. You know, when Gramps died and Gran was heart-broken – literally – she used to get terrible pains in her chest. That was the same. A page turns, Hessie. And you can't turn it back.'

Hester thought of Valentine turning the page irrevocably on Oxford. 'Shut up!' she said fiercely.

'Sorry. I'm an old grouch. Listen – can you come home with me for tea? Hattie will be there and she'll run you back in Percy's car. She's going to cook something special. Please say you will. I just cannot stand watching Percy watching Hattie all evening!'

It was heaven-sent. If Hester had believed in a personal god, like Alice did, she would have sent up a quick thank-you. As it was, she said un-graciously, 'Well, if you need the company . . .'

'Not just any company, Hessie. You.'

The Pettifords were like that. They made you feel special.

* * *

Actually, it was fascinating watching Percy Westbrook watch his fiancée. It took Hester's mind off Valentine for almost an hour. He was one of the most unattractive men Hester had seen, but the crossed eyes meant that he could watch Hattie's face with one eye and her waist with the other. The odd thing was that the Hattie of the kitchen – who cooked with a frilly apron and commanded Doffie and the two girls to peel and scrape and stir and wash up – was quite different from the Hattie of the living room, who rearranged the table, brought in flowers, and pecked at Percy's face whenever she passed him – which was often. The Hattie of the living room made her tummy concave, arched her arms like a ballerina and seemed to be able to put two inches on her bust. Whereas the Hattie of the kitchen was just fun. Hester was not used to having fun in the kitchen. She was beginning to understand why Valentine had come here last month to tell them that he was leaving Oxford. Aunt Doffie was so sweet. Pretty, too. Not fiercely intelligent like Mother, but perhaps more approachable. And Uncle Ted was blessedly quiet. Not carping at everything all the time. In fact almost silent. She loved the way he forbore to interrupt the chatter of the women, murmuring beneath it to Alice, 'Darling, pass me the pepper, could you?' It was so completely different from Percy Westbrook's apparent inability to speak – unless you counted his grunts, which could have meant anything. What on earth was Hattie Pettiford thinking of? She could have anyone.

Hester recognized that her own thoughts were mimicking the way Aunt Doffie and Hattie talked.

She breathed slowly and deeply. She must not become shallow like them; Val would not approve. And yet he had chosen to come here and tell them before he told anyone else.

Ted leaned forward. 'You all right, Hester? Not feeling faint, are you?'

She jerked her head up and looked at him. His clear grey eyes were concerned for her. He wasn't handsome, but he looked so nice. So very, very nice.

She said, 'It's rather warm.'

'Come on.' He stood up. 'Let's take a turn in the garden. It's what they do in those books you read. And it's not raining.' He laughed and put his arm down for her to lean on, then led her past the table and into the hall. Aunt Doffie had left the lights on: the kitchen, hall and stairs were all bright and cheerful. Hester thought of the hall at Deanery Close: dark, tiled, cold. She hoped she wasn't going to cry.

'Too much reading perhaps, Hester.' Ted opened the front door and the smell of damp fields and woods rushed at them. 'When the bluebells are out you must come and stay. Alice will have left school by then and she will be so pleased to see you.'

Hester could think of nothing to say; the silence was broken only by the crunch of their feet on the gravel drive. Ted led her around to the back of the house where Percy Westbrook had parked his car. The light from the kitchen window illuminated it theatrically.

'It's called a family saloon,' he said regretfully. 'But there won't be a family. Just as well, I suppose.'

Hester wondered what he was talking about. She felt bound to say something. 'He must be rich – Mr Westbrook. Alice says he's got a tennis court. But he's only a railwayman, like you and Father.'

Ted laughed. 'His mother has a tennis court – and probably this car as well. As you so realistically put it, Hester, he is only a railwayman like Reggie – your father – and me.'

Hester was embarrassed. 'I'm so sorry, Uncle Ted. I didn't mean ... it's just that he's ... well ...' She reverted to a previous thought. 'Hattie could have *anyone*!'

Ted laughed again. 'Ah, Hester. Hattie knows what she wants, my dear. She's had enough excitement, obviously. Now she wants security and safety. And Percy can give her those.'

'Yes, I understand that. But it's not just that, is it? He looks at her. And she – she sort of performs for him.'

Ted stared at her, startled. 'Of course! You've put your finger on it, Hester! Absolutely! She performs. She's acting a part, isn't she? Good Lord. What happens when she forgets her lines?' He laughed, but she could tell he was serious, and she couldn't think of a serious reply. Yet didn't *she* act a part a lot of the time? And what happened when she could not act any more?

'She'll probably come to see you, Uncle Ted,' she replied.

He was startled again. Then he took her arm and they walked back around the house.

'We'd better go in. It's starting to rain.' He drew her under the porch and began to stamp his feet on the doormat. 'Why don't you stay the night here, Hester? You seem a bit under the weather.

You could have a lie-in tomorrow.' When she did not immediately answer, he said, 'No way of letting your parents know, I suppose. Never mind. Just a thought.'

It was a wonderful thought. They were all so kind and welcoming. And there would be boiled eggs for breakfast and a fire in the living room. 'Actually, Val will know where I am. He dropped in to see me at school today and suggested that I stay with you.'

'Ah, he's breaking the news, is he?'

Hester almost sobbed again at this reminder that the Pettifords already knew about Val's enormous, shattering decision to leave Oxford.

Ted sighed. 'You know, I never thought he'd do it. Not when push came to shove.'

She did sob then, but from terrible sadness rather than petty jealousy.

Ted put his arm around her and held her tightly. 'You know, Hester, he might well leave his studies behind, but he can't leave his brain behind. He'll go on learning, whether he wants to or not. There's no throwing that away.'

Hester sobbed and held on to him as if she were drowning.

Doffie came into the hall and said, 'Oh Ted, is she all right?'

'It's Val. He's come home to tell them all. She's going to stay the night with us.'

'Yes. Let the storm blow over.' Doffie came the other side of Hester and held her too. Hester felt completely protected. 'Come on, little lass.' Aunt Doffie's voice was like warm water rippling over her. Little lass – how lovely that sounded. 'I'll go and find you some nightclothes. You can have a hot-water bottle and slip into bed straight away. Alice won't be long.'

She gave herself up to them. It was wonderful. In the background she could hear Hattie screaming with laughter and Percy grunting appreciation. Alice came out of the living room carrying a loaded tray of dirty crockery. She raised her brows and Aunt Doffie said, 'Hester's not too good. She'll be in bed by the time you go up, darling.' And Alice's face lit up with pleasure.

They loved her. They really loved her. Alice was right – they were linked. Probably for ever.

As Doffie came downstairs, frowning slightly, Ted was waiting for her at the bottom.

'Well done, Doff. She needed that. Poor little sausage.'

She paused, holding the banister, leaning back slightly. 'Oh Ted, thank you for helping Hester. I thought you were still angry about Hattie and Percy.'

He said, 'That's not your fault, Doff. Hester made me realize . . . Hattie makes up her own rules as she goes along. We don't. But we must take her as we find her.' He tried to laugh. 'Bloody Hattie and her bloody awful fiancé!' He held out his arms, and Doffie fell into them.

Seven

The two girls were deeply asleep, Hester neatly tucked into her side of the bed, her dark hair unbraided but lying smoothly over one shoulder, Alice spreadeagled across the rest of the space, looking as if her limbs were flying off in all directions. She had talked quite seriously to God when she crept in by Hester's side, asking him outright to make Hester happy. She did so without diffidence, because it must surely be all right to ask a favour for a friend. She slept with a faint smile curving her mouth. Life might be a bit worrying at times, but it was also very interesting. She could hardly wait to see what would happen next.

What happened next was gravel from the drive clattering against her window.

Alice was awake instantly, because it had happened often during the War, when one of the shunters had come out to fetch Dad for an emergency in the marshalling yard. Her room was right over the front porch and a natural target.

She knelt and leaned across Hester to pull back the curtains. Someone was down there – she couldn't tell who it was. She opened the window and hung out.

Valentine whispered hoarsely, 'Let me in, Alice, can you?'

She froze for an instant. Then she looked down at the bed, intending to wake Hester. But Hester was sleeping so peacefully that she decided against it. She closed the window, slid off the bed and padded across the room, along the landing and down the stairs to the front door.

Val almost fell into the hall. He was weeping. She took his weight and he held on to her shoulders and sobbed into her neck. She whispered, 'There, there. It's all right.' They were words her mother had used when she fell over as a child, and they sounded ridiculous to her. She patted his back and he held her fiercely and tried to talk. He sounded like an animal caught in a trap.

Alice managed to spare one hand and flailing arm to close the front door, then she began to shuffle him towards the living room. He was soaking, his jacket heavy with water, his shirt clinging to his body. It must be raining.

'Come on now, my lamb . . .' Her mother's words again. 'Come on. Let me take your jacket. Come on.'

She kept coaxing and tugging him towards the embers left in the grate. She pulled out a dining chair with her foot and lowered him into it. He still clung to her, and she doubled over to accommodate him. And then suddenly he raised his head, grabbed her by the neck and planted his mouth on hers.

She almost jerked away, controlling herself just in time. He wasn't kissing her, he was sobbing into her mouth, communicating something . . .

something awful. When he finally slid away, leaving a trail of saliva on her chin, she said more urgently, 'Val, what has happened? They were angry – I realize that. But things like that don't worry you.'

He dropped his head on his chest, trying to control his breathing. She loosened his grip and stood up to switch on the light. Val flinched as the overhead light illuminated everything . . . the bloodied nose, the swollen eye.

'Oh Val . . . oh my dear. Oh Val.'

He spoke at last. 'Switch off the light!'

'Let's get your jacket and shirt off first. Come on. Let me help you.'

Between them, they somehow got rid of his jacket and shirt. More injuries showed up: welts across his thin shoulders, a puncture mark under one arm.

He was shivering. 'He took off his belt and strapped me, Alice.' He looked up at her. 'Can I stay here?'

'Of course.' She was horrified. Uncle Reggie was a jovial man. Surely he wasn't capable of hitting someone. 'I'll get some water and a face-cloth.'

She went into the kitchen and filled the kettle, then reached down the first-aid tin and cut some pieces of lint. The TCP was upstairs. She bit her lip and decided to leave it. Through the cracks of the hatch she could hear Val weeping again. It was terrible. Val, who was always in control. Not now.

She took everything in on a tray and began to dab his face. 'It's not too bad. It's the shock. You need tea and blankets. We had a course at school.'

She made tea and forced him to drink it. The

weeping had stopped now, but he had gone into another world, staring at nothing, shaking spasmodically in the aftermath of the sobs.

Alice glanced at the clock; it was past two. She whispered, 'Come on, Val. You can sleep for six hours. Come on.'

He blinked. 'Where?'

'In my bed, of course. It's warm. You need warmth.'

'But –' He stared at her wildly. 'He said I was queer!'

She tried to smile. 'Well, we've always known that.'

'Have you? Oh God.'

'It's nothing to worry about. It's because you're so clever. It's always made you odd man out.'

'Odd man out? Is that what he meant? Odd man out?'

'What else?'

He blinked again. 'He meant something else as well. I can't sleep with you.'

She frowned and then shook her head, confused. 'Listen, Val, I don't know what you're talking about. But I'll go and sleep with Mum and Dad. You can have my place. Next to Hester.'

He looked wilder still. 'Hester? Oh . . . she's here, isn't she?'

'You came to see her, didn't you?'

'No. It was you. Hester – that's different.'

She was still in the dark, but said in a motherly voice, 'Of course it is. Now come on. Otherwise someone will wake up and there will be a fuss.'

That got him on to his feet again. She came behind him and helped him up the stairs ahead of her. Her bedroom door was wide open and the landing light revealed that Hester had not moved. Valentine gave a small sob, and as Alice held up the bedclothes he slid next to his sister and lay rigidly on his back, clutching the eiderdown to his chin. Alice leaned towards his ear.

'I'm going downstairs again to clear up. No one will know about this unless you tell them.'

'Thank you.'

'Go to sleep. You're safe and warm. No one can get you. And Hester is with you. She loves you better than anyone else in the world . . .' Alice spoke in a singsong voice, words coming from nowhere. She recognized their truth afterwards. She had, of course, always known that Hester loved Val with her whole soul.

After she had cleared up downstairs, she looked into her room again. Valentine was curled against Hester, his eyes closed, his lips vibrating on each outgoing breath. Alice stared at them and wondered what it would be like to have a brother. Or better still, a sister. Then she crept into her parents' room and insinuated herself next to her mother. Doffie encircled her with a protective arm, muttered something unintelligible, and let her own sleep engulf her daughter.

When Ted woke the next morning to find Alice sleeping with them, he demanded an immediate explanation. He went next door in his pyjamas and stared at the sleeping Ryecrofts. Then he came back and winked at Doffie before going into the bathroom, so they knew it was all right.

Alice and Doffie went downstairs to put the kettle on and pass plates and cups through the hatch. Alice did not tell her mother the whole story, but Doffie was concerned anyway. When he came downstairs, Ted seemed to think it was all a bit of a joke; Doffie was less amused. They sat around the breakfast table while Alice gave her edited account of the night's happenings for the second time. Ted crept upstairs again to look at Val and Hester and found them still deeply asleep in Alice's bed; he came back down, his grin a little doubtful.

'I suppose it's all right? The two of them?'

Mum poured her fourth cup of tea and dropped three saccharin into it. 'It's not that so much, Ted.' She swivelled her eyes warningly towards Alice. 'It's just that ... Well, we can understand there was a row. Of course. He's a brilliant lad and the Ryecrofts must have pinned their hopes ... but to actually run off and come here. It's a bit much. How would you feel if Alice buzzed off to Deanery Close every time we had a row?'

'She wouldn't,' Ted said stoutly.

Alice turned the conversation. 'The thing is, Mum, he didn't come here to *us*. He knew that Hester was staying and he came to *her*!'

Doffie nodded her head. 'Yes, that makes sense. Of course. You're right, Alice. He wasn't running away from his family. He was running to it. Is that what you mean? Is that what I mean?'

Ted was tickled. 'Darling Doff, of course that's what you mean. Especially if it will make it all right with the Ryecrofts. Because . . .' He lengthened the last syllable tantalizingly, then put his hand on the back of Alice's. 'Listen, sweetheart. There's a job in the office. You needn't take it. Especially after what happened last night ... it could be difficult for you. But if you think you can cope—'

She was overjoyed, her worries about Valentine completely forgotten. 'Of course I can cope, Dad! I want to start soon! I want to be a breadwinner!'

Doffie looked as if someone had kicked her. 'So soon! I thought we'd have a bit of time together.'

'Mum – we will! Every evening and every weekend!' Alice turned to her father. 'Is it someone's secretary, Dad?'

'Yes. Junior typist, mainly working for a man called Bernie Berry. He's in charge of all the lost luggage and claims for it. There's a lot of filing, as well as shorthand and typing.'

'Is he nice?'

'Very. A truly good man. But there is a snag, Alice. I don't know how much it will affect you, but Bernie is Reggie Ryecroft's assistant. You'd be working in the same office as Reggie.'

Doffie said, 'Oh no, Ted. No, she can't do that.'

But Alice was overjoyed. 'Don't you see? I can make it better for Val. Our families have always been linked. It's right. It's meant to be.' She wanted to tell them that God had arranged it all, but Dad wouldn't like that.

'He's not a kind man, Alice. I don't want to put you against him, but he has a great many faults. And it could be awkward for him, too. He might feel he has to be stricter with you because of the link. He would not like anyone to accuse him of favouritism,' said Doffie.

'Mum, I know all that. But – this is fate. And I cannot fly in the face of it. You must see that.'

Doffie did see that. She sat back in her seat, worrying her bottom lip. And then, as Ted went on to tell Alice that the department was called the

General Accident and Claims department, she reached for the teapot again.

Alice sat there, bubbling with excitement. She had covered up for Valentine and now she was in a position to make it all right for him with his family. God was definitely listening.

She took a tray of tea and toast up to her room and put her hand on Hester's shoulder. Hester woke slowly and luxuriously, then did the most marvellous double take at the realization that the person in bed next to her was not Alice. Her jerk of surprise woke Valentine. For a moment, Alice thought he was going to throw a defensive arm across his face, but he took in the situation and lay on his back, eyes closed.

Alice explained, 'There was a row. He came to find you.'

Hester swallowed visibly and looked down at her brother's face. His injuries were obvious. His blond eyelashes were damp. She drew a deep breath.

Alice said quickly, 'Listen. Have some tea. Mum and Dad are catching the ten-thirty bus to go shopping in town. I'll scramble you eggs when you come downstairs.'

She turned and left the room. She had made it all sound so simple for the sake of Mum and Dad, and now Hester. But the fact remained that Valentine had been damaged. Damaged by his own father. And Alice was going to work for Valentine's father.

For the first time, she began to have doubts.

She went downstairs and stood at the front door while Mum and Dad went down the muddy lane towards the church, where the Cheltenham bus would stop. She felt suddenly grown-up. She was in charge of the house, in charge of a secret. Mum turned and called something and she shouted back, 'No, I don't want to come with you! Enjoy yourselves.' She wished she could tell them not to have any more rows; to stay together until death did them part, and even then to be together somewhere.

She discovered she was weeping.

Eight

Hester did not dare sit down. She had found her parents at the kitchen table eating their midday meal of stewed mutton and turnips. Her mother had answered her timid knock, then had immediately turned back down the passage and resumed her seat. Her face was ashen, and though she said nothing, her mouth worked uncontrollably. Hester saw immediately that she had not touched her plate of food, so she certainly was not chewing.

Reggie ignored his wife and daughter, and concentrated on cutting up the tough meat. Hester stood with her back to the gas cooker; she wondered whether she might be about to fall down. She and Valentine had worked out very carefully that it would be better if she came alone and pretended she had no knowledge of Valentine's state. Hester had tried to explain to Alice that it would be much, much better if they all pretended ignorance about the full extent of what had happened, although they could not ignore his black eye or his swollen nose. Alice had agreed to everything. She was not as outraged as she might have been. The picture of her mother

102

throwing a cup of scalding tea over her father was still very fresh in her mind. After all, everyone lost their temper at some time or another. And if Hester could begin to paper over the cracks, Alice herself could go on with the good work when she started her new career.

After what seemed an eternity, Dorothy said in a gasping sort of voice, 'You don't know, Hester dear. Valentine is missing. His bed has not been slept in.'

At last a clue. Hester tried to sound reassuring. 'He came to find me, Mother. He's quite safe.'

Reggie's head jerked up at that. He fixed his daughter with a cold blue stare. Hester told herself she must be careful. Very careful. 'What time did he arrive? Did he walk through the night?'

'I don't know, Father. I'm afraid Alice and I slept rather late.'

'And he was there? Downstairs?'

Hester shook her head slowly, as if confused. 'I think he was in the bathroom. I'm not sure. Anyway, he came downstairs.'

'Did he have breakfast with you and Alice? Was he dressed? What did he say to Ted and Doffie?' The questions came slowly, inexorably.

'He did not want anything to eat. He wanted to go to the library for some books. Aunt Doffie and Uncle Ted caught the ten o'clock bus, but he said the same things to them as he said to us.' Hester put a surreptitious hand behind her back and held on to the stove. 'He said . . . you were displeased with him. He'd left Oxford for good and you were angry about it.' She shook her head slowly. 'I think he wanted to tell me so that I could come home and reassure you. He seems quite his usual self.'

The basilisk stare softened and Reggie looked down at his plate. 'I think the mutton is tough, Dorothy,' he said.

Dorothy blinked, looked away from Hester and prodded her meat. 'I'm inclined to agree with you, Reggie dear.' She looked up again and smiled. 'Hester, sit down. I'm going to fetch another plate. See what you think.'

Hester pulled out a chair and sat down, putting her hands beneath the table. If her father saw them shaking he would know.

He glanced at her and almost smiled. 'It's cold out, is it, Hester?'

'Yes.' She sought desperately for something else. 'Considering it's almost Easter it's quite chilly.'

Dorothy put a plate in front of her. 'Easter is a very treacherous time,' she commented. Hester glanced up to thank her and saw that, though her face was still pale, it was somehow less white. Hester smiled at her, trying hard to convey reassurance. Then she speared a piece of turnip and put it into her mouth. It was almost cold and rather too hard. Her mother had never been really interested in cooking; but then she was interested in books and theatre and music, and her embroidered altar cloths were beautiful. Aunt Doffie was a good cook. Hester ate another turnip. It was also true that Aunt Doffie was interested in books and everything else. And though she did not embroider altar cloths, she knitted all the time.

Hester sighed and began on the mutton.

Out of the blue, her father said, 'So you did not notice his torn shirt? I assume he has gone to the library wearing it?'

Hester crammed a lump of meat into her mouth and chewed till her eyes watered.

Dorothy patted her back. 'Don't try to speak until you've swallowed that, my dearest. My goodness, you must be hungry. Did Aunt Doffie not give you any breakfast?'

Hester thought guiltily of the breakfast tray Alice had brought upstairs; and later of the three of them in the kitchen, Valentine making scrambled eggs and she and Alice doing the toast. She had said impulsively, 'Wouldn't it be fun if the three of us could live together like this all the time?'

She wiped her eyes and shook her head, and when she could speak she said, 'Aunt Doffie and Uncle Ted caught the bus into town. Shopping. And something to do with the wedding.'

Reggie went on eating, but it was clear he was waiting for a reply. Dorothy tried to give her more time. 'Wedding? Who is getting married?'

Reggie said briefly, 'Harriet Pettiford. Val told us in February.'

Hester felt a chill. She swallowed convulsively and felt the lump of meat in her gullet. Reggie lifted his head and nailed her with that awful look of his again. Yet his eyes were the same colour as Val's, and his hair had been the same straw yellow . . .

'Well?'

She did not pretend forgetfulness. 'He tore his jacket on the bushes. I did not see his shirt.'

Dorothy said quickly, 'He fell over. Caught his shirt on the edge of the stove. I did it to my cardigan the other day. Nasty sharp edge.'

Hester tried not to show how startled she was; surely Mother did not have to endure Father's wrath too? She caught her mother's eye and said quickly, 'I wondered why your cardigan was laddering.' She looked around the kitchen. 'It is awfully cramped in here. Perhaps if we moved the table against the wall it would be better.' She found herself almost believing that Val and Mother had torn their clothes on the stove.

'And where, pray, would Valentine sit then?'

But Reggie was smiling, because her suggestion practically proved that the kitchen arrangements were lethal.

Hester almost blurted out that Valentine would not be living at home any more, then took another forkful of mutton, chewed and smiled at her father. He nodded at her approvingly.

'Obviously I was wrong, Dorothy. The mutton cannot be too tough. Hester is thoroughly enjoying it.' He became benign. 'And how was Alice? Regretting her hasty decision to leave school?' Hester could not speak, so he continued pontificatingly. 'I think she made the right decision. She is not a real scholar. Rather a shallow girl. Of course, the Pettifords were all the same. I should know, I lived at Leadon Markham for over five years. Yes. I was thirteen when I went there and almost nineteen when I was promoted into the office. The old lady thought of nothing save the next meal and washing the clothes. And as for Mitzie . . . well, she definitely had a one-track mind.'

Hester raised questioning brows and her mother interpolated, 'Mitzie was Hattie's mother. It's short for Millicent.'

Reggie grunted. 'Should have shortened it to minx. And that would have been a kindness.' He caught Dorothy's eye and shook his head. 'I'm not saying Alice is like her, and Doffie's a good enough soul.'

Dorothy said firmly, 'Doffie is a wonderful woman, Reggie. And I am sure Alice will turn out the same.'

'Maybe. Maybe. Time will tell. Ted doesn't believe in thinking much. And she is like him in many ways.' He sighed as if with regret. 'No, I think she at least recognizes her own limitations. She will probably do well in a clerical post somewhere.'

Hester swallowed the rubbery mutton and said in a cheerful tone, 'Uncle Ted has got her a job in the office, Father.'

There was a split-second of silence when she was terrified she had antagonized him. Then her father smiled. 'Mr Berry is short of a typist. I wonder—'

'I think that was the name Alice mentioned.' Hester pushed her plate away; she had done it justice. 'It was a funny name. Like a comedian's.'

'Bernie Berry. Yes, he is a bit of a comedian. She'd do very well for Bernie Berry. Very well indeed.'

'And you could help her, Father. Keep an eye on her . . . that sort of thing.'

Suddenly Reggie Ryecroft tipped his head back and laughed. It was such an unusual event that Hester and her mother exchanged alarmed glances. But it seemed genuine enough.

'So I could, Hester. So I could.' He smiled. 'Shall we break the habit of a lifetime and have a cup of tea? To help the mutton on its way.'

He laughed again. Hester thought she must remember to tell Alice how delighted he was that she was to be employed in his office.

Valentine and Alice watched Hester walk into Deanery Close, and then did not know what to do next.

Valentine said, 'I should have gone with her. If he goes for her . . . I might kill him.'

Alice laughed. She could not get used to this new Valentine, beaten and humiliated. The old Valentine had always seemed to be in control of every situation; everyone was in awe of him because he was so clever, even Uncle Reggie.

She said, 'Of course he won't go for her. She's a girl. And your mother will be there – it's their dinner time.'

'Yes. You're right. It must have been a moment of sheer madness. He's never laid a finger on me before. And Hester – and Mother – he's so proud of them.' He turned to look at her. 'Alice, you've been marvellous about this. I'll never be able to thank you properly.'

She was surprised. 'I haven't been marvellous at all. I just did what had to be done.'

'But you didn't blab it all out to your parents. They have no idea . . .' It was half a question and she shook her head decisively. 'I would hate anyone except you to know what happened.' He tightened his mouth. She had not realized he was still so close to tears. She put a hand out and he caught it and put it to his face. 'Alice, I'm a fool. I didn't realize it. When I first told you – was it back in January? Anyway, I thought it was all going to be so easy. D'you remember I thought your father would get me a job too? And then I said you and I would get married and be happy ever after? D'you remember?'

'Of course I remember. You were in a wonderful mood. You made everything sound so real—'

'I kept saying that, didn't I? I wanted everything to be real. I was such a fool thinking it was all a bit of a joke. But one thing was true and real, Alice. I want to marry you. Will you marry me?'

'Val, stop it! You know very well I can't marry you!'

'Why not? You know me better than anyone else – better than Hester, even!'

'But we're not in love, Val. You have to be in love to get married!' She frowned. 'You do agree, don't you?'

'But I want you very badly. Terribly badly. In fact . . . Alice, you're my only hope.'

Alice was totally bewildered. 'Listen, Val, be sensible. You are still shocked. You've done an enormous thing, leaving Oxford. You've had this terrible upset at home – well, don't look like that, it *was* just an upset when all's said and done. I could tell you things that have happened at home . . . Anyway, don't keep talking this way. You'll regret it when you realize . . . Val, stop! We're in the street. You cannot kiss . . . Val!' She fought free and kept him literally at arm's length, her mittened fist pressing into the hollow above his clavicle.

He was almost weeping again. 'Alice, I'm sorry. It's just . . .' He made a visible effort to control himself, then took a deep breath. 'Listen, let's walk. Cut through to Westgate Street and down to the river.'

'All right. But no more trying to kiss me, Val. We're not like that.' She was intensely embarrassed, but determined. 'If you're going to keep on about getting married, we can't be friends. And that's that.'

He said nothing, but as they started to walk past the cloisters he did not take her arm or even walk close to her. There was a rather fraught silence while they trudged through College Court and into Westgate Street. By the time they reached the bridge, Alice was hot and flustered and wished only to get back to the bus terminus and go home.

Val stared across the fields at the gypsy encampment, and she followed his gaze. He had been there that night when she'd gone to tell Hester she was leaving school. She knew men went there to kiss the gypsy girls.

He said dreamily, 'I could rent a caravan. I could stay there.'

Alice was horrified. 'They've got fleas, Val! Anyway, if you go back today I think you can patch things up. We must see what Hester says.'

'I don't want – I can't bear the thought of going back, of submitting to that bully—'

'Val, he's your father. And there's Hester and Aunt Dorothy.'

He was silent for a long time. The thin March sunshine held no warmth. Alice shivered. 'I wonder whether the daffs are out at Newent.'

'That's probably where they are.' Val jerked his head in the direction of the encampment.

'They'll be picking like demons so that they can be back here this afternoon to sell them.'

'Probably.'

Silence settled on them again. A farm cart trundled past them, loaded with cabbages. Alice felt some of Val's despair seep into her. She had wanted to unite their families. Perhaps it would make sense to agree to some kind of secret engagement. There had been a girl at school who had confided that she was secretly engaged to an American soldier. It had come to nothing. In time this too would come to nothing. She bit her lip. It wouldn't do.

He said slowly, 'Alice, I want to explain. It's as if . . .' His voice was almost unbearably hesitant. 'It's as if I'm in a deep hole. A really deep hole. My family is in the hole too, but we're not together.' He forced a laugh. 'Perhaps we're in separate holes. I don't know. But from the bottom of my hole, I can see the sun shining and you and your parents . . . you're all there. You're happy and busy. You don't know I'm in a hole, so you treat me as if I'm there with you. And sometimes I want to shout and tell you about the hole and ask you to pull me out . . .' He laughed again. 'Perhaps that was why I tried to force myself on you back there. I was trying to get out of the hole.'

'Oh, Val.'

'It's all right. Don't look like that. Actually, Hester often comes into my part of the hole. And I think Mother too . . . But I thought that if I could get out I might help them to get out as well.'

'Oh, Val,' Alice said again, distressed.

He turned back to the parapet and leaned over,

looking at the turgid flow of the river beneath. She looked at his profile and remembered what Hattie had said: that he looked like Leslie Howard. He certainly had a thin face, a good chin and an aquiline nose, but it did not add up to Leslie Howard.

She thumped the parapet with her mittened fist. 'Listen, Valentine Ryecroft! If Hester gives you the all-clear, you must go back home. Then you must get a job like your father had – like my father had. A clerk – a booking clerk, perhaps – at one of the stations in the division. Where you can have digs. Start a new life.' She took a breath. 'My father will help you. I'll have a word tonight. I want to talk to him about going into the office, so I can ask him then. And everything will calm down and it will work itself out.'

He did not move; she thought his profile lifted slightly.

She said, 'You think my family's playing at life, don't you? Laughing and happy. But we're just ordinary. We're not different – we have rows and things. We're probably in a hole and we don't even realize it! We just get on with what has to be done. Washing up and planting potatoes and – and everything.'

She could have wept then, because she suddenly saw that getting on with things was special. She was so lucky. And Valentine wasn't.

He said, 'Am I allowed to hold your hand?'

She slid her mitten closer to him and he took her wrist, slipped off the mitten and held her hand tightly.

She said, 'It's going to be all right, Val. This is not the end of the world.'

His mouth lifted. 'I know. Give me a minute, then we'll go back and wait in the cathedral for Hester.'

She moved closer to him. 'I've got half a crown. We could have a cup of tea and a scone at the Tudor Tea Rooms.'

His head turned and he looked at her, then burst out laughing. 'See what I mean? That's *exactly* what I mean! And you still don't see it!'

He tucked her hand inside his elbow and they began to walk back towards the cathedral.

Hester was already there, sitting in the middle of the nave, staring across to where Edward was entombed. When she heard their footsteps she turned. Her face lit up at the sight of her brother and she stood and came to meet them.

'It's all right! Val, it's all right! I remembered exactly what we'd rehearsed and it worked splendidly!'

Val held out a hand, but she made no attempt to touch him. He said, 'Are you all right?'

'Of course! The main thing is, so are you. Mother tells me you ripped your shirt on the edge of the stove, so we're going to rearrange the kitchen to give us a bit more room. Father wasn't keen at first – guess why? Because there would not have been a place for you at the table!' She beamed. 'Anyway, Mother solved it. You and I are going to be next to one another.'

Val took a deep breath and glanced at Alice.

'So it was all in code. The place at the table means—'

'Exactly! That you still have a place at the table!' Hester did the tiniest jump. 'Please say you'll

113

come home, Val. Only for two or three weeks. Then you can look round and—'

'It's all right, Hester.' Valentine's smile was weary. 'Alice has it all worked out. Uncle Ted will get me a job at a station somewhere. I shall live in the station house just like Father did, so he can have no objection to that!'

Hester paused. Then she said, 'Of course. Oh, Alice, you are so clever! Father will be flattered that Val wants to follow in his footsteps! Oh, it will work! Val, I'm sure it will work. So long as Uncle Ted can find a suitable post.'

Alice said ebulliently, 'He found me a job, didn't he?'

'Yes. I told Father about that too, and he was really pleased and said he would keep an eye on you. It couldn't be better, could it?'

Alice said, 'Our families have always been linked. It couldn't be any other way.'

'Like the Capulets and Montagues?' Val's smile was definitely weary now. 'Kindly remember, little Alice, how the story ends.'

'Death. I know. But that was only because it was a play. If Shakespeare had worked it through to its natural conclusion – everyone happy – it wouldn't have had a proper ending.' She frowned and shook her head. 'You know what I mean.'

Val grinned. 'I know what you mean, Alice Pettiford. You mean you have no intention of dying or letting anyone else die!' He sighed with great exaggeration. 'Will that half a crown stretch to coffee for Hester too?'

'Of course.'

'Come on, Hester. Listen, you can have my books. And my essays too, if you want them.'

Hester gasped. 'Oh Val, would you? I'll definitely get in to Oxford then!'

'Yes, you probably will.'

He crooked both his arms, and after a second's hesitation Hester took one and Alice the other. As they marched out through the west porch and across the Close towards the Tudor Tea Rooms, Alice echoed Hester's words of that morning.

'Wouldn't it be great to live together and do things together like this?'

Nine

Bishop Hooper's Mansions in Gloucester had been leased to the Great Western Railway for many years. It stood on the corner opposite the Cattle Market and was flanked above its imposing front porch by two enormous oriel windows, from which there were superb views of the weekly cattle drives through the city. By moving the files which were stacked on the window ledge, it was possible to crawl to the front and peer up the road to the old theatre one way and the Catholic church the other. One of these windows belonged to General Accident and Claims, the other to the Staff Office. The Staff clerk was Dugdale Marsden – known to Alice for as long as she could remember as Uncle Duggie – who had run away from boarding school at thirteen, not to join the circus but to join the railway. The General Office clerk was Reginald Ryecroft.

Alice parked her bike next to her father's in the grubby little backyard, which had once housed horses and maybe a carriage, and entered by the back door, where the messenger was dealing with the morning's post. He glanced up from the rack of pigeon-holes, saw that she was not important and went back to his work. Alice fidgeted on the other side of one of the enormous tables, which seemed to symbolize railway waiting rooms and offices. She was wearing a new dirndl skirt she had made herself and a blouse made by Mrs Mearment, topped by her old jacket, also made by Mrs Mearment from a car rug. After six years of school uniform she felt overdressed.

She glanced at her watch. Quarter to nine. She had always visualized coming into the office with Dad and being introduced to the people she did not already know. But Dad was on earlies, and in any case had told her there mustn't be a sniff of favouritism. She would go in the back door and tell the messenger that she had to report to the Staff Office and knew her way. Dad had not told her what to do if the messenger ignored her.

She glanced sideways at the back stairs which led to the offices. She knew the layout fairly well, because Dad had shown her around on a Sunday when only the Control Office worked. The landing at the top of the stairs was the entry to all the offices and was called the long landing. First was the tiny cubby hole inhabited by the Chief Clerk, an old man called Mr Mucklesmith who had come up through the ranks and was as nervous as a kitten. Then there was a bigger office with a view of Market Parade, where the Divisional Superintendent held court. He was a gentleman. His father had been Superintendent of the Line and had always encouraged his son's love of the railway system. The father was called Sir Basil, but his son was ordinary Mr. In fact, Dad often referred to him fondly as 'old Eddie Maybury', and was proud of the fact that they shared a forename. Everyone liked Mr Maybury; he was tall and good-looking, with the sort of round face that was somehow instantly familiar. When he'd had his moustache he'd looked a bit like Joseph Stalin, but luckily he had shaved that off now.

Next to him was his assistant's office. The assistant hadn't been there long – the previous one had drunk himself to death because of the War, but Dad said this one was all right. His name was Richard Oliver. He was old, probably as old as Mr Mucklesmith, and he had worked himself up in the same way too. But Dad said he knew what he was doing.

Beyond those three offices was the Control, where Dad worked, then the General Office, where Uncle Reggie held sway, then the Staff Office, where Uncle Duggie smoked his pipe to try to hide his smelly feet.

Alice wondered whether she could simply slide past the table and go upstairs without actually speaking to the messenger. She wanted to see Uncle Duggie well before nine o'clock, so that he could take her into the General Office and show her where she was going to sit without too much fuss and bother.

She took a sideways step and the messenger spun round from the pigeon-holes, still holding an envelope.

'Where d'you think you're going?' he snapped.

He was really old. He had spent the best part of his working life up at the station sweeping platforms, and had come indoors thankfully when his bronchitis forced him to lean on his broom most of the day. His name was Parfitt. Alice suddenly realized she had no idea if that was his first or last name.

'I – I—' She was terribly nervous. She mustn't let Dad down. She should have eaten breakfast, because now she felt sick.

Unexpectedly, Parfitt's face creased in a smile. 'It's Alice Pettiford, isn't it?' he asked. 'You dun't remember me, do you?'

'I might do . . .' People didn't like not being remembered.

'I were up the station. When you was a toddler you came with your mum. Neville Chamberlain were visiting the Gloucester Aircraft. You shook 'is 'and.'

'I remember that,' Alice said, smiling. She had been more than a toddler. It had been after the Munich crisis and she had been nine or ten.

'I came and took you to the front so you could shake old Chamberlain's 'and.'

'Yes, I remember!' Her smile widened. 'Thank you ever so much, Mr Parfitt.'

'Pleasure. I 'eard you was coming to work 'ere. First day, is it?' Alice nodded. 'Now you don't want to be nervous. Mr Marsden is a very nice man.' Alice nodded again. 'D'you want me to come upstairs with you?'

'I know the way,' Alice said. 'But thank you.'

It did not seem that he was used to being thanked, because his smile was now a beam; it couldn't go any further up his face. He watched her climb the staircase and called out, 'I remember your Grandad. Lovely gentleman, 'e were.'

'Oh –' Alice paused and looked down. For two pins she could have cried. 'Thank you so much, Mr Parfitt.'

'Only the truth. Your pa's the same. And now you.'

119

Alice gulped. 'Yes. Yes, that's what I thought. Exactly.'

She managed another smile, rather watery, and went on up the lino-covered stairs to the long landing. It was empty and echoing. Halfway along on the left, the main staircase – beautifully proportioned, of polished oak – led down in three flights to the tiled foyer. Visitors used that entry. But someone was climbing the stairs. The sound of slow footsteps indicated someone old and not very able. Alice hurried forward.

'May I help you?' she called into the stairwell. And then felt a complete idiot, because the person climbing the stairs so laboriously was probably her own age. He lifted his head to look at her: his hair was very thick and glossy black, which she hated – Brylcreem Boy, Dad would call him – but his face was young and open, and somehow quite lovely. She looked over the balustrade at the top of the landing and gazed down at it. It was round, brown-eyed, snub-nosed. And smiling. He looked like a very young Mr Maybury. Perhaps he was Mr Maybury's son. But no, Mr Maybury was only about thirty – he could hardly have a son of sixteen or seventeen.

All this went through Alice's head in half a second, if that. Then, more consciously, she realized that the boy had not said a word. He just stood there, holding something obviously heavy and smiling up at her as if he had never seen anything like her before. Which, of course, he had not, because they certainly had never met. If they had, she would not have forgotten him.

By this time, Alice felt totally confused. She withdrew slightly and straightened her shoulders.

The hairy material of the unlined jacket made by Mrs Mearment scraped her neck. She swallowed.

He stayed where he was and said, 'Are you the new recruit?'

She loved that. He didn't call her the new girl. She was a recruit.

'Yes. I'm on my way to the Staff Office.'

He was galvanized into action. 'I'll show you.' He took the stairs two at a time, still laboriously, but much quicker now. As he joined her, she saw he was carrying an Aladdin paraffin stove. 'Just been to the cellar to fill it,' he panted, putting it down and holding his side. 'Now I have to light it out here and wait for a moment until it stops smelling. While that happens I go down again and fill the coal hod.'

'But it's Easter. Do you need all that heat?'

'Yes. We don't get any sun on the oriels until midday and it's very cold. Mr Ryecroft says he can catch cold at home in his own time.' He grinned, sharing the joke. Alice laughed. She could imagine Uncle Reggie saying that.

'You work in the General Office, then?'

'I'm the junior clerk. I do a lot for Mr Berry.'

Alice felt her face lift. 'Oh, how –' she searched for a word and came up with 'coincidental!' It sounded so pretentious. 'I mean, I am supposed to be typing for Mr Berry.'

He said, 'Yes, I know. But I thought you might be – you know, grammar school and everything. And Mr Pettiford's daughter, too.' He ducked his head, embarrassed. 'Everyone knows your family.'

'Gosh, I hadn't realized.' First Mr Parfitt and now – 'What is your name? Mine is Alice Pettiford. But I expect you know that.'

He lifted his head to nod, then said simply, 'Joseph Adair.'

She knew exactly how he felt. When you were forced to speak your name aloud like that, it always sounded ridiculous. Alice Pettiford. Joseph Adair.

She wanted to tell him it was a lovely name with a definite ring to it, but obviously she could not. Perhaps she should have said how pleased she was to meet him, and that it would be good to know someone in the office where she was working . . . but she could not say that either. In the end she made a silly giggly sound and told him she had better go. He skipped ahead of her and opened the door of the Staff Office, and there was Uncle Duggie on his knees in front of an enormous iron stove, riddling out the ashes.

He looked over his shoulder. 'Oh, hello Alice. I thought you'd be along in a minute. Come and give me a hand with this, will you?' He stood up, dusting his hands. 'Oh, you too, Joe. Have you met Alice Pettiford?'

'Yes, sir.' Joseph Adair hurried forward. 'Let me do that.'

But Uncle Duggie held up his hand. 'Don't worry, Joe. Alice is a whizz at lighting fires. Nearly set the house alight when she was only eight. Germans didn't need incendiary bombs when Alice Pettiford got hold of matches!'

Alice had to laugh, although she would rather Uncle Duggie didn't make too much of her infant escapades in front of Joseph Adair, who was so clearly capable and efficient.

Uncle Duggie was dusting the knees of his trousers now. He glanced up and said, 'Off you go, m'lad. If Mr Ryecroft catches you in here you'll suffer for it, and so shall I!'

'Yes, sir.' Joseph Adair hung on to the enormous brass door handle. 'I'll probably see you again, Miss Pettiford.'

She was already feeding paper strips through the bars of the stove. 'Oh, please call me Alice. No one has ever called me Miss Pettiford before.'

His smile was wonderful to see. He closed the door gently and was gone. Alice felt a curious sense of loss. Uncle Duggie said, 'Right, I'll apply the match to the blue touchpaper, young Alice. I've no wish to set the flue alight.'

As he stood next to her, she could already smell his feet. It wasn't unpleasant; she associated it with him coming to tea with his young lady of the time, playing cards during the evening and yarning with Dad about railway matters while the young lady helped Mum wash up.

He said, 'Listen, Alice. About names. Call Joe Mr Adair when Reggie is around. And for God's sake, don't call Reggie uncle. He is either sir or Mr Ryecroft. And however friendly Bernie is, he is Mr Berry. Got it?'

'Yes, Uncle – I mean Mr Marsden.' She grinned. 'It's a bit of a joke, isn't it? Are you all frightened of Uncle Reggie?'

'Not exactly frightened, but he can make life tricky. And he could make it damned unpleasant for you, my girl. Go along with the joke, for your own sake.'

She knew what he meant, of course. After what had happened to Valentine, it was obvious that Uncle Reggie's sarcasm could develop into something much worse. But that's why she was here – to

123

be a bridge between the two families. Wasn't it? She tried to remember just why she had left school in the first place. That was one reason, anyway. If she was going to be a successful bridge, she would have to go along with a lot of things Uncle Reggie said and did. But that was all right, because he liked her.

Uncle Duggie got out some papers and began to ask her questions, to which he generally knew the answers, such as full name, date of birth and parents' occupation. 'Your mother's occupation is obvious, of course,' he said, removing his pipe from clenched teeth and gazing into the bowl. 'She is a saint.'

Alice laughed obediently, and Uncle Duggie replaced his pipe and said, 'Identity number.' And Alice, with some newly discovered sentience, thought suddenly, Uncle Duggie is in love with Mum!

'Well, that's it, Alice. You are now on the temporary staff of the Divisional Superintendent. You will be able to use privilege tickets immediately in your own name and you will be eligible for passes in six months. How do you feel?'

'I don't know.' She was frightened, but whether by her unexpected sentience or by the whole signing-over of her life, she had no idea. Uncle Duggie – Mr Marsden – stood up and clapped her on the shoulder, and then shepherded her out through the door and on to the long landing again. Joseph Adair was lurking by the Aladdin stove, which was percolating its oily smells through the diamond-shaped holes on its top.

Immediately, she stopped feeling frightened.

'Did the fire take all right, sir?' Joe asked,

glancing at Alice, then looking away again very quickly.

'Fine, Joseph. Hope you got yours going too. It's a nippy wind and Mr Ryecroft feels the cold.'

Alice wondered why, if that was so, it was always cold in Deanery Close and he refused to light any fires there.

They went into the General Office. It was far more cluttered than the Staff Office; there was an enormous desk, obviously Uncle Reggie's because its chair had its back to the stove. At angles to that there were two tables, so that the three enclosed the heat. The table nearest the door held two typewriters, the like of which Alice had never seen before. There was another similar machine at one end of Uncle Reggie's magnificent desk. The oriel window ledge was packed with files. Behind its mica doors, the stove roared. Alice blinked in bewilderment as Uncle Duggie gave her what he called 'the grand tour'.

'Got it, Alice?' He turned to leave. 'Keep an eye on her, Joe. Make sure Miss Webster shows her the cloakroom and includes her on the doughnut list.'

'Certainly, sir.'

Alice stammered, 'You're all so kind. But I don't think . . . I mean, I'm not sure that I can – can *manage*!'

'You'll manage, Alice.' Uncle Duggie tamped his pipe absently on Uncle Reggie's desk. 'Just remember your grandfather.'

But that was the trouble; she couldn't.

The morning was a complete muddle. Miss Webster arrived and turned out to be in her late twenties, as tall as Alice, and pale, with an aristocratic nose and haughty eyes. When Alice was presented to her, Miss Webster asked what sort of books she read and Alice told her about *Mrs Dalloway*. Miss Webster said, 'I met her once, you know – Virginia Woolf. Before she drowned herself. She was on the London train. I recognized her because she was so like me.'

There was a photograph of Virginia Woolf on the back of the library edition of *Mrs Dalloway*, and Alice looked at Miss Webster with renewed interest. Yes, she had the long nose and patrician expression and rather sunken eyes.

'I say,' she murmured admiringly. 'Did you speak to her?'

'No. But it was dark and I could see her reflection in the window, so I could really study her. She seemed very anxious. Haunted.'

'Yes. Well . . .'

'Quite.' Miss Webster removed her hat and kid gloves and began on her coat buttons. 'It's going to be a pleasure having a permanent typist in the office. Poor Mr Berry has been reliant on Joe and me for far too long. We've got our own jobs, after all. It's simply not fair.'

The door opened, and Parfitt came in with the post and put it on the desk. He greeted Alice like an old friend. Joe began to open the letters. The door opened again and Uncle Reggie entered, followed closely by a short round man who was introduced as Mr Berry.

Uncle Reggie was in a jovial mood. 'Ah! Miss Pettiford herself in person. No less. In fact very much more. And how are we, today of all days, Miss Pettiford?'

This was the Uncle Reggie she knew, and she had difficulty in replying without calling him by that name. In fact, she discovered when the morning was nearly over that she had not called him anything at all. On the other hand, it was easy to call Mr Berry by his name because he looked like a berry, round and shiny.

When Uncle Reggie drew his post forward and began to dictate to Miss Webster, Mr Berry came to the table where Alice was staring in horror at the typewriter.

'Now look, m'dear. I'm going to do what I usually do. Write out my letters by hand and then give them to you to type out neatly. While I'm doing that, Joe will show you the works, as it were!' He grinned. 'We used to be called the Works Department, so that's rather apt. But we deal with a little bit of everything here, much too much for you to take in all at once. So I suggest that Joe shows you the filing system first of all.' He waved a stubby hand at the office. 'All the letters that come in have to match a file. They should have a number on them. If not, you just have to plough through until you find their file – takes time, I'm afraid. Joe has already started.' He took her arm and led her to the window ledge. 'Stand as close as you can and watch what he is doing. You will pick it up easily.'

In fact she did not pick it up at all, mainly because when Joe started to explain what he was doing, Uncle Reggie boomed, 'Can't hear myself think, Mr Adair!' and he had to drop his voice to a whisper. But now and then he would flash her a smile and point to a number and she saw what he was doing. She hoped she never had to do it herself.

Halfway through the morning, Miss Webster was summoned by a bell to Mr Maybury's office and suddenly Uncle Reggie's joviality was at an end.

'These University men! Completely selfish!' He watched as Miss Webster put away her notebook and took another from the drawer. 'Kindly inform our reverend Superintendent that you were in the middle of taking dictation from me!'

She stood up without a word and left the office. Uncle Reggie sighed deeply and then said, 'Ah, well. That's why you are here, Miss Pettiford. Let's see what you're made of, shall we? Have you brought a notebook?'

'Yes.' She produced the shorthand notebook she had used at school. 'I'm not very fast . . .'

'Just keep up as best you can. Dear Sir, Referring to yours of the tenth inst., I shall be glad if you will investigate the possibility of a temporary points failure at the junction with the Dymock line on the date in question. I am requesting the Divisional Engineer to interview the ganger concerned with a view to—' At this point, Alice found a pencil and began. He was by now on another letter, this time to a member of the public who had lost a suitcase. '. . . Will let you know as soon as my searches of the LPO have taken place. You know what the LPO is, I suppose, Miss Pettiford?'

'Lost Property Office?' she hazarded, her voice breaking.

He smiled. 'Exactly so. Exactly so.' He leaned back. 'Now, I am going to be telephoning. Is there anything I can do to help anyone? That's good. Carry on.'

Alice looked at her hands. They were shaking. On the other table, Mr Berry was talking into his telephone. It was cacophony. Opposite her, Joseph Adair was writing like a crazy person. How could he keep it up? She looked again at the typewriter. It had three banks of keys instead of four and they came from two arches, one on the right and one on the left. It was called an Oliver. The same name as the Superintendent's assistant. She wondered dully whether he owned the firm. What was she going to do? What on earth was she going to do?

Joseph leaned over the table. He was clutching two pieces of paper sandwiching a sheet of carbon. Somehow, back to front and upside-down, he rolled the sandwich into her machine. The top paper was imprinted with the old GWR crest. This had been crossed out and replaced by 'British Railways, Western District'. She stared at it hopelessly. Another sheet of paper appeared. It was covered in Joseph's clear schoolboy script. It began, 'Dear Sir, Referring to yours of the tenth inst., I shall be glad if you will investigate . . .' She read on. All the letters dictated by Uncle Reggie were written out in longhand. She glanced up at Joseph Adair gratefully and he smiled at her. Tentatively, she put her fingers on the home keys and slowly began to type. The letters were in the right place; there were two shift keys, one for capitals, one for numbers. She could do it. She could do it. She looked up and smiled at Joseph, and though her eyes were damp, she was happy. She was so busy that she hardly noticed Joseph disappearing, and when a cup of milky coffee arrived at her elbow with a paper bag containing a doughnut, she stared up at him as if he were a vision.

'How absolutely lovely!' she breathed.

He grinned. She thought of the boys she knew; they would say cockily, 'All part of the service.' Joseph said nothing. He simply moved to Uncle Reggie's desk and poured him a coffee from the big enamel jug he was carrying, then on to Mr Berry's desk. Miss Webster came back and said, 'Oh Joe, I need this. Thank you!' But nobody stopped working. Uncle Reggie stood up and made for the door, saying 'Duty calls,' and Mr Berry put down the phone and commented, 'Trouble at Severn Tunnel Junction,' and Miss Webster groaned and typed on furiously.

Quite suddenly, the morning was over. Miss Webster put a cover over her Oliver and donned her outdoor clothes in a way that reminded Alice of the time she had seen the Sadlers Wells ballet at Cheltenham Opera House. She then handed Alice her car-rug jacket and, keeping her back to Uncle Reggie, said in a low voice, 'I'll cast an eye over those letters when I get back from lunch, don't worry.' Much more loudly she said, 'I very much like the jacket, Alice. I've seen them in Cavendish House. Are you going home for lunch? I'll walk with you to the bicycle shed.' She turned on her heel and said, 'After you, sir,' and waited until Uncle Reggie had departed. He went down the main staircase and she escorted Alice down the back one.

'You've done well, Alice. You don't mind if I call you Alice? We tend to use forenames among the lower ranks!' She rolled her eyes humorously. 'I'll get back early and retype those letters if there are any errors.' She opened the door on to the chill Easter wind. 'He's going to be a bit hard on you –

no favouritism, that sort of thing. Just grin and bear it. Most railwaymen are lovely.' She smiled sentimentally and turned up the street towards the shops. Alice gazed after her adoringly. Then she ran into the yard, grabbed her bike and pedalled furiously out to Lypiatt Bottom. She had an hour and a half, but she wanted to be back early for the afternoon. To see Miss Webster again. And Joseph Adair – Joe – who had saved her life. And she hadn't even thanked him.

Mum said she should take him something; some daffs, maybe. But you didn't take flowers to a man. 'Dad will know. You can take it tomorrow.'

Alice had hardly stopped gabbling since she got home, even through her stew. Now she said, grinning, 'I think Uncle Duggie is in love with you.'

Doffie burst out laughing. 'Duggie Marsden? What on earth makes you say that?'

'I know things like that. I've got a sort of second sight when it comes to feelings.' She was splutter-ing with laughter, but her wagging finger proclaimed that she was also serious. 'I know things that people themselves don't know. I think Hester is a bit in love with Val, for instance.'

Doffie stopped being amused and turned her mouth down. 'Stop it, Alice. You don't know what you're saying.'

'Oh, I do. I know nothing will ever come of it. Ever, ever, ever. But it's true. And Val probably feels the same way. But he would never admit it.' She sighed. 'That's why he's in such a muddle.' She took another mouthful and chewed, while Doffie sighed too and slid another carrot on to her plate. Alice speared it, opened her mouth and

131

then paused. 'That's probably why he asked me to marry him!' she said, surprised.

'He what?' Doffie was astounded – and annoyed. 'He came here, slept in the same bed as his sister, and had the nerve—'

'Mum, you know it wasn't like that. You saw him. But what you didn't see was that Uncle Reggie had beaten him. He was a nervous wreck.'

Doffie quietened instantly. 'I suppose I'm not surprised. Reggie Ryecroft has a really sadistic streak in him.' She stood up. 'And my daughter is working for him!' She went through to the kitchen and opened the serving hatch. 'You know, darling, you can always leave. You don't have to stick it out for Dad's sake.'

Alice spooned the rest of the gravy to one side of her plate.

'It's not like that, Mum. I think Mr Berry is going to be very nice. And Miss Webster is really, really nice. And the junior clerk is nice too.'

'I thought you were the junior clerk.'

'No, I'm the junior typist.'

'And who is the junior clerk?'

'Someone called Joseph Adair.'

Significantly, Doffie said nothing.

The afternoon sped by. Mr Ryecroft – Alice was already thinking of him formally – glanced through the letters she had typed and smiled sideways at Miss Webster.

'I take it you retyped these?' he asked.

She glanced up from her machine, where she was still working on Mr Maybury's reports. 'Sorry? Oh, your letters. I checked them for you. They are perfectly all right.' She continued to type at a rattling speed. Mr Ryecroft read the letters again and almost reluctantly put them on the pile for signature. Joseph Adair did not look up from his work and Alice, who had been holding her breath, let it go in a puff that sent her carbon paper skidding across the table. She snatched it back and fitted the next paper sandwich into her typewriter.

Mr Berry ambled across the office and put another three letters by her side. 'Sorry about these last few, Miss Pettiford. But that's the lot for today. You must be tired out.'

Mr Ryecroft said genially, 'I wonder whether Miss Pettiford could be early in the morning, Mr Berry? Apparently she is a genius at lighting fires and I notice that Mr Adair would never gain his scout badge in that activity.'

Joseph kept his head down. Alice was so angry for him she could have burst, but after counting five slowly as Mum advised – Mum, of all people – she said brightly, 'It will be a pleasure.' She tried to add 'sir', but it would not come.

But she had spoken the truth. It would be a pleasure, because outside on the landing, Joseph Adair would be trimming the wick on the stove.

Ten

Joseph Adair was seventeen on May 15th, and on the following Sunday six of them celebrated by taking the train to Lydbrook Junction and walking up to Symonds Yat to admire the view and then having tea at Mrs Hobbie's house. Mrs Hobbie was a relative of Miss Webster, and was renowned for her boiled eggs, cucumber sandwiches and dough cake.

'It will be in the nature of an expedition,' Miss Webster told Joe. 'Stout shoes and macintoshes, just in case. And tea will be on us.' She glanced at Alice. 'We'll work it out properly in Miss Warner's office. No need to worry.'

Alice knew she was lucky to have been taken under Miss Webster's wing. Miss Warner was Mr Maybury's secretary and was unofficially in charge of all the girls. She could be difficult. But she treated Miss Webster as a near-equal rather than an underling, because when Miss Warner was busy, Miss Webster stood in for her and took Mr Maybury's dictation. The female expedition members consisted of Miss Webster and Miss Pettiford from the General Office and Miss Jenkins from downstairs. Miss Warner declined gracefully, saying she could not manage hills. And Miss Ford was a Sunday School teacher. 'I take a Sunday School class also,' Miss Warner informed her loftily. 'But for Mr Adair's sake I would have arranged a stand-in for this week.' Miss Ford blushed, and everyone knew her defection was nothing to do with Sunday School. 'A chap, more like,' Miss Jenkins said into Alice's ear.

The male threesome consisted of Joseph himself from the General Office, plus Toby Fletcher and Dennis Fluke from the Control Office. Ted Pettiford described them as 'the lads' and told them glumly that given fifteen years they might just about grasp the purpose of the railways. They guffawed at this, which made Ted look glummer than ever.

Alice was bubbling with excitement.

'The train is early, Mum,' she warned. 'I'll have to leave here by seven. I'll leave my bike in the office and run round to the station. Miss Webster and Miss Jenkins are walking. They both live in the same direction. Stroud Road somewhere.'

'Surely you can use Miss Webster's first name, darling? You've been there a month now and she calls you Alice.'

'I don't know what it is and she never suggests it. Everyone calls her Miss Webster, not just me.'

'What about Miss Jenkins? She's still in her teens, isn't she?'

'Yes. She said I could call her Janet. And I will – I think.'

'Janet Jenkins,' Doffie mused. 'How thoughtless of her parents.'

Alice said, 'You're so down on the office people, Mum. They're all lovely. Honestly.'

'All I said was that the name Janet Jenkins is unfortunate. Supposing Dad and I had named you Petula?'

Alice giggled. But she knew she was right. Mum was terribly critical of everything to do with the office. When she had heard that Uncle Reggie had given Alice the job of lighting the stove every morning, she had wanted to go and see him to complain. Luckily, Dad's expression had squashed that idea immediately. Alice's idea of bringing everyone closer together was a slow job. She hadn't seen Valentine and Hester since that day in March, and Mum and Dad still argued and niggled ... though Dad had not sent either of them to Coventry again. That was something.

Meanwhile, every day was exciting and different, and yet the same. Joe had showed her how to light the paraffin stove, which she had named Fido for no reason at all. But now everyone called it Fido and talked to it coaxingly – Come on, Fido, stop that dreadful smell and get burning ... Not that they needed Fido so much now the weather was getting warmer, and the stove was allowed to go out in the afternoons. But it was cold in the mornings still, and anyway she loved getting to the office before anyone else – except Joe, whose train from Cheltenham arrived at eight-fifteen. He was usually already in the cellar by the time she had hung up her coat, and she would grab the heavy iron coal hod and leap down the front stairs, swinging on each of the posts and jumping the last four steps with a frightful clatter so that Joe would know she was on her way. He always filled the bucket for her, but she had to carry it because it was more manageable than Fido. So they staggered upstairs, exaggerating the steepness, panting laboriously, smothering their laughter in case Mr Ryecroft had arrived early. He had caught them on the second landing once and asked them what was so funny. His question had amused them even more, so they had to grit their teeth to stop themselves bursting with silly giggles. They did not know why they were so light-hearted. Why everything was such a delight. Why the business of fetching fuel was such fun. But Mr Ryecroft had waited for a reply.

Joe had said inspiredly, 'Apparently, sir, I have smut on my nose!'

Alice had made a sound like bath water running away. Mr Ryecroft had said coldly, 'Kindly wash and brush up before coming into the office, Mr Adair. And Miss Pettiford – hurry with the stove, it's very chilly this morning.'

He did not approve of the birthday outing, and wanted to know why Mr Berry could not accompany them. But Mr Berry was a model-railway enthusiast and there was a fair on in Tetbury.

'Why don't *you* come, sir?' Miss Webster enquired sweetly.

'Because it seems to be for youngsters,' Mr Ryecroft replied, then looked at her. 'Although of course you are going, Miss Webster.'

He rarely directed his sarcasm at Miss Webster, simply because it had little effect. This time she laughed and said, '*Touché!*' And after a moment, he too laughed. Alice found it fascinating. How on earth had Miss Webster attained the dizzy heights so securely guarded by Mr Ryecroft? Could anyone do it, with practice?

As if in response to this thought, he seemed to

rely on Alice more heavily during the week before their outing. Several times she was near tears; then, on the Wednesday, he told her sharply that she would have to finish her filing faster, otherwise they'd be borrowing Miss Ford again, which apparently they had done before her arrival. She scrabbled through it in time to help him with that day's correspondence, but got no thanks for it. Instead, he leaned back in his chair and said musingly, 'There's a precedent somewhere for this particular claim. A firm down in the forest. Accident with one of their trucks . . . happened about a week after I arrived in the office. I was in Mr Berry's chair then and dealt with all the claims, accidents or not.' He pursed his lips. 'Could have been 1925 onwards. See what you can do, Miss Pettiford.'

She said timidly, 'Have you got the name of the firm, sir?' She hardly ever called him sir, but he liked to hear her say it.

He frowned. 'No. You'll have to get the steps and go on top of the cupboard.'

Mr Berry called out, 'Probably in the cellar.'

Mr Ryecroft did not deign to look round. 'I don't think so. Go to it, Miss Pettiford.'

She went to it without much hope. The files on top of the cupboard were in a mess; they were grey with age and dust. Her nose ran and her eyes watered. She balanced on the steps, sifting helplessly through the detritus of years.

Suddenly Mr Ryecroft stopped dictating and said, 'What a splendid view we have of Miss Pettiford's legs!' He put the tips of his fingers together and swung his chair slightly. 'My goodness, Miss Pettiford. Plenty of calf muscle there.

If only Gloucester sported a ladies' rugby team!'

She felt her face redden and stayed very still, praying that Joe would not spring to her defence. The silence was deafening. They all recognized Alice's humiliation, they all knew that the sally was as near to an insult as he could get, but they did not know what to do about it.

Then, unexpectedly, Mr Berry stood up and pretended to peer appreciatively. He put a hand on Joe's shoulder and bent his head. Alice closed her eyes, which were watering profusely. Mr Ryecroft smiled.

Mr Berry said in a jolly voice, 'I say, you're right, sir! Betty Grable doesn't stand a chance where our Alice is concerned, does she?'

Mr Ryecroft knew that the tables had been turned and his smile disappeared. Miss Webster put down her pad and pencil, rolled some paper into her machine and began to type faster than usual. Her lips were thin and disapproving. Joe kept his head down and was careful not to look at Alice's legs. Alice straightened, rubbed her hands on her handkerchief, blew her nose fiercely and went back to sifting.

Mr Ryecroft said, 'I have not finished the last letter, Miss Webster.'

'Oh? It seemed as if you had.' Miss Webster picked up her pad and read back the last line.

Ten minutes later, he had in fact finished and she put down her pad, rolled out the final letter from the typewriter and put it in the tray for signature. Then she stood up.

'Come along, Alice. We'll go together and fetch the coffee and doughnuts this morning. Give Mr Adair a break, as it's his birthday.' And she took

Alice's coat from the peg and handed it to her before Mr Ryecroft could say a word.

Alice followed her down the front staircase, only just holding back her terror. But as Miss Webster opened the swing door, she took her arm.

'Don't be frightened of him, that's the secret,' she said directly. 'You did the right thing keeping quiet. If Bernie hadn't saved the day, his words would have hung about pointlessly.'

Alice gulped. 'It's different for me. I've known him for ages. He used to call me his little chickadee.'

Miss Webster almost spat. 'How sickeningly patronizing! Still, I suppose you were only a baby. Listen, what we'll do, we'll have our coffee in the milk bar and then take theirs back. It's my treat, and we'll have two doughnuts each!'

Alice loved being part of this little conspiracy. They sat on the high stools and the barman asked them what had happened to Joe. Then he topped up their cups, and Miss Webster told her that when Mr Ryecroft was out of the way, Alice could use her Christian name.

Alice almost choked with sheer pleasure. 'Actually, I don't know it,' she confessed.

'Hardly anyone does. It's Helena.' She smiled. 'Mr Maybury calls me Helena sometimes.'

'I say.' Alice was very impressed.

'Keep it under your hat.' Miss Webster – Alice still thought of her as that – lifted her cup in salute. 'Here's to us, Alice! Now . . .' She looked serious again. 'Do you like Georgette Heyer?'

Alice always told Miss Webster about the books she read, and Miss Webster had nearly always read them too. If she hadn't, she made a point of going to the library and getting them, which was the best compliment of all.

Alice nodded. Miss Webster said, 'I've got loads. I love her, and Mother always gets me the latest for birthdays and Christmases. You can borrow them.'

'Oh, Miss Webster.'

'Helena.'

'Helena.'

'I'll bring a couple this afternoon. We'd better be getting back.'

'Oh dear.'

'He'll be all right now, you'll see. We've raised the flag and he knows it.'

The best of it was that that afternoon, before Mr Ryecroft or anyone else got back from the dinner hour – except Joe and Alice, Joe rang the station master at Awre Junction on the internal telephone, known as the Bus Line, and asked him about the accident. 'Our Miss Pettiford is having to compile a report for Mr Ryecroft and we are unable to turn up the file.'

There was a silence, then Joe grinned. 'Certainly, Mr Lewis. Here she is now.'

He passed the receiver to Alice, and before she could put it to her ear a voice boomed through it, 'Don't tell me that's Will Pettiford's girl?'

Alice cleared her throat. 'Actually sir, Will Pettiford was my grandfather. My father is Ted Pettiford.'

'Good God in His gracious Heaven! Where did them years get to then, eh? Ted old enough to 'ave a girl in the office? I remember Ted when I was a porter down the Golden Valley Line. 'E were a lad clerk then and used to polish the station lamps for me. Good lad, 'e were. And now his little girl . . .' The voice became nostalgic. 'So you're carrying on the family tradition, are you? And in the General? Don't envy you that, my girl. Is 'e there? A-breathing down your neck?'

She wondered whether loyalty demanded that she asked who ''e' was. But she laughed and said, 'No. Not back from dinner yet. That's why Mr Adair thought of ringing you about that accident.'

'Well now. What is it you want to know? Anything for a Pettiford, I'm telling you. Just mention—'

Joe was making frantic signs, so Alice said quickly, 'The name of the firm concerned. And he's coming. Now.'

Mr Lewis got the message. 'Turner Iron Products. Newport. Monmouthshire. 1926.'

'Oh Mr Lewis, thank you so much.'

'Put the phone down now. Quick!' said Joe.

She did so just as the door opened and Mr Ryecroft came in. She finished tidying her half of the table while Mr Ryecroft gave a weather report, saying it was 'treacherous' and he wouldn't be surprised if they all returned from this ill-advised expedition with streaming colds, because Miss Pettiford appeared to have one already.

Remembering Miss Webster's – Helena's – advice, she said nothing to this and squeezed past Joe to climb the steps yet again. The file was definitely not there. She climbed down and went to the oriel window and fingered through the T's. And there it was. Dusty and dog-eared. 'Turner Iron Products, private wagon derailed, June 10th 1926.' She pulled out the folder and placed it carefully on the edge of Mr Ryecroft's desk, then went back to her typewriter where Mr Berry's neatly handwritten letters were waiting.

'My goodness! Better late than never, eh, Miss Pettiford? We might have to wait for our coffee and our files, but they come in the end!'

The door opened and Miss Webster came in. Mr Ryecroft said no more.

Sunday dawned brilliantly. High cirrus clouds in an ice-blue sky, the air so clear it hurt Alice's chest as she pedalled furiously into Gloucester. The lanes were full of buttercups on their long-branched stems, reaching out to flick her as she passed. She stood on her pedals to get up the Pitch and then waited, panting, at the lights before soaring down into the city, the public gardens on one side, the almshouses on the other. Gran had said, 'I don't mind them there almshouses up London Road, but don't let them put me in the workhouse – don't let them do that!' Why had she begged a child for such a favour? Thank God for Hattie, who had left her boarding school at Ross and come to live with Gran. Alice spared the Victorian cottages a glance as she free-wheeled gloriously into the quiet Sunday-morning streets. She could not imagine Gran anywhere but in the cottage on the banks of the Severn river, and now that Hattie was back again there was no need to worry.

Alice shoved her bicycle into the shed and carefully shut the yard door, then scooted up George Street as if she hadn't a minute to live, which was ridiculous as she was much too early. There was a call from behind her and there were Miss Webster and Janet Jenkins, arm in arm, swinging along as if they were moving to music, Miss Webster holding out her spare arm for Alice as if she were one of them! And she was! She took the arm and fell into step without any wrong-footing at all, and they landed up at the booking office window perfectly synchronized, breathless, smiling, 'like three little pots of petunias' as the ticket inspector said when they made a rhythm out of showing their privilege tickets and going through to the platform. And there were the Cheltenham lads waiting for them: Toby Fletcher, Dennis Fluke and, of course, Joseph Adair.

The railcar meandered unhurriedly along the banks of the Wye, so the passengers could enjoy the view and even greet some of the anglers who were making the most of this delightful Sunday morning. Alice sat sideways on one of the long seats, making sure her cotton dress was tucked over her knees and hugging her cardigan around her, only half listening to Miss Webster as she pointed out landmarks to the others. The sun sparked off the water and made her think of summer holidays spent at Weston-super-Mare. They had usually gone for a week in August during Alice's school holidays; this year she would be lucky to get a week off. New staff were allowed one day's annual leave for every month they had worked. She wondered whether they would count April – if not, that would only leave her May, June, July and August. Four days. Dad said he would see what he could do, but she didn't want that.

Joseph spoke behind her. 'Do you know the forest at all, Alice?'

'Not really. My grandad was station master at Leadon Markham, but that's really right on the edge of the forest. Dad knows it well. My mum says it's a foreign country with its own laws and language!' She laughed.

'Well, actually, I know what she means. Mr Maybury took me on one of his trips around the old lines when I joined. I had to work the ganger's trolley, and then when we stopped I took notes from him.'

'You're brilliant at shorthand.' She smiled shyly. 'I should know.'

'I wasn't at first. Lad clerks had to have a speed of a hundred words a minute and I could only manage eighty. But they took me anyway.'

'Why did you want to join the railway?'

'I'm not sure. Perhaps it's in my blood somewhere. It's obvious why you did. Definitely in your blood.'

She nodded. 'Dad. Yes.' She glanced at him. His dark eyes were like velvet. He had the nicest face she had ever seen. 'What did your dad do, Joe?'

'He was in the Marines. But he was killed right at the start of the War.'

'Oh, Joe. I am so sorry.'

'For asking a perfectly normal question?' He smiled. 'Perhaps that's why I joined the railway. To be normal.' He shook his head and said more seriously, 'I needed a job, a steady job. You know . . . Mum.'

She almost told him then. About her terror that one day Mum would leave Dad, and that she would have to go with Mum, and then they would need money and – and perhaps a go-between. But they were interrupted by Miss Webster, calling their attention to the fact that they should be getting ready as they were nearly there, and the moment was lost. Later, she was glad. How could she have thought their circumstances were similar, when she had a father and he had none? He must have felt responsible for his mother since his father died. Of course that was why, in spite of his boyish looks, he was so mature. He made Toby and Dennis look like idiots. Which, as Dad had told her last night, they were.

The trek up to the top of the hill was hard going. Dennis trailed his mac behind him like a dog's tail. Janet hung on to Toby on the steeper bits; Toby was the biggest of the three boys and had played rugby for his school. Miss Webster went ahead of them, in case anyone thought she was too old for this sort of thing. Her elegant legs seemed to make light work of the climb.

Joe said admiringly, 'We're so lucky to have her, Alice. It's awful in the Train Office and Janet's got no one to chat to in the Staff Office.'

'But Mr Marsden is so nice,' Alice protested loyally. 'Heaps nicer than Mr Ryecroft.'

'Yes. But those feet . . .'

Alice said, 'It's probably a medical condition.'

'It is. It kept him out of the War.'

'I didn't know that.'

'Miss Warner told me. I think she's in love with him.'

'Oh!' She nearly told him that she thought Uncle Duggie was in love with her mother. Again, later, she was glad she hadn't.

He said, 'I'm sorry. That was gossip, wasn't it? I get into the habit of collecting bits of things like that, to tell my mother. She doesn't go out much, you see.'

'Oh, I'm sorry about that. But that's not gossiping, is it? It's trying to get your mother interested in things outside.'

'Well, yes. And it doesn't seem so bad when she doesn't know any of the people I talk about.'

Alice nodded understandingly, then stopped and held her side. 'Have to get my breath,' she explained.

He stopped too and the others went on. They looked back the way they had come. The view was superb: the forest, girdled by the river, was a pillowed mass of spring green.

Joe said, 'Funny to think that under all that foliage there are still all the little lines that ran to each colliery. They took some up for the War effort, but there's still a lot around.'

'If you had to pump a ganger's trolley around, you should know!' Alice laughed.

'It was such hard work,' he confessed. 'I'd joined the month before and I think Mr Maybury wanted to give me a treat.'

'Some treat!'

'Yes. But it was good. It gave me a . . . feel for the railway. You were probably born with it. I had to learn it. Perhaps Mr Maybury knew that.'

'Dad likes Mr Maybury. He respects him.'

He looked sideways at her. 'Your father is quite a character, isn't he, Alice?'

She was immediately on the defensive. 'How do you mean?'

'Well, Toby says he won't answer bells. If anyone wants him they have to come and talk to him in his office.'

Alice was surprised. 'I didn't know that.'

'It's what Toby says.'

147

'Funny. Gran – my grandmother – told me once that when the squire went past, Dad would never lift his cap like the other boys. Always said he was as good as any man in the land.'

They smiled at each other, acknowledging the oddities of all adults, then turned and scrambled after the others. When they reached the promontory of Symonds Yat itself, they were holding hands.

You could stand and admire the view for so long, and after that Toby and Dennis reverted to school-boy silliness and pretended to push each other off. Miss Webster made them stand still while she took a photograph of everyone with the sheer drop behind them, then said briskly, 'Time for tea, I think. Mrs Hobbie is expecting us at three and it's nearly that. So best foot forward.' She said to Alice, 'Ridiculous lads! Perhaps they haven't yet learned that to fall from this height is certain death.' The 'lads' heard her and took up the cry. 'Certain death to you, Fluke old man!' 'And the same to you, Fletcher the Retcher!' they chanted at each other.

'Oh, for goodness' sake!' Janet protested. 'And what has happened to the helping hand, Toby? I notice Miss Webster and I don't get any assistance, like Alice is getting!'

'Oh, I do beg your pardon, Miss Jenkins!'

But there was still no helping hand, and the two women walked together, discussing the fact that the young men of today did not know the meaning of chivalry. Alice and Joe brought up the rear. But though they exchanged smiles occasionally, they no longer held hands.

Boiled eggs had never tasted so good. Alice did Dad's trick and upturned her empty shell to present it to Joe. Then everyone was doing it and laughing inanely. Then Mrs Hobbie brought in a fatless fruit cake – 'I saved some dripping for 'en, but did go off' – with candles stuck into the top, and they all sang to Joe and demanded a speech.

Blushing, he said, 'I don't know what to say. To have such good friends and such a good time . . . I don't know what to say.'

Dennis leaned sideways and said into his ear, 'Try "thank you".'

'Oh! Yes, of course! Thank you so much! Miss Webster, for arranging it all, the rest of you for coming. And Mrs Hobbie for a wonderful cake! Thank you!'

They clapped and laughed, and then Joe cut the cake and passed it around. Miss Webster produced the birthday card she had made everyone sign. Janet Jenkins daringly kissed his cheek, and Toby and Dennis pumped his hand vigorously. His face was red but he looked happy. Alice stood slightly apart, next to Miss Webster, and smiled. Miss Webster said quietly, 'He's a good lad, Alice. You've got just a year. Make the most of it.'

Alice looked round, startled. 'A year? What will happen then?'

'He will be eighteen, Alice. National Service.'

'Oh.' For a moment she had imagined a dreadful illness. 'But there's no war.'

'No. Thank God.' She smiled. 'And he's well used to looking after himself.' She laughed. 'Not many men can, you know. Mr Maybury has one manservant, a cook, and someone to do the rough. Just for one man.'

'Well . . .' Alice was struck by the fact that Miss Webster seemed to know about men. Especially that she realized that Joe was much more mature than most boys of his age. She said, 'Don't forget that Mr Maybury isn't just a man. He's a gentleman.'

Miss Webster pretended to be surprised. 'Alice, I am shocked. You are not your father's daughter!'

They both laughed. That was the best of Miss Webster; she was always one jump ahead. Alice watched her press some money into Mrs Hobbie's hand, and wondered why she had mentioned Joe's National Service with such foreboding. One year. Already, after just one month, it was difficult to imagine the General Office without him. And, as the General Office was her life at the moment, that meant it was difficult to imagine life without him.

She looked across to where he was allowing Dennis and Toby to josh him about something. He was like a grown-up man indulging a couple of puppies in their playfulness. She went over to them.

'Joe, come and look at the backward view. Over there must be Speech House, where all the forest laws are made. And there's a sort of lake – can you see it?'

He joined her willingly. 'One of the ponds, I expect. The open-cast mines were often allowed to flood once they were exhausted.'

'You certainly learned a lot on your trip with Mr Maybury.'

'Not that. I knew that before. My grandmother spoke about the forest. I wish she were still alive – I'd like to ask her one or two things.'

'Such as?'

'Oh . . . nothing really.' He shrugged. 'Why she hated it so, I suppose.' He tightened his full mouth. 'And why she treated my mother so badly.'

Alice was silent for a while, hardly able to take this in. And yet Valentine was obviously worried that Uncle Reggie might ill-treat Aunt Dorothy. But a mother and daughter?

Joe turned to her and said earnestly, 'I try to make up for it, Alice. Can you understand that?'

'Of course – of *course*!'

'Only, you know – Dennis and Toby – what they were saying just now.'

'I didn't hear. They're awfully silly, anyway.'

'They're always calling me a mummy's boy. That sort of thing.' He laughed rather painfully. 'I don't take any notice.'

'Of course not! How ridiculous!' She was furious. She promised herself she would have nothing to do with Dennis Fluke or Toby Fletcher in future. 'Dad says they're just a pair of idiots, anyway!'

'Does he?' Joe brightened. 'I thought it was only the bright ones who went into the Control Office.'

'Who told you that?'

He smiled slowly and said, 'Actually, Dennis and Toby.'

They both laughed.

As they started back down towards the station and the train home, something really good happened. It was even more tricky getting down the rock than getting up, and Toby took Miss Webster's arm while Dennis took Janet's. Alice

151

noted this and waited for Joe to catch her up before reaching for his hand.

He held it tightly and said apologetically, 'What an idiot. I must have a form of vertigo or something. Didn't notice it on the way up. Thanks, Alice.'

She went slightly ahead, stopping at the steeper bits and holding his hand firmly. She was filled with a powerful sense of protectiveness; a deep pleasure that she was able to help him. There had been the transcribed shorthand notes; the phone call to Mr Lewis at Awre. And now she could quite literally offer a helping hand.

They arrived on the platform at a run and stood there panting, smiling at each other. She thought how wonderful it was when a strong person revealed a weakness. To her.

But later, tired after the cycle ride to Lypiatt Bottom, she remembered Miss Webster's words like a gypsy's warning. Just a year. Only a year.

Eleven

Hester was amazed how much she missed Alice that summer term. Alice had made the monochrome of school life into a technicolour extravaganza . . . well, perhaps not quite that, but certainly she had added colour. Without Alice, Miss Plant no longer looked like George Eliot, in spite of her looped hair and long nose. The melodramatic romance of Fräulein Schmidt, who had married her Jewish husband when they met in Heidelberg University and smuggled him out of Germany on a false passport, paled against the reality of him being interned as an alien all through the War and Frau Schmidt changing her title to Fräulein so that she could teach in a school near the internment camp. What had been romantic became terribly ordinary. Even though she had been in the Lower Sixth, Alice had still behaved like a third-former, sliding down the banisters, getting out on to the roof of the labs to sunbathe. Hester remembered her response to Dr Grey's stock phrase, 'What do you mean by it?' She recalled Alice's spread hands as she said, so reasonably and logically, 'But Dr Grey, we had to get out on the roof to put out those incendiary

153

bombs, which was rather horrid. Why can't we use the roof for something pleasant?'

Hester found herself smiling reminiscently at some of Alice's escapades, though at the time they had irritated her to death. And then she realized that Alice's absence was to her own advantage. She could work twice as hard; she could even take on some of the reading which she had always considered such a waste of time when Alice did it. She wished she could see Alice and get a book list from her. But then, Alice probably never kept a list of the selection she and her mother borrowed so haphazardly from the library. She remembered that when Alice and Aunt Doffie had gone to the cinema together to see a film taken from a book, they had always borrowed the book afterwards and talked about which was the best, the book or the film. Hester found herself reading *Random Harvest* and *Mrs Miniver*. When she and Alice eventually got together, she must ask about the films. There was something showing at the Picturedrome with Humphrey Bogart and Lauren Bacall . . .

But the summer went gloriously on and she did not see Alice. There was a letter from her in late July:

Dear Hester,
    Can you come for the weekend? I have such a lot to tell you. I am typing this on my Orrible Oliver. Only just getting the hang of it.
    Love Alice.

Hester showed it to her mother, who smiled widely and said, 'Do go, Hester. It would do you

154

good. Now that Valentine is down at Leadon Markham you have no young companions. You and Alice always got on.'

'I thought she might come home with Father for tea or something now and then,' Hester said.

'Oh, I don't think so. Do you?'

Hester shook her head dumbly. Since the 'business' with Valentine, she and her mother seemed to agree tacitly about many things. It had not occurred to either of them that Alice was now out of bounds to Hester.

Reggie looked at the invitation with smiling interest.

'So impulsive. Very like her mother. And when, I wonder, did she use company property and time to type this personal note? Ah-ha. We must investigate.'

Dorothy tried to put that right immediately. 'If she is anything like Doffie, it would not have been in company time. And surely such a short note is permissible if typed in her own time?'

Reggie sighed with obvious disappointment. 'I suppose so. It is ... interesting, to watch Miss Pettiford rise to certain baits.'

Hester was surprised. '"Miss Pettiford"? Do you call Alice "Miss Pettiford", Father?'

'Certainly. Just as I call Miss Webster "Miss Webster". And Mr Berry "Mr Berry". And Mr Adair "Mr Adair".'

'And she calls you ...'

'Sir, of course. What else would you suggest? Uncle Reggie? I am not a relative, Hester, so that would be inaccurate.'

Hester did not think she could bear any more of her father's pontifications. She said jokingly, 'I

155

do hope she will call me Hester and not Miss Ryecroft when I go for the weekend.'

Reggie lifted his bushy brows. 'My dear girl, surely you realize there is no question of you spending time at Lypiatt Bottom now? Not while Miss Pettiford is working for me. It wouldn't do. It simply wouldn't do.'

'But Father –' Hester ignored her mother's warning look, 'Alice and I have been friends since we were – babies, practically! You can't mean that it is over?'

'That is exactly what I mean, Hester.' Reggie frowned. 'I am surprised you have not realized it. The same applies to Ted Pettiford and myself. To Dorothy Pettiford and your mother. When we were all on an equal social footing, it was quite different. Now that Alice Pettiford is one of my clerks, it would be difficult – impossible – for any of us to cross the divide.' He saw her bewilderment and said forcefully, 'Hester, would you expect me to take Mr Maybury – my Superintendent – out for dinner? To invite him here? Would you expect that?'

'I – I don't know. I've never thought –'

'Of course not. It is unthinkable. Just as it is unthinkable that you continue your childhood friendship with Alice Pettiford. It would put you in a most invidious position. As if you were acting charitably.'

'Oh!'

'Now, child, go to your room and compose a suitable reply to Alice Pettiford.'

'I don't know what to say!'

'Perhaps you can visit Valentine on that particular weekend.'

There was not a particular weekend mentioned, but to visit Valentine, which until now had been expressly forbidden, was sop enough. Hester retired into the hall, then hung on to the newel post, shocked by this sudden termination of friendship. What would Alice think? Or say? Or do?

Through the kitchen door she heard her father say sternly, 'Dorothy, I do not brook argument in this case.' Whenever had Father brooked argument in any case? Hester frowned and listened harder. 'Not so ... Unreasonableness does not enter into this, my dear ... There are rules, there are limits. Alice – Ted – they knew it when she came into my office.' Another pause while her mother murmured something else. Hester gripped the newel post and whispered, 'Don't, Mother. Please don't.' Then her father said roughly, 'You are my wife, Dorothy. Never forget it.' The table grated on the quarry tiles as it was pushed, and then there was a small gasp and, seconds later, a male laugh.

Hester went upstairs. She remembered seeing her father kiss her mother once before; claiming her. She supposed it was better than ripping her cardigan on the edge of the stove.

She wrote two letters to Alice; one for her father to see, another to send to Alice. The first one said:

Dear Alice,
  I am afraid I cannot visit you at weekends as I have a great deal of studying to do now, especially in Latin. I do hope this finds you well, as I am at present.
    Affectionately, Hester Ryecroft.

The second one said:

Alice,
    Father is not keen on me coming to Lypiatt
any more – it will make it awkward for him at
work. I do hope I will see you before next
winter. Give my fondest love to Aunt Doffie and
Uncle Ted and the same to you.
    Your friend Hester.

She secreted the second letter beneath her
blouse, next to her skin, and took the first one
downstairs.

'"Affectionately"? I think you should change
that to "Sincerely yours". Otherwise it is fine. Well
done. I am glad you understand the position.' He
looked across the kitchen table at Dorothy, who
was sitting very still, breathing evenly. 'On second
thoughts, let the affection stand. After all,
it means little.' He pushed the letter into its
envelope and stuck it down. 'I will treat you to a
stamp and post it, Hester.' He pocketed it and
smiled. 'And I will purchase a return privilege
ticket to Leadon Markham for Saturday. How
does that sound?'

'Thank you, Father.'

'Don't thank me, child. Your mother needs
news of Valentine and you can bring it for her.'

'Oh, Mother.' Hester was so full of joy she almost
forgot that poor Alice was actually going to receive
the first letter. 'Mother, shall we take a walk? Round
to the park, perhaps? It's a lovely day.'

'Your mother is tired, Hester. She is going to
have a lie down. Off you go and enjoy your walk.
You are looking pale.'

'Oh –' Hester said yet again. She had wanted to talk about Valentine. And her mother would not meet her eyes. 'Yes. Perhaps that would be nice. And I could post the letter then.'

'I told you, that is my treat. Together with the railway ticket.'

Hester went into the hall. It was six-thirty. There was no way she could catch Alice or Uncle Ted and give them the proper letter. She drifted out of the front door and along the Close. She must remember that she was going to see Val on Saturday. That would make up for everything. She would go to the cathedral and stand in the nave and thank God for her brother.

Alice had always loved the cavernous cathedral. She used to run along the whispering gallery and through the cloisters as if they belonged to her. Val loved it too, because it was like the inside of a drum and resonated with every sound, especially the long low organ note that you heard with your feet as well as your ears. Her mother loved it for the right reasons: because it represented all that was awesome and wonderful about God. Hester had always felt alienated by its history, the stone figures of dukes and kings, the terrible story of Edward II, whose body was brought here from Berkeley Castle to be honoured at last. To Hester its enormous columns and arches, fan vaulting and windows spoke of a strange indifference. More than that; an uncaringness. She stood at the top of the nave facing the choir stalls and shivered. The letter inside her blouse stuck to her damp sweaty skin, reminding her that tomorrow Alice would get the cold missive her father was posting.

From the organ loft there came a tentative note, then another. Then a voice. Mr Makin was giving a lesson. Hester stood very still, letting the single notes drop around her. She knew she was going to cry; she wanted to cry; she wanted to stand here and be washed by melancholy. And somehow she couldn't.

She took a deep breath, then let it go in a bubbly sigh and began to walk slowly down the nave. Suddenly, in the shadow of the huge columns, she saw Alice. It was so like the answer to an unspoken prayer that she gasped and stood stock-still, staring, hardly believing that at – probably seven o'clock, now – on a Wednesday evening at the end of July, Alice Pettiford could be waiting for her in the cathedral. She had opened her mouth to call out before she realized that Alice was not alone. She was with a boy.

Hester continued to stare. Alice with a boy. Alice, who had always scorned Diana Townsend and Grace Leith for being 'boy mad', who had found her romance between the covers of books, who had said, 'I never want to marry. I want to look after my mother.' Which was the craziest thing to say, but Alice had said it with such conviction that Hester had never questioned it.

And here she was. With a boy.

Hester stared intently. He looked terribly young. Slicked black hair, round face. Val had a long narrow face, so obviously intelligent that you forgot he was the image of his father. Round faces belonged to schoolboys. He wasn't as tall as Val, and was more thickset. He wore grey flannels and a tweed sports jacket, a white shirt and a dark-blue tie. Alice laughed suddenly and took his arm – they were the same height. He laughed too.

Hester did not know what to do. Alice was meeting a boy – this must be what she wanted to tell her. It seemed sordid and horrible to Hester, and somehow typical of Alice. Not that Alice was sordid and horrible, but just when you were expecting a wonderful chat with her about books or Hattie's wedding or dear Uncle Ted, the chat would turn out to be about something quite different, trivial and uninteresting. And, frankly, rather trite. Her father had forecast this very fate for Alice, and Hester was angry with her for being so – so obvious. She wrinkled her nose and watched them laughing together, then remembered with great thankfulness that she was seeing Valentine at the weekend instead of Alice.

Suddenly, as if she heard the thought, Alice half turned, lifted her head and saw Hester. Her face, already smiling, seemed to burst with pleasure. 'Hester!' she called. The name reverberated around the columns and across the choir stalls, and for a moment the organ stopped playing and Hester could imagine Mr Makin, alert and listening.

Alice rushed forward, half pulling the boy with her.

'Oh, Hester! What a bit of luck! I very nearly suggested in my letter that we ought to meet in the cathedral. Then I thought Mr Ryecroft – Uncle Reggie, sorry – might see it and wonder what on earth was going on! And I wanted to take Joe along the whispering gallery and we've just done that and come down to do the cloisters and here you are!'

'Here I am,' Hester agreed, ignoring the boy and smiling indulgently at Alice's open face.

Alice turned to him. 'I told you, Joe. We often share thoughts. Not exactly telepathy. Not thoughts, exactly – actions, impulses.'

'Actually, I'm going for a walk,' Hester said calmly. 'I just looked in for a moment—'

'There you are!' Alice was triumphant. 'That's what I meant! D'you see, Joe?'

Hester could see that Joe did not see at all. But he smiled and nodded, and Alice suddenly understood his embarrassment.

'Joe, I am sorry. Hester – sorry too. Hester, this is Joseph Adair. He works in the office and he has saved my bacon many a time! I would not have stayed if it hadn't been for him.' Her smile was almost watery as she looked at him. Then she drew a breath and went on. 'And Joe, this is my best friend, Hester Ryecroft. We've known each other since the cradle. We'll probably be buried side by side!' The other two looked startled and she added quickly, 'Sorry, I'm getting carried away. I just wanted you two to meet and I couldn't think how it would happen and now it has.'

Joe held out his hand. 'Pleased to meet you.' It sounded awful there in the nave with the organ encasing them in sound again. He shook Hester's hand and added, 'I would have known you anyway, Miss Ryecroft. You are so like your father.' Hester almost snatched her hand back, though she had been thinking that it was a good dry handshake, not like some of the boys, whose handshakes were horribly damp and fishlike.

'It's Val – my brother – who looks like my father. I am like my mother,' she stated firmly. He looked crestfallen, and for Alice's sake she had to say something halfway decent. 'I have heard of you,

Mr Adair. My father speaks most highly of you.'

For some reason both Alice and Joseph Adair laughed at this. It made Hester feel left out.

Alice said, 'Listen, it's pay day tomorrow and I've still got two bob from last week. Let's go and have tea somewhere.'

Hester had no intention of prolonging the meeting over tea. She smiled kindly. 'Alice, dear, it's past seven o'clock. And I don't think two bob would buy a dinner at the New Inn, do you?' She laughed – not a joyful laugh like Alice's. This laugh held a hint of condescension. 'In any case, I must have a short walk before going home. It's been nice meeting you.'

She half turned, but Alice grabbed her. 'Hester, when are you coming for a weekend? You might as well tell me now and then we can plan to do something. A swim at Wainlodes? A cycle ride? Whatever you like.'

Hester had a moment of complete indecision. The letter inside her blouse crackled a reminder. She could explain everything here and now. Or she could leave it and let Alice receive the formal note which Father would post later that evening.

She smiled dismissively. 'I've already written and posted a reply. Will you give my apologies to Aunt Doffie and Uncle Ted? I can't manage anything until after the interviews, Alice. I know you understand.'

In the silence that followed, Hester made her escape. They watched her hurry along the nave, lit by the changing colours filtering through the stained glass, and then disappear into the shadow of the porch.

Alice looked at Joe. 'She doesn't want to go on being friends, does she?'

Joe hardly knew what to say. Their own friendship was so new and fragile. He was frightened that the wrong reply might blow it away.

She misinterpreted his silence. 'She's not usually like that, Joe! She can be sharp and awkward, but underneath she is always . . . there.'

He swallowed. 'It was me, wasn't it? She thinks I am pushing her out.'

'Of course not! How ridiculous!' She flushed warmly. His words acknowledged the closeness of their friendship. But perhaps that was what it was. Hester felt pushed out.

Alice said briskly, 'Come on. Cloisters next. Then we'll have to go back to the office to pick up my bike. You should get back on the eight-fifteen. Your mother has been on her own all day.'

'Yes.' Joe had hardly mentioned his mother, yet Alice seemed to understand the complexities of his situation.

He followed her to the strangely small door that led into the cloisters, and duly marvelled at yet another ornate ceiling and the curiously modern little basins known as lavatoria, where the monks had washed. He loved it when Alice became enthusiastic; she took him with her. 'Can't you just imagine them all – those rope things they had round their waists and the way they tucked their hands into their wide sleeves. D'you think they were drying them after using a lavatorium? Or just scratching their elbows?' She laughed, and he had to face the truth yet again. He loved her.

Hester walked into Westgate Street and straight back up to the Cross. She had intended going to the bridge and watching the gypsies go about their business, as Val so often did, but the heart had gone from her. It was only the thought that her father might still be upstairs with her mother that kept her from home. She lingered by Denton's window, looking at the furs and thanking God that she was not interested in such trappings. She stopped feeling tearful and became angry. How dared Alice go down such a predictable path? Presumably she would marry her boyfriend and they would struggle through their lives just as Mother and Father did; just as Uncle Ted and Aunt Doffie did. She paused, frowning. Uncle Ted and Aunt Doffie were not like Mother and Father. And yet they were. They had rows, Alice had said so. And they kissed, and Uncle Ted bent Aunt Doffie backwards. And they went upstairs on Sunday afternoons for a lie down.

She turned from the window and walked up Northgate Street towards Hare Lane. After all, what did it matter? There were only two things she really wanted: to go to Oxford, like Val; and to take him back with her.

Twelve

It was the August Bank Holiday and the weather was poor. Hester had a cardigan over her summer frock and her school blazer over that, and she was still not really warm. As the railcar stopped at Newent, she hung out of the window, half hoping that Val would have come this far to meet her. But that wasn't Val. He waited for people to come to him. She sat back down in the sideways seat that left enough room for bicycles. A woman jiggled a gigantic perambulator expertly, cutting off a child's cry as if by an electrical switch.

At Leadon Markham the line ran alongside the little river which, clear and shallow, provided the perfect school-holiday playground for the local children. Hester had been here often as a small girl and thought she recognized Timmy Fieldfare wading among the big stones, building them into the inevitable dam. Then she realized that Timmy would be eighteen by now and probably doing his National Service. She flopped back down on to her seat, determined not to be waiting eagerly by the window when the train came to a stop. It occurred to her suddenly that the juvenile Joseph Adair would no doubt be due to do his National

Service next year too. And then perhaps Alice would want her friendship again. In the week since they had met so unfortuitously in the cathedral, Hester had convinced herself that it was Alice who no longer wanted their friendship. It helped to think that, especially when she remembered the note she had written for her father to post. She cringed at the thought that Alice may well have shown the note to Uncle Ted.

The brakes on the railcar started to squeal and she made her way to the door, making sure that the woman with the perambulator was before her. A porter hurried forward and took the front wheels of the pram; the woman lowered the handle and then jumped down on to the platform. There was no sign of Val.

The porter was doubling as ticket collector, and held Hester's ticket up to the invisible sun. 'You be Miss Ryecroft? Our Mr Ryecroft's sister?'

'Yes.'

'He's expecting you. You'll find 'im in the booking office. Balancing books. Lucky for 'im they 'aven't asked for July's returns.' He made a sound of disgust. 'You youngsters was never taught to add up, was you?' She said nothing and he grinned forgivingly. 'Go on with you. The door en't locked. Put the kettle on and make 'im a cup o' tea. 'E could do with it, I reckon.'

'Oh.' Hester looked around her and moved towards the lavatories, before remembering that the door to the booking office was at the back. She was bewildered. No one spoke of Valentine Ryecroft like that: critically, disparagingly. Val was a genius; an academic. What on earth did that oaf mean by implying he could not add up?

She knocked on the door, noticing the gleam of the brass handle. Nothing happened, so she opened the door and looked in. Val was sitting on a high stool at the side of the counter. The window was firmly shuttered. He was bent over an old-fashioned ledger. He looked so achingly familiar and there was nothing she could do about it. If only they were like other brothers and sisters; if only he would stand up and throw open his arms, grin and say, 'Hello Sis, great to see you . . .'

He said, 'Hester, I know it's you but I can't look up else I lose my place. This is hell. Sheer un-adulterated hell. If I can't do it in the next ten minutes I'm leaving it and we'll go.'

'Don't be silly, I don't mind waiting. I'll make some tea.' Somehow his greeting made up for everything. It was so natural and sweet and welcoming. And he *couldn't* add up. She reached for a ghastly sooty kettle and went to the tap at the back of the office, filled it and put it on the oil stove. There was Mazawattee tea in its tin with a spoon sticking out; there were cracked cups and saucers, condensed milk and sugar. While Val muttered and perhaps swore over his work, she laboriously made tea and poured it out. Her hands were filthy from the kettle; there was a burn on her thumb. It was a labour of love.

Val shoved everything away from him with a furious, exasperated grunt. 'Bloody, bloody, bloody, bloody, bloody, bloody—'

Hester put her hands over her ears and wailed, 'Oh Val, don't!'

'Well, I can't do it, Sis. Now I know how you feel about the bloody Latin. It's not difficult, but you can't get it—'

168

'You said I was all right! You said I'd done well! You said—'

'You can do it, you did do well. But you don't get it. It's not in you!' He grinned. 'Don't let's talk about what we can't do. Let's have the tea and then go down to the river and paddle! Then I want to show you something.'

She was amazed, both by his grin and his suggestion. She saw suddenly that in spite of the curses, in spite of the oaf of a porter and the columns of figures, he was happy. Incredibly, Val was happy.

He sipped his tea, closing his eyes ecstatically and breathing in the steam. 'Delicious!' he pronounced. Then he put down the cup. 'Did you notice my door knob? I usually polish it on a Monday morning, but I gave it an extra buff this morning just for you!'

This was wonderful, but also inexplicable. 'You mean you have to polish the brass?'

'Of course. All the oil lamps. Change the mantels on the gas lamps. Water the hanging baskets. Weed the flower beds. Make the tea. Date the tickets – have you seen the machine, Hester?' He showed her the machine, inserting a piece of paper so that it clamped its jaws on it and left the date imprinted at the top. 'Isn't it great? We don't get that many passengers, but it's such fun using it.' He picked up his cup again and drank. 'I know most people by name now. And the farmers – they bring their stuff in most mornings; mushrooms and raspberries and peas and beans – I know them well. And they know me. They laugh like drains when I tell them my name, but they don't forget it!'

'I thought . . . you know . . . it's a bit . . . menial.'

He finished his tea and put the cup in the yellow-stone sink. 'It's living, Hes. With people. Real people who do real things.'

'Oh, Val . . .'

'I know, old girl. I know how you feel and how Father feels. But I have to go my own way. Say you understand.'

She did not. She asked about the figures.

'We have to produce them every month. Someone comes from the accounts office and picks them up. I had to do May's, June's and now July's. Luckily Dugdale Marsden came out for May and June. He's the Staff clerk and I think Uncle Ted must have had a word with him. He did them himself in about ten minutes. Pretty shame-making, isn't it? I shall get it eventually. I'm absolutely determined about that.'

She went to the high stool and sat on it. The ledger had dates at one side, then two columns. Money coming in and something or other going out.

Val came and looked over her shoulder to explain. 'Goods . . . passengers . . . that means tickets. And goods means invoices to farmers there. See what I mean? There's so much of it. Honestly, Hester, I've done it six times now and each time I get a different answer and it never tallies. It's supposed to tally. That's the whole point.'

'Of course. And you're sure you've entered every ticket sold and counted the money properly?'

'You sound like Duggie. But yes, I think so. I mean, I can't be sure. But almost sure.'

170

She shook her head slowly. 'I've never known you like this, Val. You're usually so decisive. You sound like Alice!'

'Well, that's the best compliment you could give me, Sis! Knowing how fond you are of her—'

'Not so much now.'

'Why, what has happened?'

'Well, nothing really. She's working and I'm at school. You know.' She turned on the stool. 'Let me have a go. We're not in a hurry, are we?'

'Oh, no. It's my day off, but I would probably look in tonight to make sure Seth has been all right on his own.'

Seth must be the porter. Val seemed to actually like him. She shook her head again and started on the columns. They did not tally. She demanded to count the takings. Val unlocked the safe and handed over the sugar-paper bags. 'You can't start counting this lot. It will take for ever.' She reached for the scales and put the bags one on each side.

'I didn't realize . . . How did you know to do that?'

'Haven't you ever noticed the scales at the post office?' Hester replied.

She found the discrepancies: several of them. Put shillings and half-crowns from one bag to the next. Went back to the figures.

'I think that's it,' she said triumphantly.

Val didn't believe her. 'It can't be. You've been fifteen minutes by that clock. Let me see.'

She tallied the figures aloud, slowly.

'How did you learn to do this? Why can't I do it?' he said in amazement.

'At the Deanery Infants school. We had a game. Someone started off in the front row with two numbers and the next person had to add them together and say another number, and the next person—'

'Yes. All right. I do understand that.' He looked at her with down-turned mouth. 'Of course, Mother sent me to that private place. We did art and poetry and acted plays.'

She looked at him and started to laugh, and he clapped her shoulders and laughed too. They so rarely, so very rarely laughed together. It was wonderful.

Val got his jacket with the leather patches and they went outside. He gave the keys to Seth, then they crossed the barrow crossing and walked past the line of cottages and down a field towards the river. It was still grey, and a splatter of rain dampened them before they reached the line of willows. Hester could not believe that they would paddle; it was the sort of thing she had done with Alice, never with Valentine. He kept talking the whole time, trying to tell her everything. He continued while he sat on the bank, took off his shoes and rolled up his trousers.

'Come on, Sis. Buckle your sandals together and put your socks in your pocket. You must paddle in the Leadon. Everyone does.'

She said defensively as she followed him, 'I've done it before. When I came with Alice to see Gran and Gramps. We used to play with the village kids. Timmy Fieldfare—'

'Of *course*! You knew old Mr Pettiford, didn't you? What was he like? He's almost revered down here. And Patience – people used to go to her rather than the doctor!'

'Patience?'

'Old Mrs Pettiford's name. You know, Alice's grandmother. She lives at Epney now, down on the river.'

'I didn't know she was called Patience. How odd.'

'Why?'

'I don't know.' Hester laughed. 'Just odd.'

Valentine stopped mid-stream, the clear water almost to his calves. 'Isn't this good, Sis? I mean, *good*!'

She was surprised to hear herself saying, 'Yes. Yes, it is. Dear Val, you're getting better all the time, aren't you? I think you've been ill. Overwork, and this . . . thing . . . with Father.'

He looked at her. 'He's never hit you, has he, Hester?'

'No.'

'What about Mother?'

'I don't think so.' She thought about the torn cardigan, but said nothing.

Val smiled gaily. 'I might have to go back home and kill him if ever he laid a finger on either of you,' he said.

'Don't worry. He wouldn't.'

'I can't imagine how things are for Alice. I'd phone her, except that of course Father would be there and would know. How is she?'

'Well, as I said before, I don't see much of her. But I think she is very happy. Actually . . .' She looked at him. 'Father does not want me to see her any more. He says it will make it awkward in the office.'

Valentine returned her look and understood everything immediately. He said, 'That's a pity. You'll miss out on all that family thing. Hattie's wedding, too.'

She opened her eyes wide. 'I'd forgotten Hattie's wedding. Alice will be a bridesmaid, I suppose.'

He moved to the bank and sat down with his feet in the air. 'Come and dry off now, Sis. Mrs Seth said she would put us out some bread and cheese at midday. Then I want to show you something.'

'What?' She sat by him and waved her feet too. It was all so delightful. 'You said that before. What is it?' She looked at him apprehensively, 'You haven't bought a car, have you?'

He laughed. 'Not likely! You know how much I earn. Anyway, who wants a car? No, I've found something. You'll have to wait and see.'

They waved their feet companionably for some time, then put socks and shoes back on and stood up. Daringly, Hester put a tentative hand on his arm; after a surprised glance at it, he crooked his elbow, patted her hand in a – yes, in a *brotherly* way, and they walked back across the field and went into the first of the terraced cottages.

He explained that Mrs Seth would be out, 'doing' up at Markham Hall.

'I want you to meet her some time, Sis. You've heard the saying "salt of the earth" often enough. But she is. One of these days I'm going to lick her.'

'What are you talking about?'

'To prove my point. She will taste of salt. I know it.'

'Lot's wife,' she said, entering into the spirit of the thing.

He roared with laughter and propelled her ahead of him, through the door into the kitchen. It was twice the size of their kitchen at home, most

174

of the space taken by a large scrubbed table, one end of which was laden with food. Along one wall there was a shallow yellow-stone sink, a gas cooker and a long shelf, stacked with plates and bowls and hung from beneath with cups and saucepans. The floor was quarry-tiled; there were no curtains or rugs, or cushions on the chairs. Yet it seemed to offer more comfort than all the rooms in Deanery Close put together.

Hester stood by the table and looked around. She lifted her head to the wooden ceiling, closed her eyes and took a deep breath. 'It smells of soap. And – and cabbage.'

'She's forever scrubbing. And she cooks cabbage every damned day!'

'It's lovely. It's not a trapped smell – stale or left-over.'

'Oh no. The cabbage is growing half an hour before it goes in the pot.'

She looked at him, her eyes shining. 'I can see why you're happy here.'

Val went to the table and started hacking at a loaf. 'Cut some cheese, can you, Sis? Wrap it all in one of those towels. And some of the apples. They're last year's Russets.' He took a white enamel canister from under the sink. 'Cold tea,' he explained. 'We'll have a picnic.' He packed everything into a calico bag and slung it on his shoulder. 'You know, Hester, it's very hard to imagine Father living in Leadon Markham and not being . . . different.'

'Maybe he was when he lived here. He's always felt linked to the Pettifords, so he must have felt happy with them. Just as you do with Mr and Mrs Seth.'

They wandered outside, crossed the railway line again and took to a narrow lane almost masked by enormous fronds of cow-parsley. 'Watch out for the ditches. We're on the edge of the forest here and all the roads have to be well drained.' Valentine re-shouldered the bag and looked sideways. 'Do you know about the forest, Sis? It was used in Edward the Confessor's time for hunting. And when ships were needed for wars, it was where the ship-builders got their timber. Oak. And then there was the coal . . .'

She listened avidly. Val so rarely talked to her like this. His Latin lessons were terse, almost brusque.

'They make their own laws, you know. At Speech House. And they look after their own too, laws or no laws.'

'What do you mean?' She sounded like a child, breathless for the rest of a story.

'Things have happened here.' He stopped and looked around. The lane bore to the left, and forking from it was a track into suddenly dense foliage; ferns and thickets of thorn bushes were flanked by a wall of trees. 'These trees guard a thousand secrets!' He rolled his eyes comically and she laughed. They took the track and held their hands high to avoid the thorns on either side. 'Seriously, Hester. Many an unwanted baby is buried here. And when one of Seth's cousins decided to open up a surface mine the other day, he came across a man's arm.' She gave a little scream of horror and he added, 'Look on the bright side. There was nothing else to go with it!'

She did not know how serious he was being any more, but it was odd how menacing the thatch of fern and thorn had become. But they struggled on into the forest proper, where Valentine stopped again and let her catch him up. She caught her breath, because everything was so suddenly changed.

'It – it's like the cathedral,' she whispered, as if she were indeed in a house of God. 'The height of those trees ... and this path ... like a nave running through. Oh Val, how beautiful.'

'I knew you'd appreciate it.'

'This is what you wanted to show me?'

'Yes. But this is the general picture. There is something else, something particular.'

She said no more, and after a while he went on again and she followed. The little path led them further into the forest, showing them impenetrable stands of trees intertwined with brambles and head-high ferns. Suddenly the path opened into a clearing, with the grey sky above them. And as suddenly as it had started, the path gave out; it had led them to another arena of springy leaf mould, but there was apparently no way on.

'Oh, Val.' She was disappointed for him as he searched along the perimeter of the clearing for another way through. 'Don't worry about it. Let's stay here and have our picnic. I'm really tired, aren't you?'

'No and yes. Or yes and no, as the case may be.' He never used to make this kind of meaningless small talk – Hester guessed it must come from Mrs Seth. He had found a stick now and was thrashing at the ferns with it. 'It's a month since I came here, and I can't quite remember ... If we entered the clearing at six o'clock, it was at quarter past three.'

'What are you talking about?' She laughed. She had already found a flat rock which would be ideal as a picnic table. She sat down, crooked her legs and pulled the skirt of her cotton dress down to her ankles.

Val looked round, grinning. 'Directions. Think of the clearing as the face of a clock. Might be ten past three, actually. Gosh, Hester, you look as if you're posing for a portrait.'

She rested her chin on her knees. 'Do I?'

'Yes. Stop it this minute, otherwise I shall think you have become a minx since Easter!' She straightened her legs with a jerk, blushing, though she could not think why. 'That's better! Now come along, little Sis. This is the remnant of the old railway line. It's absolutely clogged with growth, of course, but it's there underfoot and we can move along slowly until we come to . . . it.'

She got off the rock and stumbled after him, somehow embarrassed beyond words. It was a most uncomfortable fifteen-minute struggle, which she would have protested against loudly before. The old railway line was there, but it provided traps of its own; the sleepers had mostly sunk into the leaf mould for lack of ballast, but here and there they were proud of the surface, and twice she tripped and half fell. But she said nothing. And then the trees fell away again, promising another clearing. Which it was, in a way. Lying before them, fifty yards across, was a lake. A black pool, coloured by the coal beneath it.

Valentine reached back and took her hand. 'Don't ever do this in the dark, Sis. You'd be in the water before you knew it, and they do say that no one has plumbed the depths of this particular pond.'

Hester shuddered, and held her brother's hand tightly, as if even now she might slip into those still depths. The idea held a fascinating attraction – just as once, when Alice had insisted on climbing the cathedral tower, she had felt a distinct pull from the ground far beneath her, and had been forced to grip one of the gargoyles so tightly that it almost broke off in her hand. 'Oh Val, this really is a surprise.'

'This isn't it. It's part of it, but there's more to come. We have to skirt the pool just here, but then there's a path and it opens out. Don't be frightened.'

But she continued to grip his hand tightly, and edged with some exaggeration round the muddy bank. She could not take her eyes from the water, and when Val eventually stopped she looked up and gasped again at what lay before her. The forest had fallen away and wrapped a protective arm around – what on earth was it? A cottage? It was a dwelling of sorts, but it was so covered in moss and climbing flowers that it seemed to be growing there.

She released her hand at last and put it to her throat. 'Val, what is it? It's like Hansel and Gretel. What *is* it?'

He was delighted with her reaction and grinned. 'It's a railway coach. And it's empty. This is where we'll have our picnic. Now tell me it wasn't worth fighting for! All those brambles shield it from anyone else. What do you think?'

She was ecstatic. She ran forward and almost pitched into the water, but then ran further up the bank and stood outside the door, holding out her arms as if she would embrace the coach.

'I love it, Val! It's ours! Our very own house!' She turned, glowing. 'Can we get in? Is it locked?'

'Yes. And I have got the key.' He produced the old-fashioned T-shaped coach key and held it aloft like a talisman. Then he climbed five shallow, rickety steps to the door, unlocked it and pulled it open. 'Your palace awaits, Your Majesty!'

She climbed the steps slowly. She could see that the coach had been adapted at some point, and there was a large space behind the door which was actually furnished with deckchairs and a table, and a strange old-fashioned corner unit which she knew that Alice's grandmother would call a whatnot.

She whispered, 'Val, it's wonderful. Is it really yours?'

'No. But for today it is ours. Not mine. Ours.'

She looked at him, her eyes were like stars. She knew she was beautiful. 'Will you carry me over the threshold, Val?'

'I shall be honoured.'

He did not pretend to stagger under her weight. He swept her into his arms and stepped carefully through the doorway. Very gently, he lowered her into one of the deckchairs. Then he kissed her forehead.

'Let's have that picnic,' he said.

Hester ate her share, although she was not hungry; happiness was filling her whole being and she did not need food. They sat in the deckchairs – gingerly, because the canvas had rotted in places – and gazed out at the dappled water and the leaves dancing crazily above it.

Valentine said lazily, 'If Alice was here, we'd be listening to some story about the Lady of Shalott.'

Hester felt a small prick in her happiness. She wished she could make some Alice-like suggestion; something daring and completely crazy. Juice from her Russet was sticky on her chin, and she wished she could wash it off.

She said suddenly, 'Let's go swimming! What do you say, Val? Shall we? Shall we go swimming?'

He laughed. 'You don't mean it! What if I said yes?'

She stood up. 'I'd say, come on! I'll race you!' She pulled off her cardigan and began to un-button her dress. He turned his back, still laughing, and began on his shirt buttons. She kicked off her sandals and ran down the steps in her underwear. Once down the bank, the grass gave way to squelchy mud and she screamed as it oozed between her toes.

'Coward!' yelled Valentine. 'You're not going to do it!'

'I am! I am!' Hester half skidded the rest of the way and was suddenly up to her knees in icy water. 'Oh, Lordy! It's cold! Oh Val—' And then quite suddenly something wriggled beneath her sub-merged feet, and with a terrific scream she lunged forward into a frantic breast stroke. 'There's something there! On the bottom! Val – something touched me!'

She rolled on to her back, kicking up spray as if to beat off the Loch Ness monster. Val was stand-ing on the grass in his pants, bent over with laughter. Hester was furious.

'You – you *devil*! You're not going to get in, are you?' He shook his head, still choking with mirth. 'That's the meanest trick!' she spluttered, but she was used to the cold by now and nothing else had wriggled anywhere near her. Hester laughed too. 'Actually, I wish you could see yourself! You look simply ridiculous in those old pants! They come below your knees – almost combinations!'

He made a sound like a lion's roar. 'Nobody speaks to me like that – not even you!' He lifted his fists in the air, pawed the ground with one bare foot, then raced down the bank into the water and completely disappeared. Mud surged to the surface. Hester stopped laughing and tried to stand up; she was out of her depth. She trod water and waited for him to bob up. When he did not, she called uncertainly, 'Val? Val, stop playing the fool! Where are you?' Nothing happened. She took a huge breath and upended herself, reaching out with her arms, kicking forward. There was nothing.

Then she felt it again – a wriggling movement, starting this time at her hip and working quickly down her leg to her right foot.

She surfaced on a rush of hysteria, and there was Valentine, next to her, grinning idiotically and blowing mud bubbles into her face.

'I thought you were drowning,' she said weakly.

'You thought I was the hand of a dead man, grabbing your foot, dragging you down to a watery grave to lie by his side for ever!' he crowed. He swam into the middle of the pool. 'Come on, let's swim to the other side and back. We mustn't be much longer. What time is your train back?'

'Five-fifteen.' She tried to recover that

happiness of a few minutes ago. But she had thought he was drowned and she had had a glimpse of a world without him. She swam level with him and said, 'If anything ever happens to you, I shall kill myself.'

'People who threaten suicide never do it. Anyway, you're strong, Hester. You'd survive a lot.' He turned on his side and grinned at her. 'Killing myself isn't actually included in my plans.'

'What are your plans, Val? Will you come back to Oxford with me?'

They slithered up the bank and on to the grass.

'No. Never that. But I thought I might borrow Seth's bike, come back with you and cycle out to Lypiatt to see the Pettifords for an hour. I haven't seen them since that time in March.'

She laughed. 'Neither have I.'

'Yes you have. You were at school with Alice.'

'Oh, Alice. Yes. I haven't seen Uncle Ted or Aunt Doffie.'

They went back inside the coach, both cold now and coated in mud. Hester began to have qualms about her reception back home unless she could get clean. Valentine dragged his trousers over his legs and sodden pants, then pulled on his shirt. Unwillingly, Hester put on her dress and buttoned it with shaking cold fingers.

He said, 'You should keep in touch with them, Sis. They've been good friends to us.'

Hester mumbled something unintelligible.

'What?'

'I told you before – I am not allowed to go and see Alice any more. It would make it awkward for Father at work.'

Val paused in tugging on his socks, and looked

up. 'You're not going to take any notice of that, are you?'

She glanced at him. 'I don't think Alice is very interested in us any longer, Val.' She said in a rush, 'She's got a boyfriend. And that is all she cares about now!'

Val looked stunned. He stared at his sister as if she had turned into a monster. Hester stood up and went to the window; the overcast sky above the trees looked suddenly menacing, and she wondered whether it would rain. At least that would give her an excuse for her bedraggled state.

Val said, 'You mean . . . she's got a friend who – who happens to be male?'

'I suppose so.'

'Is he from the grammar school?'

'No. He works with her. In Father's office.'

'Oh. Well, that's all right then. Colleagues. Father thinks it's funny to make something of it, does he?'

She shrugged. 'Father has said nothing about it. I met them in the cathedral one evening.'

'One *evening*?'

'Well, after tea. I was going to post a letter . . .' She remembered as she so often did that Alice had received the other letter, the letter approved by Father and posted by him. 'You know how Alice has always been about the cathedral.' Val said nothing; he had always called the vast building his 'present refuge'.

He said quietly, 'That time last March when we had breakfast, the three of us, out at Lypiatt – I thought we might have lived like that. Some time.'

'So did I.'

'Perhaps you and I aren't intended for such

simple pleasures, Hester. At least we've got each other.' He came to her and put his arms around her damp shoulders. 'Take care, won't you?' Then he released her with a sharp sigh. 'We must go. And I won't come back with you. No point in going out to Lypiatt. I'd have had to see Mother too, and then there'd probably be a row afterwards. Not worth it.'

She waited at the bottom of the steps while Val locked the coach. Then they tracked back through the forest and eventually, after what seemed like hours, emerged on to the track which led to the lane and Leadon Markham.

Hester leaned out of the window of the railcar and waved until she could not see Val any longer. Then she sat down and stared at her muddy legs. Alice had deserted them – she was certain now of that. But she and Val were still together. And that was all that mattered.

Thirteen

That same August Bank Holiday Monday, Alice and her mother got up with Ted – who was on early turn in the Control Office – and went out in the dawn-damp field which led to the bluebell woods to pick mushrooms for their breakfast. Doffie had wanted Alice to have a lie-in, but these were days of fizzing excitement for Alice. She slept deeply and dreamlessly, and when she awoke she wanted to be up and out and doing something. Usually the something, of course, was getting early to the office so that she and Joe could talk. No longer did Joe have to fetch paraffin for Fido, no longer did Alice have to lug coal upstairs for the stove. Even when it was downright chilly, heating was simply not allowed in Bishop Hooper's Mansions from the end of May until the end of September.

The friendship between Alice and Joe, which had started that first day, had steadily grown stronger. Now it did not matter where they met; their friendship was an accepted thing in the Mansions. They were the two babies, Joe just seventeen, already an established member of staff; Alice trailing the Pettiford colours, still just sixteen. They were known collectively: 'the two young 'uns down in the General with Mr Ryecroft'.

The friendship was still new enough to have some boundaries, however. Joseph was not Alice's boyfriend as yet. They shared an exclusive half-hour each morning and sometimes an hour in the evening, but apart from that Sunday outing to Symonds Yat, their weekends were still spent in their respective homes. Neither of them minded yet. They knew that eventually they would reach the first secure niche; they would go to the pictures together, either on a Friday night or a Saturday matinée. That would be a serious milestone from which they could either go on or retreat, but not stay the same.

Meanwhile, they both looked forward to each working morning, and they were satisfied with that. They had not yet reached the point where every moment apart was agony. In fact, moments apart were times of terrific anticipation. Their weekends were never spent languishing and love-sick. Joseph had quite a lot to do at home for his mother; and Alice still enjoyed her mother's company and her carefully disguised diplomatic role in the house in Lypiatt Bottom.

There had been no quarrels since Alice had started work, and she knew that was partly because her father felt much more secure. She was able to understand when he talked of the whereabouts of rolling stock; she loved to tell him the latest office gossip gleaned from Miss Warner and filtered through Miss Webster. What had not occurred to her was that her mother might feel left out in the course of this sudden rearrangement.

However, as they combed the meadow that rather grey Bank Holiday morning, Doffie was animated, almost excited.

'I was thinking, Alice. If Hester is coming for the weekend, she will be able to see you in your bridesmaid's dress. Mrs Mearment popped over last week and said it was ready for the first complete fitting.'

Alice made a sound which could have meant anything, and then dashed over to investigate a sighting of a fairy ring. It was a complete circle of toadstools, small and grey, soon to disappear in sun or rain. Alice called to her mother and stood in the middle, turning slowly with closed eyes.

Doffie appeared, smiling. 'What did you wish?'

'You know you mustn't ask that! How can it come true if I tell you?'

'But you know what I wish!'

'Do you still wish the same thing? When you stir the puddings or get the wishbone?'

'Of course.'

Alice hopped out of the ring and hugged her mother soundly. 'I do love you, Mum! You know that, don't you? If anything – happened ... I would look after you.'

'Oh, darling!' Doffie tipped her head back to look into Alice's face with some dismay. 'So morbid! And it's all a ploy to get you out of telling me your wish!'

Alice sighed deeply. 'It's not, actually. Because in a way I am wishing for the same thing. Which makes me sound terribly selfish. But I don't think it is, really. Not when you dig down a little bit.'

'Sweetheart! Stop! It's never selfish to wish for happiness. When we're happy we sort of glow in the dark. That must help other people.'

'I hope so. It just makes me feel quite dreadful that ever since I was born all that time ago, you have been wishing the same wish, whenever you got the chicken wishbone, whenever you stirred the Christmas pudding ... every birthday ...'

'To wish that one's child will always be happy is fairly silly, really.' Doffie was trying to be sensible, even as she stepped into the fairy ring and closed her eyes. There was a little silence, then she stepped out again. 'After all, we know that we can't be happy all the time.'

'Deep down we can. Well – I suppose unless something terrible happens, like Gramps dying and Gran wanting to die too.'

Mum, not known for her rapport with Gran, said, 'The funny thing was, I didn't think they were particularly close. She nagged him terribly.'

'She nags everyone, Mum. You know that.'

'But he did find it – her – irksome.'

'Irksome? That's a funny word to use. What makes you think that?'

Mum stooped to scoop up a snowy white button mushroom.

'He used to talk to me. He wanted to travel. He wanted a car. A sports car. He asked me whether I'd like to go to France.' She stooped again; there was a small drift of mushrooms following a line of cow-pats.

Alice was disconcerted. In the last three months she had absorbed the fact that her grandfather was almost revered by other railwaymen. It was hard now to imagine him finding Gran 'irksome' and asking his daughter-in-law – of whom Gran disapproved – to go abroad with him. After all, Mum was only related to him by law, not blood.

She said, 'Why didn't you go?'

'Gran would never have forgiven me! You know that.'

'But did you want to go?'

'Alice, it's hard for you to imagine, I know. But then – I never wanted to go anywhere without your father.'

The words hung in the grey morning air, speaking sadly, nostalgically, of a time long gone.

Alice felt a catch in her throat. She wanted quite desperately to tell her mother about Joe, but it was still so fluid, so tentative. What if she was mistaken?

Doffie laughed lightly and changed the subject. 'Now, what do you think about making a definite date with Hester. Mrs Mearment says—'

'Actually, Mum, it's a bit difficult. I think Hester is so wrapped up in school work—'

'Darling, it's the summer holidays.'

'Yes, but that makes it even more difficult.' Alice had rehearsed several reasons for Hester's defection, none of which held much water. 'I rather think she is spending a lot of time in Leadon Markham with Valentine, now that he has left Oxford and is working over there. She thinks it will please her parents . . .'

Mum glanced sideways at Alice. 'She always enjoys coming here, Alice. After Deanery Close, I rather think our house is like a hotel!'

'I'm not sure any more. I think Hester has left me behind.'

It was the wrong thing to say, but she couldn't tell Mum that Uncle Reggie was probably behind

Hester's dreadful letter, and that probably Hester would never come to Lypiatt again. Mum was quite capable of bearding Uncle Reggie in the public domain of the office and 'having it all out into the open'. Alice cringed at the thought.

But when she saw her mother's face she felt terrible, really terrible. Her eyes were full of tears and her nostrils almost closed – when she was angry they seemed to inflate. She looked positively stricken.

'Oh, darling.' Doffie put out a hand and Alice took it. 'Darling, you mustn't be hurt. You could have done it – maybe not Oxford, but another University! You could have taken Hester on and beaten her, I am sure of it! And later – there will be other opportunities. We know University isn't always the way ahead. Look at the way Val gave it all up. Hester might do the same.'

'Mum, stop it. I don't mind. I'm not hurt at all. Maybe I've left *Hester* behind – has that occurred to you?'

Doffie looked into her eyes, searching for the truth. The tears subsided. Alice kept smiling, willing her mother not to be upset. And at last Doffie shook Alice's hand, let it go and clasped her gratefully.

'I don't think I could bear it if you had any regrets.'

'I haven't. Honestly.'

'I haven't either. Whatever you do, so long as you are happy then so am I.' She gave Alice a tight squeeze and released her.

Again, Alice almost told her mother about Joe – about the joy of being his friend, the joy of anticipating seeing him every weekday morning. And some evenings too, when Joe decided to wait until the six-twenty.

Doffie said, 'I have to admit that one of the reasons I wanted you to stay at school was so that we could have the summer break together. Today is lovely, but I am a greedy woman and I want tomorrow and tomorrow and tomorrow . . .' She danced across the field and Alice followed her, laughing, deciding to wait until she could introduce the subject of Joe – well, officially.

Mrs Mearment said, 'Well, I know I'm more biased than this bias binding, Alice, but in my 'umble opinion you look prettier than Princess Margaret Rose done up in all 'er royal finery. What have you got to say to that?'

Alice, well used to Mrs Mearment's convoluted compliments, giggled appreciatively and Mrs Mearment, ever the clown, got up from her knees and bowed with much hand-flourishing.

Mum said, 'Actually Alice, you do look rather nice. I didn't realize you'd got a waist because I'm always looking at your legs – which, by the way, are particularly good!'

Alice laughed again, gratefully. She had never quite forgotten Mr Ryecroft's description of her rugby legs. And though the days of the hand-span waists were over and done with, nevertheless a good waist was well worth having for Joe's sake. Her laugh died to a smile. How strange that she should be pleased about her personal appearance because of Joe.

'Shall we have a cup of tea?' Doffie suggested. 'I made some lemon-curd tarts with the last of the lard and they're not bad.'

'I'm sure they're absolutely delicious,' Mrs Mearment said loyally. 'Alice, if we're going to have tarts you'd better slip out of the dress.'

'Hang on just a few moments more, Mrs M.' Doffie plumped up the armchair cushions for Mrs Mearment. 'Hattie is always late, but she did say she'd come and see the dress this afternoon.'

'Unless she's playing tennis with Percy,' Alice said naughtily. The other two laughed uproariously at the thought of Percy running around a tennis court. In fact, running around at all.

'Actually, there *might* be a tennis party up at the Leckhampton house.' Doffie looked through the window at the deserted lane. 'It is Bank Holiday Monday, after all.'

They sat down, Alice on the edge of a hard chair with the skirt of the rose-coloured dress spread around her. Mrs Mearment told them about the Reverend and Mrs Hyde, who were planning a trip to Brighton.

'I said to Mr Mearment, Brighton, I said. What would they be up to in Brighton for a whole week?'

Doffie raised her brows enquiringly.

'Well, my dears, surely Brighton is for weekends only?' Mrs Mearment tittered meaningfully.

'Oh!' Doffie tried to swivel a warning glance in Alice's direction without her daughter noticing. 'Actually, Mrs M., they've got a niece in Brighton. Towards Hove, I believe.' She got up. 'Was that a car? Yes – Percy and Hattie! I'll put the kettle on. Alice, you open the door. What a surprise for them!'

It was. Percy took it calmly enough, but according to Mrs Mearment, Hattie's screams would be heard in Tewkesbury. She wanted to hug Alice, but did not dare come close to the dress.

'Darling! You look absolutely wonderful – I just cannot believe it's you! And you'll never guess – we've decided to be married in Leckhampton after all. The church at Epney is a bit out of the way and dearest Mamma wanted all her friends to see me . . . and now they will all see you as well! Oh, Alice, I'm so proud of you! You've always been like a baby sister to me. I'm going to cry. Percy, sweetheart, hanky – hanky now!' She buried her face in his handkerchief and turned into his shoulder. He squinted through his pebble glasses and laughed indulgently. Doffie ushered everyone into the sitting room and fussed around with small tables and plates of lemon-curd tarts.

Alice said to Mrs Mearment, 'It's always like this when Hattie comes. Can you come upstairs and help me off with the dress? Then things will calm down.'

Mrs Mearment undid pins and then took the dress gently over Alice's head. 'I don't like to say anything, dear. After all, it's none of my business. But Mr Westbrook seems a strange choice for your cousin. She's so very attractive and he—'

'He's very kind to her,' Alice said hastily, before Mrs Mearment could make the sort of personal comment that would need overt disapproval. 'The car is in her name. And the house is very grand.'

'Have you seen it?'

'Not yet. Percy's mother is a semi-invalid and not at all keen on visitors.'

'But you're not visitors in that sense. You're family.'

'We shall see it soon, I expect.'

Mrs Mearment draped the dress reverently on a hanger. 'Of course. Of course you will, dear. Meanwhile . . . you are pleased with the dress?'

'Oh, I am, I am. Thank you a hundred million times! I feel quite beautiful in it!' Alice finished buttoning her cotton frock and looked up into Mrs Mearment's solid square face. 'Mrs M., do you think Mum is all right? I don't see so much of her now, of course, and this morning, when we went out for mushrooms, I felt a bit . . . anxious.'

'How sweet! The boot being on the other foot, I mean. Only the other day your mother was saying that she didn't have to worry about you any more because you were with your father all day. And here you are, worrying about her!'

'I hardly see Dad, actually. But I see Mum even less. What does she do all day?'

'Well, it's been plum picking, hasn't it? Her and me, we've been over at Harris's farm helping out. Then we come home and make jam with the Pershores and bottle the Victorias. Just like we always have.'

'But the War's over. I know we're still rationed, but things will get better.'

Mrs Mearment went to the window and looked down the garden, where they had 'dug for victory'. She said slowly, 'Perhaps the War will never end for us, Alice. Your mother and I are too old to change now. The War was a way of life.'

Alice felt suddenly sad for Mrs Mearment, who had no children and a husband who didn't care tuppence for her. The War had given her something to do, something important. Coats from car rugs. But it wasn't like that for Mum.

They went downstairs and Hattie swept them all

along on the tide of her enthusiasm. There were nylon stockings for Doffie and a silver ankle chain for Alice. Only last week Doffie had pronounced that ankle chains were common, but she clapped her hands delightedly as Alice clasped the chain into place.

'About time you drew attention to those legs!' she said. 'Probably not with those sandals, though.'

'I've got some white satin pumps that will go beautifully with that dress,' Hattie said. 'They're a high heel but you'll manage them. I'll bring them round and you can practise.'

Alice could have wept with gratitude. Now she would be able to lift the skirt of her beautiful dress as she got in and out of the wedding car and show off the shoes and the silver chain to perfection.

Hattie began to tell them 'the latest'. Old Mrs Westbrook had let them have a room they could decorate and furnish for themselves, and they had chosen a three-piece suite, a standard lamp, a coffee table.

'The lamp and coffee table are utility, of course,' Hattie said disparagingly. 'But the suite is pre-War. From the manor house at Guiting. You can imagine what it is like. Hide, my dear. Thick hide.'

'Doesn't matter how many scratches ... it simply shows off that it is good stuff,' Percy added.

'Absolutely quite, Percy darling. Doffie, don't keep pressing these tarts on me, sweetie. I've got to think of my figure. I simply must get into that cross-cut dress.' But she took another tart, and another after that. When Hattie turned her head to peck Percy's cheek, Alice could see a fullness beneath her chin which had not been there when she came home at the beginning of the year.

Hattie wanted to hang on until Ted came home, but Percy explained that his mother was expecting them for tea. Hattie pouted, but allowed herself to be tucked into the car and driven away. 'Poor Hattie. It's beginning already,' said Doffie.

'What?' Alice asked.

'Well . . . you know. The cheap utility furniture and the battered old-fashioned leather sofa. I've heard that Mrs Westbrook is very careful with her money.'

'But Hattie was so *happy*.'

'Yes. Of course.' Doffie grinned. 'In fact, absolutely quite!'

They both laughed.

They were interrupted by the sound of a car outside. Doffie automatically looked around for whatever Hattie had left behind. But it wasn't Hattie – it was Dugdale Marsden in his pre-War Flying Standard, which he had hung on to since 1939.

'Duggie!' Doffie actually put her hand to her throat like a film heroine as they went out to meet him. Alice was sure that a messenger from the office could only mean one thing.

But Uncle Duggie was instantly reassuring. 'It's all right, Doff. No bad news.' He grinned amiably at Alice and patted her mother awkwardly on one shoulder. 'I had the phone put in – when I was in charge of the firewatchers, d'you remember? Ted rang. There's been an accident on the Andoversford line. He'll be home when he can, but it won't be this afternoon.'

'Oh Duggie. Is it bad?'

'Passenger or Goods, Uncle Duggie?' asked Alice.

'Goods. Coal wagons. Jumped the points and blocked the line completely. No lives lost.'

'Well that's good . . .' Doffie did not seem to know what to say next, and the three of them simply stood there under the grey Bank Holiday sky, silent and smiling.

Finally Alice said, 'Poor old Dad. He will have a long day.'

Doffie ignored that and said suddenly, 'Dug, come on in and have a cup of tea. It's all laid up because Hattie and Percy have just been.'

'That would be lovely, Doff. I'm not keen on bank holidays. Nothing happening, no papers.'

'I've made some lemon-curd tarts.'

Doffie led the way into the sitting room. It had the used-up look of visitors just departed. Mum gathered teacups on to a tray and went into the kitchen to replace them.

Uncle Duggie said heartily, 'And where is your young man this afternoon, Alice? I expected the two of you to have made the most of a day off.'

Alice said quickly, 'He's not my young man, Uncle Duggie. And – and Mum doesn't know about him.'

'Oh.' He was surprised. 'Hasn't Ted – hasn't your father—?'

'No.'

'Oh dear. He fears the worst, does he?'

'The worst?'

'Your mother's disapproval.'

'No. He just – I mean, there's nothing – but it might be better if you didn't mention—'

'My lips are sealed, Alice!'

Doffie came in with fresh tea and tarts. 'Why are they sealed, Duggie? And sealed against what?'

Duggie laughed easily. 'We've struck a bargain, Doff. Alice doesn't tell you about my goings-on in the office, and I don't tell about hers!'

Doffie made a sound of mock exasperation and began to pour the tea. There was another silence, during which Alice wondered what she could say about Joe. Then Doffie said, 'This reminds me of that time at the tea dance. D'you remember?'

'The day you met Ted.'

'Well . . . yes, I suppose it was. I met Reggie Ryecroft too, of course. And poor old Clarke . . .' She glanced at Alice. 'He was Chief Clerk, darling. He died.'

'Oh.' Alice was feeling distinctly odd and did not know why.

Duggie accepted a cup of tea and inhaled, his eyes blissfully closed. 'The cup that cheers . . . Did you know, Alice, that I took your mother to that tea dance and she deserted me for your father?'

Mum laughed. 'I thought your lips were sealed!'

Uncle Duggie sipped his tea. 'Was it a secret, Doff?'

Alice glanced quickly at her mother. She looked warm.

'Not really,' she said.

Duggie smiled at Alice. 'Perfidious Albion,' he said. 'And Dastardly Doffie!'

The banter continued, with Doffie's face growing rosier by the minute. They were both talking to Alice, yet she felt left out. Even when her mother told her to fetch her dress to show Uncle Duggie, she knew as she held it against her and

199

smiled at their compliments that they weren't in the least interested in the wedding.

The strangest thing of all was that during the two long hours of his visit, Uncle Duggie's feet did not smell at all.

Fourteen

Hattie's wedding day dawned grey and windy. Alice was awake at seven, and could tell before she opened the curtains that it was not wedding weather. The wind rattled the casement and the light was gloomy through the lime-green curtains. She turned over and humped a disgruntled shoulder. The weather put the finishing touch to all of it: Joe was still on holiday at Wainlodes, six miles away but it might as well be sixty; Miss Webster – Helena – had done something to her back, which meant the long walk from St James's station to Leckhampton church was out of the question; worst of all, Dad was simply terrified of giving Hattie away and making a speech afterwards, and the weather needed to be particularly sunny to reassure him. Last night Mum had said for about the fiftieth time, 'Listen, Ted, it doesn't matter what you say. Everyone will be concentrating on Hattie.' And he had said, 'So if I start on Hey Diddle Diddle, it won't matter?' Doffie had not even smiled, but had said, 'You know what I mean. This obsession with your speech is a form of vanity and conceit!' And he had clammed immediately.

It was all too much. Alice felt she could not bear it. Even Hattie had lost some of her pizzazz. She kept pouting and telling Percy he did not love her any more, and when he tried to kiss her and re-assure her she told him not to spoil her hair or her make-up. On the very few occasions when she was without Percy, she clung to Ted's arm as if she might be drowning.

They ate a scratch breakfast before eight o'clock, then Doffie and Alice folded their outfits and slid them into the big case they would use for their week in Weston-super-Mare. Dad changed into the pearl-grey lounge suit chosen by Hattie and immediately started pulling at the jacket and humping his shoulders uncomfortably. He wanted a cup of tea before the car arrived, but Doffie refused to make it on the grounds that he might spill it on his new waistcoat. He folded his lips into his mouth – the image of Gran – and obviously wished he had not broken his silence in the first place.

The car came. It had belonged to Percy's father and was pre-War and majestic. Percy drove it with exaggerated care, so that he nearly always ground the gears and applied the brake too fiercely. He did not get out or switch off; the Pettifords hurried out frantically, Ted clutching the case, Alice and Doffie carrying various paper bags. When they reached the main road, Doffie dis-covered she hadn't got any confetti. 'Can't reverse,' Percy shouted. 'Won't need any.' Ted, sitting next to Percy, rolled his eyes. The wind blew a scud of rain against the windscreen. Alice wanted to cry.

It continued the same way, with Hattie in

hysterics at one point, old Mrs Westbrook locked in her room and Percy's best man already drunk in the breakfast room. And then, amazingly, things started to improve.

Alice, in her rose dress with a circlet of daisies on her head, holding a tight posy of clarkia and bachelor-buttons in her lace-gloved hands, came shyly into Hattie's room just as the slipper-satin, bias-cut dress slithered over her hips. They stood facing each other; Alice fair and slender, Hattie dark as a gypsy, full-bosomed, voluptuous.

'Alice. My little Alice.'

Alice swallowed. 'I'm taller than you!'

'You are beautiful, darling. Delicate and precious. Oh, Alice, I do love you!'

It was the first time since the wedding arrangements had begun that Hattie was not preoccupied with herself. The moment did not last. She turned to the old-fashioned pier glass in the corner of the room and almost screamed in dismay.

'This damned dress makes me look fat! Here – here and here!' She took handfuls of fabric and flesh and pulled at them furiously.

Doffie said, 'For goodness' sake, Hattie! You are not fat at all! Let me hook you up . . . there . . . now stand straight. Look at that. You are stunning – absolutely stunning. Hedy Lamarr . . . Constance Bennett . . . Rita – Rita – I've forgotten –'

'Hayworth,' Alice supplied. 'Mum's right, Hattie. You do look marvellous. And . . . and I love you too.'

'Do you?' Suddenly Hattie looked pathetic. 'Do you really? I sometimes wonder . . . if it weren't for Gramps and Gran I would have been in an orphanage, you know.'

'Then doesn't that prove how much they loved you?' Doffie stepped back. 'Now let's get the veil on. Alice, put down those flowers and pass me the pearl cap.'

Finally it was time for Doffie and Alice and Enid to go to the church. Enid was Percy's unmarried sister and was the second bridesmaid. She wore thick glasses like her brother, but, unlike him, was merely plain rather than downright ugly. The wonderful thing was that she thought Hattie was marvellous and smiled all the time. The best man drove them to church in his car, and as they walked through the lych gate a few spectators clapped and murmured compliments about the pretty dresses. Then they waited in the porch. Enid's nose was bright red, so Doffie got out her compact and powdered it. Her smile widened. The best man left them and went to take his place in the top right-hand pew next to Percy. There was nothing to do except shiver and listen to the organ music seeping through the inner door. A few late arrivals passed them, smiling and complimentary.

At last the wedding car drew up, and Ted got out and put his hand inside to help Hattie. Someone leapt around with a box camera. Hattie stood, fussing about getting her veil over her arm. Then she leaned on Ted and they came through the lych-gate and up the gravelly path to the porch. Doffie said, 'Now, now, Enid,' and Alice realized that Enid's smile had temporarily disappeared and she was almost weeping. Hattie gripped her sheaf of lilies as Doffie arranged her veil carefully, then whispered, 'Everything is fine, Hattie. God bless you, darling.' As Hattie slid through the inner door, the ushers pulled both doors wide and the organ blasted forth the wedding march.

Things happened so quickly after that it was hard for Alice to sort it all out. There was a skidding crunch behind her on the gravel and she glanced over her shoulder just in time to see Joe Adair prop his bike against a buttress. She beamed at him and he blinked, not recognizing her at first in her dress, then smiling uncertainly as he slipped past her and disappeared into a back pew.

As Alice and Enid followed Hattie up the aisle, faces turned and peered, and there were little gasps of surprise and pleasure at such a riot of beauty and colour after seven years of austerity. Alice recognized a few people: Mrs Mearment, of course; the Reverend Geoffrey Hyde and his wife, smiling sedately; Ditcher Harris, glorious in his suit with his red neckerchief tucked into a top pocket; Alice looked up, then down, uncertain in her white satin court shoes. She thought she had seen Uncle Duggie and next to him – yes, it was – dear Miss Webster – Helena – with, incredibly, Miss Warner. How had they got to Leckhampton? Uncle Duggie, of course. Dear Uncle Duggie, even though he had probably come to see Mum and was not in the least bit interested in Hattie or Percy. And of course, behind her, out of sight but very much not out of mind, was Joe Adair. He must have come home from his holiday early in order to attend this wedding. And she knew quite well who he had come to see.

Alice felt her face lift; in fact, she felt her whole being lift and was surprised her feet could still touch the ground. Wafting around her were words, comfortable, well-known words, about joining together this man and this woman – who were Hattie and Percy, of all people. Then about holy matrimony being an honourable estate instituted by God, and Jesus turning water into wine when he was a wedding guest – Alice risked a humorous glance up into the vaulted roof of the church at that, because although Percy had agreed to provide a glass of wine for the toasts, any other beverages had to be ordered at the bar and paid for by the consumer! And then came the all-important questions to Percy. Alice hardly held her breath for his answers; of course he would keep her in sickness and in health and forsake all others. It was when the priest turned to Hattie that she found herself holding her flowers much too tightly. Would Hattie be able to keep this whole peculiar alliance going until death did them part? There was so much she had to do – obey him, serve him and forsake all others . . . But her voice was strong and confident when she replied, 'I will.'

Ted gave her away; Enid took the lilies and stepped back while Percy fitted the heavy gold ring on to Hattie's finger; they all knelt and then the priest said loudly, 'Those whom God hath joined together, let no man put asunder.' Alice felt a sudden shock wave pass through her. What a fool she had been. Mum and Dad had made these promises too. How could she have thought they might split up? It wasn't possible.

There was a hymn while the signing in the vestry took place, and then it was time to go. The triumphal organ notes cascaded around the congregation, who stood informally and relaxed now to watch the happy couple walk out of the church. People smiled and waved, and leaned out to touch Hattie's veil, clap Percy's shoulder, whisper to Alice that she looked lovely. She saw Joe – he must have been standing on his hassock – and risked a small wave. And there, on the groom's side, side by side, were Valentine and Hester Ryecroft.

She almost stopped in her tracks, so unexpected were they. She had not seen Valentine since that awful March day when, amazingly, he had listened to her advice to follow in his father's footsteps and apply for a job at one of the country stations. She had almost forgotten the terrible thing done by Valentine's father, and when she did remember, it somehow seemed that Valentine's father had very little to do with Mr Ryecroft. When the letter had arrived from Hester, she had thought that it was the end of the connection between the Ryecrofts and Pettifords. Yet here they were, surely reaching out to her. She smiled, and Hester waved discreetly.

Everyone milled around while a few photographs were taken for the local paper. Old Mrs Westbrook got into her car, now being driven by Percy's best man, and sat holding her stick and staring ahead of her blankly. Enid and Alice posed together, then with Hattie. Hattie and Ted were photographed together, then Hattie and Percy, then Hattie by herself looking soulful.

As Alice stood by her mother, suddenly Joe appeared from nowhere. Alice smiled and said hello, and Joe took her hand and shook it gently.

'Mum –' There was nothing for it. 'This is Joseph Adair. From the office.' She turned to Joe. 'This is my mother.'

He shook Doffie's hand, not quite so gently, as if trying to pump sincerity through the palm. 'You're very alike,' he said.

'Thank you, Joseph.' Doffie gave him one of her smiles and he blushed. She said, 'It was good of you to come.'

'Miss Webster came too. I spotted her. And Miss Warner.'

Alice nodded. 'Yes. I must introduce them to you, Mum. It's good of them to come, too. I thought you were still at Wainlodes, Joe?'

'I borrowed a bike. I'm going back now – my mother is there on her own. It looks like rain and the chalet has a leak.'

They both smiled, as if at a secret joke. Doffie registered this and more, and her expression was suddenly sad. She said, 'I did not realize there was all this interest in Hattie's wedding!'

Joe said, 'Well, you know – Will Pettiford's granddaughter and everything.'

'He is still remembered?'

'Oh yes.'

Helena Webster appeared behind Joe, with Miss Warner on her arm. Doffie knew Miss Warner, and felt she knew Miss Webster too. They immediately launched into an easy dialogue, leaving Joe and Alice to smile at each other.

'Mr Ryecroft did not come?'

'No. But his son and daughter were here.' Alice looked around. There was no sign of the Ryecrofts now.

'Never mind. At least they came.'

'Yes, that's what I thought. Did you have a good week, Joe?'

'It was fine. Mother looks better for it.'

'Oh, good.' Helena was leaning over, asking about the court shoes. 'They're Hattie's.' Alice lifted her skirt and looked down at the high heels, knowing that Joe would not like them. 'I'm not keen, actually.'

'My dear, they look wonderful!' Miss Warner nodded approval.

Joe said shyly, 'They make you look . . . grown-up!'

Everyone laughed except Doffie. Miss Warner said, 'Literally so. They make you much taller, Alice.'

She nodded ruefully; she was quite tall enough already.

Joe said he had better leave. He shook hands again and said he would see Alice and Miss Webster on Monday. Suddenly he turned to Doffie. 'Would it be possible . . . would you care . . . my mother would be delighted if you would come to tea. You and Alice. One Saturday, perhaps?'

There was a pause. Helena looked at Alice and then at Miss Warner. Alice looked at Joe, and then past his head to where Hattie was fussing with her veil yet again. Doffie covered the pause with a little laugh of pleasure. 'How kind, Joseph! Are you sure? I would love to meet your mother.'

'Oh yes! And she would love to meet you! And – and Alice, of course!' Joe was bright red, but determined. 'We could have toasted teacakes. And perhaps listen to the band in Montpelier Gardens.'

They arranged it then and there. The Pettifords

were off to Weston-super-Mare in two weeks, so it had to be next Saturday. Nobody suggested it could wait until they came home. Helena Webster nodded approvingly and Miss Warner managed a smile.

Everyone knew what this meant. Joe had jumped well past the first date at the cinema. This was official. This was the meeting of the mothers.

Alice did not care how embarrassing her father's speech was or how overbearing old Mrs Westbrook was either. This was the happiest day of her life.

Fifteen

Hester longed for it to be 1947. It was the year she would go to Oxford. And it was the year that Joseph Adair would go into the Navy for a long time . . . Well, certainly long enough for Valentine to 're-establish contact' – Hester's phrase – with Alice.

She had not realized until that August Bank Holiday outing that Valentine felt anything but a kind of generous tolerance towards Alice Pettiford, and, at first, the idea of him nourishing any stronger feelings appalled her. But then, as the winter drew on, she realized how absolutely marvellous it would be if Valentine and Alice got married and she went to live with them. It was their only chance of realizing the dream of living as a threesome. She recalled the three of them in the kitchen at Lypiatt Bottom, getting the breakfast that awful morning after Valentine had been beaten by Father. The feeling of . . . rightness. At last, she understood why Alice had wanted to bind their families together. And – obviously – they could not be more bound than if two of the three were married.

It was Hester who had suggested that she and

211

Val should go to Hattie's wedding.

'I wouldn't have thought of it, actually.' She and Val were sitting on the right bank of the Leadon, dabbling their feet in the clear shallow water before starting on their second trek to the ginger-bread house. Hester was carrying the sandwiches, Val the cold tea. Mrs Seth had added one of her apple turnovers. 'If you wuz to stop a-long 'ere you could 'ave cream on it,' she suggested. They had never told her about the gingerbread house; they liked to think it was still their secret. Though Hester knew that Val would never have found it on his own, she would not ask who had taken him there in the first place. It could have been Seth, of course.

Val had said easily, 'Too nice to be indoors, Mrs Seth. Besides, you and Seth like your Saturday afternoons to yourselves.' He laughed and so did she. Hester wondered why.

Hester repeated, 'It simply would not have crossed my mind to go to Hattie Pettiford's wedding, except that I heard Mother say that she wondered whether we should go. Just to the church, of course. We haven't had an invitation.'

'Mother said that?' He lifted his knees to his chin. The Leadon water was icy, even in the height of summer.

'Yes. I was surprised too. But Father would have none of it. He was quite nasty about it.' Hester breathed in sadly. 'When he kisses Mother, it doesn't seem like a loving thing. Not like Uncle Ted and Aunt Doffie.'

'No. It's a reminder.'

'How do you mean?'

'He's reminding her who is master and who is servant.'

'Val!' Hester was aghast.

'You must have realized. In this case, Mother had no right to make a suggestion.' He frowned. 'I wonder why. Normally, Father would enjoy going to the church and then making some derogatory comments about it afterwards.'

Hester said nothing; the thought of her mother as a servant was just dreadful. But . . . the way he bent her backwards – not romantically, like Uncle Ted and Aunt Doffie, but possessively, and as if he wanted to hurt her.

Then Val said, 'I don't see why you and I shouldn't go if you're keen, Sis. Though it's been so long since we had anything to do with the Pettifords.' He started to pull on his socks and grinned slightly. 'I rather like Hattie Pettiford. She's almost brazen. Everyone in the family knows she's marrying Percy Westbrook for his house and his money and his car. She couldn't possibly love him.'

'He's a railwayman, isn't he?'

'Yes. There is that. She might be trying to pull herself back to her roots.' Val tied his shoelaces and snorted a laugh. 'He's like someone from a comic film. Cross-eyed, thick pebble glasses, never speaks a word. He's a bit like Father, in that he wants to master Hattie. But I doubt he'll have much success.'

She asked the question she had asked Uncle Ted. 'Why has he got money if he works on the railway?'

'I think it's family money. Hattie is going to live in his mother's house. It's never going to work.

213

She – she's so full of life. She'll die of boredom.'

Hester said thoughtfully, 'She'll probably take a lover.'

Val exploded with laughter. 'What do you know of taking lovers, little Sis?' He stood up and pulled her with him. 'Come on. Let's get to the gingerbread house and have a swim in the pool.'

'What did you call it?' Hester asked triumphantly, because when she had named it the gingerbread house he had scoffed unmercifully.

'You know what I called it! And yes, we will go and see Hattie Pettiford getting married to Percy Westbrook. Now, are you satisfied?'

'Oh, I am! I am!' She leaned against him while she put on her sandals. A little while ago, she could not have done that.

They did not tell their parents where they were going; it was just another of their outings. Dorothy was delighted by their days out together, Reggie tolerated them. He usually had a message for Valentine. This time it was, 'Tell him I haven't rented out his room yet!'

Hester met Val at the station and they carried on to Cheltenham. From there it was a long walk up to Leckhampton church. Val commented, 'Not wedding weather at all. Hattie's veil will blow everywhere and she'll be as cross as two sticks.'

Hester laughed. 'I did not realize you knew her so well. But you're quite right. It will matter terribly to her that the weather is windy.'

Valentine said, 'I'm not sure myself how I know her. But I do. Sorry to sound like Father, but there isn't much to know, really, is there?'

'More than you think. When she left school and came back to live with her grandmother by the river, she was pretty marvellous, actually. I remember how awful it had been for Alice, staying in the cottage and going to the cemetery every day. We were only six. She told me about her gran crying all the time . . . it was hard for a six-year-old. Hattie came home and cried with her – much louder and oftener than Gran, too. And then, gradually, she made Gran laugh again. And she got the job in the bank and then brought her friends home, and when the War started she used to take Gran with her when she was singing at dances and things.'

'Singing?'

'All right, crooning. Whatever you like to call it. She made sure Gran was all right before she went off with that band.'

'How do you know all this? You were only six yourself.'

'Well, Alice and I talked a lot. Chattered, really. I missed that at first. But of course, this time next year I'll be going away, so I'd lose that anyway. And I've got you.' She hugged Val's arm, but then dropped it as she felt his lack of response. She thought it might be because she was probably going to Oxford . . . could he be regretting his decision? She said tentatively, not for the first time – water dripping on the stone of his resistance – 'You could come with me, Val. Finish your final year.'

He glanced at her, understanding what she was trying to do, but completely certain. 'You know I won't do that, Sis. Can't you see? I'm happy!'

And he was. He was looking forward to 1947 as much as she was.

By the time Doffie had fussed with Hattie's veil in the porch, she looked untouched by the skittish little wind blowing the leaves around the church-yard. Hester, craning her neck to look round at the raffish crew who must be Hattie's band of musicians, thought she looked exactly like Hedy Lamarr. Her dark hair was parted in the middle and swept back in wings to join a pearl headdress, which held her veil in place. Hester's eyes went to Uncle Ted, so upright, shy and modest, so kind and wise, so handsome in his grey suit and throttling stiff collar. Alice was the luckiest girl in the world to have a father like Uncle Ted; she was completely unappreciative.

Alice. Alice was in rose-coloured satin, with tiny green velvet bows going from Peter Pan collar to waist. She looked years younger than seventeen. Well, she wasn't seventeen until November, any-way. She wore a little green velvet cap on her head; it turned her undistinguished straw-coloured hair into gold. Hester bit her lip. She had always been the attractive one; now she saw that Alice, too, could be beautiful. As her gaze swept over Alice's green cap, she saw that some-one else on the groom's side of the aisle was looking at Alice too. It was that boy – Joseph Adair. Ridiculous name.

Valentine saw the bridal procession as a whole: a spectacle to be re-run in his head at a later date, savoured again and again. As the word 'spectacle' registered in his thoughts, he frowned slightly. He was here as a spectator. He had always been a spectator. It was just a word, of course. Spectacles had to have spectators. Audiences were essential to all performances, after all. He smiled as the 'speaking parts' began and the wonderful evocative words rolled through the ancient church. When Percy agreed to plight his troth, his voice was unexpectedly loud. Assertive. Hattie's, too, was strong. Val looked sharply at the back of her head. He knew – in spite of her apparent confidence – that she was not sure about this marriage.

Afterwards, he and Hester stood outside in the wind and watched as photographs were taken and people chatted in groups. Aunt Doffie spotted them and came over for a word.

'So *good* of you to come!'

Val said bluntly, 'You have always been a second family to Hester. And then – last spring . . . I've never thanked you.'

'How are you liking Leadon?' Aunt Doffie had not known the full extent of last spring's horror and, it seemed, Alice had never told her.

'Very well. Very well indeed. They still talk of Will Pettiford.' He smiled at her, and she smiled back.

'I know. He was a very special man.'

'Uncle Ted takes after him,' Hester blurted.

Aunt Doffie's smile widened as she turned to Hester. 'He does indeed.' She took the girl's hand as if to comfort her. 'How is your mother, my dear?'

'Very well, thank you.'

'I haven't seen her for such a long time. She too is special.'

Someone took Doffie's arm and introduced her to one of the Westbrooks. Val watched her as she was almost blown from group to group. He imagined Uncle Ted and her ... he closed his eyes against the thought, and Hattie's voice came suddenly, from almost underneath his bowed head.

'Valentine Ryecroft! Darling boy! How wonderful of you to come to my wedding!'

He opened his eyes, let her take his hands and pull him even closer, into a spurious privacy. She could not stop talking; it was one of the things he had so enjoyed about her before. Her – what had Hester called it? Her chatter. It was as insouciant as Alice's, yet also ... knowing.

'What did you think of the wedding? No, seriously, I want to know. You are the only one here whose opinion means something, so just tell me! My hair is such a mess and I've got toothache! Can you imagine it? Every other bride in the world has a headache! I have to have toothache!'

'You are beautiful,' Val said in a low voice. 'You are the most beautiful woman I have ever seen. I am sorry about the toothache, but it makes no difference. You are radiant.'

'Oh my God, I adore you for saying that. And meaning it – I know you mean it. That day – at Ted's – didn't you just so admire Ted? I love him so much, Val, so much it is unnatural!' She breathed a laugh. He could not understand why people were allowing her to be monopolized in this way. 'But that day, I knew there was something *we* shared, Val. I was drawn to you instantly. Tell me you felt it too!'

He thought back. Yes, he had felt it. He nodded, never taking his eyes from the dark velvet brown of hers.

She said, 'I don't know whether I love Percy. You know that too, don't you?' She did not wait for his nod, but put her lipsticked mouth to his right ear. 'Listen, Val. Come and see me. Come and see me soon.'

Someone spoke to her and she drew back and smiled secretly at him. Then she turned and was gone, and he stood there, his empty hands still held before him. He watched her flit from group to group like Aunt Doffie, and then she was lost in a cloud of confetti and rice as she was led to the car by Percy.

Yes, he was still watching. But there was a promise of more. Was he going to be part of the Pettifords? After all, Hester had always been almost one of them. And he was a member of the station staff at Leadon. They came from Leadon . . . he could do it.

Hester appeared at his elbow. 'That awful man! D'you know, he actually kissed me! It was disgusting!'

'Who was that, Sis?' He took her arm absently and they followed the crowd on to the road.

'The ghastly Percy Westbrook, of course! Didn't you see? They were trying to have a word with everyone. She spoke to you and he spoke to me! Ugh!' She shuddered dramatically.

'Never mind. Let's go and have a cup of tea somewhere along the Prom. Then we must get back. It's going to rain.'

They swung down into the Bath Road. Hester chattered almost as vivaciously as Alice, and he listened contentedly. As they sat over tea and toasted teacakes at the Gloucestershire Dairy, Hester sighed happily. 'Gosh. The future's going to be good for us, Val. I feel it in my bones!'

He felt it too. He smiled at her, and did something he had never done before. He leaned across the table and put his lips briefly to hers.

Sixteen

Looking back, Alice found it hard to remember exactly when her friendship with Joe flowered into a love affair known about by everyone around her, and – on a personal level – into the intense intimacy which often engulfed the two of them so completely that they even felt each other's joy and pain.

Joe's invitation was, of course, the public announcement everyone had been waiting for. He might just as well have put a notice in the local newspaper. Most of the office staff had assumed that the friendship between the two juniors would 'come to something', and their pleasure was almost smug. Only Uncle Duggie cautioned Alice to 'take it steady, my girl'. Mr Ryecroft ignored the whole thing. At home, he said once or twice that he had known all along that Alice Pettiford would marry as soon as she was out of a gymslip – she did not have the brains for anything other than marriage. His wife cast him a strange look, but said nothing.

Mrs Adair was pretty and quite small, with a flushed face and fluttery hands. Mum was nervous too and very keen for a return visit. Mrs Adair said she would come before the days started getting shorter, but there was a bus strike when the Pettifords got back from Weston-super-Mare, and in the end she put it off until the spring.

When Doffie and Alice paid their visit, they all sat in the upstairs sitting room of the terraced house in Cotswold Close, eating toasted teacakes with a choice of honey or strawberry jam, and a meringue each from the corner shop. 'Joe queued up for them,' Mrs Adair confided, then flushed as Joe started to tell Doffie that it had been no trouble.

After their visit, Doffie sighed as they settled themselves on the train. 'Well, that was nice,' she said as they chugged out of St James's station. 'I do hope Mrs Adair will be able to come to us.' When they got to Churchdown she said, 'How long has Joe been looking after his mother?' And when Alice confessed she did not know, Doffie said sadly, 'It must have been when his father was killed.' They both stared out of the window in silence until they got to their station, where they unlocked their bikes. Only then, cycling home through the summer-sated lanes, did they slough off the feeling of sadness that surrounded Joe's mother.

As far as Alice was concerned, the Weston holiday was just an interlude. They swam, walked and went to the theatre, just as they always did, but Alice was somehow disconnected from all of it.

Then it happened for the first time. It was Alice's birthday, and Joe took her to the Opera House to see the Fol-de-Rols. It was the first variety show she had seen, and she was not particularly thrilled. But tenderness flooded through her because she saw that Joe was enjoying it, and she knew even then that it was an evening she would never ever forget. The final act was an impersonator, who blacked up as Al Jolson and sang, 'Though April showers may come your way . . .' At the end of the song, amid the applause, Alice and Joe turned and looked at each other. Alice could feel her eyes burning in the dim light of the auditorium. And Joe's velvet brown eyes seemed to let the fierce blue of hers into his head . . . into his soul. They were locked in intimacy and could not look away. The applause died and the compère walked on stage as the curtains closed behind him, and still they looked. Alice felt her eyes filling just before she saw that Joe was weeping. She reached for his hand and held it tightly, and very gradually their tears subsided. He smiled slightly, ruefully, and turned back to the stage. She did the same. She was exhausted. It was as if for an instant they had changed bodies and souls. And she knew, with an almost terrible certainty, that Joe Adair could never be happy without her.

Christmas was wonderful too. The office – except for the Control – closed at lunchtime on Christmas Eve, and everyone was invited into Mr Maybury's office for a glass of sherry and a mince pie. Someone had a box of crackers and they all drew straws for the paper hats. Mr Oliver arrived late, having been to the market; he was carrying a bunch of mistletoe which he put to good use immediately. Alice was amazed at the way everyone let their hair down. Mr Maybury kissed Helena and Miss Warner, and would have kissed

Alice and Janet too, if Miss Warner had not stood in front of them like a guardian angel – or like a dragon, as Dad said later. Joe waited till it was nearly time for his train, then produced his own mistletoe and pecked Alice's cheek when she went to fetch her bike. They had never kissed properly. Their connection in the Opera House had made kissing redundant.

'I'll see you in two days,' Joe said. 'I hope – I hope you have a lovely Christmas.'

She pulled the cuffs of her gloves over her coat sleeves; she knew he and his mother would go to church on Christmas morning, and then stay in and listen to the wireless. His loneliness lay heavily on her heart.

She said, 'I think we're going to see Hattie on Boxing Day. I expect someone at Leckhampton has a bike. I might be able to cycle down. Just to say Happy Christmas to your mother. That is, if she wouldn't mind.'

'Oh, Alice!' It was as if she'd given him the keys to Heaven. 'She'd love it. She thinks you're nice, really nice. She keeps saying that. Could you? Could you really?'

She knew it would not be easy. Neither Mum nor Hattie would think much of her disappearing, but she said blithely, 'Of course. It would be good to get out of the house for a while. I'll do my level best!'

They both laughed. They walked slowly to the station together, and Alice waved goodbye as Joe's train drew out. Lately, she had not enjoyed this small ritual and had not known why. Today she knew. In five months' time she would be waving goodbye to him for two years. She remembered

Helena Webster's words and shivered. She had already used up over half of their precious year together.

While Hattie was dishing up the Christmas pudding, Alice asked as casually as she could whether she could borrow a bicycle and call on Joe.

Ted was unexpectedly furious. 'If that silly young idiot wants to see you, he knows where you live!'

'Dad, you know that his mother isn't very well—'

'It's all I hear! That damned stupid Toby calls him a Mummy's boy, and he's not far wrong!'

She could feel her temper rise at that. Old Mrs Westbrook sat on the sofa like a buddha, the epitome of a mother with her son well under her thumb. Doffie leapt to Joe's defence. 'If he's good to his mother, he will be good to our daughter!' she snapped.

That did it for Ted. 'I had no idea they were married!' he said sarcastically, then immediately softened as Percy came into the room. 'You'd better go then. You can probably borrow Hattie's old bike. But be back for tea – she's gone to no end of trouble!'

She went, but as soon as she reached the little side street at the bottom of Leckhampton hill, she saw that the Adairs had visitors; an enormous pre-War Lanchester was parked outside number eight and a uniformed chauffeur sat in the driving seat.

Joe must have been looking out for Alice, because he came running up the road as she sat uncertainly on her borrowed bicycle, one foot on the kerb.

'I was afraid you'd turn and go back when you saw the car,' he panted. 'It's my grandmother's sister – my Great Aunt Eve. She's really stuffy. She did not warn us – it's a duty visit – she is staying with the Garston-Smiths at Stroud. Come and be introduced, then she might clear off!'

Alice was going to make a joke about being good at frightening away unwanted visitors, but Joe was obviously in no mood for jokes. She left the bike where it was and went with him up the front steps and into the little-used sitting room. Alice could sense poor Mrs Adair's panic. She sat at one side of the fire, a shawl clutched around her narrow shoulders, her hair in disarray. She was delighted to see Alice; in contrast to the visitor, who turned down her mouth when she was introduced and said, 'A colleague of Joseph's? I had no idea women worked on the railways.' Alice smiled and held out her hand, and after a second's obvious surprise, Great Aunt Eve took it and held it limply, before announcing her departure.

'We've had our little talk, Rose. I am glad you understand the position. My sister should have made it clear years ago, of course. She was always indecisive.' She gathered up her bags and gloves. 'And as you were not expecting anything, you are not disappointed!' She smiled. 'What a true saying that is! Expectations nearly always lead to dis-appointment.' She nodded at Joe. 'We probably won't meet again, my boy. I suppose you must take after your father; you have very little of the Chatterton colouring or features.'

At last, Mrs Adair spoke. 'He is the image of his father,' she said quietly but with pride. 'And he is just as kind and thoughtful.'

Great Aunt Eve looked surprised again, but said nothing. Joe opened the door for her, and followed her into the narrow passage to do the same at the front door.

'Goodbye, Aunt,' he said. 'It was kind of you to call.'

Alice went to the netted window to watch the chauffeur leap from the car and lead his mistress by hand down the steps to the pavement, as Joe returned to the house. Behind her, Mrs Adair said faintly, 'I'm glad he looks like an Adair! My poor mother had to suffer from the Chattertons!'

There was a soft thump. Alice looked round, and saw that Mrs Adair had slumped sideways against the arm of her chair. She seemed to be unconscious. The awful thing was that Joe coped with it so matter-of-factly and efficiently. Obviously it happened quite often. When he had used the sal volatile and spooned some sweet tea into her mouth, he continued talking as if nothing had happened. Alice was glad she could not stay to tea. 'Hattie wants us all around the table . . . you know how it is. It's been grand to see you, Mrs Adair. I do hope you will be all right.'

'She's fine,' Joe said robustly. 'And we're back to normal tomorrow. Too much excitement . . .' He saw her to the door, and suddenly his defences were gone. 'Alice, when I'm called up, can you keep an eye? Just visit her now and then, perhaps.'

'Oh Joe, of course. You know I will.' Her gut twisted agonizingly. 'I cannot believe—'

'I know. Don't think about it. It will spoil everything.'

'All right. You'd better go back in. Get her to eat something.'

He nodded. 'It was Great Aunt Eve. She wanted to talk privately. Heaven knows what she said. If it was to tell Mum that Grandma left us nothing, it was no surprise, we already knew that. Perhaps it was the way she said it.'

Alice felt she could not bear it. She was going back to paper hats and crackers, and Joe and his mother had nothing.

She said, reminding herself, 'You've got each other, Joe. That's what counts.'

Which was absolutely true.

And then, quite suddenly, it was 1947. Alice remembered last New Year's Eve, when the boats in the docks had sounded their sirens for the first Eve since the War had finished, and the shunters in the marshalling yard had let off an enormous detonator. She remembered wondering whether it had been a message from God. She had been such a child then.

January and February proved to be dark days in every sense of the word. Joe could never stay on until the later train, as his mother 'got in a state' once the curtains were drawn. The weather was appalling, ice and snow delayed the trains and he never knew when he would arrive at work or at home. Alice left earlier each morning so that she could meet him at the station; with frozen hands and toes they would walk down to the office together, before fetching the coal and the oil stove. It was in the cellar that Alice fully realized Joe's desperation.

'I shall be posted to Corsham first of all. That's where the square-bashing takes place.'

She hardly knew what to say; her own dread of his absence was submerged beneath his obvious misery. She made a small sound, halfway between plea and reassurance.

'I know, Alice. It was me who said we must forget it. But suddenly it's 1947 and I can't forget it any longer. What are we going to do?'

'We must take it day by day. Now. And then. If only we can do that we won't spoil what's left and we won't be swamped by what's to come. You might be posted somewhere near home. In an office.'

For a moment he was comforted. 'Wouldn't that be wonderful?'

The enormous cellar was lit by a single naked bulb. They stared at each other in the dimness, hopeful and frightened. Alice whispered, 'If only we could skip the next two years.'

'Alice . . . Alice, could we go away together? Perhaps at Easter? Just the two of us.'

She was startled. 'I don't know. Where?'

'It wouldn't matter. Just to be together. All the time.'

'What about your mother?'

'I know. But she will have to manage when . . . you know.'

'My parents wouldn't allow . . . perhaps if they came as well . . .'.

'Oh Alice! You know what I mean! Together! You and me. All the time.'

'What?' She frowned at him, then realized. Her eyes filled. 'Joe, don't say any more. I can't say no to you. I love you too much. But I don't want to.'

'How can you say you love me?'

'I do. But what you are saying . . . it's wrong.'

He was silent; she felt a separation from him
which she had never experienced before. He
passed her his handkerchief and turned to pick
up the oil stove.

'I won't say any more then. You must do what
you think is right, even if I don't agree.'

She hardly knew how to bear it. They staggered
upstairs with their loads and went about the business of warming the office. She glanced at him
now and then; she knew he was in pain, and his
pain rebounded into her so that she had to
breathe deeply and consciously.

In April, cold and wet and somehow hopeless –
Alice was reading poetry in bed each night and
knew exactly what Eliot meant by 'the cruellest
month' – a most surprising thing happened. Ted
was sent to work in Paddington for a whole year!
Not only that, but Mr Maybury himself drove out
to Lypiatt Bottom to tell them personally. Luckily,
Miss Webster had already warned Alice.

'I can't tell you what it's about – something
good, I promise.' She smiled. 'My mother
would not be happy about an unheralded visit
from the Divisional Superintendent, so I rather
assume—'

'Oh yes,' Alice said fervently.

'These bachelors simply do not understand,'
Miss Webster said, her smile becoming indulgent.
'And Mr Maybury is worse than most. He
suggested taking your father home tomorrow
evening, and when I pointed out that Mr Pettiford

would have his bicycle, he said he would put it in his boot!'

'Oh . . . but how kind. How sweet.'

'Yes.' The smile trembled away. 'Yes, he is a very sweet man.'

'I am supposed to be going home with Joe tomorrow,' Alice said. 'To say goodbye to his mother.'

'My dear, go ahead. It is the best thing. They will tell you all about it when you get home.'

'Yes. Yes, of course.'

But Alice wished she could have been there to see the big black Armstrong Siddeley jog sedately down the lane, with Dad's bike bursting from its boot. As time ran out for Joe and her, she wished it away even faster. It was like waiting on a railway platform for a train to pull out. She thought that once he was there and she was here, it would somehow be different, not such a ghastly strain. She would still go to Cheltenham once a week – just as she went to Gran's – to visit Mrs Adair and cook her a meal. They could talk about Joe. It had to be better than this.

The evening was as dreary as she had expected. She had made scones the night before and took them in her saddlebag, with some evaporated milk with which to make ersatz cream. Mrs Adair became flushed and animated; she ate half a scone and drank half a cup of tea. Alice thought that, since her husband died, she had probably been only half a person. When Joe said that Alice was going to visit her regularly once he was gone, she said bravely, 'We'll wait for the better weather, dear, then we'll have a walk. Montpelier Gardens – we used to walk there and listen to the band, didn't we, Joe? You will be able to picture Alice and me walking together past those lovely marigold beds.'

'That sounds grand, Mrs Adair. And perhaps my cousin will drive you to our house to have that cup of tea.'

Mrs Adair's eyes flicked from left to right. Joe said quickly, 'If you're strong enough, Ma. Only if you're strong enough.'

'Yes, of course,' Alice added quickly.

She cycled home. It was six miles and the wind was against her. It took her an hour, and towards the end she stopped seeing the damp hedgerows and could only think of getting home. She wondered whether there was anything wrong with her. Before she had left, Joe had held her so tightly and kissed her hard on the mouth, trying to force her lips apart, and she had pushed him away and jumped on to her bike and pedalled down Bath Road as if the devil himself were after her.

Mr Maybury had long gone. Doffie and Ted were sitting on opposite sides of the fireplace, looking at each other. It seemed that Ted had been accorded a great honour. He had devised a new system for finding coal wagons and marshalling them in fewer but bigger marshalling yards.

'I didn't *invent* it, Doff,' he protested in between her torrent of words. 'It just developed over the years—'

'Never mind that, darling. You did it. You are the one they want in Paddington to start off the national scheme! You are the one who is going to London, to stay in a hotel –' she scrabbled among the papers on the table, '– Number six, Sussex Gardens to be exact – to work out the charts for the rest of the country—'

'Just the western region, Doff,' he put in again.

'And to show other controllers—'

'Oh, Doff!' But he was grinning. 'Stop being so damned *proud*!'

'I can't.' She laughed and got up to hug him. 'Come on, Alice! Come and congratulate your poor old father here.'

They almost smothered him, and he enjoyed every minute of it. Alice wondered fleetingly what the office would be like, not only without Joe but now also without Dad. Then she decided that she was the most selfish person on the earth, and hugged him harder than ever. And in the midst of all the congratulations, there was a knock on the door and there were Hattie and Percy, grinning, right on cue.

'How did you *know*?' Doffie shrieked.

The house was full of voices and laughter. Hattie never went anywhere quietly.

'How did *you* know? That's the thing!' She released herself from Doffie and smoothed her skirt over her abdomen. 'It doesn't show yet, so how on earth –?'

There was a moment's pause, then Doffie exclaimed, 'Not—?'

'Yes! What else?'

'My God, when?'

'Tell them, Percy baby – I have to keep using that word! Isn't it an absolute scream?' Percy grunted something and Hattie interpreted, 'October, darlings! An autumn baby, in good time for Christmas! And no one can say we had to get married either, because it will be just past our first anniversary!'

Neither Ted nor Doffie said anything for a long moment. Alice knew they wanted to remind Hattie that she hadn't wanted children and neither had Percy, but with him standing there it was all rather difficult.

Alice said, 'Congratulations! How lovely!' She managed to kiss Percy on the cheek, then hugged Hattie. 'I'm going to be an aunty! Well, sort of.' She grinned into Hattie's dark eyes. 'We thought you must have heard our news – Dad is going to work in London for a whole year!'

Hattie's face fell. 'What? You can't go away, Ted. Not now. Not when I need you most!'

'Darling, you'll have me and Alice!' said Doffie.

Hattie said, 'Yes, I know. But I simply want everyone. My whole family. I want Gran to come and live with us. And Alice to stay every week-end—'

Percy grunted and Ted said sternly, 'That's enough, Hattie! Sit down quietly, the baby won't appreciate all these histrionics. Alice, put the kettle on.'

'We've brought champagne, haven't we, Percy baby?'

He produced a bottle from beneath his great-coat, explaining that it was left over from the wedding.

'Oh, all right then,' said Ted. 'You can have some too, Alice.'

Doffie unearthed glasses and they sat around talking and talking. It was past midnight when Percy finally insisted on making a move. As they were leaving, Hattie darted back to say quickly, 'I know what I said and I know what he said. But we're both so happy. You do realize that, don't you?'

Ted glanced at Doffie and nodded.

Hattie made for the front door again. 'And she – old Mrs Westbrook – she's delighted.' She grinned wickedly. 'I don't have to wash up or do anything any more! I'm the mother of her grandson!'

Percy revved the car triumphantly as he drove back down the lane. As they closed the door, Doffie said, 'Alice – bed.' Ted said, 'I don't get it,' and Doffie replied quickly, 'Later, dear,' and shooed Alice up the stairs.

She went thankfully. She needed to talk to God. If He thought He was sending Hattie's baby as a replacement for Joe and Dad, He really did not understand His own creations very well.

Seventeen

Parting with Joe was like a physical wound. It healed, but there would always be a scar – Alice knew that, even as she tried to slot back into her office and home routine. Mr Berry knew it too, and was kindly concerned for her, almost as if she were indeed an invalid. Everyone else, Miss Webster and Mum, even Hattie and Dad – especially Dad – kept reminding her quietly that he would be home on his first leave in six weeks, and that even if he was posted abroad it was only two years.

'Two years, sweetheart.' Mum was all concern, tears in her eyes, remembering how it had been when she had fallen in love – how she felt now with Ted about to go away to London. 'I know it sounds ages, but you're at the beginning of everything and it's not long. I promise you, it really isn't.'

'I know, Mum. Of course I know.' Alice met her mother's gaze full on. 'I could bear it for myself. I will do. You know that. I have you – I have everything.' She swept her arm around their living room, glanced out of the window at the clematis clambering over the crab-apple tree. 'It – it's him.

His whole being is here. It's like depriving him of water.' Tears poured down her face. 'I'm sorry, Mum. Truly sorry. But I am so frightened he will not be able to cope.'

Doffie gathered her up and rocked her, then held her away and spoke with total confidence.

'Alice, I don't know your Joe very well. But that's good, because I am still seeing him objectively. He will survive this, darling. He is strong. He is strong in a steadfast way. He has a core that won't change. It's possible that you will change, but Joe will not.'

'Neither will I! Never, never!'

Doffie clasped her again. 'I know. At first I was worried, but then . . . I am glad you have met each other. He is a good person, Alice. A really good person.'

Alice was so thankful that her mother knew that. She wiped away her tears, and it was she who suggested they should go and pick bluebells.

Helena spoke to Alice in the cloakroom, at the tiny basin where they washed up the coffee cups. Alice was dry-eyed, but Helena knew how she felt; everyone knew. She put a gentle hand on Alice's shoulder and said, 'Time will fly, Alice. You'll look back and realize it was just a tiny fraction of your life.' Alice nodded dumbly and dried the cups as if her life depended on it.

Mr Berry seemed to know how she felt. He brought her a buttered roll; real butter and home-made bread. She ate it with her coffee, and thanked him with a bunch of cowslips the next day.

He said, 'My favourite flower, Alice. When I was

a boy we used to pull the blossom carefully – like so – and drink the nectar.'

Alice nodded, animated. 'Hest—' She glanced back at Mr Ryecroft's desk and then went on, 'My friend and I . . . we used to do that.'

She felt another pang, this time for Hester. And for Valentine.

It was good when Ted came home at weekends. Alice and Doffie would cycle to meet him, Alice expertly steering his empty bike alongside her own, and they would cycle back, three abreast, through the lanes, which were burgeoning that year after a wet spring. Ted loved it. He would pedal away, no hands on the handlebars; sometimes, he was so happy to be home that he would even put his feet on the handlebars. Doffie prophesied disaster – but even when, predictably, he wobbled into a ditch, he could not be subdued.

'Nothing like going away to appreciate your home,' he said. 'Remember that, our Alice.'

'Yes, Dad.' She had to grin back at him. He looked so funny, with mud dripping from his hair and Mum fussing over him, saying they'd never get his suit cleaned for Monday morning.

At last, the six weeks were up and Joe came home for seven precious days. But there was no peace for him; home was almost too precious, too ephemeral. He clung to Alice on Lansdown platform, breathing in the scent from her hair, telling himself he was a rotten coward and wondering how the men must have felt knowing that they had to return to the trenches, or the air, or the desert . . . He closed his eyes and hung on to Alice more tightly than ever.

She sensed his mood immediately and tightened her own grip on his shoulders. When they drew apart, he said, 'Mmm, you smell so good.'

She said in a hoarse voice, 'It's Cuticura soap. I always use it.'

He nodded. 'I know.' He tried to smile. 'Mine's carbolic. Not quite so fragrant!' They laughed. He shouldered his kitbag and they started up the wide avenue towards Cotswold Close.

Joe looked like a stranger in his best tiddly suit. He explained how they folded the trousers and put them in their hammocks to preserve the strange horizontal creases. He told her about the cookhouse and the incessant drill and the 'heads' and the liberty boat. He had to explain to her that though they were still landlubbers, everything was the same as on board ship. 'We wash our smalls in a bucket. I knew about all of this because my father was a marine and lived on board all through the War.' He swallowed. 'Well, until he was killed, of course.' He squeezed her hand. 'How is Ma?'

'A bit subdued. Naturally. If I said anything else, you would know I was not telling the truth.' Alice smiled at him, hoping for one of their special moments. It did not happen. 'I've been to see her three times.'

'Oh, Alice, thanks. Have you had a walk in the park?'

'No. I'm going to leave that to her, Joe. I can't risk anything.'

'Of course not – I don't expect . . . the people

next door, Mr and Mrs Trotter, they know about Mum. If she knocks on the wall they will come in.'

'She's not keen on them.'

'I know. But what other choice is there?'

Alice hesitated. 'Joe, if she were ill, I think Mum would have her with us. Nurse her for a while – that sort of thing.'

'Have you asked her – has she suggested it?'

'No. But I think she would do it.'

Joe said sceptically, 'People don't. Not when it comes to it. They're always too busy or something.'

'I'll mention it. Mum's not just people.'

'I didn't mean any criticism—'

'I know . . . it's all right, Joe. Really.'

Rose Adair was in the kitchen when they arrived. A savoury smell filled the room, and her face was flushed with cooking and radiant happiness.

'I've done a stew, Joe!' She hugged Alice. 'Alice, I've done a stew! Mrs Trotter brought in some best end of neck yesterday, and I simmered it and let it get cold, then took off the fat and put in onions and carrots! Just like I used to when Pa was here, Joe! Just the same!'

It was delicious. They sat around the table, dipping bread into the clear broth and spearing vegetables on their forks. Mrs Adair smiled and smiled and Joe told her about the barracks.

'It's like having your father back again,' she sighed happily. The aura of sadness around her had gone. Alice was delighted and thought Joe would be too. But when he walked her back to the station, he was almost entirely silent. It was left to her to tell him about dear Mr Berry and awful Mr Ryecroft.

'Have they replaced me yet?' he asked at one point.

'No. Someone is coming in from Bourton-on-the-Water. To get office experience.' She hadn't wanted to tell him that.

'No one is indispensable. Isn't that what they say?'

Alice said robustly, 'Not to the railways, perhaps. But everyone is indispensable to someone. You know that, Joe. You are indispensable to me. I am indispensable to you.'

He peered down the line at the home signal. She said insistently, 'You do know that, don't you?'

'Of course.' He straightened and gave her his attention. 'Of course I know that. Romeo and Juliet. Yes?'

'Yes.' She'd used that analogy before – but not about Joe. She frowned. 'Let it be Joe and Alice. I'd prefer to be us. Not like anyone else. Unique.'

'All right.'

It was too pat; he was playing a part. He handed her into an empty compartment and slammed the door. She hung out of the window. It had been like this six weeks ago when he had left, and her heart clutched all over again; but this time she was seeing him the next day. They had a whole week.

It was nine o'clock when she got home. Uncle Duggie's Flying Standard was parked outside; the windows were rolled down and the familiar smell of his feet wafted out. Alice realized that she had wanted Mum to be on her own, waiting for her. She put her bike in the shed and went through the back door, hoping that Duggie would even then be going out of the front one.

'Damn,' she said under her breath.

Doffie and Uncle Duggie were standing by the dining-room table, looking at some photographs. Doffie was laughing.

'Oh, Alice. Come and see. Duggie has been clearing out and has found these old snaps. Look – Reggie Ryecroft and Dad. Paddling in the Leadon brook – can you imagine Reggie?'

It was left to Uncle Duggie to say, 'How was Joe, Alice? Is it getting him down?'

She heard herself say, 'I don't think so. He seems fine. Mrs Adair had made a stew.'

Mum enthused a bit too much, as if to cover the fact that she hadn't asked after Joe. She explained to Uncle Duggie that Mrs Adair was practically a recluse.

'Not quite.' Alice was angry with her mother. 'She must have gone out to get the meat and vegetables for the stew.' But even as she spoke, she remembered that Mrs Trotter next door had provided the ingredients.

Uncle Duggie said he had to go, but that Doffie could keep the snaps. He said goodbye to Alice and went to the front door; then there was a pause. Alice stared blindly at the photographs on the table; it would be all right in a minute. Mum would come back in and ask properly about Joe, and Alice could pour out her worries and her mother would somehow make them go away.

She shuffled the photographs and found one of her father – a family photograph: Gran, Gramps, an attractive young woman with a mass of dark hair and a low-cut blouse, no doubt the incorrigible Mitzie, and in front, sitting on the ground, a young Dad, holding a baby who must be Hattie. She picked it up, smiling sentimentally.

Underneath it was one of Uncle Duggie kissing Mum.

Alice stared for a moment, knowing it meant nothing, then shoved it to the bottom of the pile, stacked them neatly and went into the hall. Uncle Duggie was having difficulty starting the Flying Standard. He got out a handle and Doffie went out to help him crank the engine to life. They were laughing.

Alice said, 'Joe, it's not the same. What's happened?'

They were sitting at the top of Cooper's Hill, where the famous cheese-rolling took place. It was Sunday and they had been out all day on their bikes. Joe was going back to his 'ship' in two days' time.

He was immediately filled with remorse. 'I'm sorry. I'm so sorry, Alice. I thought I was doing all right. It's just . . . I don't know which is the real world. Here or there. But we're all right . . . we are all right, aren't we?'

'Of course.' She wrapped her arms around him; he was trembling. 'Of course we're all right. It's just that . . . I wanted to make you happy—'

'Oh God, you make me more than happy, Alice! What is happy, anyway? You make me want to – to live. That's the important thing. To want to live.'

She clutched him closer. It had never occurred to her that there should be a reason for living. Maybe a purpose. Never a reason. But Joe's mother was without a reason – Alice saw it suddenly. And just as suddenly, with horror, she knew that Rose Adair would die, simply because there was no reason to live. And Joe was her son; her blood was in his veins.

She said suddenly, 'Joe, I want us to be together. Like you said before in the cellar. Now. Here.'

'No, Alice. It is enough that we are side by side—'

'Joe, I am not saying this for your sake. It's for my own sake. I have grown away from my mother. My father is in London all the week. I need you.'

'Darling, we can't. Supposing . . . there could be a baby, Alice. And you here alone to cope with it. No.'

She pressed her mouth to his insistently. She pushed his hand inside her blouse. She did not know about the mechanics of sex, and when – after a long time – she prevailed, she was shocked when she saw him unbutton his trousers and pull them down. She had to bite back a scream when he pushed himself inside her; the pain was ferocious, and she clung to him then simply to bear it.

Afterwards, he wept and she comforted him. It had done nothing for either of them; it had made him humble, and Alice just wanted to go home to her mother. When they cycled back down the hill, she was sore and felt unutterably bleak. She insisted that he should go on into Cheltenham and let her cycle home alone. Contrarily, she was terribly hurt when he finally agreed.

It took her a long time to negotiate the lanes; long enough to face the fact that he could have been right. She could be pregnant.

Eighteen

Two days later, Joe returned to Corsham. The following week, he rang the office at six-thirty to tell Alice about his posting to HMS *Hermes*. She knew by then that there was no baby.

They had arranged that she would wait in the milk bar until everyone had left, then return to the office via the front staircase to wait for his call.

'Sometimes there are queues for the phone box. It could be a bit later.'

'Don't make it any earlier. If Mr Berry misses the Stroud train—'

'I know. I won't. I love you. You were right about – you know. I feel we're married. I feel . . . settled.'

Alice had never felt quite so unsettled in her life. Even kissing was something they had rarely done before; there had been no need for any kind of demonstration of their love. Since the day at Cooper's Hill, she had been constantly hugging him, kissing him, telling him she loved him. Whenever they were alone he had slid his hand inside her blouse and cupped her breast. They could not have gone on like that; in a terrible way, it was a relief when he went.

She got back to the office and stood over Mr

Berry's phone, willing it to ring. Joe was two minutes late and his voice came over the phone urgently. 'Is that you?'

'Yes. How are you? Have you heard anything? Are you all right?'

He was shouting. There must be a jostle of sailors outside, all wanting to phone their families to tell them about this posting. His voice reverberated against her ear.

'Say that again, Joe. I can't—'

'I'm fine, darling. Really I am. I wish we were together. Lying together. I love you so much. I want you. Are you all right?'

'Yes. This morning.'

There was a pause, and she could hear other voices pressing against her ear.

He said, 'That's good.' He sounded disappointed. Perhaps he could have got compassionate leave if she had been pregnant.

'Yes, it is, isn't it? I've been so relieved. I can't tell you.'

'Have you?' There was a wistful echo in his voice, then he said, 'Of course – of course. I am too.'

'Have you got your posting, Joe?'

'Yes. It's HMS *Hermes*. I'm sorry, darling.'

She gripped the phone. It smelled of tobacco and she coughed. He had spoken of various ships and commissions. *Hermes* was a minesweeper. There were minefields all over the world's seas and oceans.

She said, 'Do you know where you'll be going?'

'It's the Far East.'

'Oh!' There were no words to voice her distress. He would be gone for a long, long time.

'Listen, can you come to Plymouth? We've got two days in barracks. Getting equipment and kit. There will be evenings.'

'When?'

'Next week.' His voice was being drowned by others. He shouted, 'I'll write. Take care. Can you go and see my mother? Take care . . .' He was gone suddenly; the receiver replaced with a rattle. She took out her handkerchief and slowly wiped the mouthpiece of Mr Berry's phone, before replacing it on its cradle. She thought of him in the phone box, with the press of bodies all around him. She shuddered. Joe hated it; and so did she. And now she had to find a way to get time off next week. Mr Ryecroft had been particularly sarcastic since her father had gone to London. Alice knew before Helena Webster told her that he was bitterly jealous that Ted had been singled out.

She went to see Mrs Adair the next Saturday afternoon. She had hoped that Mum would come with her, but Dad couldn't get home until Saturday and Mum was going to meet him off the London train and take him to tea at the Cadena.

'Do come, Alice love,' she said. 'It's a sort of anniversary. We met at the Cadena tea dance twenty-five years ago on Saturday.'

Alice thought of Uncle Duggie and his feet. She tried to look quizzical. 'Then you won't want any gooseberries around!'

'Oh darling – as if!' But Doffie didn't really mind. She admitted herself that she felt positively girlish about it. She remembered aloud how Ted had swept her off her feet. Alice felt something close to revulsion, but hid it with a smile. There was something wrong with her, that was for sure.

* * *

Mrs Adair looked as if she had been put through the mangle; you didn't notice how thin she was until she stood sideways. But she was delighted to see Alice.

'Dear girl, I knew you'd come. And what's this? Flowers? Oh, how lovely! And a cake too – from your mother? That is so kind.'

She was in the living room, with a view of people passing by behind the railings on the pavement outside. It was chilly, but there was no fire in the range. Alice went out to the coal house and brought in four buckets of coal and some kindling. She laid a fire, then fetched a blanket and wrapped Mrs Adair up before making tea.

'I'll do some hot-water bottles when I go. Then you can light the fire in the morning. I thought the man next door was going to see to that.'

'I told him not to bother. No need for a fire at this time of year.' Mrs Adair smiled. 'I need never worry that Joe won't be properly looked after! You are a good girl, Alice.'

'No. No, I am not.' Alice thought how sad it was that only ten days ago she could have accepted that compliment. She was no longer a good girl. She told Mrs Adair about Plymouth. 'I'm so afraid that Mr Ryecroft won't let me go.'

Mrs Adair's face became more pinched than ever. 'Surely he could not be that unkind?'

'It's my father. He's getting at my father through me. But of course I'm not telling Dad . . . anything.'

'No, you mustn't worry him when he's working away.' She smiled. 'For the same reason, you must not tell Joe about the fire, Alice. Please.'

Alice smiled and shook her head. 'All right. But you promised Joe you would take care of yourself. Remember that.'

Mrs Adair nodded smilingly, and Alice cut her another slice of cake.

A letter came from Joe on Monday morning. He was already in Plymouth, in the Naval barracks at Devonport. They were sailing on Friday, for Singapore.

Alice was horrified. So was Doffie.

'Of course you have to go to see him, love. I don't like it, but you can't let the poor lad go all that way without saying goodbye. I'll come with you.'

'No!' Alice was determined. 'No need for double expense. I'll go on Thursday morning, say goodbye to Joe that evening –' her voice quavered alarmingly, '– and come back on the mail train.'

'Darling, you can't. Not by yourself. Please let me come with you. I'll say goodbye, then I'll go and sit in the station waiting room – I won't be in the way, I promise.'

'Mum, I've got to be as brave as he is. He is alone and I must be alone. You do see, don't you?'

Doffie gazed at her, anguished, then said, 'I suppose so.' She got up to open the door. 'Let me go and see Reggie, then. I'll make sure you have Thursday off. Let me do that, love.'

But that really was beyond the pale, and it would never have worked, anyway. Mum simply had no idea. Alice even managed to laugh about it, when she told Helena Webster what her mother said.

Helena was her usual understanding self.

'Yes, it would probably have made him even worse. He would seize the chance to upset your mother as well as you!' They were in the ladies' cloakroom at the office, and Helena had been staring closely at her face in the tiny mirror above the sink. Now she closed her powder compact with a snap. 'Leave it with me, Alice. I'll have a word with Mr Berry when Mr Ryecroft goes to dinner. Then this afternoon, make sure you have to take some obsolete files down to the cellar, and don't say anything until I tip you the wink.'

'He'll know I've put you up to it.'

'No, he won't. I promise you that.'

Alice did exactly as she had been told. She came back from her own dinner break, red-faced in the summer heat, and had to suffer the usual uncomplimentary remarks from Mr Ryecroft. She had already made a pile of files dated before the War, and went through them with Mr Berry before 'descending into the depths', as Mr Ryecroft always said. She stacked them alphabetically by the light of the single bulb, trying not to think of how she and Joe had cemented their friendship down there. If only they had stayed just friends . . .

She went slowly back up the stairs. The General Office door was propped open to allow a draught to cool the overcrowded office. She heard Helena's voice, calm and clear and very cold.

'You can call it that if you like.'

And then Mr Ryecroft's, spluttering with indignation. 'I do! I do call it that! You are threatening to uncover some inadvertent misdemeanour I may – or may not – have made many years ago! I call that blackmail!'

Mr Berry said gently, 'We're not blackmailing anyone . . . sir. We are pointing out that in the past you obviously bent the rules. We're asking you to do it again. We're all very fond of Alice and Joe. A day off, just to make their farewells . . . it's not much to ask, surely?'

Alice shrank back against the wall and prayed that no one would emerge into the corridor and ask her jovially what she was doing skulking outside the door of her office.

Mr Berry had hit the right note, and after a grunting pause, Alice heard Mr Ryecroft grudgingly admit that perhaps a day off . . . in the circumstances.

Helena said, 'That's settled then. But before we leave the subject, perhaps the same circumstances could be applied to our general attitude to Alice.' Alice could imagine Helena fixing Mr Ryecroft with her ice-blue eyes. 'Her father has gone and now Joe has gone. She needs our support. She needs our . . . kindness.'

'Well, of course,' Mr Ryecroft was blustering. 'The girl has always been close to me. Second daughter. She practically lived at my home when she was a child. Probably thinks of me as a replacement father.'

Helena said nothing. Her policy had worked well.

The weather held and on the following Thursday there was a glorious sunset. Joe and Alice watched it from the dockside at Devonport. The liberty boats were coming and going, but Joe had given up his rum ration for a month to be on the last one. Alice held his hand and shivered. The journey down had seemed endless and it would be worse going back. She felt sick with fear.

For the umpteenth time, she begged him to take care of himself; he promised he would and extracted a similar promise from her. The whole evening had been spent making these meaningless exchanges, but ordinary conversation was out of the question. She had told him about his mother, and he had admitted miserably that since his father had been killed she had 'given up'.

'I suppose in Victorian times it would have been called a decline.'

'But that was really tuberculosis, Joe. What does the doctor say?'

'He thinks it's her mind. It might be. I don't know.'

The last liberty boat bumped against the dock, and another Ordinary Seaman touched Joe's shoulder. 'Time we weren't here, mate.'

Joe straightened himself with an obvious effort. 'Don't forget me, Alice.'

'As if I could!'

'You know where the taxi rank is?'

He had told her a dozen times. She nodded, and then put her arms around him. He stood stiffly until she drew back, then shouldered his kit and moved into the queue for the ladder leading to the boat. She waited until his cap disappeared; he did not look round again. She had never been so unhappy in her life. During the long journey home she tried to quash the terrible thought that Mrs Adair might have passed some of her weakness on to Joe.

'Is Uncle Reggie playing up?' asked Doffie.

They had cleared away the tea things and were

meant to be reading. Except that Alice had not turned a page for ages, and Doffie had noticed.

Alice looked up, relieved at having her thoughts interrupted. 'No. He's sort of sulking, I think. But that's all right, because it means he has nothing much to do with me.' She forced a slight smile. 'Anyway, if he so much as glances across at me, Helena gives him one of her looks!'

Doffie smiled too, and shook her head slowly. 'She's got some kind of hold over him. Has he got a thing about her?'

Alice could not resist telling her mother about what she had overheard.

'Mr Berry and Helena were . . . I don't know, sort of shocked. He'd made a mistake, I think. Or it could have been he was bribed.' She shrugged. 'I don't know. He told them they were blackmailing him—'

'Good Lord above! Did he really say that?'

'I think so. I was listening outside the door.'

'Alice!'

'I didn't mean to. Anyway, it worked. Helena can be very fierce at times. And Mr Berry is so gentle and reasonable. Between them they . . . well, they fixed it.'

'I love them both.'

'So do I.'

'But you're still so unhappy. I know how hard it is, love, but don't pass on this unhappiness to Joe. He is having to bear it for himself and for you—'

Alice burst out, 'It's the other way round, Mum! He – he's sort of *sinking*! Honestly, it's awful. Like Mrs Adair.'

Doffie considered this, sitting with her chin on her hand, thinking. Then she said firmly, 'Joe's not like his mother. She is grief-stricken, but she is also ill. Joe is simply grief-stricken. He will get better.' She looked up. 'He will, love. With your help. When you write, ask him the sort of questions that will force him to look outside himself. About the food and the weather and what kind of colleagues he has—' She had made Alice laugh, and corrected herself. 'All right. What the crew are like – is that better? And then when they reach land, you will need to know his first impressions.'

Alice nodded, but without conviction. 'You see, Mum, he's in a black pit. He doesn't want to have to look up and think I'm dancing around in the sunshine. I need to be there, in the pit, with him.'

'What on earth made you think of that?'

'Val said something like it once.'

'And he's all right now. He took an interest in things outside himself.'

'Yes, I suppose he did.' Alice stared through the window at the evening sky. 'I haven't seen Hester since Hattie's wedding. I wonder whether she got the Oxford scholarship.'

'I wonder.' Doffie too stared through the window. 'The thing about not seeing too much of people is . . .' she smiled wryly, 'you can't quarrel.'

Alice knew exactly what she meant, but pretended not to. 'Hester and I never quarrelled,' she said. She stood up. 'I'll make some cocoa.'

'And next Saturday I will come with you to see Mrs Adair, and we'll think about trying to have a word with her doctor.'

Alice smiled properly. It would be good to do something for Mrs Adair; almost as good as doing something for Joe.

She was stirring the cocoa powder into the frothy milk when Percy's car drew up outside. He almost hurled himself into the house. Doffie's face was a picture of anxiety.

'She's had it!' Percy stood there, holding his side and panting, though he had taken just ten steps to reach them. 'A boy – Edmund.'

Doffie screeched, 'How are they?'

'Perfect. Both of them. She had no trouble at all. She is a natural mother.'

He had never said so much to them before. They both stared at him, Doffie with her hands clasped beneath her chin as if praying, and Alice still stirring the cocoa.

'Oh Percy,' said Doffie. 'How wonderful. Congratulations.'

He grinned. They hadn't seen that before either. 'Mother says he's the spitting image of me!'

Mum gave a high-pitched giggle and said, 'Glasses and all?'

Alice laughed so much she cried. Percy did not join in.

Nineteen

Hester did not get a scholarship to Oxford.

She could not wait until the weekend to tell Val, and cycled out to Leadon Markham with the tears drying on her face in the September breeze. Seth was doing a stint in the booking office and sent her over to Mrs Seth, who told her that Val had gone for a walk to some pool he'd discovered in the forest. Hester declined 'a nice cup of tea', and left her bike in the front garden while she followed the now well-known track, finally emerging into the clearing where the gingerbread house was framed by greenery. The sight of Val sitting on the steps was too much; she stood forlornly before him and let the tears pour unchecked down her face until they dripped off her chin.

Val said, 'Oh damn and blast it, Sis. Don't tell me. They've turned you down.' When she did not reply, he got up, went to her and held her to him. It was the calm she had wanted, but it did not stop the tears; they flowed even more freely. He said into her ear, 'Listen, they offered you that place in Bristol. It's a damned good University, it's closer to home, you'll be with girls who – maybe – aren't quite so ambitious . . . you won't follow in my foot-steps. You've broken the pattern, Hester. It's better this way. Much better. You'll realize that soon.'

Hester tried to realize how much better it was for the rest of that day and week and month. Her mother reinforced Val's words at every turn. Her father said nothing. He refused to go with her to Bristol to inspect her room, collect her book list, meet her professor. Moreover, he would not allow Dorothy to go either. Miss Plant came to the rescue and drove her there, introduced her to a tiny bird-like lady in the bookshop at the top of Park Street – 'Miss Galligan was here in my day, Hester, she knows every book in the shop' – and took her down into the war-torn city, to the docks, then up to the magical suspension bridge and the camera obscura. 'You're going to enjoy it, Hester,' she said in a tone that brooked no argument. 'I did and so will you!'

'I had no idea, Miss Plant—'

'Your mother was at the teacher-training college here, Hester. Surely she has recommended Bristol?'

'We – we don't discuss things. And Mother has not been well.'

Miss Plant looked at her sharply, but made no comment.

Valentine was delighted. 'Thank God for common sense! I've never met your Miss Plant, but obviously she has a head on her shoulders!' He was in the booking office, the window closed, the rain drumming on the roof. 'So just one more week to go, Sis. Happy?'

'Yes. And yes again!' She drew up one of the tall

stools and slid the monthly return towards her. He grinned and pushed over the ink stand and pen. He had long since mastered the columns of figures, but he never enjoyed the task and the sums often failed to tally.

As Hester started adding up, she said, 'And that awful Joe Adair is right out in the China Sea somewhere. So you could bring Alice to see me.'

He stared at her admiringly. 'Clever girl. What about Father?'

She was silent while she wrote in her total. Then she looked up. 'Father won't know what we are doing any more, Val. Will he?'

He shook his head slowly. 'Not quite so simple, Sis. Mother is still there. He won't hesitate to use her to whip us to heel.'

She was too excited to be cast down. Her mood had swung from despair to euphoria in four short weeks. And she knew her father well by now.

'He needs an audience, Val. Mother tries to keep it away from me, but he makes sure I know what's going on. If I'm not there, it won't be such fun any more—'

Val was alert, flushed. 'What does he do to her? For God's sake, Hester! Why haven't you mentioned before that you've seen what he's doing?'

'I haven't. Not exactly. There are . . . noises. She cries out sometimes.'

Val's face contorted furiously. 'The swine! D'you mean he hits her – beats her – what?'

Hester's face flamed. 'No, of course not. He . . . it's . . . you know, they're married, aren't they? And she doesn't always want . . . but of course she has to, because of something-or-other rights. He's always talking about them.'

'Conjugal rights.' Val's voice flattened suddenly. 'Oh God, the swine.'

'She's all right, Val. Thin, of course. But she was always thin. And as I have said, if no one is there, there will be no point in – in – forcing her.'

Val groaned and put his head in his hands. Very gently, Hester touched the straw-coloured hair.

'Val, please. We can't go on being unhappy. So many good things are happening. I met Uncle Ted at the station. He told me that Hattie has had her baby! And that awful Percy Westbrook told Aunt Doffie that the baby looked like him, and Aunt Doffie asked him if that included the glasses. Can't you just imagine Aunt Doffie saying that? She's completely mad!'

He looked up at that. 'It's early. It wasn't due until October. She told me so.'

'Well . . . only four weeks or so, then. She's all right. Uncle Ted has been to see her. She had it at home.' Hester smiled. 'Uncle Ted was so sweet and concerned. She's only his niece, after all.'

'She thinks of him as a brother.'

'Does she?' Hester raised her brows. 'You seem to know a lot about her.'

'I went to see her a few times last autumn and Christmas. You remember, she invited me – at the wedding.'

'I didn't know.'

'She doesn't like Percy Westbrook. She should never have married him.'

'Well, she did,' Hester retorted sharply. 'And now she's got a baby.'

'Yes.' Val stood up. 'D'you mind if we don't do the gingerbread house today, Sis? It looks like rain. Listen, if you like, I'll come back home with you. Say hello to the ancient p's.'

Hester wasn't as pleased as she felt she should have been. As they sat opposite each other on the old push-and-pull railcar, watching the rain pimpling the shallow surface of the Leadon, she knew they were thinking separate thoughts. Val had put his bike into the brake; he did not need it to get from the station to Deanery Close, so Hester guessed he was planning to go somewhere else.

'You could carry on and see Alice later,' she suggested hopefully.

'I might do that.'

She leaned forward. 'Val, when I've gone, can you try to patch it up? I know she's pretty unhappy, but I can't do anything. You could.'

'I thought we'd already discussed that. I'm to bring her to Bristol to see you. Yes?'

'Yes. But . . . will you?'

'Of course. Why this doubt?'

She sat back, not satisfied. 'I'm not sure. You – you're like quicksilver.'

He lengthened his face in mock solemnity and intoned, 'I will go to see the Pettifords and invite Alice to accompany me to Bristol. How's that?'

She smiled unwillingly, but insisted, 'And you'll take over from me?'

'I'm not sure about that, old girl.' He smiled back. 'Seriously, I'll do my best. No one can do more.'

Val arrived at Leckhampton House at eight o'clock. It was getting dark and had been raining steadily for several hours. Percy's sister Enid answered the door, and was naturally cautious about taking this dripping visitor upstairs to see Hattie.

'She'll be feeding Edmund and settling him for the night. I'll have a word with Percy—'

'Please don't disturb him, Enid. You remember me. Valentine Ryecroft. I've called on Hattie before. We're very old friends.'

'Percy is reading the evening newspaper to Mamma.'

'Well then he won't want to be disturbed. Listen, I'll be ten minutes. That's all. I'll just slip – yes, I do know which room.' He was already halfway up the stairs, smiling down at her re-assuringly. His face felt unnaturally stretched. He ran along the landing to the last door and burst through it unceremoniously, then stood gazing at the scene before him, mesmerized by the clutter of recent maternity. The bed, which had been all pink satin, framed by pink-shaded lamps, was now sternly clinical, with white pillowcases and counterpane echoing the plain white cot next to it. The fragrance that had lingered here before was replaced by a milky smell. On the dressing table, the enamelled brushes and mirrors had gone and cotton-wool balls were piled up, reflected in the swing mirror. Reflected too was Hattie, sitting in a low nursing chair, feeding her baby. Val gazed, transfixed by this new image of her. Her head was bent low over the child, her rich black hair framing the two of them, plus her enormous white breast.

She had not seen it was him and said, 'Oh, Percy darling, I've told you, I would rather feed Edmund on my own.' But she was smiling, not cross or distant as she had been in the past when talking about Percy.

Then she looked up and saw him, and her face split with a smile.

'Val!' The baby lost her nipple and for a moment there was a fuss while she cooed and rearranged him more comfortably. Then she looked up again, still smiling. 'Val, you remind me of that time with Ted and Doffie. You're absolutely soaked! What on earth brings you here at this time of night?'

'It's only just gone eight.' He came round and knelt by her. 'My God, Hattie, you look wonderful. I've missed you so much. Do you realize you haven't let me see you for months?'

'Darling boy, you would have fallen out of love with me if you'd seen me all huge and ugly.'

'Rubbish. You know I'm besotted.'

'Yes.' Her smile widened. 'I didn't really understand, though. Not until I fell in love with Edmund. Look at him, Val. Isn't he wonderful?' She lifted the baby up high. All Val could see was her breast. She said, 'I absolutely adore him – I know I keep saying that about everyone. But this is different, Val. I was born for this and didn't even know it!' She lowered the baby and looked into the tiny face. 'Shall we have the other side now, sweetheart?' She fiddled around with her clothing. 'You see, Val? It comes naturally to me. The midwife simply cannot understand how I know what to do all the time!' The child grabbed the other nipple and sucked frantically. Hattie flinched. 'It hurts at first. A bit like sex, really.' She laughed joyously. 'Well, this is real sex, of course. Isn't it?'

'Hattie, you told me the baby would be born in October.'

'A bit early, that's all. Keen to get to know me.'

'Work it out, darling. We were together at Christmas. Percy took his mother to see her brother in Ledbury and you telephoned the booking office—'

'Oh, dear boy! Wasn't it marvellous? I think Enid suspected something, but she didn't say a word.'

'The baby is mine, Hattie. Face up to it.'

She tore her gaze away from Edmund and looked at Val, surprised. 'Does it matter, darling?'

'Of course! You can't stay with Percy now! We'll go away together, Hattie – France or Spain or somewhere.'

She laughed incredulously. 'Sweetheart, we'd drive each other mad! Oh, you are so sweet – I love the idea. But it wouldn't work. Now that I've got Edmund, all that . . . excitement . . . is in him. Anyway, Val, it's all in your head. Edmund is Percy's child. He looks exactly like Percy did at this age – his mother has a picture, it's simply amazing.'

'Hattie, all babies look the same when they're swathed in shawls and things. Work the dates out for yourself.'

Suddenly she was stern. 'Val, stop that. We had a wonderful time together, but it won't happen again.'

He gave a cry, and she reached out with one hand and put it across his mouth. 'I said stop it! Percy will be here any minute and I don't want—'

He jerked his head free. 'What about what I want? You can't block me out of your life for ever!

263

I am the father of this baby you say you're so in love with!'

'No, you are not. And you have to accept that, Val. You have to go along with things. Can't you see that? All this striving and fighting ... sit back on the edge of the bed. There are things that are far more important than you and me. There is Edmund.' She pushed him away and he fell back on his heels. Then, in the face of her immediate pre-occupation with the baby, he scrambled on to the end of the bed. And just in time, because at that moment the door opened again and there was Percy, pebble glasses, protuberant ears and all.

'Enid said you'd got a visitor.' He turned to Val. 'Bit late in the day, isn't it, young man?'

Val enjoyed purposely misunderstanding the remark. 'Yes. Sorry I haven't been before – most remiss. Greetings from my sister and parents, of course.'

Hattie laughed joyously. 'Darling Percy means that your visit is practically a midnight one!' Her eyes glinted at Val, then she turned her face up to Percy. Her hair fell back. The extra flesh she'd put on when she had so enthusiastically eaten for two had not all gone, and she was voluptuous. Val stared at her avidly. Percy leaned down and kissed her. Val wanted to hit him.

He said abruptly, 'I must go. There's a train at nine-thirty.'

'And just you get out of those wet clothes as soon as you can, sweetie.' Hattie was laughing up at him knowingly. 'We don't want you catching pneumonia now, do we?'

He made for the door, then stopped and

turned. 'Anyway, good to see you. And Edmund, of course. Congratulations.'

Her smile was reflected in the mirror; it became soft. 'Thank you, Val. Dear Val, I'll always love you.'

Percy was used to it, of course, but his hand slipped to her breast. Possession was, after all, nine points of the law.

Enid was waiting nervously at the bottom of the stairs. She said, 'Is everything all right?'

He nodded curtly, then paused. 'Thank you, Enid.' She was like Percy, ugly and unappreciated. He leaned forward and pecked her on the forehead. 'Look after her, won't you?'

Her face flamed with embarrassment, and she did not move from the newel post, even when he opened the front door. Val grabbed his bike and pedalled furiously down the long hill. The station was unbearably grim in the autumn rain; a foretaste of the winter ahead. He thought of Hattie's laughter, her upturned face, like a sunflower. And suddenly he knew he had done it: he was part of the Pettifords. Whatever she said, however small she saw his contribution, he was – quite definitely – the father of her son.

He looked at his reflection in the window of the railcar. He was grinning like a Cheshire cat.

Twenty

It was almost Christmas again. Ted was going to get a whole week's leave and Doffie was as excited as a schoolgirl.

'Mum . . .' Roles were suddenly reversed and it was Alice who was advising caution. 'He's supposed to be collating all the information he's collected to present to the Line Superintendent. He'll be working—'

'I don't care!' Doffie was jubilant. 'He'll be here! Someone will be here!'

Alice felt guilty at the implication – of loneliness. She knew she was no company during the long dark evenings, and at weekends she had to visit Mrs Adair and Gran. She had seen baby Edmund only three times since his birth, and one of those had been at his christening.

'There's Mrs Mearment,' she said weakly.

'Well, of course.' Doffie laughed. 'But she's not exactly Dad, is she?'

Alice's conscience forced her to say defensively, 'Uncle Duggie pops out now and then on Sundays.'

Doffie sighed. 'Yes, I know . . . But he's not Dad, either.'

This should have been a reassuring exchange, but somehow it was not. Doffie looked at Alice and suddenly hugged her close. 'You of all people should understand. Oh, I know Dad isn't thousands of miles away, like Joe, but he's not here any more – not even at weekends, usually.' She drew away slightly. 'Love, take heart. Joe won't be away for ever. And once Christmas is over, you're somehow going towards him instead of watching him move away. Does that make sense?'

Alice nodded bleakly. It made perfect sense. It was simply that sometimes she wondered whether she and Joe had lost something vital that day on Cooper's Hill.

Miss Webster had been taking dictation from Mr Maybury for two hours and Mr Ryecroft was not pleased. She came back into the office flushed and frowning slightly, obviously not quite herself. Mr Ryecroft sat back in his chair, placed his fingertips together and gave her a sardonic smile.

'We wondered whether you had been taken by ambulance to the Infirmary.' He glanced sideways at Alice. 'Our Miss Pettiford was becoming quite anxious. Yes, quite anxious.'

Alice followed Helena's advice and said nothing.

Mr Berry cleared his throat. 'Joking aside, my dear, are you all right?'

'Perfectly, thank you, Mr Berry.' She glanced at her watch. 'I'll have to start on Mr Maybury's report after lunch, I think. In fact, I'll leave now – with your permission, of course, Mr Ryecroft. I find two hours' solid dictation rather tiring.'

She did not give Mr Ryecroft time to refuse

permission. She dumped her notebook on top of her typewriter and was out of the office like a whirlwind, grabbing her new hooded raincoat from the back of the door as she went.

Mr Berry cleared his throat again, and Mr Ryecroft said, 'Well – rather odd. I don't associate Miss Webster with jack rabbits.'

Alice said, 'She's not well. May I go after her?'

Mr Ryecroft looked unusually flustered. Illness in females only meant one thing to him. 'I suppose so. But you must be back before two o'clock, Miss Pettiford. If Miss Webster is going to be all afternoon on Mr Maybury's precious report, someone has to type my letters.'

'Of course . . .' Alice hesitated, then added, 'sir'. It wouldn't hurt to butter him up. For Helena's sake, of course.

She dashed down the front stairs and caught Helena in the foyer. She was putting on her raincoat and adjusting the hood.

'It's raining,' she said with some disgust. 'Oh Alice, I wish you did not have to go home. We could have another coffee at the milk bar, and talk.'

Alice thought of her mother, probably already preparing something hot and sustaining, ready to be put on the table the moment Alice's bicycle appeared at the kitchen window.

'It's all right, Helena. Mum won't mind me staying in town for once. Anyway, I have to be back early this afternoon, so perhaps it will be better if I don't go home.'

Helena looked at her sharply. 'Are you sure? Your mother is so sweet, I hate to think of her being anxious about you. What about Duggie

Marsden? Would he drive out and let her know?'

It was Alice's turn to look up sharply. Helena elaborated. 'He's the only one with a car and nowhere much to go.'

'I suppose he could eat my dinner,' Alice said reluctantly.

'Come on –' Helena was already back up the stairs and turning left for the Staff Office. Alice followed her none too closely.

'Duggie, dear . . .' Alice had never heard Helena talk like that to anyone. 'Would you be an absolute angel and pop out to Lypiatt Bottom with a message from Alice?'

Uncle Duggie looked past her at Alice. 'What's happened?'

It was all most difficult. Helena was so determined and Alice so uncertain. But Helena won the day, and they eventually ended up in a corner of the milk bar with hot chocolate and cheese rolls.

'Do you do this every day?' Alice asked, feeling almost like one of the *femmes du monde* featured in Helena's Georgette Heyer books.

'Oh no. Mother and Father both work, and usually I go home and peel the potatoes for the evening, feed the cat – you know the sort of thing one does.' Alice smiled weakly. Since when had she been any help whatsoever in the home? On the other hand, her mother didn't go out to work like Mrs Webster did. 'Now and then I treat myself. And today I'm going to treat you!'

'No – no – you're much too generous—'

'You're here for my sake, so it's only fair.' Helena put her roll back on its plate and took a deep breath. 'Alice, listen. This must be kept well under your hat. But I have to tell someone. And you know everyone so well. Me especially.' She smiled ruefully. 'I've always felt you were like a younger sister.'

'Oh, Helena—'

'That's why I want to talk to you – must talk to you. Something has happened. Quite unexpectedly.' Alice realized Helena's face was very red. 'Though, of course, not really unexpectedly. But – it so often happens – one has these romantic notions and nothing comes of them. After all, I am a signalman's daughter. A typist. And he is – well, important.'

'What has happened?'

Helena replied baldly, 'Mr Maybury asked me to marry him! This morning! Alice – be careful!'

Alice had jumped in her seat, almost upsetting her cup of hot chocolate. She made little squeaking noises; she clasped her hands, unclasped them again and reached across the table.

Helena took her hand and held it tightly. 'It's incredible, isn't it? Rather like a romantic novel.'

'*Jane Eyre.*'

'Something by Ethel M. Dell, more likely!'

'Stop trying to diminish it, Helena! He is a darling man – we all know that. And he has chosen you. It shows that he has the most wonderful taste. And you will be marvellous as his wife. You're so dignified and well-read and charming and absolutely lovely!'

'Oh my dear girl! We really do sound like characters from a novel! Oh Alice. What shall I do?'

'Well, it's so obvious. Unless . . .' Alice looked apprehensive. 'You do love him, don't you?'

'Very much. I loved him from the moment he appointed me. He's got beautiful eyes, and after all, they are windows to the soul. And he's kind. He knows Miss Warner is losing her sight, but he pretends she is overworked and sends for me. Oh yes, I love him. I dream about him. When Reggie gets on my nerves, I dream of marrying him and living happily ever after.'

'So you've said yes?'

'Not yet. I told him I must think about it. He kept kissing and kissing me—' She broke off at Alice's gasp. 'He's been doing that since last Christmas, under the mistletoe. But I thought – well, I certainly did not think he would want to *marry* me. I thought . . . you know.'

'And would you?'

Neither of them could bring themselves to voice the actual details. Helena said slowly, 'I might have done. Eventually. He is the only man for me. That's why this is so wonderful.'

'Oh, Helena.'

Helena suddenly smiled. 'So you think I should say yes?'

'No, of course not! I think you should marry Uncle Duggie. Or even Mr Berry.'

'Bernie Berry has a wife and Dugdale Marsden has always been in love with your mother.'

Alice's eyes opened wide, and Helena said quickly, 'Don't be embarrassed. Miss Warner told me – there's no gossip or anything. They went out together quite a lot. Then she met your father and that was that. I thought you knew.'

'Well, yes, in a way. He joked about it once. But I can't believe it . . . we've sent him out there and she is on her own.'

Helena laughed. 'Come on, Alice. Your parents are so in love it's crazy. I mean, after all these years.'

Alice thought of the times when her father had sent her mother to Coventry. It didn't happen now, because he was never there, but it used to happen.

She shook her head. Impossible to think of her parents in love, as she and Joe were in love. She reverted to the topic in hand. 'Anyway, of course you must say yes.'

'Well, in that case I'll have to leave work. You realize that?'

'Oh! Yes, I suppose . . . oh Helena, I shall miss you terribly.'

'Not if you were working in a new job. You'd be too busy to miss me – or worry yourself silly about Joe.'

Alice looked down at her plate and crumbled her roll. 'I couldn't leave Bishop Hooper's Mansions now. It would be like leaving Joe.'

'Oh, my dear girl.' Helena reached for Alice's hand again. Then her voice became brisk. 'I'm not talking about leaving the Mansions. I'm talking about taking on Miss Warner's job.'

Alice was aghast. Helena said, 'I know. It sounds a bit too much, doesn't it? But Miss Warner will be retiring next year. Her sight is awful and as soon as I go, so will she.'

'But I'm a junior typist!' Alice protested.

'So who do you think should get the job? Janet in the Staff Office? That poor soul up in the commercial section?' Helena leaned forward. 'Listen, Alice. You're a good shorthand typist. You've got the hang of all the office procedures.

272

You know everyone up and down the local lines and they know you. Even poor old Reggie knows he can rely on you now. And next April you will have been a railway servant for two whole years.'

'I couldn't do it. Mr Maybury is—'

'A lovely man – you said it yourself. You could do it, Alice. It would give you something to work for. Something else to think about. Sometimes you look quite wizened with worry!'

Alice looked up, shocked. Then they both laughed.

A letter came from Joe. They had cleared another minefield around Singapore. The explosions were enormous. He missed Alice terribly. He was not even halfway through his time.

Alice was reading the flimsy single sheet at the breakfast table. She looked up for a moment and stared through the window at the bleak view of the garden. Joe had been in the Navy almost six months and was there for another eighteen. He was twisting time just as she was, wringing it out as if to make it flatter and smaller.

Doffie said, 'Time you weren't here, Alice. Be extra careful today, love. There's ice on all the puddles. The postman came off his bike twice coming down the lane. He seemed to think it was my fault.'

'For living here, I suppose.'

'Perhaps so.' Doffie brought in Alice's wartime pixie hood and matching gloves and held them in front of the fire. 'Is everything all right with Joe?'

'Yes.' She glanced at the letter again. 'He says his mother is going to stay with Great Aunt Eve for Christmas.'

'Oh, what a relief! I did wonder. She could come to Hattie's, but she would hate every moment.'

'Yes. But she really loathes Great Aunt Eve. Last Christmas when she turned up, Mrs Adair fainted.'

'Oh Lord.' Doffie held out the hood and gloves. 'I wonder whether she ever had good health. Maybe before her husband was killed she was all right.'

'I don't think so. It just got worse afterwards.'

Alice put on her outdoor clothes and kissed her mother goodbye. Doffie was bright-eyed this morning. It could be because of Christmas and Dad coming home. Or it could be because she had seen Uncle Duggie yesterday. Alice had said nothing about Helena and Mr Maybury, so it could not be that.

The roads really were icy that morning and she was late arriving at work. She took off her hood and coat on her way upstairs and swung them on to the back of the door as she opened it. The new junior lived in Berkeley and was hopeless at lighting fires, so Alice had to do Joe's old job as well as her own. She did not mind; in fact she welcomed the extra work. She knew the filing system well now and frequently stayed late to read up on past claims, accidents and the ubiquitous 'general works'. And she had perfected lighting both stoves; even Uncle Reggie admitted that.

But that morning was different. As she reached up to the row of coat hooks, she realized that the office was already warm. Sure enough, the flames were licking the doors of the stove, and the paraffin heater glowed over by the oriel window.

Mr Berry stood up from it. 'Is it smelling?' he

asked anxiously. 'I left it in the corridor for ages, but I fancy I can still smell it.'

'It's fine. Why are you here already?'

'I came early so that I can get away at three. The phone was ringing – Mr Ryecroft's phone. Someone wanted to speak to you, my dear. Wouldn't say who he was or what it was about. Since then he has rung again and said he would try in ten minutes.' Mr Berry glanced at the clock. 'It's almost that.'

Alice felt her heart and mind racing. 'Was it – did it sound – could it be about Joe?'

'I don't think so. They would have left a name, surely?'

The phone rang. Alice stared at it. Mr Berry picked it up.

'Hello . . . Yes . . . Yes, she is here now. May I know who is calling her?' He raised his head and covered the mouthpiece with a sooty hand. 'A Mr Trotter. Do you know him, Alice?'

'Yes.' And instantly she knew why he was ringing. She took the receiver in both hands and pillowed her left ear into it. 'Hello, Mr Trotter. It's Alice Pettiford. Is it about Mrs Adair?'

He was not used to a telephone; she could imagine him standing in the kiosk in Bath Road, head down, peering at the coin slot.

He said roughly, 'Thank God. She's not our worry, you know, my girl! Someone has got to take charge and it's not going to be me or the wife! She'll set fire to that place and we shall go up with her! He shouldn't have left her there all on her own, she's not fit!'

'What has happened, Mr Trotter? Please try to tell me before your tuppence goes.'

275

'Hammered on the wall, she did. About six o'clock this morning, it was. Six o'clock! I ask you! The missus went in. Scalded herself, she had. Both arms. Don't ask me how. The missus put butter on for her – hands, past the elbows – raw meat, she said they looked like. Went in at seven-thirty – nice cuppa tea, can't say we haven't done our bit – and she's flat out on the floor. Thought she were dead at first. Police came. Sent for an ambulance. She's in the General. That's all I know.'

'Oh poor Mrs Adair. I am so sorry.' Alice was almost relieved. At least Mrs Adair was not dead. How would she have told Joe? 'Listen – will you thank Mrs Trotter and tell her I'll go to the hospital immediately.' The phone went dead before she finished. She looked up helplessly. 'It's Joe's mother. She's in Cheltenham General.'

Mr Berry was all concern. He told her what to do. There was a train at eight forty-five which she could just catch. He would make sure her mother knew where she was. He would tell Mr Ryecroft . . . it would be all right. He helped her to put her coat back on, reminded her to take her bike on the train.

'Can you manage, Alice? Helena would come with you if you waited.'

'Oh no –' She almost told him about Mr Maybury. 'No, I couldn't ask her. I'll be back by midday. Tell Mr Ryecroft I'm sorry.'

She was gone, pedalling along George Street into the station and right up to the booking office with just a minute to spare. The train was from Cardiff and was going to Birmingham. Alice paced the corridor, then went into the brake van to stand by her bike, ready to lift it out at Malvern

Road. Once off the train, she pedalled furiously to College Road, where she wedged the handlebars into the railings of the playing field and ran across the road into the hospital. It was nine-twenty. Probably three hours since Mrs Adair had ... whatever had happened.

The Sister in charge wanted to know whether she was a relative, what her name was, and how well she knew the patient. Alice wanted to push her aside and rush down the long ward to the curtained cubicle at the end.

She said bravely, 'She will be my mother-in-law. Her son is in the Far East.'

Sister looked her up and down and then nodded curtly. 'She is very ill. You can stay ten minutes. We are trying to get in touch with an aunt.'

'Oh.' That would be Great Aunt Eve. 'They don't get on very well.'

Sister did not choose to hear. She walked briskly between the beds and lifted aside one of the curtains. A nurse stood up and nodded several times in response to Sister's whispered questions. Alice had eyes only for Joe's mother. She was propped on pillows, the bedclothes coming to her waist, both arms lying on top, bandaged from fingertips to shoulders. Her eyes were closed, but her lips moved and tiny sounds came from them.

'She will hear you and probably understand,' Sister said. 'Ten minutes.'

Alice took the place of the nurse and leaned forward over the bed. 'It's Alice, Mrs Adair. Alice Pettiford.' She waited. The murmurings ceased and it seemed as if Mrs Adair was listening. Alice said, 'You're going to be all right. They say you're going to be all right.' She waited again, and incredibly the parched lips opened and Mrs Adair said clearly, 'Stay with me, Alice.'

'I will.' Alice wished she could take one of the poor bandaged hands in hers. She leaned closer. 'I promise.'

'Joe . . .'

'Yes. We'll tell Joe. He'll come home and look after you. We'll all look after you.'

The lips smiled. 'He's a good boy. He loves you dearly. So like his father.'

'I love him too, Mrs Adair.'

'He's not ill, you know, Alice.' The eyes opened and gradually focused. 'I am, but he's not.' Alice nodded. The voice went on. 'Great Aunt Eve told me I was ill– . . . egitimate. I don't like the word.' She frowned and tried to shake her head. 'When she came last Christmas she told me. That's why my mother could not leave me her estate.'

Alice stared, assimilating this with some difficulty. She whispered, 'Oh, Mrs Adair. She should not have told you. That was cruel.'

'Yes. The Chattertons are cruel. But not my mother. She would never have told me. Just that she loved my father, and they had a honeymoon in a railway coach. Isn't that romantic, Alice? In the forest. In a coach.' The lips smiled again. 'Like Cinderella. A pumpkin coach.'

Alice wanted to say something reassuring, but could think of nothing. Tears filled her eyes.

Behind her, Sister said, 'I'm afraid you've tired the patient. I must ask you to leave now.'

Mrs Adair made a weak sound of protest and Alice said, 'I'm sorry. I have to stay with her. I have promised, you see.'

There were some near-threats, but Alice took a leaf from Helena's book and said nothing. Sister eventually withdrew, saying, 'Another few minutes only. And that is my final word.'

Alice did not even thank her. She kept her gaze on Mrs Adair, as if she could keep her alive by looking at her. And for three long hours she succeeded.

By that time, Doffie had arrived and told her in a low voice that Helena was waiting too. Doffie leaned over the frail figure and whispered re-assurance, just as Alice had done. And it was Doffie who said, 'Darling, she's gone. I'll go for Sister. Say goodbye to her.'

Afterwards, Alice recalled that her mother made no attempt to hold her or offer comfort. She treated Alice as someone who could manage. Helena took her hands and said, 'Oh Alice – poor Joe.' And that was it. They were all so sad for Joe.

Perhaps that was when Alice began to feel angry. It was as if the weight of anxiety she felt for Joe was increased with the weight of everyone else's concern. The only person who did not add to the load was Great Aunt Eve, who thankfully turned up at the hospital the next day and took over all the funeral arrangements.

'No good waiting for the boy,' she said imperiously to Alice and her mother, who had come to see Sister about what would happen next. 'And we cannot have a full family funeral in the circum-stances.' Doffie looked up questioningly and Alice grabbed her hand and held it hard. 'But she was a Chatterton, after all, so there will be room for her in the family vault. A quiet ceremony, I think. In the private chapel at the Hall. I will see my brother about it. Luckily, his wife is dead so she cannot object.' Doffie's eyes opened wide. Alice squeezed harder still and she remained silent. Great Aunt Eve surveyed the two of them without pleasure. 'You are very welcome to attend. I believe there is a train service to Dursley, and James – the chauffeur – can meet you there.'

Alice said, 'I don't think—' but Doffie interrupted.

'Joe would expect Alice to go. She will represent him on behalf of his railway colleagues.' Doffie could sound grand at times, and Great Aunt Eve looked at her properly for the first time.

So Alice went, and Helena went with her. Alice did not shed a tear, neither did anyone else. Rose Adair, the result of one weekend, one secret and romantic tryst, had barely rippled the surface of life's pond. Except to leave a son.

Later that day, when Alice was going to bed, she broke down. Doffie tried to put comforting arms around her, but Alice would have none of it.

'It's all such a *waste!*' she wept, making for the stairs and the privacy of her room. 'I don't want any more to do with it! Sadness and awfulness everywhere! And when Helena leaves it's going to be worse! And I suppose Joe will come home now and it will go on and on. The thing is, she couldn't *help* being a burden! She was ill – all the time, she was ill! And no one realized!' She clung to the newel post. 'She didn't realize herself. She told me she was ill then added "–legitimate". She was illegitimate, so they would not acknowledge her! It's just not *fair!*'

She expected Mum to follow her and suggest

her sharing the double bed, where Alice could draw comfort into her soul through a kind of osmosis. But Doffie stayed in the hall, looking up at her with another kind of sadness.

Twenty-One

Joe did not come home. *Hermes* went on to Hong Kong, but Joe stayed in Singapore in the Naval hospital. In between treatments, he stared out of the window at the enormous harbour. The Chinese nurse who had seen it all before many, many times described it as a 'world of his own'. Just once he looked at her questioningly, and she leaned down and spoke slowly to him.

'Your world is a long way away. And you do not want it any more. So you make another one. Your very own world.'

When the cablegram came, he stared at that too.

She said, 'This means you can go back to your world. It is your mother's gift to you.'

But he shook his head. His world had gone; thrown away in an agony of self-harm. He might well have gone back to his mother had she lived, but he could never go back to Alice.

It was much later that he wrote to her: a stilted letter, hovering between familiarity and formality.

Dear Alice,
    Thank you for looking after my poor old ma. I do not think she would mind being dead. She

282

believed in life hereafter, so expected to meet my father. He was the one good thing that happened to her. I am grateful that you went to the funeral arranged by my mother's family. I am in hospital in Singapore undergoing treatment for a disease caught from one of the girls here. I cannot explain anything. Try to forget I ever existed. I am thankful that you are not tied to me any more. You deserve better. Thank you again.

    Yours most sincerely,
    Joseph Adair.

He did not get a reply and was glad.

Christmas was centred around Edmund. Hattie invited all the family, and, much to everyone's surprise, Valentine and Hester Ryecroft were included for tea.

'I did ask them for lunch as well,' Hattie said, lounging on the brand-new sofa with Edmund over one shoulder. 'But dear Hester is cooking the lunch for the family and they both thought it was best not to come until afterwards.' She giggled. 'Reggie is playing up, I expect.'

'Anyway, darling,' Doffie said, 'you can't expect Mrs Westbrook to cook Christmas lunch for all of us and two complete strangers.'

'Oh, she just loves it. It's given her a new lease of life.' Hattie smiled down at the burping Edmund. 'Since Edmund was born, we are so happy here . . . I just cannot tell you! And anyway,' she looked back at the others, all smiling down at her sentimentally, 'Enid is out there helping her.

And Percy is doing all the drinks. And Alice says she's going to wash up.'

Doffie said, 'She must be in her eighties now, Hattie. After all, Percy is over fifty.'

Hattie giggled. 'I know. I'm an old man's darling! Isn't it a scream?' She passed Edmund to Alice. 'Have a cuddle with your Auntie Alice, sweetie-pie. Mummy must go and change into something that doesn't smell of milk.' She stood up, a hand in the small of her back. 'Doffie darling, come and see the suit I bought at Cavendish House last week. It's absolutely New Look, the skirt almost to my ankles and the jacket has a little pleated peplum.' She leaned over Ted and kissed him on the forehead. 'Darling, stop worrying. Is it about Val and his sister? I invited Val for Enid. Don't ask me why, but she's crazy about him!'

Ted was completely bewildered. 'I'm not worried about the Ryecrofts, Hattie! And how on earth does Enid know Val?'

'He calls now and then. Since the wedding, actually. Brings her flowers and things.'

'*Enid?* Valentine Ryecroft brings Enid flowers?'

Hattie spoke in a stage whisper. 'So that she won't let on to Percy!' She led Doffie out of the room and up the stairs, still giggling. Ted and Alice looked at each other.

'Sounds ominous. Typical Hattie,' Ted said.

Alice said, 'Oh dear. He's bringing back that last bottle. Where's that muslin stuff Hattie uses?'

Ted helped out. Then he kissed Alice's cheek. 'You really love that baby, don't you? It's the first time I've seen you looking happy since that damned boy sailed off to Singapore!' He made it sound as if Joe had gone on an adventure holiday.

Alice said, 'I enjoy the simplicity of it. The feeding and the changing and the bathing. It's so basic. D'you remember when Val left Oxford and told us he was looking for reality? I think I know what he meant.'

'Rose Adair . . . all that business. Got you down, didn't it?'

'I suppose so. Poor Mrs Adair.' She looked down. 'Hello, Edmund Westbrook. Are you all right now? Would you like a little sleep?' She beamed at her father. 'Oh look, Dad. He's smiling.'

Upstairs, Doffie was trying on Hattie's new suit. Hattie clasped her hands.

'Darling, it makes you look positively "county". You're so much thinner than me and it hangs beautifully.'

'You'll soon be back to normal, Hattie. Don't worry about it.'

'I don't. I really love being pregnant.' She glinted at Doffie. 'Yes . . . I am. Again! Isn't it just marvellous? I must be fetid!'

Doffie was stunned. 'I think you mean fecund, darling. And you can't be pregnant again! Edmund is not four months old yet!'

'Well, of course, I'm not certain. And yet I am! I know!' She put her arms around Doffie and hugged the tweed shoulders convulsively. 'Sweetie, I think I'm going to have lots of children! I had no idea how marvellous it is! And I thought Edmund would be the only one. And this time – this time it must be Percy, because there's been no one else! No time for anyone else,

285

in fact!' She was laughing, waltzing Doffie around the pristine white bed.

'Hang on – wait – what are you saying?'

Hattie whirled herself away and on to the bed, which bounced alarmingly. She lay back laughing, then controlled herself, breathed deeply and patted the counterpane.

'I always intended to tell you, darling. We're as close as most sisters. And I have to tell someone. Edmund is Val's child. I've told him otherwise, of course, but he knows it in his heart.' She put a swift finger to her lips at Doffie's shocked expression. 'Percy has not got the slightest idea, Doffie. And he must never have. I should have sworn you to secrecy.'

'My God, it's not likely that I will tell anyone! Oh Hattie!'

'It's all right, sweetie. Absolutely all right. I suddenly wanted a baby – just like you prophesied.' She pulled Doffie down beside her. 'So I let Val do what he wanted to do – had to practically give him lessons!' She laughed again. 'And of course, it happened.' She sobered suddenly. 'Perhaps if I'd waited it would have happened with Percy. But he told me –' She giggled. 'He told me he could only fire blanks. So I didn't wait.' She sighed. 'You never know what to do for the best in this life, do you, Doffie?'

Doffie found her voice. 'You certainly do not.'

'Well, if I'm right and I'm pregnant again, then Percy is obviously fetid as well.' She giggled. 'All right, fecund. Which is marvellous, because Percy is so good at . . . it.' Doffie blushed immediately and Hattie went on, 'For goodness' sake, darling, we're both married!'

Doffie said, 'I cannot believe what you are saying. I know you are – well, a woman of the world, Hattie – but this isn't right. Val and Percy are both being led by the nose—'

Hattie was convulsed again and Doffie continued sharply, 'It's all very well, but how do you think Ted will take this?'

Hattie was still at last. 'You promised. You said you wouldn't tell a soul.'

'But Ted is your closest family.'

'Listen, Doffie. You don't want to upset Ted. Oh damn, I wish I hadn't told you now. You must promise again. Ted must never know.' She knelt on the bed, took Doffie's golden head in her hands and kissed her hard. 'It's just that I find it so easy to love people, darling. I love you. I love Alice. I love Ted. I love Val. But I love Percy. Especially if he has given me another baby.'

Doffie, shocked by the impulsive kiss, drew away slightly. She looked at this beautiful niece-in-law, who saw no need for rules and regulations, who was truly hedonistic. And yet who desperately wanted children.

She said in a low voice, 'Of course I won't tell Ted. Or anyone else.'

'Oh, Doffie, I think I love you best of all!' Hattie scrambled off the bed and pulled Doffie with her. 'Oh, I'm so glad I've given you that suit. You look so wonderful!' Doffie started to protest again. 'All right, if I'm not pregnant I'll have it back again. But wear it now. Knock Ted out. He might be seeing someone up in London – who knows. But if he is, then he'll come running when he sees you looking like this!'

Doffie knew she should have changed into her

new woollen dress. But Hattie had a way of carrying everything before her. Doffie even wondered whether it was a possibility that Ted was seeing other women . . . after all, he had been invited to dinner by the Assistant Station Master. Doffie shook herself and the long skirt swayed around her ankles.

The two women went down to lunch, arms around each other.

There were no trains, so Val and Hester cycled from Gloucester and arrived red-faced and breathless after the hard pedal up Leckhampton hill. The afternoon was already darkening. Val stood out in the garden looking down at the lights coming on in Gloucester and thought of his parents ensconced in the drawing room, with a meagre fire keeping the windows clear of frost and a small pile of presents. His mother had not gone to the cathedral that morning; Reggie had told him jovially that she had stopped 'all that nonsense' some time ago. 'Made her giddy and ill, as you well remember, my boy.' Val had taken to calling on his parents at weekends, and could have charted his mother's regression as a steady downward line on graph paper. He did not know what to do about it and was hoping that Hester would think of something over the Christmas holiday. So far she had found it difficult to talk about anything but her work; somehow Miss Plant had never fired her imagination like Professor Tibbolt. Val wondered whether she was conforming to the point of being in love with her teacher. To his surprise, he felt a small pang of some emotion he could not name.

It was wonderful to leave the frosty garden with its stupendous view and go indoors to total warmth and almost decadent comfort. The smell of food made his stomach clench with anticipation. Hester was no cook, and the chicken and vegetables they had eaten earlier had been very ordinary. His mother was the same. Whereas the Pettifords imbued their cooking with . . . something else he could not name.

Hattie was more beautiful than ever; plump as a pigeon and practically cooing like a dove. Aunt Doffie was suddenly different; as stunning as ever, with her mass of blond hair, but very slim and chic; he wondered how on earth Uncle Ted had won her heart. But he was pleased to see Ted; he had a lot to thank him for and made up his mind to try and say something during the course of the evening.

They told him Alice was in the kitchen, still coping with the mound of washing up from lunch. He went to find her. She stood at the deep stone sink, which was ridiculously full of steaming suds, the sleeves of a blue Viyella dress pushed beyond her elbows, her hair secured behind her ears with two combs . . . and she was crying.

Val said, 'Either you fall off your bike in front of me or you practically drown in washing-up water! You are absolutely determined that I should do my Sir Lancelot role, aren't you?'

She did not look round. 'Go away, Val. Please.'

'No.' He reached for a cloth. 'I'm going to dry these while you dry your eyes. Then I'll have a go at the sink and you can dry and listen to my words of wisdom.'

'Oh, shut up!' she said. But there was a tiny smile in her voice.

He put his arms around her from behind and lifted her bodily away from the sink. She gasped. He put her down on the other side of the table, and then, quite involuntarily, buried his face beneath her hair and kissed the nape of her neck.

'Val!'

'Sorry. Sorry. I forgot my lines. Right. Now let's take that tureen first, otherwise everything is going to topple to the floor, and it's probably family china which is completely irreplaceable. And we'll clear a space here and put it carefully down . . . so . . . then start on the dinner plates.'

She said in a small voice, 'Where's Hester?'

'Sitting by your father, talking about Bristol. Hattie is acting her sleepy seductive part for Percy, who still looks down the front of her dress whenever he can. Your mother is doing sterling work with Enid and Mrs Westbrook—'

'Where's Edmund?'

'Presumably in his cot, having an afternoon nap.'

'He makes sense.'

Val looked over his shoulder; her face was smudged with tears. 'What do you mean? How can a three-month-old baby make sense?'

'Nothing else does. If it weren't for Edmund—'

'You'd what? Commit suicide?' She said nothing and he asked sharply, 'It's not as bad as that, is it?'

'Rose Adair was anaemic. She was also illegitimate. When her aunt told her, I think the shock probably took away what little strength she had left.'

He made a little sound of surprise, but said, 'More probably you are dramatizing the whole thing. It doesn't matter any more, Alice – that sort of thing. We've just fought an enormous war and no one cares any more whether they're legal or not, so long as they're still alive.' He turned back to the draining board and finished drying the plates, then tied the tea towel around his waist and went to the sink.

She was silent at that, then pulled a hand-kerchief from her sleeve and scrubbed at her face.

'Sorry, Val. I have to be cheerful most of the time. Now and then—'

'Yes.' He rinsed off some cutlery. 'Lovely to have hot water on tap.'

'Isn't it?' She stood up and found another tea towel. 'They're all so happy. Mrs Westbrook – Enid – Hattie and Percy –'

'Yes.' He went stolidly on, reminding himself that he was part of the happiness.

'And you – you're happy still?'

'Yes. And before you ask, so is Hester. All that business about her not getting to Oxford . . . she's all right now.' He smiled at her conspiratorially. 'I rather think she's in love with her prof.' He chuckled, rinsing his hands under the tap, letting out the water. 'Who, funnily enough, is called Tibbolt.'

She raised her brows. 'I don't get it. What's that got to do with a bag of beetroot?' He spluttered and she explained. 'One of Gran's sayings. Oh dear, I haven't chatted to her yet. Must go. Thanks a million, Val.'

He caught her arm. 'Don't you remember likening our families to the Montagues and

Capulets? Don't you remember Tybalt in *Romeo and Juliet*?'

'What? Oh, I see. The name of Hester's professor? Yes, strange. Another of those ghastly coincidences that seem to be everywhere.'

'It's happened, Alice. The two houses are joined for ever, whether they like it or not.'

'What do you mean? Val, I have to go.'

He was on the point of telling her; he knew it. And then, somehow, he drew back. He recalled the amoral Hattie inviting him into her boudoir-like bedroom and seducing him so blatantly. Anyone would have done to father her child. It had been no real marriage between two houses. He snorted a laugh at himself, pulled Alice closer and kissed her.

She was sufficiently surprised not to pull away immediately; he slid his hand along her sleeve to hold her head and thread his long fingers in her hair. Hattie had taught him well and she still did not pull away. When he released her, she looked at him with dazed eyes and then began to cry again.

'Is that what you still think? That you and I could bridge the gap? Oh Val – you don't know – you do not understand.' And she turned and ran out of the kitchen.

After a while, Val went upstairs and into the familiar bedroom. Edmund was asleep with upflung arms and damp dark hair. Val stared down at him. He was so like Hattie that it was impossible to see anyone else. But Val knew.

Very gently, he picked the child up and sat on the edge of the bed, holding him carefully while he grunted and stretched and woke up. Dark eyes gazed into pale blue. Val leaned close and whispered, 'Hello, Edmund. You'll never know it, but I am your father.'

The child stretched luxuriously and smiled.

Twenty-Two

Once Ted returned to Paddington, 1948 began dismally for Alice and her mother. Doffie talked of getting a job, and meanwhile threw herself into an orgy of cleaning and painting, first the house and then the church. The Hydes helped where they could, but they were both elderly and the Reverend Geoffrey's main contribution was holding the ladder, while Doffie climbed up with a paintbrush tied to a broom handle.

Ted, home for a weekend in February, was angry. 'He simply wants to look up your skirt!' he said. 'I've never liked him – he's the reason I don't attend church.'

'What poppycock! You don't go to church because you had too much of it when you were a lad! You're bored by church! All you care about is your bloody wagons and your priority lists and stabling capacities and—'

'How do you know about stabling capacities – is it Alice? So you listen to Alice but not to me. Thanks, Doff.'

Unexpectedly, she began to cry. Ted knew that she rarely cried when she was angry. 'What?' he asked irritably. 'What now?'

She was a long time telling him, and he was a long time understanding her because of the great tears that choked her. Eventually he understood and took her hand, holding it limply until she calmed down. If it crossed her mind that a year ago he would have taken her into his arms, she barely registered the thought. She had known she would have to tell Ted some time. After all, Alice was his daughter.

Doffie had been clearing the grate before Christmas and had found a half-burned letter which Alice must have thrown away the night before. Joe had caught some horrible disease from prostitutes, and . . . well, that was that. He had called everything off.

She pulled her hand away and reached into her sleeve for a handkerchief, then dried her face. 'I couldn't spoil Christmas. I had to pretend to Alice that everything was all right. She was putting up such a brave front. I couldn't tell her that I knew, and if you'd known it would have been twice as hard.' She blew her nose vigorously. 'And actually . . . I didn't expect that from Joe Adair. No, I thought he was a clean-living boy who—' She was stopped by Ted's hoot of derisive laughter.

'Oh, Doff. You have no idea, have you? He's in a different world, miles away. He's desperate. His mother dies. He sees things happening, people dying all the time from the aftermath of the War. These girls . . . it's not the sex he's after, it's comfort. Human comfort.'

She raised her intensely blue eyes to his. 'I thought you didn't have much time for him. You called him a mother's boy—'

'I did not call him anything, Doffie! Those

stupid boys – Toby Fletcher and Dennis whatsit – in the Control called him that, and he was worth a dozen of them.'

'Oh, God. We should have done something.'

'He had to do his National Service, we couldn't have kept him out of that.'

'Valentine Ryecroft didn't go.'

'He failed because of his weak chest, you know that.'

'Well – we could have had his mother here, at least. I would have nursed her. It would have given me a purpose in life.'

'What the hell are you talking about, woman? She was nothing to us. She might have died here, and then you'd never have forgiven yourself. Why are you going on like this?'

Doffie stood up and walked into the kitchen.

Ted followed. 'You're muttering – I can't hear you.'

She filled the kettle. 'Nothing. It's nothing. It's just . . . I can't help Alice. You're not around . . .' She banged the kettle on to the electric cooker. 'I should get a job.' She half smiled at him. 'Any more jobs going in the office, Ted?'

He ignored that, thinking she was joking. 'I'll tell you one thing. When I get back into the Control, I'm going to pull strings to get young Val Ryecroft into the office. I was talking to him at Christmas. He's got vision, has that young man. He's not confining it to the Great Western, either. He sees the country's railways as a whole – plus the roads, even the canals. He could build a system that would connect us all – the tiniest villages and the biggest cities.' Ted was not even looking at her; his eyes were on the window, where the heavy grey light suggested snow.

Doffie sighed. 'Yes. Well, Reggie will never let him into the office. Not while he's there.'

'I know. But there's something afoot with Reggie. Eddie Maybury was telling me. Of course, he knows everything that happens in the office – the division, in fact – through Helena Webster. What a match that will be.'

'Made in Heaven,' Doffie nodded, thankful to find a topic of common interest.

'Made in his office, more likely. Underneath the mistletoe, Christmas before last. French kissing, they call it.' He laughed knowingly. Doffie turned her shoulder to reach down cups and saucers. He would never have spoken like that to her a year ago.

'So what is Reggie up to?' she asked pointedly.

'Getting himself another job, probably. Bernie Berry and Helena found out something about our Reggie. He's scared they'll let the cat out of the bag. Bernie thinks he's trying to get himself another job.'

She poured the tea. 'I know about that. Alice thinks that Reggie had been up to something over a claim. That's why he let her have the day off to go to Plymouth.'

'If you know it already—'

She picked up the tray and went on as if he had not spoken. 'So in his turn, he is blackmailing that firm – whoever it was – into giving him . . . what? A seat on the board? A partnership?'

'Something like that.' Ted had always admired Doffie's quick understanding; but in this case, it made him feel resentful.

She picked up her tea and sat in the armchair

by the fire. 'I see what you mean. It would leave the field clear for Val.'

He misunderstood. 'For God's sake, woman! Can't you stop matchmaking for one little minute?'

Doffie looked at him, and he knew that for two pins she would have thrown her tea at him just as she had before. The row had been brewing for weeks, ever since he'd come home for Christmas. It had been escalating all afternoon; Ted knew she was deeply angry and aggrieved, but had no idea what he had said to offend her.

Just then, Alice arrived home from a depressing afternoon with Gran, who had burned a hole in her ancient saucepan when boiling a pig's head. She heard the torrent of words as she wheeled her bicycle into the shed. By the time she got inside, the flood had abruptly stopped. Dad had sent Mum to Coventry again.

Wearily, she hung up her coat and put on her slippers. Whatever she did, it never turned out right. She did not even bother to tell God about it. He hardly ever listened, anyway.

The bright spot in February was Helena's wedding. To avoid any embarrassment for the two families, she decreed it should be a registry-office ceremony, six guests each and a sit-down lunch at the New County. Her parents and a favourite aunt and uncle made up four; Miss Warner and Alice came from the office. Eddie Maybury had his elderly parents, two sisters and their husbands.

Alice kept Miss Warner's kid-gloved hand firmly in her elbow, even when they sat in the ladder-backed chairs. She leaned close to describe the outfits.

'Miss Webster is in primrose,' she whispered. 'Her parents look really nice too. Mrs Webster is in a sort of old-rose jumper suit and Mr Webster is wearing a grey suit with a chalk stripe and turn-ups – you don't see many turn-ups now, do you?'

'Austerity suits . . . couldn't afford material for turn-ups,' Miss Warner whispered back. Miss Warner was going to clear up the office while Mr Maybury was away on honeymoon, and then retire. She was planning to join her sister in Sidmouth, who did teas in the summer. Miss Warner loved Sidmouth. No one had said a word about who would take over in her tiny office. Both Miss Jenkins and Miss Ford had applied for the job. Alice had done nothing. It was as much as she could do to turn up every day.

The lunch was delightful. Three courses, real butter for the rolls, cold meats, potatoes and salad, cabinet pudding or meringue and ice cream. Mr Maybury thanked the bride's parents for such a wonderful spread, and for their blessing on their daughter's union; he thanked everyone for coming, and mentioned his younger brother, who had been killed in action. He faltered and stammered now and then, and what with that and his kind eyes and general niceness, Alice was reminded terribly of Joe and felt treacherous tears in her nose and throat. But, as usual, she swallowed them. She knew it was her fault. That dreadful day on Cooper's Hill – she had made a mistake then, and nothing would ever be the same again.

* * *

Reggie sent for Valentine the following Monday. He used the internal Bus Line when no one was around, and spoke to him directly.

'Thought I'd have a word, my boy. How are you?'

There was a pause, then Val said, 'Is Mother all right?'

'Of course. Why shouldn't she be? And your sister. And myself.'

'Right. Sorry. First time you've telephoned me at work.'

'Yes. I have avoided doing so. Families should not really work together; it is frowned on, as you well know.'

'Yet,' Val's voice was softly reasonable, 'the railways run in so many families. Strange, is it not?'

'You know very well what I mean, Valentine. Don't argue the toss with me today, boy. I need your cooperation.' Reggie waited, but Val said nothing.

'An opportunity has presented itself.' The ponderous tone swelled into pomposity. 'It would mean leaving your mother alone in the house. I would like to talk to you about it.'

There was another pause.

'I could get off early tonight. Would that do?'

'Certainly. I will tell your mother to expect you to supper at seven o'clock.'

Reggie replaced the telephone sharply, then placed his fingertips together and sat back in his chair, smiling at the smoke-blackened ceiling.

Valentine ran over to Seth's cottage immediately and gave him the booking-office keys. He caught the three-thirty railcar and ran from the station down Hare Lane to Deanery Close, so that he could have an hour of his mother's exclusive company. She was overjoyed to see him.

'Such a treat, Val. Does your father know? Where are you off to?'

'I've been summoned, Ma. Something is afoot. I thought you might know.'

She shook her head apprehensively. 'I hope Hester is all right. She never comes home for the weekend now.'

'That means she *is* all right. I promised her I would take Alice to see her. I haven't done so. I don't think Hester minds. She is otherwise interested.' He looked at his mother and saw that she understood. They both laughed.

Dorothy said, 'He's been rather sweet lately – your father, I mean. I know he really hated Miss Webster marrying Mr Maybury and leaving the office.'

'It probably means he will use poor old Alice for his work. I wonder whether she will have to work for Mr Maybury as well.'

'Someone will have to. Miss Warner has left as well. Her sight is so poor she cannot see the keys on her typewriter.'

Val was silent, watching his mother peel potatoes and cut them into slices over a fish pie. He said slowly, 'Ma . . . I think he might be moving out.'

She was startled. 'What on earth makes you say that?'

'You say he's being sweet . . . yet he has no reason to be sweet. He is frantically jealous of Uncle Ted—'

'Val!'

'It's true, Ma. I hear things . . . you can't help hearing things on the Bus Line. He hates having to promote Alice into Miss Webster's post. He hates me working on the railway – especially at Leadon—'

'No, Val. That's not true! It's what he did him- self, remember.'

'He wanted to boast of his son being an Oxford don.'

'Val, please don't say these things. He is your father. He is my husband.'

'And I know what he does to you, too. That has got to end!'

'Val – you have no idea what you are saying. Marriage is something so private, so mysterious—'

'I suffered too, remember. I still have some scars.' Dorothy closed her eyes. 'Ma, I could be quite wrong. But we must be prepared. How would you feel?'

She opened her eyes, then put the fish pie in the oven and came to the table. She said slowly, 'I don't know how to feel any more, Val. Your father calls me a cold fish and I think he is right. I know I love you and Hester. That is all I can really be certain of.'

He got up and held her tightly against his shoulder, then sat her down. 'That is enough.' He smiled at her. 'I have discovered a very important thing, Ma. If you love one person, it helps you to love another. It's a bit like an infectious disease.' He kept smiling, willing her to laugh, and eventually she did.

Val laid the table and cut bread and butter, chatting all the time just like Hattie did, covering everything with a blanket of comforting words. It was almost time for Reggie's arrival when he discovered his mother had forgotten to light the gas for the fish pie.

They were both laughing helplessly when Reggie came in, bringing with him the sharp tang of vinegar from the pickle factory.

'Something smells good!' he said, putting his hat on the newel post and hanging his coat on its peg. 'Let me guess . . . fish pie?'

Val was amazed; the pie would take ages in their ancient cooker. But his mother continued to laugh.

'That's cheating, Reggie darling,' she said. 'You know very well we always have fish pie on a Monday!'

'So we do, so we do.' He came to her, held her chin and kissed her. 'My goodness, I wish I could bring a sparkle to your eyes like your son does! You are looking well, Dorothy.'

Val waited for her to go still, which was the only way she knew to be submissive. But instead she cupped her husband's face in her hands. 'Ah, Reggie. How could I look otherwise? You care for me so carefully.'

It was an unfortunate choice of words; Valentine laughed and so did she, and Reggie thought they were laughing at him. But he recovered his composure and sat down to question Val about what he called 'the state of play' at Leadon.

'What about the station master's daughters?' he chortled. 'I don't expect he has got anyone to compare with the notorious Mitzie Pettiford. But you never know.'

Valentine did not remind him of what he already knew: the station master could only ever

303

be seen at the local pub, where he declared he was drumming up business from the local farmers. He was a bachelor, and as far as anyone knew had no children. It seemed that Reggie wanted to talk about the past.

'Tell us about Mitzie, Pa. I understand from Seth she used to swim in some of the pools left by the diggings.'

Reggie laughed. 'She certainly did. And in the buff! Poor old Will Pettiford had a job with her, right enough.'

'What happened to her?'

'Died, I heard.' Reggie frowned. 'A girl like that ... promiscuous ... comes to no good.' He looked up. 'Anyway, why ask me? How would I know? All I'm saying is, she disappeared.'

'Poor Mrs Pettiford,' Dorothy said softly.

'Poor Mrs Pettiford indeed. She was a harridan, if ever there was one! No wonder Mitzie left.' He sighed. 'Sometimes it's the only thing to do.'

Val put his hands beneath the table and crossed his fingers. 'I wonder,' he said musingly, 'what would have happened if I'd done my National Service. Gone right away, like that junior in your office – Joseph Adair.'

Reggie said jovially, 'You'd never have stuck it, my boy. You couldn't stick Oxford, so you certainly wouldn't have stuck the Army.' He sniggered. 'Doesn't sound as though Mr Adair has been able to stick it either. Apparently he's got some foreign disease – malaria, I think Miss Pettiford said – and he's in hospital in Singapore.' He sighed deeply. 'She's useless now. A promising typist – gone.'

Valentine raised his brows encouragingly and

Reggie nodded at his own words. 'It's as I've always told you, my boy, you cannot continue with friendships when you work together. Had she never set her cap at him, she'd still be good at her job. Mr Maybury will need a new secretary when he gets back from his honeymoon –' he guffawed sardonically, 'though what sort of honeymoon he can be having with Miss Webster, who is so high and mighty she can't always catch what people say to her—'

Valentine looked at his mother as he said, 'Bit of a cold fish, Pa?'

Reggie slapped the table. 'Exactly, my boy! A cold fish indeed. However, I wish Miss Pettiford had taken a leaf from her book. There could have been a good future for her in the Gloucester division. She was always getting up ladders to show off her legs, spending hours in the cellar with him lighting the oil stove and fetching coal—'

Dorothy said firmly, 'The fish pie will be ready now. Would you like to dish up, Val?'

There was a pause while plates were fetched – icily cold – and the pie placed on the table. Dorothy served Reggie and then Valentine. They ate silently; the potatoes were still hard, but Reggie did not seem to notice.

After two helpings he sat back, hands on stomach. 'I needed that.'

Valentine pushed aside his plate, knowing the moment had come. Dorothy had long ago given up on her portion; thankfully, she took her plate to the draining board, where Reggie would not see it and nag her about wasting food.

Reggie smiled benignly across the table. 'I know you are wondering why I have asked you to come

305

home tonight, Valentine. Well, my son, two things. Firstly, your name has been put forward for a special post in the Divisional Superintendent's office in Gloucester.'

'Your office, you mean, Pa?'

'Obviously, my boy. Try to concentrate. This is something quite new, designed to promote men with promise. As such, of course it is an honour.' His smile broadened. 'I am proud of you, Valentine.'

Val flapped his hands. 'I'm not quite clear—'

'The post entails the gaining of experience in all departments. The Control Office, the Trains Office, the Staff Office, even the commercial side. You would spend probably six months in each of these departments—'

'What about your department?'

'Mine too, of course.'

There was a pause. Dorothy's eyes were wide and bright, and she appeared to be holding her breath.

Val said, 'You have always cavilled at family working in the same office.'

'Which brings me to my second point.' Reggie turned his gaze on to his wife. 'Not to put too fine a point on it, my dear, I have long felt my talents are not being fully used as a railway servant. I am not a discontented man, as you know, and would never have actively sought anything different in life. But the opportunity has come to me unsought. Unlooked for. As much an honour as Valentine's. A firm of iron workers in Newport, Turner's – mining, smelting, fabricating – a firm I have had much to do with in the past, have been impressed by my administrative and diplomatic skills. They have offered me a place on their board of directors.' He leaned back and stopped smiling. 'Obviously, I turned it down. I could not move my wife to South Wales in her state of health. And I could not leave her alone here. So that was an end to the matter.'

Dorothy leaned towards him, a sound of protest preceding what she intended to say next, that she would move wherever her husband went. But before she could utter a word, Val nodded vigorously.

'Of course you were right, Pa. Absolutely right. But . . .' He appeared to be thinking things out as he went along. 'What if I move back home? I can look after Ma, shop and cook and clean, just as you do.'

There was an ominous silence, while Reggie wondered whether Val was being sarcastic.

Val too leaned across the table. 'Don't you see, Pa? This is all meant to be – part of a pattern. If I hadn't had the offer of this job, you couldn't go. And if you hadn't been offered your directorship, then I couldn't take up my offer! It would have been impossible to work in the same office, let alone the same department!'

Reggie thumped the table. 'Well done, my boy! You have arrived at the same conclusion as myself! That is exactly why I intend to ring Turner's first thing tomorrow and rescind my previous refusal! I knew that you would agree to come home, Val. The young rebel of two years ago has had time to think things through. I must admit, I had my doubts. I thought you might take a malicious kind of pleasure in insisting on staying at Leadon, making it impossible for me to go to Newport.' He ducked his head. 'I should have known better. We have always been a strong family. We shall never be any different.'

Val bowed his head too, though only to hide a smile. His mother looked from one to the other, hardly realizing what was happening. She wondered whether she should tell them both that she would cook, clean and shop for Val, as she always had for Reggie. But even as she opened her mouth to speak, Val's knee pressed warningly against hers and she was silent.

Reggie lifted his head. 'Well, what do you say to all of this, Dorothy? The decision is yours, my dear. Only say the word and Valentine and I will turn down both offers and I will cleave to you as I always have done.'

Her eyes filled with tears and she reached for his hand. 'I am so proud of you both. And delighted, too. And if Doffie Pettiford can manage on her own, then so can I!'

Reggie smiled again, this time with triumph. Val smiled too. He would be seeing Alice every day of every week. And Dorothy smiled. She felt as if a door might finally be going to open in her life.

Twenty-Three

Gran spread butter thickly on to a doorstep of bread and pushed the jam pot towards Alice.

'Help yourself, girl. And don't be mean. Blackcurrants were good last year and I made twenty-four pots of jam.'

'Will you use them all, Gran?' asked Alice, spooning the thick jam on top of the buttered bread.

'Oh aye. I drink a lot of blackcurrant tea. Good for you, so they say.'

Alice had a whole file in the office on the transport of blackcurrant cordial from Lydney by rail; vitamin C was all the rage. She nodded and took a big bite of bread. She had not had much appetite lately; the worst of it was that she couldn't tell Mum about Joe. Not ever, really. And Joe seemed to be disappearing from everyone's memory. Doffie did not even ask how he was any more.

Not that she could tell Gran much. But at least she could talk about him; say his name; wonder aloud how he was getting on. And enjoy the food Gran always found for her.

Gran put the poker in the fire and riddled

furiously. The fire flared up and she drew her chair closer.

'Next week we'll put a potato in the ash pan. You always used to like a potato when you was a nipper.' She looked at Alice, remembering the six-year-old girl who had stayed by her side for the first few terrible days after Will had gone. She watched as Alice chewed and then said, 'He's not coming back, is he, our Alice?'

Alice stopped chewing. Her cheeks bulged like a hamster's; slowly, her eyes filled and overflowed, and then she choked. Gran held a hand beneath her chin, caught the regurgitated food expertly and threw it on the fire. Alice put her hands over her face.

'Oh Gran,' she groaned.

Gran said nothing more. When Alice finally took her hands away, there was a glass of black-currant tea at her elbow, and next to it an almost clean handkerchief. She used it, hiccuping, blowing and scrubbing for some minutes. Then she smiled apologetically.

'Sorry, Gran. I can't tell Mum or Dad. They would be angry with him and I couldn't bear that.'

Gran said, 'It happens all the time. Some flowers can survive the frosts. Others can't.' She pushed the glass to Alice. 'But you can, our Alice. You showed me how to do it when you was a nipper. You can still do it. You *are* doing it. Just let the days pass. Build them up one by one. They'll keep the wind and frost out.'

Alice took the blackcurrant tea and sipped obediently, smiling over the rim at her father's mother. The skin on Gran's face was grey and there was not a smooth patch anywhere; the skin over her hands was quite different: stretched, almost transparent, huge veins roped loosely across the backs.

'Miss Plant would call that mixing your metaphors, Gran. But it makes sense. Is that how you did it? Day by day?'

Gran thought back. 'Sometimes minute by minute,' she said heavily. 'I'm not saying it's easy.'

'No.' Alice nodded. 'It's not easy. And I'm not doing it very well. I don't bother at work or at home. Helena's wedding was so nice, but I was outside it in a strange way. I looked after Miss Warner and I was glad of that, because it meant I wasn't . . . at the front.'

'You've got to hide behind someone, girl. I hid behind you.'

'Did you really, Gran? I've forgotten so much.'

'You don't forget, not really. You wrap it up and keep it safe. That's all. Just like you will this. And one day you'll say to your husband, "You weren't my first love," and you might unwrap it and tell him about it. But if not, I hope you can look at him and say truthfully, "You weren't my first love, but you are my last."'

Alice wept again, but this time because Gran could not know that marriage was not possible for someone like her.

She would not let Gran see her to the front gate. The river was swollen with the February rains and it was damply cold. She pedalled furiously along the Bristol Road and into Southgate Street. Since Rose Adair's death, Alice had made a point of spending every Saturday afternoon with Gran. She knew it hurt Mum that her precious half day was not spent at home, but in a strange way

311

she wanted to punish Mum. She had no idea why.

As if time had slid back two years, she automatically turned down Longsmith Street and into Westgate as if she were going to visit Hester. The thought gave her a pang; how she would love to go back to the days when she and Hester met and talked about things that mattered, like books and poetry and the cathedral's east window buried carefully in the crypt against the German bombs. She remembered making Hester laugh unwillingly at her silly rhymes . . . the west window smiles and looks down on the nave, now that the east window lies in her grave . . . She swung her bike irritably down St John's Lane to emerge into Northgate again and storm up the pitch towards the countryside and home. And there, coming out of the old bookshop which was still lit by gas, was Valentine Ryecroft.

She was going to pass him by, but he turned and saw her and grabbed her handlebars. The bike swung around and she fell against his shoulder. They both tumbled into the gutter.

Val lay there helpless with her sprawled across him. He was shaking; at first Alice thought he was hurt, but then realized he was laughing. She pushed herself up on to her knees. Bystanders were coming over to help them.

'You silly fool!' she shouted, all her frustration and pain emerging in an enormous yell. 'You did that purposely! We could have both been injured – do you think it's funny?' He was convulsed, tears of laughter pouring down his face. The people dropped away, embarrassed.

He screwed up his eyes and held her arms. 'Oh Alice, I'm so sorry. But we're not injured and your face – you looked as if you'd seen a ghost!'

'Well, I had!' She pulled herself together and stood up, then tried to tug him up too. But he could not help himself because of the laughter. It infuriated her again. 'For God's sake, Val! It's not funny! You're wet and bedraggled and I'm probably suffering from shock and all you can do is—'

He stumbled to his feet somehow and held on to her shoulders while he got his bearings. 'I wanted to see you. To tell you. And never thought for an instant . . . and then you were there! Quite suddenly, out of the February dusk, you were there!'

She said, 'Every Saturday I am here. Going back home after visiting my grandmother.'

He said wonderingly, 'Will Pettiford's wife, Patience.'

'Yes, of course.'

'But you should have gone straight over the Cross.'

'It was one of those forgetful moments. I must have been thinking of the time I went to see Hester about leaving school.'

'You see? It was meant to be.' He was alight with excitement. 'Let's go and have tea, Alice. I have to talk to you. Seriously.'

She went, because it would take too much effort to do anything else. It would worry Doffie if she was late; but that did not matter. She let him wheel her bike and prop it up against the kerb outside Fearis's tea shop. He had money in his pocket now and he bought a pot of tea for two and some toasted teacakes. In spite of the jam sandwich at Gran's, Alice's mouth watered at the smell of the melting butter; she took the little

313

silver knife and cut her teacake into quarters. She remembered Gran saying 'minute by minute'; it made good sense – this minute she felt . . . all right.

Val said, 'I stayed at home last night. Slept in my old bed. Ate supper and breakfast with my parents. Went to work this morning and came home again.'

She looked up, surprised. He laughed at her expression and then, very seriously, told her exactly what had happened on Monday evening. 'It's a new post they are creating, Alice. And I'm the first one to fill it. What do you think?'

'It – it's wonderful!' She was genuinely pleased. 'And I can quite understand that you couldn't have accepted it if your father had still been in the General Office.'

'You don't sound unduly surprised by his . . . what would you call it, defection?'

'Mr Berry has mentioned things once or twice.' She shook her head. 'Isn't it strange, Val? Such a short time ago I would have loved all this – the gossip and the intrigue. Now, though I am so pleased for you, I don't really care.'

He stared at her, willing her to cry again and tell him everything. All she did was eat another quarter of her teacake.

He said, 'What about you? Can you cope with Miss Webster's work as well as your own?'

'I've been offered Miss Warner's post.' She glanced up; there was butter on her chin. 'I didn't even apply for it, Val. It was Helena Webster's doing. I can't take it.'

He exploded then. 'Of course you can! My God, you are ideal for it and Miss Webster knew that.

314

D'you think she would have recommended you if she thought you couldn't do the job? And how do you think I landed mine, anyway? Your father. That's obvious, isn't it? And I trust his judgement enough to take it on. And that's exactly what you've got to do.'

She stared for a moment, almost interested, then started on another piece of teacake. He was furious with her. She looked pathetic, with butter on her chin and her hair a mess.

'For God's sake, Alice! Stop being so damned self-centred – self-pitying – just plain selfish! I gather this is all about Joe Adair? Lovesick youth and all that poppycock?'

She looked up and stopped chewing. She seemed to be considering something. He waited.

She swallowed, and he could tell that the tea-cake stuck in her gullet. But she spoke through it, slowly, as if hearing her own words for the first time and facing the facts one by one.

'He's got VD. He's not coming back to Cheltenham. His mother's dead and the house was rented. There's nothing for him here any more.'

He stared at her. He could not look away. He felt a muddle of emotions, rather like the time when his father had beaten him and he had run to the Pettifords. They had thought he had run to Hester, his sister. But it had been Alice who had met him, taken him in, bathed his weals. He looked at her now and saw that she was as injured, as damaged, as he had been then. Now, if ever, was the time for logic.

He said, 'Drink some tea. You'll be all right.' And when she had he went on, 'What about you? He's got you to come home to.'

She smiled very sadly. 'I'm the trouble, actually. I'm no good to him, Val. Can't you tell that? I thought men knew instinctively. And you've had experience with girls.'

'What does that mean, exactly?' He shifted his gaze to her buttered chin. Had Hattie been boasting about her much younger lover?

She shrugged. 'The gypsies. Remember the last time I fell off my bike down St John's Lane, you had just come from the gypsies.'

He didn't like to think of that time. 'Right. So what is wrong with you that I ought to be able to see a mile off? Except the butter all over your chin.'

She stuck out her tongue and tried, unsuccessfully, to lick off the offending butter. Then she said very calmly, 'I had intercourse with Joe. I hated every second of it. So did he. I can't do it, you see.'

He sat back as if she had punched him in the chest. She smiled. 'I've shocked you. But I had to make you understand, Val. Somebody has to understand. And maybe we met tonight so that somebody could be you.'

He said slowly, 'Yes, I understand.'

She went on, 'I think God sent you.'

He breathed carefully, then said, 'Perhaps.'

A waitress approached them with a linen napkin and put it by Alice's plate. Val reached across and picked it up; he shifted his seat so that he was right next to her, their thighs touching.

'Let me get rid of that mess on your chin,' he said steadily. He leaned over and held her head, twining his fingers in her hair as he had done in Hattie's kitchen at Christmas. She just sat there.

Val took a corner of the napkin and wiped her chin. He took his time. When he had finished, he folded the napkin and put it by her plate. 'I've messed up your hair now. Why don't you go to the ladies' and tidy it?'

She whispered, 'Val, thank you.'

'You did it for me once. Remember?'

'Yes.' She looked down at the last piece of tea-cake. 'Did you feel . . . better? Afterwards?'

'Yes. Do you?'

'Yes. Oh yes. I nearly told you at Christmas. When you kissed me under the mistletoe. But it was too soon.'

'Was there mistletoe? I didn't notice.'

'I only heard the week before. He wrote . . . Oh Val, it was awful. Just so awful. And yet, somehow I knew . . . when that liberty boat pulled out at Devonport. I knew it was the end, Val. I knew. How could that be?'

He said steadily, 'Doesn't that make it better? That you knew last summer?'

She wasn't listening. 'If I'd been able to . . . he wouldn't have gone off with . . . you know . . . then he wouldn't have been so ill. He probably nearly died – he wouldn't say that, you see . . . and hearing about his mother . . . Oh Val, if only I'd been a different person. Normal. Like Helena. Helena would have lived with Mr Maybury if he hadn't asked her to marry him – she told me herself!'

He leaned closer to her. 'Alice, go and tidy your hair, darling. I'll wait for you here, then I'll borrow a bike from one of the controllers and I'll cycle home with you. Please, Alice.'

He watched her cross the room, knocking against chairs and tables as she went. She was the same age as Hester. And she had sat there and said, 'I had intercourse with Joe . . . I was no good at it.'

As he waited for her to come back to him, he was already planning to take her to the gingerbread house that spring and prove to her that she was very good at it.

Twenty-Four

Whether it was anything to do with baring her soul to Val, Alice had no idea, but that spring it seemed as if life was opening again for her. She took Miss Warner's job and put everything she had into 'looking after' Mr Maybury. Her little office was easy to maintain and he had a cleaner who also dealt with his fire – which was open and cast iron and rather beautiful – so the memories of the cellar gradually faded. She tried to do what Gran had suggested: wrap it up and keep it safe. She considered handing it over to God, but she no longer approached God in such an informal way, and of course God did prefer you to help yourself, it was all part of the free-will thing.

She went to meetings with Mr Maybury and took the minutes; her shorthand was now confident and people were helpful to her, not only because of her father and her grandfather, but because she proved to be totally discreet and straightforward. The Superintendent in Newport was particularly appreciative. He had already had dealings with the new director at Turner's Iron Products and thought that if Miss Pettiford could work for him, she could probably work for anybody.

Alice discovered an old-fashioned coffee percolator in the back of one of the cupboards and took it home for cleaning. By that summer, it seemed to be on most of the morning, not only for Mr Maybury and any possible visitor, but for anyone who put their head around Alice's door and said, 'What's that heavenly smell?' Helena told her when she popped in that she was turning into Miss Warner, and Mr Maybury made a face and said, 'Please don't do that, Alice!' They were always joking, holding hands, smiling at each other. Alice knew how they felt, but she did not envy them. She knew she could not bear all that outpouring of love ever again.

That spring, Doffie Pettiford got a job. It was at Smith's Booksellers further down Northgate Street. She worked from seven in the morning, helping to sort the newspapers, until three in the afternoon, so that she could get home by four o'clock to cook an evening meal for herself and Alice. When Alice went to supper with Helena and Mr Maybury, Doffie might spend the day at Hattie's, helping with Edmund and playing tennis with Enid. And once with Valentine Ryecroft.

Ted came home for a weekend once a month. He was now spending a lot of time in Crewe. 'I'm a glorified teacher, that's what!' he told Alice, half proudly, half resentfully. Doffie told herself that it was because of her job that she no longer worried about Ted 'meeting' someone else. That might have been the reason – or perhaps it was because when it was raining Duggie Marsden always managed to get off early and put her bike in his boot and drive her home. Duggie was as he had always been: unexciting, yet kind, helpful and –

well, adoring, almost. Doffie was flattered, it was as simple as that.

Valentine Ryecroft was doing his six months in the Control Office and enjoying it whole-heartedly. He loved doing 'turns', because it gave him more time to cosset his mother and work on the enormous colour diagrams which showed the route of every passenger train and goods train passing through the division. When Ted Pettiford called into the office, Val showed him what he was doing. Ted was amazed. 'Took me twenty years to learn what you've picked up in two months!' He clapped Val on the shoulder. 'I knew you had it in you!'

Val said, 'So it *was* you who came up with the scheme and my name?'

Ted shrugged. 'People like you will be needed badly soon, Val. Take my word for it.' He grinned. 'Let's go and see the new Miss Warner and get some coffee!'

Val thought that if he had been married to Doffie Pettiford he wouldn't be hanging around the office in his precious time off. He had called at Leckhampton the previous week to see how Edmund was coming along, and Doffie had been there playing tennis. She looked a little bit like Alice. Almost lost.

He watched Alice carefully and from afar. Too soon and he would offend her . . . too late and she might have started showing an interest in one of the juniors who followed her everywhere, like a couple of blasted dogs.

Doffie was massaging Hattie's neck and shoulders. It was a hot Saturday afternoon in July and Hattie was sitting in a deckchair by the empty tennis court, supposedly resting, but in fact uncharacteristically twitchy. She was, as she smugly put it, 'the size of Buckingham Palace and growing'. But that day, she'd had to admit she had had a headache. But she swore it had already completely disappeared under Doffie's ministrations. 'You are the only one who helps,' she said gratefully but untruthfully; she still had everyone in the house dancing attendance on her. What she meant was that Doffie was the extremely embarrassed recipient of her confidences; she loved to discuss her pregnancy in the tiniest detail, and sometimes Doffie had difficulty in listening, let alone contributing to the conversation. She finished describing Percy's latest 'technique', as she put it, and then, tipping her head to view Doffie upside-down, she asked insouciantly, 'Does Ted try anything different, darling? I mean, I know he was pretty ordinary and staid before he went to London – he was always so shocked when I told him things. But since then, I suppose he's learned a lot?'

'Hattie! For goodness' sake! Why on earth would Ted change just because he went to London? It's no longer a den of vice, you know. Just a city, bigger than Gloucester and Cheltenham put together, but still a collection of ordinary everyday people who—'

Hattie was laughing. 'Oh, darling Doff. Of course it is. You don't have to protest too much!'

Doffie gave up the massage and came round to the front of Hattie's deckchair, determined not to say another word. Hattie smiled slightly and pulled Doffie's chair closer to hers with a still-elegant foot.

'Sit down, darling. Listen to the glorious silence. Enid has taken Edmund to listen to the band in Montpelier Gardens – he just loves brass bands. Mamma is lying down, which she has to do quite often these days. Darling Percy will be reading the paper to her . . .'

Doffie murmured that Hattie was very good not to mind Percy's devotion to his mother. Hattie laughed again.

'Oh, Doff! I adore Percy, you know that. But I adore you too.' She waited, but Doffie said no more, and after a while Hattie asked after Alice. Doffie lifted her shoulders, then put her head back and closed her eyes.

Hattie said musingly, 'Sometimes I wonder whether we're on the wrong tack there. We should come into the open and tell her that we know he's gone for good and she'd better look round for someone else. Valentine Ryecroft would be quite . . . suitable.'

Doffie's neck muscles were rigid. She said, 'But unfortunately for him, he's still in love with you.'

Hattie's eyes flew open in surprise. 'Doffie? Do I detect disapproval . . . even sarcasm? Darling, he is not in love with me, never was. Nor I with him. Our little fling was over before it began, really.'

'He was here the other day, Hattie. Have you forgotten?'

'Oh, sweetie. He comes very, very infrequently, just to see Edmund. He's not really interested. Just curious.' She giggled. 'Actually, I did wonder whether to take him upstairs. But darling Percy was around somewhere and he can be quite possessive at times.'

Doffie did not know whether to laugh or cry.

She tried to be censorious. 'You are eight months pregnant, Hattie Westbrook! What *is* the matter with you?'

'So you think that would put him off? Actually, I think it might do just the opposite. I must ask him some time.'

Doffie gave up and laughed. 'You are absolutely incorrigible! How you got like this when Will and Patience Pettiford brought you up—'

'Oh, I think darling Gramps was pretty passionate, Doff! There were one or two women in Leadon who gave him the eye. Gran forgave him, of course. She would have forgiven him anything.' She sighed nostalgically and then went on, 'And then, of course, there was my mother . . .' She left the sentence hanging.

Doffie said musingly, 'Mitzie.'

'She changed her name, apparently. It was Millicent. Changing her name says it all, I think. She used to "flaunt her body" – that was what Reggie Ryecroft said.'

'*Reggie Ryecroft*? You have chats with Reggie Ryecroft about your mother?'

'Well . . . not exactly. I overheard him telling Gramps. Ages ago. I must have been about six or seven. But I've never forgotten.' She sighed. 'Funny, the things you remember, isn't it, Doff? Gramps usually only raised his voice when he was singing, but he did that day, so I stuck my little shell-like into the keyhole and listened. And I heard Reggie say that everyone in Leadon knew that Mitzie Pettiford flaunted her body. And d'you know all he meant? My mother used to swim in Bracewell's Pool. In the buff. I asked Gramps and he told me.' Her eyes became dreamy. 'I missed him so much, Doff. As much as Gran missed him, really.'

Doffie nodded, feeling they were on the same wavelength at last. 'We all did,' she said. 'I just wish I'd found a way of travelling with him – did you know he asked me to go abroad with him?'

'No, but I'm not surprised. He loved you, Doff. He really did. It was because of him that I loved you, because at first I was really jealous of you. Well, kids are like that. But since he loved you, I knew you must be special.'

Doffie was strangely moved. The two women sat silently, remembering. When Enid wheeled Edmund around the house almost an hour later, Hattie was asleep and Doffie was holding her hand, her eyes closed too.

Alice spent the afternoon picking Gran's over-ripe gooseberries and raspberries and thinning out the lettuce she had planted three weeks before. Gran sat on a kitchen chair in the shade of the lean-to which sheltered the privy and provided hanging space for baths, buckets and gardening tools.

'You'll have to take it home with you, my girl,' Gran said ungratefully, looking into the colanders of produce. 'I can't do nothing with it now. S'long as I can make my tea and broth, I'm all right. All this fresh fruit and veg . . .'

'You've always been mad on fresh fruit and veg,' Alice said firmly. 'I'll stew this lot up and wash the lettuce. You can have it with your bread and cheese at supper.'

'Keep me awake.'

'Rubbish. There's laudanum in lettuce – makes you sleep.'

'I might not wake up, then.' Gran was determined to be gloomy. She had been like this for a month now.

Alice said, 'Let's go in now. This sun is hot.'

Gran got up with difficulty. Alice knew she could no longer climb the stairs; she should have reported back to her mother, but had not done so. She tottered in to the kitchen and sat at the table by the empty range. Alice went into the scullery to light the gas for tea. She also suspected that without the range lit, Gran no longer made tea.

Alice squashed raspberries – so ripe they were almost purple – on to a piece of bread and sprinkled it with sugar. Gran took tiny bites in between sips of tea.

'You're enjoying that, Gran.'

'I am, our Alice. I am.' She finished it and sat back. 'Listen, my girl – I don't want to go to the workhouse.'

Alice was aghast. 'Whatever made you say that? There are no such things as workhouses any more, Gran! I was telling you all about the new National Health – you can't have listened to a word I said!'

'Mrs Leggatt's aunt's just gone to Westbury. 'Twas built a workhouse and 'tis a workhouse now.'

'It's an elderly persons' home, Gran. Workhouse, indeed!'

'Don't talk to me as if I'm daft, our Alice. Just promise me—'

'Of course you won't go to the workhouse – is that what you want me to say?'

'Nor the home or whatever it's called? At Westbury?'

'No. You won't go anywhere, Gran. All right?'

'What if they find me one morning? Not dead. Stroke. All my family went with strokes.'

'You're as strong as a horse, Gran. But if you feel like that, I'll get the doctor to call and take your blood pressure—'

'Don't you do no such thing, my girl! When I want a doctor I will tell you!'

'Sorry, Gran.'

'I should think so. And you can stop grinning. I'm serious. If I'm found like that, I don't want to go to Hattie's. Is that clear?'

Alice was surprised. 'Why ever not? Hattie is your daughter—'

'No, she's not. She's my granddaughter. Mitzie was my daughter.'

Alice said slowly, 'You want to come to us if you're ill? Is that what you mean?'

'Yes. Hattie will want me there. She's got money now and she'll get a nurse for me . . . there will be no peace and quiet. She will go on having babies—'

'Gran, I would have thought you would have loved all that. And anyway, how can you say such a thing – just because she's having two close together doesn't mean—'

'I can tell things like that. I've got a gift. And I would have enjoyed it all at one time, when I could help. But not now. Now I want peace and quiet. I want gentleness.'

Alice thought of her parents, the times of not speaking. She said carefully, 'What about Mum? You and she don't always see eye to eye.'

'I was jealous. I admit it. I know she's a good girl. I know, if she agrees to take me in, she will look after me.' She looked at Alice from beneath her lowered brows. 'And you're there, our Alice.'

Alice felt her eyes fill with tears. She said quietly, 'This won't happen. But if it does, you know – you know you can make a home with us.'

Gran did not say thank you. But when Alice pecked her cheek goodbye, she held the blond head close to hers.

Val was waiting in Longsmith Street, astride his new bike.

'I went to the bookshop at first. But then I wasn't sure you'd come that way and I wanted to see you.'

Alice said, 'Has something happened?'

'No. I hope something is going to happen, but it hasn't yet.'

Alice sat on her saddle again and made to push off. 'I don't want to talk again, Val. It was good of you . . . it helped me a lot. For one thing, I took Miss Warner's job. But I don't want to talk about . . . it . . . any more.'

'That's good.' He smiled amiably. 'Carry on, I'll catch you up. This bike has got three gears. Cost twelve guineas.'

She was shocked at such extravagance and suspicious of his acquiescence. He did not catch her up, however, until the top of the pitch. It was when they were coasting down the other side that he drew level.

'Can't get the hang of the gears,' he panted. 'Keeps going into neutral – nearly came off in front of a blasted car just now!'

'Serves you right for showing off. You had a perfectly good bike before.'

'Oh shut up, Alice! You sound like my father!'

That did shut her up, and she drew her lips in until she suspected she looked like Gran. Then, as they started down the lanes, she burst out laughing.

Val was still pedalling frantically in bottom gear and asked, 'What now?'

She looked at him with sudden affection. 'Nothing, really. Just that . . . everything feels so heavy. And you and your new bike make it . . . light.'

'Oh well, there's twelve guineas well spent!' But he too was smiling, his light-blue eyes glinting at her, his pale hair almost gold in the sun.

She said, 'Stop, Val. Let's change bikes. I might get the hang of it – I had a go on a bike with gears when I was at school.'

They did the swap; he knew she would succeed. It was the same as that time when Hester had taken over the monthly returns at Leadon booking office and totted them up perfectly. But Alice made it fun; he loved it when she 'taught' him how to back-pedal before he operated the tiny gear lever on the crossbar, then to test that the cogs had locked all right. 'You see, if you just go mad at it, they'll slip forward and so will you – you'll go right over the handlebars! Dad did that last year when we were cycling home from the station and he tried to go no-handed *and* put his feet on the handlebars!'

'Did he?' Val was entranced. Ted Pettiford was an important man; a man who had been seconded to work in London and Crewe. Anyway, he must be coming up to fifty. You did not try to do cycling tricks at fifty. Val's smile deepened contentedly, because apparently you could and you did.

He said, 'Listen, Alice, I want to ask you something. I want you to do something for me.' He pedalled ahead of her and said over his shoulder, 'It's in the nature of an experiment. What do you say?'

They were in sight of the church. Alice could see Mrs Hyde's sunhat bobbing between the raspberry canes in the vicarage garden. She said, 'How can I say anything until I know what it is?' She pulled in by a five-barred gate. 'Stop a minute. I can see Ditcher Harris on the other side of this field. Just wait until he goes into the next one, otherwise when we cycle past he'll want to talk and he doesn't know when to stop.'

Val got off his bike and wheeled it back. The smell of the cut grass was overpowering. He propped his bike against the hedge and climbed on to the gate next to her.

He said, 'Now?'

She nodded. 'Now. Otherwise Mum will make you stay to tea and there won't be another chance.'

His contentment deepened further. Tea. Doffie Pettiford. Maybe Duggie Marsden. 'Right, I'll go straight to the point. No embarrassment – well, we'll ignore the embarrassment.'

Alice's eyes flickered; she knew he was referring to her frigidity.

Val said abruptly, 'I couldn't do it, either. Intercourse. You know you mentioned the gypsies? Yes, I used to go to their camp. The gypsy men took me there. Not the girls. Do you understand?'

She was aghast, but she nodded, then qualified the nod. 'I know what you mean. But no, I don't actually *understand*. You – was it like Oscar Wilde?'

He smiled wryly. 'No. I was never in love with any of them. But I imagined there would be some kind of – of fellowship. In reality, I simply felt dreadful. Degraded and – I was looking for something, Alice. Something that was not an abstract idea. Something real. I think I must have deliberately degraded myself. But I'm not sure any more. It didn't work. That's all I know – it didn't work. So then I thought that sexual love wasn't for me.'

He thought of Hattie; it had worked for him then. He could make it work for Alice.

She was some time thinking about it, then managed a rueful smile. 'So we're in the same boat. Is that what you mean?'

'Yes. I think we could help each other.'

She said quickly, 'I could never do . . . *it* . . . with you, Val!'

'Not as an experiment? With rules and conditions? In a controlled situation – venue – understanding – everything?'

'What on earth are you talking about?'

'Being in a special place.' He took a deep breath. 'I've found somewhere – a magic place. No one else knows of it.' He nearly told her that Hester had named it the gingerbread house, then stopped himself. This place must be special to Alice, she must think it was their secret. He said, 'It's a railway coach. I think it must have been put there years ago, probably before the first war. I kept my ear to the ground when I was at Leadon. I think your aunt might have used it as a changing room. There's a pool almost on the doorstep, and apparently she used to swim there.'

He had succeeded in turning the sordidness into romance.

Alice said, 'Val, how marvellous! Where is it?'

'Not far from Leadon. Right in the thickest part of the forest. Secret.' He sought other words that would entrance her.

She whispered, 'Hattie told me once that her mother used to swim in a pool in the woods. It might be the same one.'

'Yes, that's what I thought.' He watched her; she was looking inwards now, visualizing the unknown aunt who was so mysterious she was almost a legend, swimming in one of the bottomless pools of the forest. He said softly, 'What about it, Alice?'

She smiled slightly. 'Oh Val, I'd love to see it.' She looked sharply at him, and he thought that she had suddenly seen through the whole seduction. But all she said was, 'But don't say a word to Mum. They're always cagey about Aunt Mitzie. She wasn't married when she had Hattie, you see, and then she died. That's why Gran and Gramps brought Hattie up.'

'There was some local talk,' he said cautiously. Surely she knew it was the most open secret ever?

She said, 'When? When shall we go? Let's go on Bank Holiday Monday, shall we? Will your mother mind?'

'Of course not. What about yours?'

'Dad will be home. They can have a row in private for once.'

He was shocked at her tone and at her disclosure. Everyone knew that Doffie and Ted Pettiford were as much in love as ever. It was

332

difficult to imagine them rowing. But, after all, they were only human.

He cycled behind her, smiling all the time. She called back over her shoulder; little bits of news about the office and the village. When they passed the vicarage, she stood on her pedals and called out, 'This is Hester's brother! He's coming to tea!' And Mrs Hyde waved at him.

Poor little Alice Pettiford. She did not realize that already she was halfway to being seduced. But as she got off her bike, showing her thigh, he stopped smiling. Perhaps it was poor Valentine Ryecroft.

Twenty-Five

Doffie was not pleased to see Valentine Ryecroft, especially with Alice. She smiled briefly and told them she had just enough potatoes for two, and only two lamb chops.

Alice said, 'Val can have mine, Mum. I'm not up to a meat dinner in this weather. There are some eggs – I'll boil an egg.' She kissed her mother on the cheek, closing the subject. 'Val's got a new bike. Unfortunately I had to teach him how to ride it.'

Before last Christmas –, before the tennis party – Doffie would have enjoyed this kind of banter. She said, 'I'll have the egg. Look, I've already dished up. Please sit down and eat it.'

Alice recognized that tone and knew she had better not argue. She also understood suddenly how that kind of self-sacrifice must annoy her father. The terrible row that had precipitated Alice's departure from school and employment with the railways had been about food and self-sacrifice. Poor old Dad. On the other hand, the glass jug of mint sauce sat in the middle of the dining table, smelling delicious; and she'd had an egg sandwich at the milk bar at lunchtime

334

and simply could not face another egg. She sat down and after a small hesitation, which showed he too knew he was not welcome, Val took his place opposite her.

'How is your mother?' Doffie asked politely, bringing in her boiled egg and bread and butter. 'I had her letter and kind invitation. I will definitely call next week. It's absolutely years – literally – since we last saw each other.'

'Yes.' Tentatively Val began on his chop. Alice was already halfway through hers. 'She has always thought a lot of you, Aunt Doffie. It would do her good to have some company.'

'I take it you are on earlies?' Doffie's tone was non-judgemental, but it still told him that he should be eating a meal with his mother, not with the Pettifords. Val understood what she meant.

'I had ordered the bike and Mother was keen for me to get it and have a spin.'

'Which you jolly well did!' commented Alice, picking up her chop and gnawing it defiantly.

Val laughed, but then went on soberly, 'She isn't well, actually, Aunt Doffie. She doesn't go out now, not even to the cathedral.' He looked sideways at the woman who was nearly as old as his mother but still had health and an enormous vitality. 'I don't quite know what to do. I thought – arrogantly, I suppose – that when Father went and I arrived, everything would be fine. But it's not.'

No one commented on this. Val knew suddenly that Hattie had told Aunt Doffie that he had fathered Edmund. They finished eating; Doffie turned her eggshell upside-down and said, 'Don't bother with the honorary aunt any more, Val. Call me plain Doffie.'

It was an olive branch, they all knew it.

Val said, 'Thank you, plain Doffie.'

They laughed together, gratefully. Doffie knew she had to make the best of things. And Val knew he must speak to Hattie, make sure of his suspicions, and if they were correct extract a promise from her never to tell another living soul. And then – maybe – he should talk to Doffie. But later, much later, depending on what happened when he showed Alice the gingerbread house. Meanwhile, he eked out his gravy with a large slice of bread and, like Doffie, made the best of things.

Joe's nurse was called Wang Lu, although he called her Louise. When his demob papers came through in May, she broke her normal reserve and told him she would miss him very much. He smiled; he managed to smile now and then.

'Probably not for a while, though.' He folded the papers into their envelope; it meant nothing now. He knew he must make plans, decide where he was going to live. These kind of thoughts were exhausting. 'I have to wait for transport. The Navy aren't going to send a flagship out specially for me!' He tried to make little jokes now and then, but she did not understand them. He said suddenly, 'There's nothing for me at home. I wish I could stay here for the rest of my life.'

'Do not speak like that, Joseff. Everything will work out. You will see.' She was going off duty and leaned down quickly to peck his cheek. The complicated starched arrangement of her cap grazed his forehead. 'The treatment will finish very soon and your spirits will return. That I promise.'

He stared after her, momentarily surprised,

then relapsed into his usual state of despair. Alice had never replied to his letter; he had not wanted her to do so, but had she sent him a furious diatribe, or a forgiving note, or something about his mother ... However, nothing at all was probably best.

News arrived in July of a troop carrier which would put in at the end of the month; there would be a berth for him. He showed the letter to Louise. She read it carefully, several times. When she looked up, her face was tight with determination, her almond eyes almost scooped under her cap, her tiny nose rigid. She put the letter with its embossed OHMS crest flat on the bed and kept her hand upon it.

'Joseff, I have a suggestion. Please listen until the end.' She waited; he nodded without much interest. She went on slowly and carefully. 'I am good nurse. Excellent nurse. I can earn living, look after you, always.' He frowned slightly. 'Yes. I know this is against the male ... er ... habit, in your country. That does not matter. What matters is that you need me. And I need you.' She withdrew her hand from the letter and moved away from the bed. 'I ask you to marry me, Joseff. There is nothing for me here, no family, no friends. All killed. If I am wife to you, I can come with you to England. Yes?' She did not wait for his reply; she had already asked all those kinds of questions, she had got all her answers. 'It is the only way for me. The only way.' She folded her hands. 'That is all, Joseff. Now you speak.'

He knew he should react in some way: he should feel honoured, flattered, appalled, embarrassed – something. He felt nothing.

'I do not know what to say, Louise. I have no home. I cannot go back to Cheltenham. I can never work for the railways again. How should we manage?'

'I have said. I can be nurse in England. I will tell you what to do, Joseff. Just as here. I will find somewhere to live. I will tell you when to go to bed, when to get up. Just as here.'

'Marriage is not like that in England, Louise.'

'Nor here. But we make our own marriage. Yes?' She took another step back, physically removing pressure on him. 'Joseff, I ask for my own sake. Because here is nothing for me. You would be giving me life. So I give you whatever I can. I cook for you and find house and clean—'

'Stop! It's no good. I cannot do it, Louise. I am sorry. I must be able to give you something. And I cannot.'

She spread her hands. 'That is all. Forgive me. I should not have asked.'

She turned and immediately left him. He had an uncomfortable feeling she might be weeping.

He did not see her through that long afternoon. On the verandah the other men played cards and smoked as usual. They had long ago given up asking him to join them. He stayed on his bed, beneath the slowly rotating ceiling fan, and let his thoughts drift along their familiar route: the oil stove called Fido, the cellar, the filing cabinets in the oriel window – and Alice Pettiford.

When supper came round – more rice – Louise still did not appear. Joe missed her. She always settled him first, sponging him with ice-cold water, making sure he had everything he needed for the night. The other men did not get such attention; they were capable of using the heads, taking baths, sorting out their own requirements. But then so was he. That was the trouble; so was he. And without Louise . . . without Louise . . .

Four days later, he told her that he had thought a great deal about her suggestion, and that if she was still keen . . .

They were married four days before HMS *Plymouth* berthed at Singapore.

Hattie said, 'Darling, you're so dreadfully boring when you carp. Yes, that *is* what you are doing, sweetie. Carping. I have told you that I trust Doffie completely. That is why I might have mentioned—'

'For God's sake, Hattie! You did not *mention* anything! You told her. You *told* Doffie that Edmund is my child!'

'I had to tell someone and I couldn't tell you—'

'I knew already!'

'Quite.' Hattie sat back as if she had won the argument. They were in the garden; the deckchair sagged perilously close to the ground beneath her weight. The hot weather continued and she was bored. Valentine's sudden arrival and his anger with her provided a welcome diversion. She smiled at him and put her hand over his. 'Darling, would you like to go upstairs? Percy is at work and Enid is looking after Edmund.'

He stared at her incredulously. 'You are practically giving birth and all you can think of is—'

'Don't say it, darling. It sounds coarse. We're above that. We've got something so special, so wonderful—'

'So wonderful that you couldn't wait to tell Doffie all about it!'

'I would trust Doffie with my soul. Can I say more?'

'No, please don't. You've said enough.' He sighed deeply. 'I trust Doffie with my soul, too. But . . . what about Alice?'

'She will never tell Alice,' Hattie said definitely.

He spoke slowly, as if to a child. 'Hattie, I hope to marry Alice one day.'

She crowed with delight. 'I knew it! I said as much to Doffie not long ago! It would be ideal, Val! Oh, do please ask her. It might snap her out of the doldrums she's in because of Joe.' She squeezed his arm urgently. 'Do it soon, Val. He's probably on the way home right now. And once he's on the scene again, she won't look at anyone else.'

'Thanks very much, Hattie dear.' He glanced at her; against the sun she looked all abdomen. He shook his head helplessly. 'I've never known any-one quite so self-centred as you. Can't you see that the only way Doffie will break a promise – betray what you confided to her – is if the promise threatens her daughter? Next question: do you think – looking at it from Doffie's point of view – I am the ideal husband for said daughter?'

Hattie gazed up at him. The sun illuminated his hair like an aureole; he was squinting against it, which made his eyes . . . well, quite piercing. She suddenly envied Alice.

She said thoughtfully, 'I see what you mean. You'll have to work quite hard, won't you?' She laughed, kissed her fingers and put them against his lips. 'She's worth it, Val. And you can do it.'

As he wobbled down Leckhampton hill on his new bike, Val felt confident that he could indeed 'do it'. He wondered how he put up with Hattie; she was incorrigible. He supposed this new baby was Percy's. He scraped into top gear and coasted along the Shurdington Road and through Brockworth into Gloucester. It took him forty minutes; he could have done it in less on his old bike. But already he was fond of this one. Alice had ridden it. And had showed him how.

The Bank Holiday arrived. Alice pretended to herself that she had forgotten all about their plan; she had not seen Val in the office, and when Toby had come in to her cubby hole for coffee, she had asked whether there were any messages for her. 'No.' He stared. 'Has that Dennis got his legs under your table? We tossed for you and I won!'

'Oh grow up, Toby!' she said, irritated. But in a way, the lack of a message was a message in itself; Val could not have been serious. Which was just as well; she had done a lot of thinking about his secret house and pool. It would be too much of a coincidence if it was the place where Rose Adair's mother had spent her honeymoon, yet if it was – she could not risk it. Or could she? Would it somehow make the whole stupid 'experiment' all right?

Then two things happened. Firstly, Dad was not on the train on Friday evening. Secondly, on Monday morning Uncle Duggie turned up in his car, with a message from Dad that he couldn't even get home for the Bank Holiday itself. And so he had come instead, to take them out. Doffie looked strange. Almost frightened.

Alice said, 'I'm ever so sorry, Uncle Duggie. I'm expecting Valentine Ryecroft.'

Doffie definitely looked frightened. 'You didn't say anything.'

'Well, I thought we would meet at the station. We're going to Leadon. He hasn't said a word, but in case he turns up –'

'We'll wait with you. We could run you to Leadon, actually.'

Uncle Duggie said, 'That would be nice. Long time since I paddled in the river.'

So they waited, and sure enough Valentine turned up half an hour later on his bicycle. He immediately agreed to leave his bike there until later, and be driven to Leadon. He eyed Doffie. 'Ted all right?' he asked.

'So far as I know,' Doffie said shortly.

'Good.'

Val sat in front with Duggie, and as all the windows were down it was impossible to hear what he was saying. Duggie pulled up right outside Seth's cottage, dropped them off and drove on. Doffie did not have time to protest; she did not even have time to change seats and sit next to Duggie. Alice and Val could hear her voice as the car drove off. 'What – where are we going, Dug – I thought you said—' And then they were gone in a cloud of dust.

Val said comfortably, as if nothing whatsoever was untoward, 'Mrs Seth has put us together a picnic. She's up at the Hall, I'm afraid, so you won't meet her. But she sent her best wishes.'

He opened the unlocked door, collected a green hessian bag and was out and off up the lane as if any delay might change her mind.

Alice was, in fact, on the point of doing so. Everything had gone completely wrong. Mum and Duggie Marsden. Dad – where on earth was Dad? As for this ridiculous experiment, she could not remember what they had agreed. Surely she hadn't said she would ... experiment ... completely? It had been a bit of a joke: the new bike and Mum being strangely unwelcoming. Perhaps Mum had guessed? But how could she?

She said, 'Actually, I'm not sure about this.'

'Then do it for my sake, Alice.' Val's voice was unyielding and he increased his pace so that she had to skip a few steps to keep up.

'I meant about Mum and Duggie Marsden – together – you know.'

'No,' he said tersely.

'Well, Dad sending a message by him like that. Mum won't like it one bit. And then practically throwing them together—'

Val laughed. 'Think of his feet, Alice! Fear no more.'

'They don't actually smell. Not when he's with Mum. He loves her, you see.'

He did not stop, but turned and stared at her disbelievingly. 'I've faced the fact that you are an incurable romantic. That's why you're going to fall in love with ... where we're going. But Doffie Pettiford and Duggie Marsden? Are you mad?'

Alice said miserably, 'They were going out together. Before Dad. Before me too, of course. He took her to a tea dance and Dad was there. She forgot him, but he never forgot her.'

Val was not surprised. Who could forget the golden Doffie? Even his own father could remember meeting her for the first time, and admitted – as a joke, of course – that the reason he had fallen for his own wife was because she was another Dorothy. He said, 'Stop worrying about your mother, Alice. She is still in love with your father and Duggie knows it.'

'But he also knows that there might come a time when that might not matter.' Alice spoke in a very small voice. 'Think of us and what we are planning.'

Val said no more, veering off to the right and ploughing through the heavy summer under-growth as if his life depended on it. He did not look round, but he knew that she was still there. She was much nimbler than Hester had been; after all, she was used to scrambling around the countryside. He wondered whether she felt like him, almost drugged by the heavy scent of the head-high bracken, excited, frightened . . . terrified.

Eventually, they broke through into the clear-ing, where the still black pool reflected the railway coach to perfection. He waited, not looking at her, wanting an entirely free opinion. But he could never have hoped for her to say what she did, and in such a tone of hushed awe.

'Yes. This is the place.'

He closed his eyes gratefully, then opened them and looked round at her.

'It is, isn't it? Absolutely the place. If it won't work here, it won't work anywhere.'

She turned and looked at him, at first as if he were a stranger, then with a kind of glorious recognition. She said, 'Oh Val. You don't know, do you? But this is so much more than coincidence. This is fate, or destiny, or whatever you want to call it. Of course it will work here.' Her face split into a smile. 'Dearest Val, let's swim.'

She began to undress almost frantically and after a split-second he joined her. This was, after all, to be no cautious and unwilling seduction scene. This was as easy as it had been with Hattie; and yet so different.

For Alice, everything became instinctive. She was certain this was the place where Joe's mother had been conceived; Rose had called it the Pumpkin Coach; a magic place, where anything might happen. It was a sort of carte blanche to do . . . anything. And she knew the magic started in the water, because it was also the place Aunt Mitzie had used. A magic pool. As she walked into the water, it seemed the perfect solution to the terrible problem of her frigidity. The hideous embarrassment of watching Val unbutton his trousers, the shock of seeing him naked . . . that was over in the most natural way, because she was naked too. They shouted with cold and held their hands aloft, laughing, unwilling to surrender to that total immersion. At exactly the same moment, they leaned forward and took off like otters through the dark water. Then there was silence while they crossed to the other side, turned on their backs and glided back. In the centre of the coal-coloured pool, Alice trod water and waited for him to come to her. Beneath the surface they explored each other with gentle hands. Alice reached across and kissed him, and suddenly he was on fire. He swam to the slippery grass of the bank with her in the curve of one arm; her legs trailing between his, her mouth constantly kissing his shoulder, his neck, his chin.

He carried her out of reach of the water and knelt above her, looking down.

'Is this all right, Alice?' he whispered, frightened now that he would spoil everything.

She drew him to her; her eyes were intensely blue, glazed with water, unseeing. She knew that there would be no merging of their souls; she did not even look at him for long. This was different; this was entirely physical, she had left her soul somewhere else. There was no pain; very soon there was total delight. She felt like a flower opening to the sun. She held him close, wrapping her legs around him until at last they both collapsed, exhausted.

And then, as they lay side by side, she wept at last for Joe Adair and Alice Pettiford. As if they were dead.

Later, when Alice laid the picnic out properly on the little table in the coach, she wanted to talk.

'It's not just sexual intercourse that is intimate, is it?' she asked rhetorically, putting one of Mrs Seth's enamel mugs on to a chipped saucer she found in a cupboard. 'I mean, when we dressed each other – you fiddling with the buttons on my dress and me trying to do up your trousers – that was intimate. They talk about intimate relations and they don't mean that sort of thing. But that's what it is, isn't it? Isn't it, Val?'

He smiled at her. 'It depends on what you mean by intimacy. When we do it again, we'll *un*dress each other. That might be even more intimate.'

For a moment she looked almost disappointed. 'Oh Val, we can't do it again. You only do experiments once.'

'Oh no you don't. You have to make sure. We'll probably have to do it today and tomorrow and the day after—'

She was laughing but firm. 'Stop right there! It was successful. That's all we need to know!'

'Had it been *un*successful, it would have stopped there. But the fact that it was successful means that it won't stop – not till death us do part.'

She was startled. Then suddenly sober. 'Val, I don't think you should talk like that. I'm eighteen.'

He smiled again; he felt drunk with power. He remembered his father telling him scornfully that he was queer, and his smile escalated into a laugh of triumph. 'Eat your sandwich and drink your tea. I forgive you for being eighteen. I am just thankful you are not eight or eighty, because I rather think I would feel exactly the same about you.'

He did not think she could resist him. When she made it clear that she was determined, he wanted to hold her down and force her.

'Alice, I know it will be all right. If you just let me—' He reached for the buttons on her dress and she slapped at his hand, suddenly embarrassed. It was the embarrassment that told her the magic time had finished.

'Val, don't you see? Surely you see? It's like Cinderella – I have to go back now. No – *now!*' She held him off. 'Listen – you could see what it was like. Before. It happened. It was God telling us that we were all right. Whole. Normal. It's not like that any more.'

'God? What has God got to do with anything?'

347

He was furious. He wanted to call her the dreadful names he had heard in the gypsy camp.

'Oh, I might have known you were agnostic!'

'I am not agnostic. I am atheist. I see you, I see me. Where is God?'

Alice suddenly felt near tears. It had been perfect and he was ruining it. 'How can you look around you at this beautiful place – the way we were brought here today for a special purpose. History repeating itself. How can you not see that *this* – *this* is God!'

His eyes were hard as he stared at her. 'Do you want to go home?'

'We haven't finished our picnic.'

He said again, 'Do you want to go home?'

She nodded. 'Yes. Let's go home. Before everything is spoiled.'

He went on staring at her, but she would not meet his gaze again. He turned from her impatiently and began to shove the remaining bread and cheese back into the green bag. And then they left.

Twenty-Six

Alice and Valentine came home on the train. No other arrangements had been made; Doffie was certain that she and Duggie had been going to meet them at Leadon, but when the last train pulled out and they still hadn't turned up, she accepted the fact that they must have gone on ahead.

At Gloucester, Valentine hailed a taxi and he and Alice drove in style to Lypiatt Bottom where, after an attempt to kiss Alice's cheek, he said goodnight and cycled off into the evening. He knew he should have apologized and admitted that his experiment was ridiculous from the outset. Body and mind were one, or should be one – and they had been for him. That was the trouble. How could he admit to Alice that because he loved her he had wanted to make love to her? It would be an admission that he had tricked her. She still loved Joe Adair.

As the thought came into his mind, he realized what he had done. He stopped his bike, thinking for a moment that he was going to be sick. But there was no easy riddance to this. He sat on his saddle, his face tilted to the sky – stars were out, although the darkness was still to come. Alice would have loved it, but neither of them had noticed because they were too full of . . . guilt. Plain, old-fashioned guilt.

He started to pedal, but the gears slipped and he almost fell off. Then he recovered, back-pedalled, fitted the cog carefully into the chain and went on, slowly and carefully, into Gloucester.

Alice could not analyse her own guilt. She did what she always did in times of trouble and got on with things, in this case making supper for her mother. There was cold beef from the day before and some cold potatoes too. Probably not enough if Uncle Duggie stayed, and she did not doubt that he would stay. She got out the mincer, clamped it on to the table and began to make a cottage pie. When that was in the oven, she went upstairs and lit the pilot light on the gas geyser, then ran a shallow bath. It was while she was washing herself with great care that she started to cry. She indulged herself for a few minutes and then scrubbed her face fiercely and got out of the bath. Halfway down the stairs, her guilt at last found voice. She paused at the landing window, where a plaster dog had been displayed since she won it at Barton Fair when she was four years old. She picked it up and held it, then put it down again and spoke very loudly.

'Joe, I'm sorry. Oh my dearest, I am so sorry.'

She stared out of the window and wished she could crank away at a handle and wind time back again. But if you had to re-live events exactly the way they had happened before, what was the point of that? She tried to find a time – a day, an hour, a moment – when the whole future course of events could have been changed. There was none. She felt that it would have been better if they had never met; if she had stayed at school and not taken the post in the General Office. They had loved each other too much. Or not enough.

She could smell the cottage pie and went on down the stairs, clutching her dressing gown to her. It was almost dark; ten o'clock.

They arrived at half past. Uncle Duggie did not come in and Mum did not stay to wave him off. She came in through the back door, her eyes wide and frightened. Alice knew immediately that she and Uncle Duggie had had – that hateful word – sexual intercourse.

'When I saw the lights – so thankful. We waited for you – Dug said no arrangements had been made but I thought – assumed . . .'

Alice did not look at her. Perhaps because of Val's crazy experiment, she no longer felt any animosity towards her mother. They – her mother and Uncle Duggie – could have been making love at exactly the same time as she and Valentine.

She said gently, 'We caught the five-thirty and Val treated us to a taxi. I made a cottage pie, in case Uncle Duggie stayed for supper.'

Doffie sat down abruptly on a kitchen chair. 'No. He had to get home. It's been a long day.'

'Yes.' Alice took two plates from the grill. 'It has rather.'

Her mother was silent, looking up, knowing too. She said, 'But . . . you're all right?'

'Yes, of course. Val wanted to show me a pool. And an old railway carriage.'

'Bracewell's Pool, I expect,' said Doffie.

'Where Mitzie used to swim?'

'So they say. Before my time.'

Alice opened the hatch and put the cottage pie through. 'Let's go and eat this, Mum. And then go to bed.'

She wished that they could talk about what had happened, console one another in some way. She wished they could go to bed and lie in each other's arms and her mother could tell her stories. And she could tell stories too.

She smiled across the table. After all, that was exactly what they were doing.

As soon as Val unlocked the front door and manoeuvred his bike into the narrow hallway, he knew that his father had been in the house; was perhaps still there. He could smell him: a slightly damp and sour smell.

His mother's voice sang out, 'In the sitting room, darling.' So Val knew he wasn't still there. Even so . . .

They had started to use the sitting room soon after Reggie's departure for Newport. The grate was much bigger than the one in the dining room and there was a chaise longue by the window where Dorothy could lie in the afternoons and 'watch the world go by', as she put it. Although it was August she had lit a small fire and was sitting close to it. She smiled apologetically.

'I know it's stifling, Val. I felt sort of shivery. Open the window if you like.'

He was sweating from the cycle ride, but shook his head. 'We had a swim. I'm quite chilly.'

She smiled and he saw yet again how thin she had become. He drew up a chair opposite hers and told her about the outing.

'I'm glad you took Alice home in a taxi, dear. That was thoughtful.'

'Selfish too, Ma. My bike was out there, remember!'

'Do you *care* for Alice Pettiford, Val?'

He took a deep breath and let it go, considering her question seriously. Then he said unequivocally, 'Yes.'

She asked no more questions, but looked content. It was Val himself who could not leave it there.

'Trouble is, Ma, she does not care for me. She is still in love with Joseph Adair – you remember Hester and Father talking about him? He was the junior in Father's office.'

'Oh yes, I remember well. I have nothing much to occupy my mind, Val, except books and newspapers. But real life . . . I remember most of what you tell me. And when Doffie called she spoke of Joseph Adair and his poor mother.'

'Quite.' Val sighed again. 'They are both objects of a great deal of sympathy.'

'Sympathy and pity run close, Val. You would not want that.'

He grinned at her. 'You are a wise woman, Dorothy Ryecroft! But I rather think Alice and Joe were beyond sympathy and pity. They were on a higher plane, perhaps.'

'That sounds wonderful. But we have to live in this world, Val. You knew that when you left Oxford. You felt you were becoming completely cerebral, didn't you?'

He stared at her. All the time, that was exactly what he had felt, and he had not found the simple words himself to explain it. He leaned over further, as if he would kneel and take her in his arms. Then he smiled wryly. 'Enough of that, Ma. Have you had some supper?'

'No. I hoped I could have it with you. Would you like boiled eggs?' She started to get up, but fell back in her chair. He leapt up and held her there.

'I will do them, Mother dear! And I'll bring in the trolley and we'll eat in front of the fire. How does that sound?' Already he was planning how he would turn his eggshell upside-down like Doffie to make her smile. And then he saw that she was in pain. 'What is it? Tell me, Mamma.' He had called her that as a small boy.

Dorothy clutched her knee and said, 'Must have twisted my leg. Something silly.'

Val lifted her skirt unceremoniously, ignoring her protests. Her stocking was ripped and there was a gash at the side of her knee. His mouth tightened; he did not ask for an explanation, but fetched water and disinfectant and some lint. She tried half-heartedly to protest; he took no notice, pulling off her shoe and then the stocking, washing the gash carefully and wrapping it in lint.

She was near tears. 'Oh Val, you are so kind, my dear. And – I know this will please you – so practical!'

Val sat on the floor and held her leg straight, then bent it. 'Yes, that does please me. Does that hurt – the truth now!'

'No, nothing is broken. I fell in the kitchen. I was going to see to it myself. Must have fallen asleep.'

He put her foot in his lap and cradled her leg.

'He was here. I knew it when I came in. His smell hangs about the place.'

She said nothing, but her head dropped as he had seen it do so often before.

'If only I'd been here, Ma.'

'It was my own fault, Val. I shouldn't have lit the fire. Sheer extravagance.'

'I paid for the coal, remember?'

'It's still his house, my dear. He pays the rent.'

'We'll get it put in my name, Ma. Or better still, we'll look for something we can buy.' His mind leapt ahead. 'I can afford a mortgage. And I know someone who will lend me enough money for a deposit.' Hattie would get it for him from Percy. He was sure of it.

But his mother would have none of it. 'He could not stop you, of course, Val. If that is what you want. But he would not let me go with you.'

'He could not stop you, Ma!'

'Darling, you always forget. He is my husband and I am his wife. I made a vow before God that—'

Val put her foot on the rug and stood up. 'I hate him,' he said levelly. 'One day—'

'Stop it, my dear. No good ever comes from hate, believe me.'

He stared down at her incredulously. 'You cannot tell me you love him, Ma. Not after everything he has done to all of us. I suppose he lugged you upstairs as well?'

'*Val!*'

'I'm sorry – I'm sorry, Ma. Forgive me.' He turned away, terrified he might weep. When he went into the kitchen to boil eggs and make tea, he could hold back the tears no longer. But worse

355

even than the hatred he felt for his father was the fear that he was like him. His clever manipulation to seduce Alice seemed little different from his father's insistence on his conjugal rights. Experiment, indeed! He put the cruet on the trolley and tried to slice the bread wafer-thin. He hated himself almost as much as – perhaps more than – he hated his father.

Much later, when he was in bed, with the sash pulled up so that he could put his pillow on the window ledge outside, he thought about what Alice had labelled so baldly 'sexual intercourse'. His mother obviously submitted to it, but any enjoyment was clearly for his father only. Hattie enjoyed it; that was also obvious – but for Hattie it had nothing spiritual about it at all. Ted and Doffie were probably the only people he knew who conjoined at all levels, physical, emotional and spiritual. Then it occurred to him that there was a likelihood, a strong likelihood, that Doffie and Dugdale Marsden had indulged in it that very afternoon. He wanted to weep again. So much copulation; so little love.

The next day, they all went back to work. Doffie found she could smile at the customers, wrap their purchases, ring up the money on the cash register and wave to Alice as she went up to the milk bar for her sandwich at one o'clock.

Valentine was on early turn in the Control Office, and took over Jack Palmer's seat and telephone with a feeling of relief. There had been an accident on the Andoversford line: a goods train had been derailed by a cow on the line; the engineer and gangers were on site and the line was being cleared for passenger traffic. He spent an hour marshalling and re-routing another train to take the coal wagons on. There was hardly time to remember another railway coach, stabled by a dark pool . . .

Alice overslept. Doffie had already left by the time she got up. She made a fresh pot of tea and stared out of the kitchen window. She too barely thought of the Pumpkin Coach; her thoughts were all of Joe Adair. She had imagined that she had banished him for ever. She had not.

Then history repeated itself. The sound of a car engine sent her to the door; it was Percy in his mother's Lagonda.

'If I stop her I can't start her again!' he called through the window. 'It's another boy! Yesterday! They're both fine! Tell your mother . . .' And he was gone, the dignified old car bucketing helplessly down the lane. Alice grabbed her bike and cycled alongside it, asking questions, sending messages, feeling so much better it was amazing. Trust Hattie to burst into all the guilt and bring happiness.

On her way back up the lane she was accosted by Mrs Mearment.

'What is it? When? How are they?'

Alice stopped and told her. Then, mischievously, she said, 'You'll never guess what they're going to call him.'

'What?' said Mrs Mearment, all ready with one of her laughs.

'Persival. Spelt with an 's' so that it's a bit different from Percy's!'

'On my dear Lord!' Mrs Mearment was spluttering helplessly. 'Gives you something else to think about, doesn't it?'

For a moment, Alice thought Mrs Mearment must know all about the happenings of yesterday. Then she realized that she was talking about the boredom of life at Lypiatt Bottom.

Twenty-Seven

The summer term at Bristol ended, to all intents and purposes, at the very beginning of July. Hester had decided to spend the first month of the holidays in Provence with her professor, Richard Tibbolt, his wife Hermione, their twins Tobias and Evadne and their nanny. Richard told Hermione that he found Hester Ryecroft completely unspoilt, 'a true innocent', he called her.

Hermione had heard that before. 'You would like to introduce her to new experiences, new countries,' she said, nodding judiciously.

'Absolutely!' He congratulated her with a kiss. 'And I thought – if you are painting, darling, she could probably help with the twins now and then.'

Hermione smiled. They understood each other so well. 'I take it she has no money? So she will be grateful for such an opportunity?'

'Absolutely!' His smile was complicit. 'She is grateful for everything. She may have had a rotten time at home. I'm not sure.'

Hermione laughed. 'You will have a marvellous time finding out!' she told him. 'I've seen you reading up on Freud. Now you're hoping her father or her brother raped her, and you can sort it all out for her!'

He said seriously, 'I could help, I'm sure of it.'

'Oh, so am I, darling.'

Richard imagined them all in the villa over-looking Bertrand's vineyard; it was a halcyon place and he adored filling it with people: friends, students . . . always a student. He and Hester Ryecroft would be sitting alone, probably on one of the surrounding hills. Hermione would be putting Evadne to bed – she was the one who made the fuss – Tobias would already be asleep. Hester Ryecroft would suddenly open up. 'I am frightened of men. You are the only one . . .' And he would look into her eyes and say, 'Tell me everything. Start from the beginning, when you were a small girl . . .' And when she had finished, he would say, 'Thank you, Hester. I feel honoured – privileged . . . You should cry. Let the tears wash it all away. Hang on to me, my dearest . . .'

Hermione brought him back to the present with a jolt. 'Richard, there's Nanny calling. It's your turn to cope with Evadne. I did it last night.'

He trooped upstairs, nursed Evadne, sang to her and stayed with her till she fell asleep. He was excellent with children. At the same time, he thought of Hester Ryecroft with her peculiar photographic memory and long, dark hair, and her strange, prissy ways which he would soothe away just as he was soothing Evadne now.

Downstairs, Nanny said to Hermione, 'He's a wonderful father, isn't he? So good with Evadne.'

Hermione nodded. She told Nanny about the first-year student who would be coming with them to the Provençal villa. 'It's part of her education, Nanny, so we must make spaces for that. But she will also help with the twins. She can walk them to the village sometimes, if you need something.' It sounded fair; Hermione was a fair woman. She knew that Richard needed this Hester Ryecroft as much as Hester obviously needed him. And Hermione needed day after long day with her easel set up in the town square, opposite the well. Last year she had started on a series of paintings depicting village life in Provence, but she had not got far because the twins had been teething and Nanny had been called home for a family funeral.

This year would be different. She narrowed her eyes, visualizing the leathery faces of the two old men who leaned closer each year across a chess board. And the boules players . . .

In France, Hester's ingrained prudishness seemed to melt with the sun. Richard wooed her with a direct passion that reminded her of Romeo with Juliet. She felt no guilt when he made love to her among the vines. She assumed that it sealed their relationship. Perhaps not marriage immediately; divorce was still considered disgraceful and to be cited as co-respondent was unthinkable. But she was innocent enough to think that Richard wanted to leave Hermione and the twins and live with her. And under the Provençal sun, that seemed a possibility. When he came to her room every night for that first week, it became a certainty to her.

However, he was completely honest with her.

'Darling girl – I love you, but they are my family. I am welded to them. You must see that.'

'Well, of course . . . of course I do. But we have spent the last week together – every night – and Hermione must know and has made no objection. So naturally—' Hester began to cry. She had cried a great deal at first; Richard had encouraged it. But it had begun to be a habit, and he was beginning to find it tiresome.

He said, 'Sweetheart, do stop. I am not turning you out – in fact, we can go on seeing each other for the next two years. It will be wonderful. Absolutely wonderful.'

'But –' Hester looked up through tear-drowned eyes. 'I would be – I would be your – *mistress!*'

'Doesn't that sound absolutely wonderful to you, my angel? I would be your lover, your mentor, your inspiration –'

She went on weeping, and after trying to soothe her as he did Evadne, he gave up and said she really must stop all this snivelling otherwise it would get on Hermione's nerves.

That did it for Hester. If Hermione's nerves mattered more to Richard than Hester's happiness, then she knew that it was simply hopeless.

She had to stay on with them until the end of the month, because she had no money for the train and ferry home, but she was hardly seen at the villa. She had taken a couple of Virginia Woolf's novels with her, and she would put one in each of the big poacher pockets in her dirndl skirt and walk until she was exhausted, then sit down and read them. She became as slim as a sylph. What was more, she stopped memorizing what she was reading; the books were not on any exam syllabus that she knew about. Instead she read them over and over again until they seemed to become part of her body as well as her mind. She thought she understood why Virginia Woolf had ended her life. One of the neighbours in the village had a swimming pool, and Hester got in the shallow end one day and walked until the water closed over her head. But she was a good swimmer and she bobbed to the surface quite easily. Richard, watching from the edge, called out, 'I think you are meant to carry heavy weights.' He smiled down at her, a smile totally without sarcasm, a quizzical smile that said he still understood. She still loved him, but at that moment, with her waterlogged clothes pulling her down, she resolved to make him pay for all of this.

Miss Plant picked her up from Richard's tall house in Clifton; Hester almost cried at the sight of the familiar, austere face. Miss Plant said, 'How was it, my dear? Were you a glorified nurse for the children?'

'No.' How could she ever, ever tell anyone what her role had been? She said quickly, 'How did you know when we would arrive? It's so good of you! Hermione – Richard's wife – said she would drive me home tomorrow, but this is so much better!'

Miss Plant glanced at her, noting the general use of forenames. Professor Tibbolt was the youngest lecturer at the University, but he was still more than twice Hester's age.

She put the car in gear and they coasted down to the suspension bridge. Nobody had come outside to wave Hester off.

'The wonderful railway network, my dear. Apparently your brother is in the Control Office and has immediate information about arrivals and departures of trains in and out of Bristol Temple Meads. He had already asked me whether I would meet you – I was only too delighted, of course – and I was waiting at the other end of my telephone for news of the midday train from Paddington. I then set forth!' She laughed and Hester laughed too, suddenly almost carefree. Dear Val. Still keeping a brotherly eye on her. She smiled through the window; at one time the thought of Val caring for her would have clutched at her heart. Now it did not. Perhaps Richard had given her something, after all. What did clutch at her heart was Miss Plant. This wonderful woman, even now winding down the window so that the hay-scented air from the Downs blew through the car, she must care too. And that did matter.

The Pettifords did not go to Weston-super-Mare that year. Ted was home for the first week of his fortnight's annual leave, but the second week was going to be spent at Plymouth in the Lara marshalling yards. His initial enthusiasm for the vast scheme was on the wane. It had evolved into a census exercise, which did not really interest him. His lists and graphs were complete and he now wanted to come home. Yet he sensed something was not right there either. Doffie had made plans for outings and picnics, but when Alice said she would prefer to stay at home, Doffie said quietly, 'Oh. Well, it doesn't matter then.'

Ted cycled into town, ostensibly to buy a new siphon for the lavatory cistern, but really to go into the office and get his bearings. Helena Webster – Maybury now, of course – was back to fill in for Alice, and offered him coffee.

'I'm really enjoying this,' she confided. 'It's as if I've never been away.'

Ted made a face over the rim of his coffee cup. 'Strange you say that. I'm exactly the opposite. Feel I've lost my place.'

'You should have insisted on your full holiday and gone to Weston. You need to be reminded of your proper routine.'

Helena listened while he explained about the census and the optimum time for taking it. Then she said thoughtfully, 'Listen, why don't you fix up a bed and breakfast down there? For the family. You could find an excuse for investigating the branch lines, couldn't you? Fowey and Looe and Newquay and Falmouth . . . Go down to the Staff Office now and get Mr Marsden to make you out passes for all of those. Alice would just love it – like exploring new territory. Go on – do it now!'

Ted went, half suspecting that Helena wanted rid of him. He could not shake off the feeling of being displaced. He had had business at Waterloo about six months ago and had watched the train from Dover disgorge its first load of displaced persons. Poles, Czechs, Ukrainians . . . nowhere to go, no family, nothing. He shook himself, remembering he certainly had a family.

Valentine Ryecroft was doing the first month of three in the Staff Office. He probably felt displaced too – no desk, a corner of the table occupied by the typist. Duggie obviously did not know what to do with him. Ted almost seized him, taking him over to the oriel window and pushing aside the files so that they could sit down.

'How goes the mapping?' He did not know

what else to call it. It was more than a graph, much more than a list of stock.

Val looked rueful. 'It's sort of . . . fallen into abeyance,' he admitted. 'My mother's not too well and with Hester home . . . finding time . . . it was easier when I was on turns.'

'Yes, I see that.' Ted jerked his head towards Duggie, who was on the phone, talking through his pipe in a series of shouts, which meant he was on the Bus Line and had to concentrate against the buzzing and constant interruptions. 'Won't Duggie – sorry, Mr Marsden – let you get on with it here?'

'He might do, I suppose.' Val did not seem enthusiastic. 'Truth of it is, Uncle Ted – sorry, sir – I've backed myself into a corner. The way I see it, there will be no use for marshalling yards in the future. Wagons will not be returned, they will wait for their return load. Looking at our main users, clients, whatever we call them, there are always sidings available for loading. Why not for making up the trains? And there's something else.'

'What?' Ted was frowning, seeing no good reason to disagree with Val's findings, yet certain that he was wrong. 'And for goodness' sake, drop the "sir" and the "uncle". Call me Ted.'

Val could not believe his luck. He had been scheming to get himself into the Pettiford family, and now Ted had bypassed his schemes and invited him in. Did not even seem to realize it was something special. Val cringed, wondering how Ted would feel if he knew about Hattie and Alice. Oh God, Alice. She avoided him like the plague.

Ted said, 'Well?'

Val blinked and came back to the present. A

draught from the door wafted Duggie's peculiar smell across the office; Duggie puffed vigorously on his pipe.

'Hester was invited to a tea party, with the staff at school – her English mistress in particular.'

'Miss Plant.' Ted nodded.

'Yes. Fräulein Schmidt was also there. It's a courtesy title only, as you probably know. Her husband was interned during the War. They have visited Germany to look for his relatives. He met other scientists. They talked, naturally. These scientists were in a race with ours – splitting the atom – they tried to hasten calculations. They have constructed a machine which can do sums—'

'A comptometer. Yes. Very useful for the monthly returns!' Ted grinned at Val. Duggie had told him about the returns from Leadon Markham.

Val grinned back dutifully. 'It will be more than that, Ted. It works on the binary system. Two answers, yes and no. By working down – or up – from that, it will be able to deal with all our clerking, all our calculations.'

'I've heard of something similar in America. But machines can never replace human beings, Val. Engines need drivers and maintenance staff, the permanent way needs gangers, engineers.'

'Yes, I am sure you are right.' Val looked through the window and wondered what Alice was doing now. He said, 'I think I've simply lost some of my impetus. That's all it is.'

Ted said, 'If there was some way that what you have done could be transferred to a picture – like a cinematic picture, constantly moving – so that every signalman in the country, every controller, would know exactly where the stock was at any given time, would be able to watch it moving, rolling . . .'

Val looked at him sharply. People underrated Ted Pettiford. They thought of him as a good solid railwayman without much imagination.

Val said slowly, 'Sir, excuse me asking a personal question, but what are you doing here?'

'I thought I told you to call me Ted? I'm on my way to Lister's. We need a new siphon. Flush won't work. I'm going to make enquiries about going on the main drainage, too. That cesspit is from the Middle Ages.'

'But . . . this is the office. It's not Lister's.'

Ted shrugged. 'On the way. And I wanted to see people.'

Val knew quite suddenly that Ted Pettiford no longer belonged to the magic circle that had always seemed to glow like a nimbus around the Pettiford family. Maybe there never had been a nimbus at all.

Ted said, 'But you're right. I must get on. Doffie and Alice will be waiting for me. We're going to see Hattie, I think. This afternoon. New baby and everything.'

'Right.'

Duggie put down the phone and looked at Ted. He seemed almost nervous. Ted stood up. 'We must have a drink some time, Dug.' He glanced at Val. 'What's this young man doing here? You should have him out, looking at what the staff do . . .' He grinned wickedly. 'Monthly returns, that sort of thing.'

Dug grinned too. But Ted's suggestion was a

life-saver. He did not know what to do with Valentine Ryecroft. He could give him an all-stations pass and send him out – to observe, or something. Meanwhile, Ted was after some passes himself. Dug took the forms from his desk drawer. So, they were going to Plymouth, were they? All of them. Doffie included. He refilled his fountain pen, drew on his pipe and began to write.

It was Edmund's birthday at the end of the month and Hattie was planning his first party. Enid had made a friend in Montpelier Gardens who also liked to listen to the band, and she was bringing her niece who was just a little older than Edmund.

'They get on like a house on fire!' Hattie told Alice and Doffie. 'So we're going to have jelly and potted beef and sponge fingers. Then we're going to play Blind Man's Buff.'

'But Edmund can't walk yet!' Doffie protested.

'Enid will carry him. It'll be fun. Come and see. We're fetching Gran, so we might as well pick you up at the same time.'

She found racquets and balls and chivvied Ted and Doffie on to the tennis court. 'You come with me, Alice darling. I've got to feed Persival, and you can cuddle Edmund and try to calm him down before bedtime.' She went through the house, Edmund on one hip, organizing on the way. 'Enid, sweetie, can you rustle up a high tea for all of us? Salad, hard-boiled eggs, perhaps. Lots of bread and that real butter my grand-mother sent up? And make a pudding, darling. Percy will be absolutely ravenous.' She swung round to Alice. 'He always is after work. Well, he always is, anyway!' She laughed and Alice felt her face warm. But she had to admire Hattie: Enid looked happy, old Mrs Westbrook was napping in the lounge and opened her eyes just long enough to kiss Edmund as Hattie bent over her.

'I don't know how you do it all,' Alice said as Hattie settled herself on the bed with the tiny Persival at her breast. 'You look so well, so full of energy.'

'I'm just good at spreading sweetness and light!' Hattie giggled helplessly. 'It's just a question of getting everyone to pull together, darling. I keep telling them I couldn't manage without them. They love to feel needed. Nanna doesn't do a thing, of course, but I have convinced her that Edmund won't go to sleep without her night-night kiss. Enid's a rotten housekeeper, but if I tell her what to do she can manage it and she's wonderful with Edmund, absolutely adores him. And Percy reads to Nanna. And looks after me.' She joggled Persival, who seemed to be going to sleep. Alice watched Edmund, who was crawling enquiringly around the bedroom. There was a long silence; contented on Hattie's side, not so much on Alice's.

Hattie said suddenly, 'My God – I know what it is.'

Alice looked up. 'What what is? Should I put Edmund in the bath?'

'In a minute. Why aren't you playing with him?'

'He's happy enough.'

'That's not the point. A few weeks ago you would have been on your hands and knees with him. You're not with him. You're not with any of us. You're . . . detached. I thought it was a family thing – you're all the same. Darling Doffie

370

worried sick. Ted pushed out. And you grieving for your first love.' She moved Persival from one side to the other. She looked back at Alice, who was very still. 'Now I know why.' She paused for effect, and then announced, 'You're pregnant!'

Alice's eyes opened wide. 'Don't be absurd, Hattie! You've got an absolutely one-track mind!'

'I've inherited it from Gran. She knows things like that. Hasn't she said anything to you?'

Alice said levelly, 'Stop talking like this, Hattie.'

But there was no stopping her. 'You must have guessed. When was your last period? Is it Val? Yes, it must be Val because there's no one else. Does he know – what does he say?' She paused for breath, then said, 'Face up to it, Alice! When did you and Val sleep together?'

Edmund was homing in to an electric socket. Alice got up and picked him up, then took him to the window to distract him. She said dully, 'Bank Holiday Monday. And we didn't sleep together.'

Hattie laughed. 'I bet!' She tried to clap her hands, squashing Persival's ear in the process. He released her nipple and cried. 'Oh shut up, Persi darling. And I'll have to think of something else to call you, otherwise it's going to be too confusing for words. What do you think, Alice?'

'I suppose so.' She turned. 'I'll take Edmund to the bathroom and get him ready.' She paused by the door. 'It's too soon. But if you're right . . . what can I do?'

Hattie leaned forward and kissed Persival's downy head. He was so like his father it was ridiculous. She said quietly, 'Marry Val. And love him and your baby with all your heart.'

'Oh . . . Hattie.'

'I mean it. Forget Joe. He wasn't for you – we don't know why and we never shall. Forget him and give all that love to Val.' She smiled. 'And I've just thought what I can call this tiny Persival. Perry. What do you think of that, Alice? A sparkling wine. Perry.'

Alice said again, 'Oh, Hattie.' And then went to the bathroom.

Much later, when Ted was talking to Percy about his latest job title, which was Chief Commercial Representative for the Gloucester Division of British Railways, Doffie was cuddling the newly named Perry, Enid was washing up and Mrs Westbrook – Nanna – had gone to bed, Alice cornered Hattie in the conservatory.

She said without prevarication, 'If you're right, do you know how I can have a miscarriage?'

Hattie was genuinely shocked. 'You mean an *abortion*? God, Alice, you can't do that, darling! This is . . . part of you! Like your leg or your arm. And anyway, it's like a – a holy *trust*! You can't do that!'

Alice could have said she was a fine one to talk; she could have told Hattie that God would understand. All she said was, 'You don't know anyone, then?'

'There used to be a woman at Leadon, but she's dead long ago.' Hattie continued sternly, 'Listen, I don't believe in rules and regulations, Alice. But the only rule that matters really is that we continue to keep the human race going. Tell Val. Go and see him tomorrow before this trip to Plymouth.'

Alice almost laughed. 'He is the very last person – not even the last –'

Hattie looked interested. 'Did he force you, darling?'

'Of course not!' Alice turned away. 'I wish I had never told you! It can't be right, anyway!' She turned back angrily, just in time to see Hattie picking up one of the precious nectarines. 'Don't you dare tell a soul! Promise me – promise me now!'

'Of course I won't.' Hattie tightened her lips and looked exactly like Gran. 'Anyway, everyone will know soon enough!'

Alice left without another word and Hattie took a bite from the nectarine.

Twenty-Eight

That autumn proved to be the wettest for ten years. Plymouth had its share and more, and the reconstruction which went forward, rain or no rain, made the place look completely derelict. While Ted was at Lara doing his census, Doffie and Alice investigated the Cornish branch lines, trudged around Barbican and the Hoe and haunted the temporary shops in the bombed city centre, buying secondhand clothes that Mrs Mearment might be able to alter into something wearable for work. After breakfast, they were not allowed back to their rooms until six in the evening, so they were almost always damp and dripping. Ted would join them at six and they would spend an hour getting ready, then go for a meal somewhere. The most successful evening was spent in the cinema, eating fish and chips furtively beneath their tumble of macs. The worst one was when Ted took them to Saltash, where there were fine views over the ancient city. Alice realized that she could look down on Devonport Docks where, just over a year ago, she had said goodbye to Joe. She had to go back on to the platform quickly and lock herself in one of the toilets. She was violently sick.

When they got back home, Alice still was not well and Doffie was frantic with worry. 'Surely you've noticed how thin she is?' she asked Ted angrily, as if it were his fault. 'I realize it's a great honour to be given Miss Warner's job ahead of girls who are older than she is, but it's also a great strain!'

Alice tried to tell her mother that the job was much easier than the one she had had in the General Office, but it came to her quite suddenly that she would not have it much longer anyway. Helena had been allowed to fill in for Alice while she was on holiday, but that was simply because she was the Superintendent's wife . . . special circumstances. She rolled her head into her pillow and began to weep. Who on earth had ever heard of a girl with an illegitimate baby working on the railway? Working anywhere. She would be put into a home for wayward women; Dad would be disgraced and Mum would be heartbroken.

By mid-afternoon the next day, Alice felt better. She told her parents that she wanted to see Hester before she went back to Bristol, and she cycled slowly into Gloucester and propped her bicycle against the kerb in Deanery Close. Valentine had gone for a walk. Hester, who had seen her coming, said, 'He wanted me to go too, but I had enough walking at the beginning of the summer to last me for a long time. Will you have some tea?'

'I'm in rather a hurry. I was hoping for a quick word with Val. Something to do with work,' Alice said.

Hester's face fell. 'Oh, Alice. What a shame. Mother is so fond of you, you know.' Alice fidgeted on the doormat. Hester said reluctantly, 'Well, he's going to the cathedral later. Mr Makin will be practising.' Alice turned to go and Hester called after her, 'Come back with him, Alice, and have some tea.' But Alice was already pedalling down Deanery Close.

He was not there; she walked up and down the north and south aisles. Evensong was not until five-thirty and it was only four. Mr Makin was talking to one of the vergers. Tourists roamed aimlessly about. She wanted to weep, to run, to wail helplessly. Instead, she stood by one of the enormous pillars, which was striped purple and yellow by sunlight filtering through the stained glass, and tried to think of God.

Just as she was about to give up in despair, a voice said, 'If it's too difficult, Alice, talk to me instead.'

She held her breath. It was Gramps's voice. How she remembered it after all these years she had no idea, but she knew that it was him.

She did not think, let alone articulate, a solitary word, yet he spoke as if she had. 'It's all right, my little chick. Of course you're unhappy. That doesn't matter. Remember the pool and the wonderful swim? You're treading water now. That's all.'

He could see into the past. Inside her head she said, 'Can you see the future too?'

He chuckled. 'Of course not. Free will and all that. I know your intentions. But you could change them at any time. Now. Tomorrow. That doesn't matter, so long as you remember to love. You might have put love aside, chick. Don't.'

At that moment, she saw Val come in through the west door. He walked slowly up the central aisle, then insinuated himself into one of the pews and sat quietly waiting for Mr Makin to begin.

Gramps had gone. A figment of her imagination, no longer there.

Alice moved away from the pillar and joined Valentine. He was surprised, even shocked, but he smiled and whispered that he was waiting to hear 'old Makin' practise. She nodded. 'Hester told me. I need to see you.'

His smile widened with pleasure and he reached out for her; she avoided his hand and sat down abruptly. She felt giddy and sick, and wondered whether she might be going to faint.

'How long have we got?' she asked.

'As long as you like.'

Alice was silent, her eyes burning into the wood of the pew in front of them. 'Alice, is it about what happened at—'

'The Pumpkin Coach.'

'Yes, the Pumpkin Coach. Because if it is, shall we agree to pretend it never happened?'

'It happened.'

'Oh yes.' He leaned back and did not try to touch her again. 'But if it is going to spoil our friendship, then I wish it had not.'

'So do I.' She was silent again, but he waited patiently. Eventually, she took a huge breath and blurted, 'Val, will you marry me? Please don't ask any questions. Just say yes or no.'

He said instantly, his whole body still and tense, 'Yes.' His hands clenched on his lap in a conscious effort not to grab her. 'A thousand times, yes.'

She was silent again, looking at her own hands, wondering if this was the right thing. At last she whispered, 'This isn't for my sake. Or for yours. It's for our families.' Somewhere inside her head, a voice whispered like an echo: 'What about the young 'un? What about for his sake?' But she added nothing.

Valentine said carefully, 'Even so . . . it would make me very happy.'

She gave him a glance, then looked back at her hands. 'I have to be honest, Val. It will not make me happy.' He made a sound, immediately stifled. She said quickly, 'It won't make me any *un*happier . . . and it will be better in a lot of ways. But you must know that I still love Joe.' She waited and then added, 'I'm sorry, Val. I have to say it. Do you want to change your mind?'

'No.' The answer was immediate. 'But why?' As he spoke, he suddenly knew the answer, and though she shrank from him, he unclenched his fists and took both her hands in his. 'Oh – oh, my dear.' He bent his head to meet her gaze. 'My dearest Alice, how wonderful.'

She knew she should be grateful; she knew there were men who would walk away from her. She tried to withdraw her hands, but he gripped them so tightly it hurt.

He said quickly, 'Listen, it will be all right. I promise you that. Unless you want . . . anything else, it can be a marriage of convenience.' Val paused then rushed on, trying to think on his feet. 'We've got to remember that we're friends. We've always been friends. We can make it work.' She was silent again, still gently pulling at her hands.

He swallowed, trying desperately to think clearly. 'Mother will be so pleased, Alice. This is what she has wanted—'

'She mustn't know!' Alice raised her voice slightly. 'She must not know about the baby. Please, Val – no one must know.'

'Alice, eventually—'

'They come early sometimes. Especially first ones. Edmund arrived before he was supposed to.' She looked up at him in agony. 'I've only missed two periods. If we can do it quickly, surely no one need know?'

'I'll see to it, my dear. Please don't worry any more. Try to be a tiny bit happy about this. For the baby's sake. Please, Alice. It will be all right, you'll see. I'm not going to let you drown – just tread water for a while. Let me take over.'

She looked up at him sharply. Then she put her hands to her face, which meant his hands came too. He thought she was kissing his knuckles. He bent his head and tried to control his tears.

When at last they stood up and walked down the aisle, Mr Makin pressed one of the foot pedals and one solitary key. The cathedral reverberated to the sound. Alice grabbed Val's arm and hung on to it, her eyes closed against nausea until they were out in the air again. She stood still and breathed deeply, her eyes still closed.

For the second time, Val ordered a taxi and took her home, with her bike precariously half in, half out of the boot. Ted was home, Doffie was not: he was grateful for that. Ted was laying a fire in the grate. 'Gets chilly in the evenings,' he said.

Val took a deep breath and asked Ted for Alice's hand in marriage. He used those words. Ted was flabbergasted. He liked Val; he respected him, too. But Alice ... Doffie had told him she was still in love with young Joe Adair. He stayed crouched in front of the grate and looked up at Alice.

'Is this what you want, love?'

She nodded. Then she knelt by him and put her arms around his shoulders. 'Thank you, Dad,' she whispered.

'Hang on – I haven't agreed to anything,' he protested. 'Your mother—'

'She will if you will.'

He looked at them helplessly. 'If it's what you want.'

Doffie made no objection except to tighten her lips, which convinced Alice that she knew about the baby. She wondered whether Hattie had told her; there was no one she could really trust – not Joe, not Mum, probably not Dad. Maybe Val ... yes, she thought she could trust Val. That was important in a marriage. At least they had that.

Alice Patience Pettiford married Valentine Stanley Ryecroft on November 7th 1948. It was the bride's birthday; she was nineteen. The Reverend Geoffrey Hyde performed the ceremony; Mrs Hyde, Doffie Pettiford and Helena Maybury between them made the church into a bower of chrysanthemums, late roses and every kind of berried evergreen they could find. It was a good year for berries, the rowan trees especially. Ditcher Harris reckoned it meant a hard winter. Afterwards, in the church hall where cider was plentiful and free, Topper Morgan laughed at such old wives' tales and Ditcher offered to 'eddycate him proper'. Outside in the church-yard, if necessary. But just then, Dugdale Marsden tapped a spoon against a glass to announce that the bride's father was about to make a speech.

Ted stood up reluctantly. He did not want to make any speeches, that was obvious, but his reluctance went much deeper than that. He had no objection to Val Ryecroft, and though Alice was still in her teens, many of the women he knew had married younger than she. Val would go a long way, so there would always be a wage coming in; and for now they had the house in Deanery Close, where they could look after Dorothy Ryecroft and Alice would be near the shops. But Doffie had told him about the baby, and he knew his little girl had had no real choice. The child had forced her into all this, removed her from what had looked like a promising career and stuck her in a back street with her new in-laws. He thanked God that Valentine had taken over the tenancy agreement from Reggie, but Reggie was here today, welcoming his new daughter, as he told one and all. Reggie was still married to Dorothy, was still Valentine's father.

Ted could have borne all this cheerfully enough, but for one thing. He was almost certain that Alice wanted none of it. Almost certain that if it weren't for the baby she would not be marrying Valentine Ryecroft. He knew, with a kind of sinking recognition, that she was still in love with Joe Adair.

He cleared his throat. 'Ladies, gentlemen and babies,' he began; that raised a smile straight away. Alice had begged him to 'keep it light'. He ran through all the thank-yous except for the matron of honour and the bridesmaid, who would be toasted by Val's best man, Toby. He said the bit about not losing a daughter but gaining a son. Suddenly, he inserted an extra line here: 'A son, moreover, of whom I am already proud, and who I am certain will lead our new nationalized railways to the forefront of world transport systems.' Ted had no idea where that came from, but he was certain it was true. Alice looked pleased and Val's usually pale face turned pink. Dorothy Ryecroft was smiling her gentle smile and Reggie, damn him, was smirking smugly. Ted went back to Alice then, hoping he could get across what he wanted to say. He called her the light of the family. 'She is and has been loved by us all – my father in his time, and my mother still.' He looked over at Gran, who wore a new toque with a half-veil so that no one could see whether she was weeping or not. 'My niece, Harriet, and all her new family, especially her two sons.' Doffie Pettiford shot Val a look at that point. He felt it like a red-hot needle between the eyes. He knew that the only reason she had raised no objection to the marriage was because of Alice's baby. Did she think he had engineered the seduction to that end? He pressed his lips together, knowing that he was quite capable of such a thing. In fact, hadn't that been the way it started out? All he could remember now was Alice swimming by his side, her fair hair dark with water like an otter's. He glanced at her now; already he knew her so well and her look of controlled despair tore at him. Hattie had said to him, 'Once the baby is born she will be all right. I promise you. That's the way it works.' It had worked like that for Hattie. He was not at all sure it would work in the same way for Alice.

They had decided against a honeymoon, but Hester had arranged for them to have a night at the Bluebird Hotel in Bristol, which was a short walk from the docks and the museum. Val wanted to know how she could afford such a treat. She said insouciantly, 'My prof is paying for it. Isn't that marvellous of him? He said he would like to take a room at the Bluebird and I asked him how he knew that my brother was marrying my friend – he just looked bewildered, so I must have said something – can't remember. Anyway, I told him it was the best present I could possibly give to you both and he said he was really delighted.'

Val looked at her sharply, and then, seeing she was sincere, laughed delightedly. 'Oh Sis, how marvellous. Thank you so much. I wish I could ask you to come with us, but—'

She blushed and he saw again how beautiful she was. He almost felt sorry for Richard Tibbolt. Perhaps, as in his own case, the seducer had become the seduced.

Percy drove the three of them to Bristol that evening. It was two days after Guy Fawkes' night and a few late bonfires marked villages such as Berkeley and Olveston. They dropped Hester at the University and then drove across to College Green. Alice began to breathe quickly. Val knew by now what that meant.

'Shall I put the window down, Alice?' She nodded, and he wound it down desperately. But the fresh air was not enough to ward off her nausea, and Percy drew up just in time. Val half lifted her out and held her while she 'heaved her heart up', as Gran would have put it.

'The sooner we get you tucked up in bed, the

better,' he said, keeping his arm round her when they got back into the car. Percy barked a knowing laugh.

At any other time, the two of them would have been awestruck by the old-fashioned luxury of the hotel. Pre-War silvered blue wallpaper still lined the walls of the enormous reception room and a chandelier hung from its corniced ceiling. Their room was similar, the carpet a little rubbed in the middle, but still more comfort than either of them had ever seen. The porter put their cases on the luggage table and departed. Val tried the doors; they had their own bathroom.

'Would you like a bath, Alice? I'll run it for you. There are salts here. Oh, and some talcum. This is special, isn't it?'

She was standing by the bed, her head down. 'Perhaps tomorrow. I'll just wash and . . .' She began to breathe fast again and made for the door. She shut it firmly in his face and he stood there helplessly, hearing her vomiting yet again. He knew nothing of pregnancy and wished that Hattie were here.

The door stayed shut for a long time. There were sounds from the other side, he did not dare try to identify them. Then a moan: despair made manifest. He put his cheek against the wood. 'Alice, are you all right? Let me help you. Please.'

Silence. Then her voice, the frightful controlled voice that he hated: 'Come in, Val. The door's not locked.'

She was sitting on the lavatory. Her underwear – stockings, knickers, underskirt – was all over the floor, covered in blood. He pulled up short and gave an exclamation of horror.

She said levelly, 'Yes. I'm so sorry, Val. You need not have married me after all, by the looks of things.'

He was aghast. 'Alice, what is happening?'

'Isn't it obvious? I've just lost the baby.'

'Christ! Are you still bleeding? I'll get a doctor – that phone in the hall – I'll call reception and—'

'No need. I was three months, that's all. It's gone, Val. That's it. It's over.' Her voice became slightly stronger. 'Perhaps I'll have that bath.'

He stared at her, aghast, until she said, 'Could you put in the plug and turn on the tap?'

He obeyed her automatically. He so rarely lost control of a situation that he did not know what else to do. At her command, he took off his jacket and rolled his shirt sleeves up to his shoulders, pulled off her dress and waited while she removed a spencer and brassiere, then lifted her bodily from lavatory seat to bath.

'Thanks, Val. Saves getting everywhere too . . . messy. You know.'

'It's amazing that you know what to do. I haven't done this before.'

'Neither have I,' she came back sharply.

Once in bed, she began to cry and then she could not stop. He held her, at first against her will, but later she clung to him and after a while she sobbed, 'Oh Val, I'm sorry. I'm being so selfish. We have both lost this baby. Haven't we? Oh Val, haven't we?'

He had barely taken in that there had been a baby. And now he had lost it.

He whispered, 'I did not realize that you loved it.'

'Neither did I. Oh Gramps . . . neither did I.'

He held her closer, terrified now that she was going mad. 'There will be others, dearest.'

But she said, suddenly calm, 'No Val. No more. Not again. Not ever.'

Twenty-Nine

Alice went into the cathedral to talk to God. Just in case Dorothy Ryecroft should hear her and think, like Val, that she was going mad. She stood next to the tomb of Edward, who had been so brutally murdered in Berkeley Castle, and thought that surely nothing could shock God after all that had happened through the ages.

She said, 'You see, I'm not grieving. That's what is so terrible. It's me who is shocked, not You. I grieve for Val – and for all the family, although we have never talked about the baby and nobody is mentioning it now. Surely they know? Surely they know it was here and now it isn't? I know nothing else. It's my whole being. I am shocked, horrified, but not full of grief.' She waited. Nothing. No one was about. She had come for fish from Eastgate market and had said, 'I'll be home in time to make the coffee, Mamma. Try to stay in bed – I know it's boring, but when I get back I can sit with you and we can drink coffee and I'll tell you everything I've seen.' Dorothy had smiled and replied, 'I would love that. But it's too much for you, really.' Did she know about the baby but not the miscarriage? Alice had to press her lips together

387

to stop herself from telling her. She wanted people to know. Yet she could say nothing. Dorothy said, 'The Christmas decorations will be going up. Only two weeks to go.'

Dorothy had a new lease of life. Val kept telling Alice this, as if to emphasize her value in the small, impoverished family. Alice knew she was supposed to bring light to Deanery Close. That was her role now. No job, no baby. Light.

Alice leaned against the tomb and closed her eyes against the winter light filtering through the windows and changing to a spectrum of colours. The familiar smells of old wood and incense were quite overpowered by the haddock in her string bag. She really must be mad, coming in here on a winter's morning when no one was about and expecting to make contact with God. Even so, she said, 'God, did You take the baby because You thought I was not fit to be a mother?'

It was the crucial question. There would be no more children, she would live as a married nun. She was not intended to be anything else.

There was a pause; in other circumstances she would have described it as a pregnant pause. God was there. And He was shocked.

Then Gramps's voice was in her head. Angry – with her. 'You know darned well that you are making an accusation there. You've been down this road before. Remember? You *asked* for free will. That means no interference. And you are actually saying that God interfered and took away your child?'

'Gramps, I'm sorry. I'm sorry. I didn't think . . . I am so ashamed. I am the one responsible. I know it. That is what is so dreadful. Don't go, Gramps. Talk to me, please.'

'All right. One more thing. Your baby was a girl. You are grieving for the loss of your daughter. Got that?'

That came as another shock. A girl. A baby girl. Yet it made no real difference. She raised her voice. 'But that's it! I'm *not* grieving! I told you – guilt, shame. No grief. That is what is so awful. It makes me more ashamed and more guilty and—'

'Shut up, Alice. Grief is a prism. Many-sided, with more surfaces even than a prism. Guilt is one side. Shame another. Sadness and regret sometimes get buried beneath the guilt and shame. Remember what your grandmother told you, when she gave you that blackcurrant tea – roll it up, put it aside for now.'

'Do you talk to Gran?'

'No. She'd try to run towards me. And that must not be, yet. She's still got something important to do.'

'What?'

'None of your business.'

'Oh, Gramps, I wish you were here.'

'I am. Silly girl. Go home and make coffee. Dorothy Ryecroft needs you.'

'Oh, Gramps . . .'

But he had gone.

Alice said to Dorothy, 'Blinkhorn's have got all their toys on show. There's a rocking horse and a doll's house. And Fletcher's have got a bike in their window. It's decorated with bells and paper chains.'

Dorothy sipped her coffee appreciatively. Doffie

had popped in yesterday and suggested that she and Hester accompany Val and Alice up to Leckhampton House for Christmas. They were all invited. Doffie was really keen. 'All we'll have to do is to get out of Percy's enormous old car and walk into the house. Then get up after tea and walk out again. You can do it easily, Dorothy. Please say yes!'

Dorothy had smiled at the vivacious and beautiful face so close to her own, and had said simply, 'Yes.'

So once again they were all under Hattie's benevolent dictatorship. Nanna Westbrook was sitting on the old leather sofa which Hattie had insisted on keeping, next to Perry, who was propped up with cushions. Dorothy Ryecroft sat on the other side of him, flushed and handsome in her patrician way. Gran was opposite them in one of the deep armchairs; she was 'resting her eyes', and her lips vibrated visibly and audibly at every outgoing breath. Ted was dispensing drinks at the sideboard, attended closely by Hester. Percy and Val were playing 'growly lions' on the floor with Edmund. Doffie, Enid and Alice were in the kitchen at the stove, the sink and the table respectively. Hattie was also at the table, sitting with a drink in front of her, laughing delightedly at Doffie's irritable accusation that she was 'oversexed'. Enid was bent so low over the sink she was almost standing on her head. She still ached for Valentine Ryecroft, but knew he could never be for her. The postman had brought mistletoe every day for the past week and would never give her the post until she had kissed him. The trouble was that Leckhampton House seemed to be filled with sexual energy, and Enid had caught it like flu. She dipped further into the pile of washing up.

Hattie crowed, 'Over-sexed? Oooh, I like that, Doffie darling. And I think you're right. D'you know, girls, I've always wanted Ted. My own uncle! What do you make of that?'

'For God's sake, Hattie.' Doffie stirred the bread sauce vigorously, her face shining with sweat.

Hattie couldn't stop laughing. '*You* know what I mean, don't you, Enid? You used to get up to some tricks with Percy, didn't you? He's told me all about it, so you can come out of that sink and face up to it!'

'Stop it, Hattie,' Doffie said. She looked over at Enid. 'Don't worry, dear. She's always been like this – it's all talk.'

The words whirled around the kitchen meaninglessly. Alice was rolling sausage meat into small balls and coating each one with beaten egg and breadcrumbs. She was close enough to Enid to see that she was weeping. Hattie was crying too, tears of laughter pouring down her face. Doffie told her off again but she took no notice. Enid pulled her hands out of the sink, put her apron up over her face and fled. Hattie called after her, 'Darling, come back! I'm teasing – you should know me well enough by now!'

But Enid had gone.

Doffie was furious. 'What is the matter with you? You never used to be cruel like this! I simply do not understand . . .' Alice rolled another ball, dipped, coated, set it aside. 'And in front of Alice, too! Sometimes I find you utterly despicable, Hattie Pettiford!'

'Hattie Westbrook, if you don't mind.' But Hattie had stopped laughing. She loved Doffie and was hurt by her comments. 'And Alice is not so backward herself in matters sexual, Doffie! And don't you forget it!'

Doffie switched off the gas beneath the bread sauce and came towards Hattie. Alice thought that she might be going to hit her. She dipped, rolled and set aside two more sausage balls.

Hattie's voice rose in panic. 'Don't you dare, Doffie – it's because I'm pregnant again! I'm pregnant, Doffie! That's all it is!'

Doffie stopped in her tracks. And Alice stopped rolling and stared at her cousin. 'What did you say?' Alice whispered. 'Pregnant? Again? Three babies in two years? And I can't manage one in a whole lifetime! D'you hear this, Gramps? Where are you now? What have you got to say about this? How do I roll this up and set it on one side? Oh Gramps ... Gramps. Please let me die, Gramps. Please ... please ...' She put her hands to her face. They smelled of raw sausage meat and she wanted to retch. But she could not, because she was falling.

Much later, there was a conference in Hattie's bedroom. Percy was there, Doffie, Ted and Gran, Val and Dorothy Ryecroft. Not Hester, not Enid.

Hattie rounded on Val. 'Why didn't you tell us? She's had to go through this alone! We could have helped – we didn't know. When did it happen?'

Val said miserably, 'Our wedding night. In the hotel at Bristol.'

His mother stifled a cry of distress.

Doffie said, 'You poor things.'

Ted came to her and put his arm around

her shoulders. 'Our little girl,' he said. 'Our light.'

And Doffie said, 'I know.'

'What did the doctor say?' asked Val.

'Postnatal something.' Doffie looked enquiringly at Hattie, who said, 'Depression. Postnatal depression.'

Val said, 'Depression? That's nothing. Thank God she's not losing her mind.'

Doffie sobbed. 'What do you think depression is then, Val?'

Ted said, 'That injection—'

'To make her sleep,' Hattie explained. 'It's my fault. My big mouth. If anything happens to that girl—'

Percy said stoutly, 'Nothing is going to happen. She will get better. There will be another baby. Simple.'

They looked at him in surprise. He so rarely spoke at all when Hattie was there to speak for him.

Val seemed not to have heard him. 'It's not your fault, Hattie. It's mine. I should never – anyway, there won't be another baby. We are just friends.'

Everyone looked at him. He said, 'It was once. Just once. She said it would not happen again. And now I believe her.'

Dorothy Ryecroft moaned softly. Doffie put a hand on her shoulder.

At last Gran spoke. 'Leave the wench alone,' she commanded. 'She's got Will to look after her. She doesn't need anyone else at present.'

'Will? Gramps?' Hattie stared. 'You don't actually believe Gramps was there? She called his name in despair, Gran!'

Gran folded her lips. Doffie left Dorothy and

crouched in front of her mother-in-law. 'You don't think she is mad, Gran? You really think Gramps was there for her?'

'He's talked to her before.' Gran unfolded her lips and looked round her scornfully. 'He sent her to me when he left. Don't you remember?'

'Of course I remember.' Doffie remembered that time of anxiety, wondering what the enormous grief would do to a six-year-old child. She remembered pedalling down to the cemetery to be with Alice, expecting to be engulfed in tears, expecting to have to insist on taking her baby back home. But Alice had never asked that ... Alice had stayed until Hattie had returned from school to take her place.

Gran spoke as if to a backward child. 'Well then, it's as clear as day to me. Our Alice is going through a bad time. So Will is there with her. She asked him why he didn't talk to me too. He told her. It is all quite natural. Doctors don't know everything. She is just talking to her grandfather. She isn't going mad.'

They all wanted to believe her. Especially Val. Last week after choral evensong, Mr Makin had come to him and told him that Alice had been talking aloud, standing by the tomb of the murdered king and raising her voice in a kind of agony. Val did not believe in God or an afterlife, but he wanted so much for Alice not to be mad ...

Doffie, crouched before this woman who had never thought her good enough to be Ted's wife, gazed into the rheumy old eyes and smiled slightly. For the first time since Ted had gone away, she thought there was a chance that everything might be all right again. After all, Gramps had welcomed her into the family and had loved her. Hadn't Hattie said so?

She stood up and looked round at Hattie, who had hardly stopped crying since Alice's collapse. 'Come on, darling,' she said. 'Let's get you to bed. If you're pregnant again, we've got to look after you.'

Hattie stood up and flung herself into Doffie's arms. 'I can't bear it when you're cross with me! Alice is going to be all right – Gran's just told us. Come up with me, Doffie. Massage my neck like you did when I was having Perry. Where is Perry? And Edmund? Oh, Percy . . . find the boys and make sure Enid is all right. And Nanna – where is Nanna?' She trailed a hand behind her as Doffie led her out. 'Darlings, I do love you all so much. We're all going to be all right. I promise!'

The three men looked at each other helplessly.

Percy said, 'I'll get the car round. Ted, can you carry Alice? It's not cold.'

'I will carry her,' said Val. He was up the stairs in an instant, as if pursued by demons.

Ted said, 'Thanks, Percy. Sorry about . . . this.'

'Hattie will sort it out,' Percy said confidently, and was gone too.

Ted, Doffie and Gran were all staying at Leckhampton House for the night. Dorothy Ryecroft fumbled in her bag, found a handkerchief and blew her nose. She said to Ted and Gran, 'Please don't worry. Val and I will take care of Alice, and Doffie can pop in after work each day . . .' Her voice trailed away diffidently.

Gran said, 'The best thing Reggie Ryecroft ever did was marry you.'

'Thank you. Thank you, Dorothy,' said Ted.

Dorothy levered herself up and went for her coat. Ted did not follow her; he knelt by his mother. They said nothing for a long time. Then he whispered, 'Dad . . .' and she nodded and said, 'Yes.' She put a hand on his cheek. 'You'd best come home, lad.' He too nodded. She went on, 'And I want to be there. With you.'

He was alarmed. Doffie wouldn't like this.

She said steadily, 'I can't leave it any longer, Ted. I have to talk to Doffie.'

'Why? What?'

'She will take my place, Ted. I see that now. Hattie . . . too much like her mother. And other things too. Doffie, your Doffie – she is the one.'

'I see.' He imagined she was talking about passing on recipes, tips on gardening, collecting kindling, making potions. Doffie would be respectful, perhaps interested – no more. But he nodded yet again. 'All right, Ma. Tomorrow we'll all go back to Lypiatt Bottom.'

She smiled and put her head back. 'I'll stay here tonight in this chair, lad. Tell Hattie, will you?'

'Yes, Ma.'

He kissed her forehead. The skin almost crackled, like paper. She smelled of dust. It was not unpleasant.

Ted stood up. Poor old Doffie. She'd have to give up that job of hers. She would not be seeing so much of Duggie Marsden.

He felt his heart lift.

Thirty

Alice was never sure whether Gramps put aside the free-will thing and took on her burden for a while, or whether Val's careful nursing over the next week and into the New Year brought her back to a normal life. She liked to think it was a combination of the two. Gramps did not speak to her again, but she knew he was very close. She told Gran as much.

'Did I tell you that he says you still have something important to do?'

Gran was still living by the river. Doffie had to work a month's notice in the bookshop and it would take that long for Ted to untangle himself in Crewe and pick up the threads again in Gloucester. Mr Maybury would arrange it, but, as he put it, Ted had to tie up his own loose ends. Neither Ted nor Doffie were particularly optimistic about having Gran to live with them. Doffie said curtly, 'She could live to be a hundred.'

Now Gran stared at her much-loved granddaughter. She had envisaged living with Doffie and Ted and Alice. Alice would have made all the difference.

She said, 'What was that, our Alice? Important, did you say?'

'*He* said that. Gramps.'

'Ah.'

'What is it, Gran? What is this important thing you still have to do?'

Gran mumbled some bread around her gums and Alice thought that was an end to it. Outside, sleet was falling. She thought of getting home to Dorothy – Mamma, as she called her – to the fire in the sitting room and the evening paper open at the Births, Marriages and Deaths. She realized what a haven Dorothy and the house in Deanery Close had become. And Val, of course. Dear Val, who slept in Hester's bed with the door open so that he could hear her call in the night.

Gran said heavily, 'I promised I would open up to Doffie. That's what I've got to do, our Alice. Open my heart to your ma. She hasn't had a mother herself for a long year. Nor a father, either. Gramps tried to be a father to her. I never tried to be a mother. That's what I got to do.'

At one time – not very long ago – this would have made Alice smile. She might even have told Mum and said, 'Run and hide – Gran wants to be a mother to you!' And they would have laughed. But not now.

She cycled home through the gritty snow. Deanery Close was so convenient and it took her only half an hour to reach it from Gran's village. In Gloucester, the lights were on and people were still shopping. Above the house in Deanery Close the cathedral bells rang out as the ringers practised. Alice put her bike in the passage, then went outside to listen and watch the snowflakes whirl. She did not speak to Gramps, not even in her head, but she knew the guilt was beginning to recede, like a tide.

That night, as Gran got out of bed to use her commode, she fell and knocked herself out against the leg of her bed. When the milkman came at six-thirty, scrunching in the deep snow, whistling under his breath, he heard her calling. He got the key from the ledge in the porch and let himself in, made her as comfortable as he could and promised the ambulance would be there in a whip-stitch.

'I haven't slept in my bed for weeks now,' Gran grumbled to anyone who would listen. 'Sleep better in the armchair by the fire. But I felt so well . . . I don't want to go to Westbury. Is that clear, young man?'

The ambulance man told her she was going to the Infirmary in Southgate Street, where they'd see to her broken arm and have her home right away.

A week later, Gran moved into the house in Lypiatt Bottom. Hattie cried and accused Gran of not loving her. Doffie said gently, 'It's the babies, Hattie. Not you. Gran needs peace and quiet.'

'Nanna manages very well! She doesn't mind the babies! She adores them!'

'That's because they belong to her and she cuddles them every day. Gran couldn't cuddle them with her broken arm.'

'Well . . . I shall be down here all the time, whether she likes it or not. She's my gran!'

Doffie said gently, 'Of course she is, darling.

Come when you can. It will be good for you to get out of the house.'

But Hattie rarely visited. She did not want to leave the house where she was queen of all she surveyed. She would have loved to have added Gran to her retinue and organize a whole new life for her, but eventually conceded that perhaps Gran knew best.

After all, it was hard to imagine her orbiting Hattie as all the others did. That night, for the very first time, she pleaded a headache when Percy came to bed. Tenderly, he took Perry from her breast and laid him in his cot. She told him she had not finished feeding the baby; then she told him the baby needed a nappy change; then she reminded him about the headache. It made no difference. She realized, as she surrendered so pleasurably, that Doffie had been right at Christmas. She really was over-sexed.

Ten miles away in Gloucester, Val and Alice were talking about Gran as they got ready for bed. 'Perhaps in the summer we can take her to Leadon. She would like that,' said Alice.

Val nodded at her reflection in the dressing-table mirror. She had not bothered to have her hair cut for some time and she brushed it out now, thankful for its thickness. It was her best asset, after all; her mirrored face looked pale and drawn and the veins in her hands stood out mauve and random.

'Shall I massage your neck, Alice? Would it help you to sleep?'

She had been sleeping well since the start of February, but perhaps it would be ungracious to tell him so. 'Thank you, Val.'

His fingers were gentle across the clavicles, thumbs firm at the back. He watched her in the mirror. She closed her eyes. She would never hold his gaze for long. He travelled up the back of her neck and into her hair. He loved her hair. He loved everything about her. If she had gone completely mad it would have made no difference to his feelings.

He said in a low voice, 'I've never really apologized, Alice. I did not know what I was doing, not really. Destroying something between us. I have been sorry every day since.'

'Please, Val. It was my fault. You know – you must remember – that I instigated what happened.'

'But I actually . . . engineered it. The situation. The experiment.'

'I need not have complied.' It was a strange word to use. It needed explanation. 'It was the place. We had to fulfil the intention of the place. It was a magical place. Joe's grandfather had . . . had engineered it. D'you see? He had had the coach taken there so that he could seduce Joe's grandmother. And she was happy about that. She had told Rose – Joe's mother – how wonderful it was. And then there was Aunt Mitzie, Hattie's mother. She, too, complied. Can you begin to understand? As far as we know, Rose was conceived in that one visit. Maybe Hattie was even conceived there. That's why I called our baby Millie. Mitzie's name was really Millicent.'

His hands were still, laced in her hair. 'A girl? How do you know it was a girl?'

'Gramps told me. It began to get better when I

knew that she was a person. Millie. Millie Ryecroft. D'you see, Val? D'you understand?'

For a moment he was frightened. Old Makin had told him that Alice had talked to herself in the cathedral. But here she was in the mirror, pale and drawn, but not mad in the least. And supposing it were true and Will Pettiford had spoken to his granddaughter and told her . . . about Millie. Millie. He felt a sudden surge of joy that she had named their child. He whispered, 'Oh, yes. Yes, I understand. Millie. Oh, my dearest dear, why didn't you tell me before?'

'I was afraid you would think I was mad.'

'I wouldn't have cared.'

'You might.'

'No.' He loosened his fingers and drew her to her feet. She opened her eyes and looked at him in the mirror. 'Alice, tonight, please let us sleep in the same bed.'

He tried to hold her gaze, but it slid away at his words and her body tensed. He begged like a lovesick schoolboy. 'Please, Alice. Please.'

She made no reply, and eventually he released her and tried to pretend it did not matter. 'I would have provided a lap for you, my dear, that is all.'

She turned. 'What made you say that?'

'What?'

'A lap. You would provide a lap for me. Have you spoken to my mother?'

'Of course not. What are you talking about?'

'I know you talk about me. You are both worried that I am losing my mind.'

'Stop that, Alice! We do not talk about you in that way at all!'

She stared at him wide-eyed. He waited. She went to the bed and climbed in, then moved over to the far side.

'We shall warm each other, after all . . .' Tentatively, he climbed in beside her. She turned her back and he fitted himself around it.

'Can you tell stories, Val?'

'Not really. Only about Theseus. Would you like to hear about him?'

'Yes, please.'

She was asleep in five minutes. After that, he no longer slept in Hester's bed.

Ted was not reinstated into the Control Office until March. Until then, Doffie had had to manage alone and she had done so with ill grace. Alice cycled out on Tuesdays, and would have come oftener except that Doffie forbade it. 'You're doing so well again, love. Try to save yourself when you can.'

'I'm getting like Hattie,' Alice smiled. 'My mother-in-law does the cooking. All I have to do is the shopping.'

'You clean and you do the laundry,' Doffie insisted.

'Actually, Val does a lot of cleaning.' Alice glanced at her mother. 'He is so good.' She took a small breath. 'Sometimes . . . he reminds me of Uncle Duggie.' She blinked and added quickly, 'Apart from the feet, of course!'

Her mother did not smile. There was an uncomfortable little silence. Then Doffie said heavily, 'I've made mistakes, Alice. But you must know – surely you do – that there will never be anyone else for me. Only Dad.'

Alice nodded sadly. 'Yes. I know now, because of . . . well, I just know.' Hadn't she flown into Val's arms when she loved Joe? Would she ever love anyone but Joe? She said, 'I used to think that there were times when you hated each other. And that eventually you would split up. I don't think that any longer.'

'If ever that happens, it will be because Dad wishes it. Not me.' Doffie finished laying a tea tray and handed it to Alice. 'Take it in, darling. She might have dropped off in front of the fire. She is so tired.'

Alice took the tray, but stopped halfway through the door. 'Dad – he doesn't know how to cope sometimes. He feels we leave him out. I mean, apart from Percy he's the only man in the family.'

'Not now. There's Val. He likes Val.'

Alice nodded, surprised. 'Yes, he does. How strange. Perhaps Val will be the – the catalyst. Is that the word I want?' She laughed ruefully. 'I wanted our families cemented together. I wanted you and Dad to stay together. Perhaps it will happen because of Val.'

'Perhaps. Now go on in. Talk to her. I'm going to be fiddling out here.'

Things did not miraculously improve when Ted came home for good. Sometimes his insensitivity or selfishness almost overwhelmed Doffie, who was quick to point out that she had given up her job and her freedom for his mother. He tried to reassure her by telling her that later, once a routine was established, she might be able to go back to the shop for a few hours.

'A part-time shop assistant! Great!' she said.

Frustrated as always by her sharpness, he said, 'But that was what you were. It was no great career. Not like Alice's. She lost such a lot.'

'Thank you again, Ted! If you think that will make it better—'

'Keep your voice down – you'll wake my mother.'

So she took a leaf out of his book and sent him to Coventry for a whole hour. He did not even realize it.

But usually they muddled along all right, and by June had established the routine Ted had hoped for. Doffie forced herself not to resent the woman who had never welcomed her into the family, and Gran made a real effort to be 'no trouble'. It was difficult; her arm still hurt her a great deal and she missed her stewed tea and the spartan conditions in which she had lived all her life. The comfort and warmth offered by the modern house in the country seemed foreign to her, almost decadent. When the warm weather came, Doffie's insistence on open windows, fly-papers, sterilized milk, daily washing . . . she felt it was all a fuss about nothing. But she folded her old lips into her mouth and said nothing. She knew that one day, one day soon, she would have to do more than that. She would have to do what Will wanted her to do. But not yet. After all, it did not matter any more. It was all in the past, and she had learned slowly but inexorably that the past was gone and probably did not matter.

It was in June that things began to happen again. On the first Wednesday of the month, Alice and

Dorothy met Doffie in the Bon Marché and had coffee together, like dozens of other Gloucester housewives. Helena Maybury joined them, but not for long. She was working for Mr Maybury 'on the q.t.', as she put it. Miss Ford from the Train Office was officially Alice's replacement, but she did not know Mr Maybury's little ways. And the coffee pot had disappeared. They laughed together, and Alice remembered her days there without regret. She felt better and she was content. That was enough for now.

After Helena's departure, the three women arranged to go to see *Gone with the Wind* later in the month. Doffie said that Gran had been in the garden at the weekend and had picked some radishes; she sent her love.

'Is it hard work, Mum?'

'Not really. She is just . . . there.'

'Has she said anything yet?'

'Lots of things. Nothing particular. Why? For goodness' sake, tell me if there are any bomb-shells in the offing – I need to prepare!' Doffie laughed, but suddenly the laugh cut off. The lift doors had opened with a clank and two people were stepping out. Dorothy Ryecroft's back pro-vided a perfect screen for the other two women, who clearly saw the man lean over and kiss the small woman. It was Reggie Ryecroft and Enid Westbrook. Doffie looked wildly at Alice, who lowered her eyes quickly.

Dorothy said, 'I don't like surprises either. But it could be some small thing that has nagged at her mind over the years.'

'Yes, probably,' said Doffie. 'I should go. Don't forget *Gone with the Wind*. When Ted is on earlies. Then he can look after Gran while I'm out.'

They left almost immediately. Reggie and Enid were just going into the adjoining dining room; so they were lunching together. Doffie and Alice walked on either side of Dorothy; she didn't see a thing except the iron latticework of the lift ahead of them. She said, 'Oh, I did so enjoy that. D'you know, I used to think women simply wasted their time when they had morning coffee and afternoon tea! What a lot I was missing!'

Alice hugged her arm. 'We need times like it, Mamma. It's when we sort the whole world out.'

'So it is, Alice. So it is.'

The following Sunday, when all the Westbrooks were around the dining table at Leckhampton House eating their Sunday roast, Enid made her announcement. Doffie had not had time to tell Hattie what she had seen in the Bon Marché; in any case, Ted had advised against it. 'We don't want to be mixed up in any of that,' he said dismissively.

Hattie poured mint sauce over her lamb and frowned at Enid. 'What do you mean, you're going? Going where?'

'To live with my lover,' Enid announced, her voice quavering, her eyes darting away from Hattie, away from Percy, away from Nanna.

Hattie started to laugh. 'Your *lover*? Who the hell is your lover, for crying out loud?'

Percy was transfixed. Some man had touched his sister . . . Some other man.

'Someone I love and who loves me. We cannot marry. He is married already.' She tried to sound

407

composed, but her voice wobbled. 'We will be living in Wales. I will let you have my address later.' Her eyes flickered to Percy and away again. 'Perhaps you would drive me to the station, Percy dear? I have a lot of luggage.'

'I will drive you nowhere. You are going nowhere. Keep calm, Mother. I can assure you—'

Enid's voice rose a register. 'I am going today. You cannot stop me. I will get a taxi . . .' She scraped back her chair and made for the telephone in the hall. Percy made to get up too and Hattie put out a restraining hand.

'Steady on, my darling. Let me deal with this. No need for hysterics. Finish your lunch.' She smiled down the table. 'Nanna, will you have some more lamb? And a few peas? There, there, darling. Don't fret. Finish your lunch, then you can have a little nap and everything will look better.'

Nanna said, 'Enid! Of all people! She's always looked after me. She used to look after Percy too, didn't she, darling boy? She's too old for this sort of thing, too old entirely!'

Hattie said, 'Five years younger than you, isn't she, Percy dear?'

Percy looked at her with one eye; the other swivelled helplessly.

Nanna said, 'Go to her, Hattie. Make her see sense. She listens to you.'

Hattie smiled as she stood up and manoeuvred her bulk around the table. She leaned over Percy with difficulty and kissed him. 'Cheer up, darling. You've still got me.'

She went upstairs and into Enid's room without knocking. Enid was crying as she packed. Hattie watched her; in her regulation summer outfit of white blouse and pleated beige skirt she looked unutterably dull. Who on earth would want this?

Enid's weeping escalated. She gasped, 'Stop looking at me, Hattie!'

Hattie said gently, 'Let me do that, darling. Lie on the bed for a few minutes and relax. Now, what about nighties? These are just dreadful, darling. You have to think of this as a honeymoon. You must have some of mine.'

Enid, who had collapsed on the bed in a torrent of tears, lifted a ravaged face. 'What?' she sobbed.

'You can have all the black ones. I shall never get into them again. Your dear brother is determined that I shall spend the rest of my life having babies!'

'Oh Hattie, you are so lucky!'

'Of course I am, darling. Because I know what I want. When I get what I want, I move on.' She stooped over Enid and dried her face with a corner of the sheet. 'Now you are moving on. I shall miss you hideously, darling. But I understand perfectly.'

'Oh, *Hattie*!' Enid sat up and wrapped her arms around her sister-in-law. 'I shall miss you too. But . . . oh, Hattie, it's so wonderful! Like a novel. He can make me do anything – anything. I would die for him, Hattie. Die for him!'

Hattie held her close. 'What is his name? Tell me something about him, so that I can picture the two of you together.'

'He's so like Valentine. I've always loved Valentine Ryecroft, from the very first time he called on you. He used to bring me flowers and chocolates.'

'So that you would say nothing to Percy about his visits,' Hattie murmured.

'Well . . . anyway, I thought there would never be anyone else. And then, when he married Alice Pettiford, I knew there could be someone else. The same colouring, the same blue eyes, the same – the same look.'

'Where did you meet this paragon?' Hattie laughed kindly.

'I told you, at Valentine's wedding.'

Hattie frowned and lifted her head to look into Enid's eyes. 'I cannot recall anyone who looked like Val. Except – oh, Enid! Not Reggie Ryecroft!'

'Hattie, please! Don't turn against me! I know he's older. But so am I. I'm forty-five, you know!'

'I know that.' Hattie dropped her arms and moved away, frowning, thinking. How would a liaison with Enid help Reggie? Did he want to hurt Percy? He hardly knew Percy. And then she saw it; she remembered Reggie taking her on his knee when she was a child, coming to the bank when she was learning . . . She said softly, 'He's trying to get to me.'

'What?' Enid was blearily pushing more clothes into her suitcase.

'Nothing, darling. It's all right. Don't worry.'

Hattie went across the landing and fetched her black nighties, some nylon stockings, French knickers. Then she went downstairs and, while Nanna cuddled Perry and Percy took Edmund down the garden looking for caterpillars, she helped Enid to carry her cases and bags out to the taxi. She waved until it turned off the drive and into Leckhampton Road. Then she turned back, smiling, to face the music. The son and the father.

She could not imagine succumbing to Reggie's charms because he had so few, but it would be interesting to see what happened.

That night, when the caterwauling had finished, she had a private word with Percy.

'Listen, darling. No one could have stopped her leaving. I made it easier for all of us by helping her. She needs this man, whoever he is. It won't last. As soon as I've had the baby, I'll go and see them.' She kissed him, but he turned his head away. 'Percy darling, be sensible. She is your sister. You should understand that she needs sex just as you do.'

'You betrayed our family!'

She gurgled with laughter. 'Did I? Did I really, darling? It sounds so bold and dashing. I thought I was giving Enid a chance of three or four months of happiness. An extended honeymoon. Like we've had for the past three years.'

She put a hand on his chin, turned his face towards her and removed his spectacles. Without them, his eyes looked small and completely crossed. She whispered, 'You have always driven me wild, Percy Westbrook. You still do.'

'Hattie—'

'Shut up, darling.' She kissed him. 'Three months. Let her have the summer with her Svengali.'

'Svengali? Is he a foreigner?'

She laughed into his mouth. 'Oh yes, he is a foreigner.'

There was one more thing that happened during June.

Joe Adair came to Cheltenham to see the

411

solicitor who had dealt with his mother's affairs. In the pocket of his demob suit, he had a letter from his Great Aunt Eve, which confirmed that his mother was illegitimate and that her family had cut her off without a penny. But there was one thing she'd owned. Just one asset she had had and not even known about. And now it was his.

Thirty-One

Louise had managed to get them two rooms in an unfashionable area of Newcastle; it was not far from the QVH, the rapidly expanding hospital on the north side of the city where, after only eight months, she was Sister in charge of the paediatric ward. It was also close to the old technical college which was offering a two-year teacher-training course to ex-servicemen.

At first, Joe was not interested in anything in Newcastle. But by the winter of 1948, the bracing north-easterlies which had stripped the trees outside their rooms and found every crack in the window frames needled him into doing something, and after blocking the draughts with putty, he started taking walks around the Victorian area where they lived. There was something about it; not only charm, but vigour. Newcastle still had one of the biggest ship-building yards in the world, and the sound of hammers was a tom-tom beat inviting movement – energetic movement. Joe realized that he was terribly out of condition; he set himself small goals and gained a sort of satisfaction from achieving them. One November day he took a train to the coast and looked at

Whitley Bay in all its pared-down bleakness. The place suited his mood. The air suited his body. He began the slow process of engaging with a time and a place. In March he said to Louise, 'I like Newcastle. It does not pretend.'

Louise nodded, understanding instantly. She too had fitted in surprisingly well. They had ended up here purely because of the work in the hospital; the other nurses were down-to-earth, friendly enough, but respectful too. They liked her for her hard work and her unobtrusive empathy with sick children. The local shopkeepers smiled at her and called her 'pet', and besides her vegetable and rice dishes, she was now experimenting with Yorkshire puddings. People grumbled about the shortage of food, but for her this land was plentiful. So she nodded and said, 'It is old-fashioned. I like that.'

'How would you know it was old-fashioned?'

'I mean, old-fashioned like in books. Scarves and gloves and fires in the street for cooking the chestnuts ... I saw picture books at home like that.'

Their two rooms had originally been bedrooms in the small house, their kitchen also served as the bathroom, with a tiny cooker on a chest of drawers. They both enjoyed its simplicity, the view of the street from the window. Joe liked it best when Louise was at the hospital and he had the place to himself, but he did not resent her in any way and was always grateful when she cooked their food and sat opposite him with the local news-paper, while he looked at some of the books he had found in the library, which happened to be on the reading list for next year's teaching course.

She said cautiously, 'Have you made application for a place at the college, Joseff?'

He looked up and blinked, as if surprised to find her there. 'I did it last week. They have accepted me. I begin next September.'

'Are you pleased?'

He noted that she did not ask him why he had not told her immediately. He managed a smile. 'I don't know. But I wanted a place, otherwise I would not have tried, would I? So I suppose I am pleased.'

She sighed. 'Aah, Joseff.'

He saw she was disapproving, disappointed, and knew he did not want to disappoint her. 'I like the place. I like the seaside. Tynemouth is old and mysterious, Whitley Bay brash . . . perhaps I will like the course too.'

'You do well.' She finished her rice, every last grain. 'You will get an allowance for this course?'

'A grant. Yes.'

'So you no longer need money?'

He looked up, surprised. 'I suppose not. Perhaps I could pay you back a little, Louise.'

She laughed, shaking her head. She was exquisitely pretty, he registered, and not for the first time.

'No, no. It was the bargain we made. Do you not remember?' She poured a little salt from the shaker she had bought recently. 'We did not think past that bargain, did we? I expect . . . you will want me to find somewhere to live now? And –' she swallowed, 'a divorce starting?'

He was bewildered. 'But why?' Then he thought he understood, and was mildly regretful. 'You have met someone you can love properly? A doctor, perhaps, at the hospital?'

'Oh no. But you . . . you will wish to be free in case there is someone else.'

He was still bewildered. 'There will never be anyone else.' He stared at her, realizing how little she knew of his life. Perhaps it would be a good thing if she knew something.

He said, 'I should tell you – you deserve to know. Then, if you wish to go somewhere . . . on your own . . .' He paused and she waited, holding her breath. And then he told her about Alice.

When he saw her tears, he too wept. She reached across the small card table and held his hands. 'I am sorry, Joseff. So sorry. I will stay always. Or until you tell me to go.'

They slept in the same bed, just as Val and Alice did; but in spite of the cold, they did not allow their bodies to touch and Joe rarely turned towards her.

Spring was miraculous on the north-east coast that year. It was late – Louise thought there would never be a summer here – but when it came it came quickly, almost overnight. The drifts of snowdrops appeared late in the municipal parks and flourished immediately in the watery sunshine and the still, waiting weather. Massed crocuses were next, pushed aside by daffodils, bluebells, tulips. The next month the fair opened at Whitley Bay, and suddenly it was summer. It was wonderful. Louise blossomed with the flowers, smiling at everyone – patients, nurses, people in the street. The butcher let her have a small piece of beef; she made Yorkshire puddings to go with it and they were delicious. Joseff said so.

Joe was reading in the mornings, absorbing information, opinions, educational experiments like a sponge. He felt renewed and refreshed by everything he discovered; for the first time he wanted company, other people with whom he could discuss all these theories about teaching and learning and playing. He began to look forward to September and the start of his two-year course.

In the afternoons he still walked. He walked to every school in Newcastle and watched the playgrounds, the comings and goings of the children, the rhyming games, the football games, the hockey matches. On the way home, he would shop for their evening meal. One day he bought Louise a bunch of daffodils. She blushed a dusky red as she took them.

He smiled slightly. 'I did not know that Chinese people blushed.'

'You think we are so different?'

'More . . . able to cope. Grown-up. Sometimes you make me feel like a child.'

That amused her. She too was learning – to laugh.

At the beginning of June, the letter came from Great Aunt Eve. The Chatterton crest on the envelope made Joe shake slightly. His mother would have gone to pieces at the sight of such an envelope; he stiffened his neck muscles and controlled his hands. When he spread the single sheet on the card table, he saw that his aunt must have been shaking too. Her handwriting was cramped and spasmodic, but easy enough to read.

'Dear Joseph Adair,' it began. Did that mean that she considered him no nephew of hers?

Dear Joseph Adair,

I am addressing this to His Majesty's Forces and hope that it will reach you soon. I was sorry you were too ill to take the compassionate leave due to you at the death of your mother. I hope very much you did not choose to be absent because of any bitterness you may have felt towards her. As you know, I was the one who informed her of her illegitimacy. I was bound to do so. She needed an explanation as to why her mother left her nothing. It was because she had nothing. Your grandmother's marriage was arranged hurriedly by her father; the under-standing being that she would inherit nothing from her own family and certainly nothing from his. She chose not to tell your poor mother of her circumstances; shame held her in thrall. I feel sure now that you are a man, you will understand this and accept it as your lot. However, there is one very small legacy which I feel you should know about, although it is not worth anything. It would seem your grand-mother's paramour (it offends me to write thus but how else can I explain?) bought a railway coach and stabled it within the confines of the Forest of Dean in Gloucestershire. It was intended as a weekend retreat, but in fact was only used once before his death in the trenches. It must have rotted away by now. The site on which it stands was leased to him by the Freeminers of the Forest. Probably for nine hundred and ninety-nine years. More than that, I do not know. You might decide to do nothing about this strange arrangement. However, should you be interested or curious, perhaps you should contact the family solicitors, Messrs Venables and Lazelle in Oriel Avenue, Cheltenham.

Joe looked up from the letter and stared through the window at the double row of aspens lining the street. They were shaking in the summer breeze; just as he was.

Hattie's note arrived with the second post. Doffie assumed it was for Gran and took it up with her mid-morning drink made from a meat cube. Gran could manage the bathroom now, though it seemed to her an outlandish arrangement to have a water closet within the house and she always closed the lid with a wrinkled nose, and flannel-washed herself at the basin. She liked Doffie's lavender soap so much she did not rinse it off. She sat up in bed now, smelling strongly of the soap, still wearing winceyette in spite of the heat, her black toque pulled down almost to her ears.

'I shall get up in a minute,' she said, as if Doffie had accused her of laziness. 'And I'll do the dinner. Broad beans. I fancy broad beans. And a bit of bacon on top of them. Have you got bacon, our Doffie?'

'Yes. And I can pick some beans too. I'll do that while you read Hattie's letter.'

'Can't read with these glasses.'

'Or without them,' Doffie said humorously. 'Let me then. Shall I?'

She saw immediately that the letter was for her. 'Sorry, Gran. Look – Hattie's made her D look exactly like a P. I thought it was Mrs P. Pettiford. Oh dear. All she says is, will I go and see her. Today. Oh Lord, what can have happened?'

'She got her pains?'

'Not yet. She says it will be August, so that probably means July.'

'Percy's leaving her.'

'Not likely. He absolutely dotes on her.'

'True. Best get over there, Doffie.' She looked at her daughter-in-law. 'Too hot to cycle over – too slow. Go to Gloucester and get young Duggie Marsden to drive you over.'

'Young . . . ?' Doffie started to laugh, then stopped and looked at Gran. 'I can't do that, Gran. I haven't spoken properly to Duggie for nearly a year.'

Gran almost smiled her relief. 'Get along then. That Percy will give you a lift back home, I don't doubt.' She shook her head. 'Reckon his heart is kind enough, even if it is situated in his trousers.'

For a moment Doffie continued to look at Gran, then she burst out laughing. Gran smiled unwillingly and for a moment the two women were totally united. Then Doffie kissed the dry old cheek and said, 'Stay where you are. Don't dare try to come downstairs till I'm back.' And she was gone.

Gran said to the empty bedroom, 'I'd better listen to that bit of advice, hadn't I, Will? I want to be here when she gets back.'

And, like a miracle, his voice said, 'Well done, my Pattie.'

She stared across the bedroom at the shelves

which still contained Alice's books, and her eyes slowly filled with tears.

Joe came out of the solicitor's office and stood in the sunshine watching people move up and down the wide promenade, window-shopping, chatting, greeting each other; all the things people did. He was the only one in that small world, or so it seemed to him, without a purpose. He knew he was making progress: there was the place on the teaching course, the two rooms that Louise had made into a home, there were books . . . and all those schools with playgrounds and children, packed with individual futures. But it was all in Newcastle. Not in Cheltenham, or Gloucester, or the railway coach in the Forest of Dean. That was good, surely? The sooner he settled this matter of the railway coach, the sooner he could forget his roots for ever.

He realized that people were having to diverge to get past him; he was like a rock in the middle of a stream. He took a hurried step forward, caught his toe in one of the pavement flags and stumbled. He only just saved himself. 'Are you all right?' someone asked. 'Yes. Perfectly. I just missed my footing for a moment.'

He walked aimlessly on, embarrassed. That was what had happened. He had tripped, lost his footing, just for a moment. As he had done with his life – except that with his life, the trip had turned into a fall and nothing would ever be the same again.

He crossed the wide road and went into the dairy, sat down, ordered tea and a scone, then spread out a single sheet of paper on the table and read it yet again. He remembered going to the Forest of Dean for a few days after his father had been reported killed. 'A complete change,' the vicar had said when he had visited Cotswold Close to offer his condolences. 'My dear wife and I went there often. It's the trees, you know. Like being in nature's cathedral. You will find peace there.' So he and his mother had gone for two or three days and had indeed found peace – but not the romantic railway coach by the pool, where it seemed she had been conceived.

He smiled, remembering his anxiety for his mother then, thinking she was going mad, searching for a railway coach in the forest. They had never found it. And now it seemed it was her legacy to him. Was she offering him peace?

His pot of tea arrived with the scone. He ate it and wondered about going down to the forest and trying to find this blasted honeymoon coach. What had she called it – the Pumpkin Coach? Why? But though he tried to ridicule the idea, he knew he must go there. For his mother's sake. Maybe for his, too.

He walked slowly back up the prom, past the Winter Gardens, the Queens Hotel and the Rotunda, then threaded through back streets to Cotswold Close and the row of Edwardian houses with their steps up to the front doors. Seven steps, he had counted them often as a small boy. He stood and looked at the house where he had been born, and thought of riding on his father's shoulders at Christmas to buy a turkey, which they would share with his grandparents. He remembered his mother's face every time she had looked at his father. It had been alight with love. Just as

Alice's had been when she looked at him. Until the time on Cooper's Hill.

He turned abruptly and walked back the way he had come to his bed-and-breakfast place. When he had booked in last night, he had seen a bike in the hall. If it was still there . . . It was.

The landlady said, 'Course you can borrow it, son. It's my old man's and he's gone for good and all. Bring it back in better condition than it is now, and you can have it tomorrow as well!' She laughed raucously, so her 'old man' could surely not be dead, and if he had left her she did not appear to be broken-hearted about it. How marvellous to be able to laugh at the past. He joined in, then lifted the bike carefully into the road. 'I'll be back before bedtime,' he promised, and made for Lansdown Road as fast as he could. If he'd been a few hours earlier he would have recognized Doffie Pettiford cycling through Staverton in the opposite direction.

Hattie came out to meet Doffie as she pushed her bike up the driveway.

'You'll never guess what has happened!' Hattie greeted Doffie without the usual hug and kiss. 'Enid's gone. Left! And bloody Percy is blaming me! Can you believe it?'

Doffie leaned on her bike and got her breath. Hattie was right; it was unbelievable, incredible. When had she and Alice seen Enid with Reggie Ryecroft, and hidden them from Dorothy? Surely less than a week ago? If only Ted had agreed that Hattie should know about it then, they might have avoided this.

Hattie said, 'Come straight up to my room.

423

Percy is at work, of course, but I'd rather Nanna didn't see you. She'll tell him and he'll think you and I organized the whole damned thing.'

Doffie followed her, treading as lightly as she could, though Mrs Westbrook was doubtless asleep somewhere. She looked around Hattie's bedroom. 'Where are the boys?'

'I had to farm them out, darling. How could I manage without Enid, for God's sake? I'm the size of a house again, supposed to rest each afternoon . . . if only I'd thought of that when I wished Enid good luck.'

'Oh, so you did organize it?'

'I couldn't have stopped her, Doffie darling. She is absolutely besotted. And when I heard who she was going off with – well, it tickled me pink. I just had to know what would happen next! And I thought, let her have her fling – damn it all, she deserves something, doesn't she? Even if it is . . . I'll tell you that bit in a minute. Percy does not know yet and I'd much prefer him to hear it from Enid herself.'

It was on the tip of Doffie's tongue to forestall that particular confidence, but she waited.

'Anyway, darling, all I did was to wish her luck. And give her some of my nighties. And get her bags downstairs for the taxi . . . Someone had to wave her goodbye, didn't they? And I adore Enid, you know that!'

'Oh, Hattie.' Doffie sighed, suddenly feeling an enormous gush of sympathy for Percy.

'Yes, well, that's me, isn't it? But as I said to bloody Percy, let her have a couple of months while I give birth to this latest Westbrook –' she patted her abdomen, 'then I'll go and bring her home. She'll have had enough by then.'

'You know that for a fact, do you?'

The sarcasm was lost on Hattie. 'Of course. Enid is like me; she will want some tenderness as well as unlimited sex. She won't get that from Reggie Ryecroft.' She clapped her hand across her mouth, then removed it and said, 'You don't look surprised, Doffie. I said Reggie Ryecroft. Enid has gone off with Reggie Ryecroft.'

Doffie sighed again and told her about seeing them in the Bon Marché coffee house. Hattie exclaimed and hurled accusations of secrecy and Doffie said wearily, 'Blame your Uncle Ted. He said we shouldn't stir anything up.'

'Didn't need stirring, did it?'

'No.' Doffie thought of Dorothy Ryecroft, almost defeated by Reggie; she thought of Valentine . . . She said, as a last forlorn hope, 'How do you know that Reggie hasn't found someone he can really love?'

Hattie said, 'I know all sorts of things, Doffie darling. When people are pregnant, when men are cruel . . . Reggie is cruel.'

Doffie shuddered. 'Poor Enid. We can't leave her there, Hattie. Have you got an address?'

'Yes. She phoned. But I'm not going to tell anyone else, not even you, darling. For one thing, I promised her – not that that matters. But I don't want you to tell Percy. I want her to know she can trust me. Then I think she will come back home with me next month.'

'Next month? You said in two or three months.'

'Well, I told Helena Webster – sorry, Maybury – that it would be a month. When I asked her whether she would like to try being a mother.' She grinned at Doffie's startled expression. 'She is the Superintendent's wife, not the Lord Mayor of London's!' She sighed. 'We got to know each other when poor Alice was in such a state. She's not really my cup of tea – too bookish. But I knew she wanted to gain experience with children before – you know – actually trying to get pregnant. And she knows Reggie, of course. And she's met Enid. Oh, God . . . the more I think of it . . . it is a bit like letting a fox in the chicken run, isn't it?'

'Give me the address, Hattie,' Doffie said levelly.

'Not yet, darling. Helena said she would have the boys for four weeks. Let's wait till then before we interfere.'

'No, Hattie. I won't try to talk her out of any-thing. That I promise. But I think we should let her know that we can fetch her at any time.'

Hattie said in a small voice, 'It would mean I'd have to ask Percy to take me there. And he will be angrier than ever.' She began to cry. 'I can't live without him, Doffie.'

'D'you think he'd ever leave you?' Doffie said scornfully.

'You thought Ted was going to leave you! So you should understand!' Hattie was wailing now and Doffie shushed her impatiently.

'Just give me the address, Hattie. And then for-get the whole thing. How does that sound?'

Hattie thought about it. 'Very good, actually,' she admitted. She had had such exciting plans; but with Percy acting as if she was Judas Iscariot . . .

'Then come on. I've left Gran in bed, so I don't want to be long.'

Doffie copied the phone number and address into her diary and wondered what Ted would make of all this. More to the point, what would Dorothy Ryecroft make of it? Not that she could ever tell Dorothy. Or Alice, for that matter.

Joe cycled straight into the city and turned at George Street to see the station. It was the same; shabbier and dirtier than it had been when it was the old Great Western, but still bustling, still hissing steam, still alive. The staff were more or less the same, too, and he swerved the bike in a wide circle in case the ticket collector recognized him. Then he went back to Northgate Street and got off the bike to stare up at the oriel windows: the first one full of files; the second, belonging to the Staff Office, much less cluttered. He wondered whether Alice still stood there each morning doing the filing, looking up the road, thinking of things that had nothing to do with British Railways. He might come back here tomorrow morning and stand opposite the window by the Catholic church and wait until she looked . . . Then he knew he would not. He would catch the train at Cheltenham and go through to Leadon and ask around for the Pumpkin Coach. What a waste of time it all was.

He began to push the bike up Northgate Street towards the Cross, and by the time he reached St John's Lane he knew he was making for the cathedral. He told himself it was what he had intended all along. To walk around and see it again without the excited guidance of a sixteen-year-old girl . . . 'How do you suppose the monks washed their hands here . . . did they roll up those wide sleeves or . . .'

Joe propped his bike against the railings guarding one of the houses in the precinct and walked over to the west door, then hesitated because the organ was playing. He looked at his watch: seven-thirty. Not Evensong, surely? He pushed at the door gingerly; it did not squeak; he slid in.

It was a concert. A sidesman came up, smiling a welcome. 'Not too late, sir,' he whispered. 'Plenty of room. We're enjoying the last piece. It's composed by Geoffrey Makin himself. I'm afraid we could not afford to print programmes.'

'That's perfectly all right.'

He nearly left. And then someone looked around to see what was happening at the door. It was Alice. Joe dropped into a seat as if someone had hit the backs of his knees. Alice. Alice Pettiford, who had looked into his eyes and had not been able to look away. He closed his own eyes, remembering that time at the Opera House watching – or not watching – the Fol-de-Rols. That one incident had been enough for an exchange of souls. And at Cooper's Hill he had spoiled that, and had gone on spoiling it ever since. He lowered his head. Alice had led him here.

Thirty-Two

The final organ note shuddered to its conclusion. There was no applause. People murmured among themselves, and after a while Mr Makin appeared. Someone shook his hand and then people gathered around him.

Val said, 'Shall we have a word with Mr Makin, Alice?'

She said nothing. Val glanced at her and saw with alarm that she was pale and trembling. 'Alice, stay here. I'll try to get a taxi.'

She shook her head violently. 'Don't leave me,' she whispered.

'All right. What's the matter – are you ill?'

She stared straight ahead. 'Joe is here.'

'Joe? Joe Adair?'

'Yes.'

'How do you know? Is it just a feeling – a sensation?'

'He came in during that last piece. I looked round to see what was happening. He was there. When he saw me he sort of collapsed in the back pew.'

'So he wasn't expecting to see you.' It was not a question, but she looked at him wildly. Val said, 'I didn't mean you'd made some kind of assignation!' He tried to smile to lighten the occasion. 'Look, we don't have to see him if you don't want to. We can simply sit here until—'

'He'll wait too,' she said certainly. 'And ... I must see him, Val. I have to see him once more.'

'Very well. Come then.'

She let him help her upright and they shuffled sideways into the main aisle. Joe was immediately obvious, sitting entirely alone and away from everyone else. She thought: that's how it was, he was always on his own. Always.

She tried to smile as they approached him. He made no response; neither did he stand up. He looked terrified. He was terribly thin and the boyish good looks were gone. He was her age; his birthday was in May, so he was just twenty. They stopped at the last pew. Val waited for Alice to say something, but there was nothing to say and Val knew that a silence like this could be far more significant than words, so he said quickly, 'Joe, isn't it? You're home at last. When were you demobilized?'

Joe's lips moved but no sound emerged. He cleared his throat and tried again. 'A year ago.' He looked at Alice and said despairingly, 'I'm married. We live in Newcastle. I had to see the solicitors in Cheltenham. Otherwise I would not be here.'

She responded instantly. 'It's all right, Joe. I'm glad to see you. It – it had to be.'

Val said quietly, 'Joe, Alice and I are married. Last November. We live with my mother in Deanery Close. Will you walk back with us and have a cup of tea?'

Alice shot him a glance of pure gratitude. She smiled slightly at Joe. 'There – all our cards on the table, Joe. Will you come back?'

But he shook his head. He could not bear it. Not with her husband and mother-in-law. His relationship with her had never included domesticity, beyond his mother's famous stew . . . And was Reggie Ryecroft dead? He had been a cruel man and Joe wondered whether his son had inherited any of those traits.

He blurted out, 'I've inherited the Pumpkin Coach, Alice. And I don't know where it is.'

There was an almost deathly silence. Alice's face went from pale to ashen. Valentine held the back of the pew. Up by the pulpit someone laughed and someone else clapped their hands and then stopped immediately. Geoffrey Makin was holding court.

Val held Alice's elbow to prevent her from falling. He said quietly, 'Alice knows where it is, Joe. She will take you there. Tomorrow.'

She looked at him. 'Val?'

'You will remember when you get to Leadon. Cross to the down side and follow the lane until the big stone. Then strike into the woods—'

'But you will come, surely?' She was trying to tell him that he must not let her be alone with Joe Adair.

'I'm in Worcester tomorrow, my dear. I told you when we were having tea.'

'But now Joe has arrived, surely you will come?'

'You and Joe have a lot to talk about. Why don't you meet him at the station for the ten-thirty train?'

No one replied to his suggestion, and after a

while he said, 'Leave it at that, why don't you? If you change your minds, you simply don't turn up.'

This seemed to satisfy Alice. She did not say 'See you tomorrow,' and neither did Joe. They left Joe sitting there and went out as the rest of the music-lovers filtered along the aisle. Alice held Val's arm with both hands, leaning on him heavily. Once clear of the precinct, she sobbed, 'Val, thank you. You were so very honest and straightforward. Thank you.' They walked another three steps and she added, 'I don't have to go, do I? If I'm not there he will go on by himself and he will eventually find it.'

'Of course he will.' Val looked up at the sky. It was almost the longest day of the year and the stars were just showing in the light sky. He did not believe in God, yet he knew Alice talked often to some higher being, so he addressed his plea in that general direction and screamed inside his head, 'Don't let her go! Please don't let her go!' Immediately after, before he could think again, he said, 'It's good, Alice. Like a wheel turning full circle.' He swallowed. 'If you have to stay . . . with him . . . you know I will understand, don't you?'

She clung harder. 'Oh, Val – I thought it was over. If only he hadn't come back.'

He knew he ought to tell her that he would wait for her; that everything would be all right; that he loved her and that was why he was prepared to let her go. He said nothing.

Edmund Westbrook did not like being away from his home and family one bit. He missed his mother's squashy plump cuddles, his father's willingness to lie down on the carpet and play with his model cars, Aunt Enid's endless patience, interesting walks, caterpillar collecting. Even Nanna's powdery goodnight kiss. He said to Helena, 'Want Mummy.'

'I really cannot think why,' Helena said, genuinely surprised. 'Does she take you to slide on the grass and paddle and make mud pies at Wainlodes? Don't answer that, because I know she doesn't.' She looked at the two-year-old, who was sturdy like his mother but with fair hair and pale-blue eyes. 'You certainly don't take after your mummy and daddy as far as colouring goes, do you?'

'Want Mummy,' said Edmund.

'I'll tell you what. Let's feed Perry quickly, then go to hear the band in Montpelier. What do you say to that?'

'Want Aunninid,' Edmund said.

Helena said brightly, 'Well, we might see her there!'

Edmund clapped his hands. 'Aunninid!' he said joyfully.

Poor old Enid, Helena thought. Used as a free nursemaid when she was at home, and probably now being treated like a whore by Reggie. She blushed at her own thought. But in the old days when she had first worked for Reggie Ryecroft, he had 'tried it on' with her. She had a good idea of what he was like. Enid would soon be home, she was sure of that.

'Then you can help her to get back to normal,' she said to the small, blond boy, who was smiling now.

He shouted, 'Norma! Norma!' And she laughed

and gave him a kiss. Nothing much wrong with this one, even if he did spring from such an unlikely pair as Percy Westbrook and Hattie Pettiford.

When Doffie got back from Leckhampton she was tired and completely fed up. Gran was still in bed, dozing stertorously. For once in her life the old woman had done what she was told, but strangely enough this did not please Doffie either. When Ted came home and commented, 'Salad again,' it was the last straw.

Doffie said, 'I think the Pettifords are the most selfish family I have ever had the misfortune to meet!'

'What's brought this on?' asked Ted.

She almost told him about Hattie, but then, from pure awkwardness, did not. 'I seem to have to spend my whole life running round after them,' she said instead. 'Hattie's utterly useless. And your mum, who has always been so independent, has suddenly decided she likes being an invalid, being waited on hand, foot and finger, lying there like Lady Muck.'

Ted, who knew that his mother liked none of those things, took the stairs two at a time. Doffie followed him, and found him sitting by the bed, holding Gran's hand, looking distinctly worried.

'She's not well, Doff,' he said. 'I think I'd better go for Dr Stringer.'

It turned out that Gran had had a minor stroke.

Doffie felt terrible. 'She must have been like this all day!' She stared at the doctor in distress. 'She's had no lunch, nothing to drink since her meat drink this morning . . . and I didn't even realize!'

'She'll probably come round before bedtime. You might be able to feed her something then. I'll get the District Nurse to pop in. She needs washing and changing.'

'She's wet?' It was the last straw for Doffie.

Gran did in fact open her eyes when Doffie and the nurse between them gave her a bedbath and changed the sheets. She smiled at Doffie, and said something incomprehensible.

Doffie said, 'Yes, Gran, you're all right. Ted's home. Try not to worry.'

Amazingly, Gran obeyed her daughter-in-law again and actually smiled as she closed her eyes. Doffie said to the nurse, 'Is she going to be all right, really? Because if you think for one minute that something might happen, then I must send for her two granddaughters.'

The nurse seemed surprised. 'Of course she's going to be all right, Mrs Pettiford. It's a very minor stroke. She'll probably have forgotten all about this tomorrow. Just you see.'

And she was right. Ted and Doffie took it in turns to sit with Gran through that night, and at five-thirty, when the sun beamed in through the window above the porch, Gran opened her eyes and said clearly, 'I could do with a cup of tea.'

Ted leaned forward, grinning like a cat. 'Oh, so could I, Ma! Will you make it or shall I?' And Gran cackled.

But the nurse was wrong about one thing; Gran knew what had happened. She knew she had lost a whole day and night. And she was grateful for waking up again.

'I still got time, Ted,' she said, leaning forward to sip her tea as he held it steady.

'Lots of it, Ma.'

'Dunno about that. I do know you haven't put sugar in this tea. And when I say sugar I don't mean that saccharin stuff.'

He staggered downstairs again. He was bushed. And he would have to go in, even if he was going to be late. Doffie wouldn't understand. But when he woke her half an hour later with a cup of tea and told her he was just leaving for work, all she said was, 'Surprise me.' So he kissed her as passionately as he knew how. But she shoved him away and said, 'Too much of that in your family, Ted.'

He had gathered that she had seen Hattie yesterday, and wondered what was going on there.

Doffie told Gran about Enid and Reggie as unemotionally as possible. Gran was agog. Her eyes gleamed and she lay back on the propped pillows, breathing in the information and almost patting it into a life of its own.

'Well, it sounds a pretty kettle of fish to me, our Doffie! I wonder what he sees in Enid Westbrook? Now, if he'd tried to get at you in some way . . . he always thought a lot of you. Jealous of our Ted, that's what it was.'

'Oh, Gran, that's nonsense.'

Gran did not follow it up. 'So Hattie's going to let her sister-in-law have a fling until after the new babby arrives. Is that it?'

'I reckon so. But I really feel I must try to telephone Enid before then. Just in case.'

'Yes, maybe. When are you expecting our Ted?'

'The usual. Three-ish, I suppose.'

'What does he say?'

'I didn't tell him. We were too worried about you to worry about Enid Westbrook!'

Gran was silent, looking inwards, then she said, 'I think now would be a good time. You need to know something, our Doffie.' She squinted up into her daughter-in-law's face. 'I wanted to tell our Ted. But Will showed me that you were the one. Ted would have to do something – fight it out, perhaps. I don't know, I ain't sure. But you . . . you can hold it in your head. Keep it secret, unless it has to be told.' She looked fierce. 'Can you do that, our Doffie?'

'I don't know what you're talking about, Gran. I suppose I can keep a secret.' Doffie smiled slightly, recalling her promise to Hattie never to divulge the paternity of Edmund. 'Unless it has to be told, of course.'

Gran closed her eyes, nodded as if to confirm this, then said bluntly, 'Our Mitzie . . . Hattie is so like her. So full of life that you forget she is ungood.'

' "Ungood"? What does that mean, Gran?'

'Well, she ain't wicked. She wouldn't hurt anyone, not really. Not meaning to, like. But she ain't good, either.'

Doffie smiled and put her hand over one of Gran's. 'Yes. I understand.'

'Mitzie couldn't believe it when he said he adored her then hit her across the face. She were like a – a wild creature, see, our Doffie. We had such lovely summers then, and she used to live outdoors. Sometimes in that old coach down by Bracewell's Pool. She'd stay there till snow was on the ground some years. She was – she was—'

'Uncontrollable,' Doffie supplied.

'But no harm to her.' Gran's voice was pleading. 'No harm. Not really, our Doffie. She had ... lovers. Farm boys, even gypsies. But she weren't a whore. Whatever he said, she weren't that.' She opened one eye. 'Do you believe me, our Doff?'

Doffie thought of Hattie; she moved her thumb over the back of Gran's hand, feeling the veins. 'I believe you, Gran.'

'He called her that all the time. He said she deserved what she got. He said the babby could be anyone's. When Hattie were only a nipper, he came back to the station house. Mitzie had long gone. We thought he'd come to see Hattie – acknowledge her as his daughter. But it was just more arguments and shouting.'

A single tear emerged from one closed eye and found a channel through the wrinkles on Gran's face. With her free hand, Doffie wiped it tenderly. She said quietly, 'We're talking about Reggie Ryecroft, aren't we?'

'Aye.'

Doffie closed her own eyes in horror. Reggie Ryecroft was Hattie's father – and the father of Val. Which meant that Val and Hattie were brother and sister. And they were Edmund's parents. She squeezed her eyes into slits, forcing her brain to accept the facts. And immediately one fact emerged from the others: Gran must never know that Val was Edmund's father. Doffie felt sick.

Gran's voice went on inexorably. 'Reggie always talked a lot of nonsense about purity in women.

He admired you for two reasons. Purity, and the fact that you were Ted's – he's always been jealous of Ted. That was why he married Dorothy Tait. She 'as the same name as you, and she were a virgin . . . well, an old maid, really. And now Enid Westbrook. Hattie's sister-in-law and never been with a man in 'er life.'

'Oh dear God,' Doffie whispered.

Gran opened her eye again. 'You won't tell Ted, will you, our Doffie? 'E would try to kill Reggie, and that would not do.'

Doffie put her cheek to Gran's hand, so that that sharp eye could not see her expression. 'I promise I won't say anything, Gran. Ever.' The deed was done, Edmund was here.

'I didn't say for ever, my girl.' Gran's voice was still sharp. 'I said unless you 'ave to.'

'All right, Gran. Unless I have to.'

Doffie waited. After a while, Gran's shoulder relaxed; she was asleep. Doffie sat up. She must not think about this; not for a while, anyway. She had to concentrate on Enid. It was worse than either she or Hattie had realized. She must get to the phone box and telephone the number in her diary. Now. Before Gran woke up.

Val and Alice did not talk much that night; neither did they sleep. Alice started off the night curled into Val's back, as usual, but during the small hours she moved away until she could feel the edge of the bed beneath her cheek. In the morning, when Val told her he would take a later train to Worcester so that he could walk her to the station, she demurred instantly.

'I have to put my mind towards Joe.' She

glanced at him, begging for an understanding she did not have herself. 'I must not let myself think of us, because – because then I won't go.'

'What if he's not there?'

'I'll walk back home again.' She looked confused, bewildered, but she had thought of everything. 'I have told your mother. She knows I might not be back.'

He was aghast. 'Not ever?'

'At least tonight.'

He was appalled; out of yesterday's confusion had come this hard-headedness. Alice might actually be leaving him.

She put a hand on his shoulder. 'We will talk about it properly, when we know.'

He wanted to shout, 'Know what?' But he said nothing. Instead, he reached slowly into his pocket and took out the key to the coach and gave it to her.

She whispered, 'Val . . . I'll never forget this.'

He sighed. 'I won't either.'

At seven-thirty Val left the house; he need not have gone for another hour, but he could not stand being near Alice when she was already so far away. He walked towards Hare Lane, then veered back and went to the cathedral. He did something he had never done before. He knelt and prayed.

Joe was there. He was waiting by the booking-office window; he had bought two tickets to Leadon. 'I did not think . . . you could have had a privilege ticket,' he said.

'That's fine.' Alice fiddled with her purse and he said quickly, 'No, please. You are doing me a service.' But she found the money and gave it to him. He said uncertainly, 'If you insist . . .' He no longer knew what was the correct thing to do. 'The weather is not so good,' he added formally.

'It won't matter. It's magical, you see.' Alice led the way on to the platform. 'You will see for yourself. Then you will know why Rose wanted to find it. And you will know why your grandmother allowed herself to be taken there all those years ago. And why my Aunt Mitzie . . . cavorted there.' She glanced at Joe, but he was not even smiling. 'It's a happy place. It's literally out of this world. Things happen there that could never happen anywhere else. Do you understand what I mean?'

'Not really. But if you say them, they must be true.'

She looked at him and saw that he was putting himself entirely in her hands; had it always been like that? She could barely remember. But for now, she was – as the American film stars often said – 'calling the shots'.

They got on the little push-and-pull and settled into the side seats next to two bikes and a crate of pigeons. The cooing of the pigeons and the shouted remarks of the cyclists made conversation unnecessary. At one point Alice looked sideways at Joe and saw he was smiling. The magic was working already.

Doffie pressed button A and replied to the dull 'Hello' on the other end of the line.

'It's me, Enid. Doffie Pettiford. Hattie gave me your number and I felt bound to phone, my dear. You see, I know Reggie Ryecroft rather better than a lot of people. Are you all right?'

There was a short silence, then a sudden burst of weeping. Doffie was alarmed. 'Don't let him hear you, Enid –'

'He's gone to a meeting,' Enid sobbed. 'Doffie, can you come and get me? Please? Before he gets back? He's taken my clothes. I think my arm is broken – it's so painful. He keeps phoning me. I don't want him to ring and find the phone engaged – oh Doffie, I'm so frightened. He calls me names – terrible things – oh Doffie –'

Doffie was horrified. She had not imagined it could be so bad. And Enid, in spite of not wanting the line to be engaged for long, kept talking, pouring confidences into Doffie's ear. 'I told him Hattie would come and get me after the new baby is born and he laughed his head off. He wants that. He wants her here, under his thumb, like I am. Two of you – he keeps saying that. Two of you. Two . . . I can't say the word, Doffie. It's horrible.'

It was indeed. His own daughter. Is that why he seduced Enid in the first place? To reduce her to a pulp and then show her off to Hattie? And why? As a dreadful warning? Doffie gripped the phone so hard she thought it might shatter. She put two more pennies in and said quickly, 'I'll be with you as soon as I can, Enid. Try to be ready to leave—'

'All my things are gone, Doffie! Bring clothes—'

'I will. I'm going now.' Doffie replaced the receiver and leaned her forehead against the little mirror in the kiosk. She hardly knew what to do. The address in Newport meant nothing to her. A taxi would cost the earth and there might not be a train for ages. She found two more pennies and dialled the number of the office, then got through to Duggie.

'I know what I said . . . Yes, yes, Duggie, I know . . . But this is nothing to do with you and me. I'll have to explain in the car – can you leave now? We must be in Newport before Reggie gets back from whatever bloody meeting he's gone to.' Duggie was cautious, not to say unwilling. Doffie had hurt him enough. She need not think he was at her beck and call any hour of the day and night. She had led him to think—

She interrupted, 'Duggie, I am sorry for what happened. I have regretted it ever since. But this is different. Hattie's sister-in-law is with Reggie Ryecroft in Newport. He has beaten her, taken her clothes, she is degraded completely and this after less than a week. I have to get her home. And you are the only one I know who has a car.'

After a while he said, 'All right. I'll be with you in under an hour.'

She thought wearily that Ted would see Duggie's help as interference, as complete madness. She fumbled her way out of the kiosk and went to ask Mrs Mearment if she would sit with Gran until Ted got home.

The magic of the Pumpkin Coach came slowly. Alice had forgotten what a battle it was to get there; the ferns had grown together thickly since last year and the old tracks were securely hidden. She cast around for over an hour before she found them and then she had to go ahead, beating down the undergrowth, until suddenly there it was, waiting for them. When she had seen it last year for the first time, the trees had been heavy with foliage, ready to fall during autumn. Now, in June, everything was fresh and green and vigorous. Bindweed had grown across the door of the coach, and Alice had to tear it away before she could fit the key into the lock and open it up. She went inside while Joe stood uncertainly on the steps. The deckchairs were where she and Val had left them; the two cracked saucers she had found in the cupboard were still on the table. She went down the corridor to the bedroom: there were mothy-looking blankets in a pile; the pillows were long gone, the mattress ticking stained and torn. Had she dreamed the magic? It certainly was not in here.

Joe's voice came from the deckchair sitting room. 'Alice, the sun has come out. This is how it must have looked to my grandmother. Come and see.'

It was the most natural thing he had said so far. She joined him and they stared across the pool to the dense thicket on the other side. She remembered the icy, silken feel of the water as it slipped past her arms and body; she remembered Val . . . she must not remember Val, so she imagined Rose's mother instead. Had it not been a Machiavellian seduction at all, but rather a true love match? He must have left the coach and its plot to her before he died, and she had left it in turn to her illegitimate daughter, perhaps to make up for an impoverished childhood. They would never know.

Joe said, 'It is so important to see this place, Alice. Can you understand what it means to me?'

She nodded and whispered, 'And it has come from your grandfather, Joe. Your blood grandfather. That is important.'

'You mean, my mother wasn't *that* illegitimate!'

444

Automatically he put an arm across her shoulders as he looked sideways at her, smiling, then laughing. She was terribly aware of the arm, of his shoulder, of his face almost on a level with hers. She laughed with him, but then spoke quietly.

'You remember the time at Cooper's Hill?'

He made a sound in his throat and she said, 'Don't be embarrassed. We have to talk about it. That's why we're here. We have to . . . get it out of the way, Joe. So that we know.'

'Know?'

'What to do next. For the rest of our lives.'

'I thought we would have to talk about the venereal disease. How I could be unfaithful—'

'That was something that happened. We could have coped with that. The problem with us, Joe, is what did not happen.' She made up her mind suddenly. 'Joe, let's swim. Right now. Will you?'

'I will do whatever you say. I love you, Alice. I love you almost too much.'

She nodded. 'I know. I love you in the same way.'

They undressed to their underclothes and walked down to the pool, then waded in. They were holding hands.

Thirty-Three

That afternoon, as a surly Duggie drove Doffie
Pettiford along the riverside road through
Blakeney, Lydney and Chepstow to steep-sided
Newport, as Ted arrived home and took over from
Mrs Mearment and felt, as he had so often felt,
bewildered and angry by Doffie's half-baked
excuse for going off with Duggie to fetch Enid
from somewhere or other, and as Alice and Joe
swam very slowly across the coal-black pool,
noting the dappled sun on their heads, the deep,
earthy scent of the water and knowing exactly –
for the first time for three years – what would
happen next; it was then that Hattie's pains
began.

Hattie's first two births had been, as she put it,
like shelling peas. She had imagined that all labour,
all births were the same, and that women
dramatized them for their own ends. But this pain
was like nothing she had ever known. It wanted to
rip her in half; it nearly succeeded. She was lying on
her bed; it was a very pleasant day, not too hot nor
too cold, her ankles weren't quite as bloody awful as
they had looked yesterday, Percy had made love to
her last night, tenderly and sweetly, and she had

446

wept with the pleasure of it, with knowing that he still wanted her and, more than that, that he loved her. From the moment she'd first met him in a dance hall at Fairfield airbase, she had found him the sexiest man in the world. His eyes, crossed as they were, seemed to bore into her very soul. He had a way of looking down the front of her dress so that her heart hammered audibly. And his hands, large and capable, were everywhere. He had punished her for helping Enid by keeping away from her; last night had been sweet indeed.

But now he was at work, and Nanna was resting and the boys were with Helena Maybury and Enid . . . Enid was probably having the time of her life with Reggie Ryecroft.

The pain echoed around her body and then began to gather itself again. She screamed at the top of her voice, 'Nanna! Come quick! Nanna!'

Old Mrs Westbrook stumbled through the door, asking what on earth all the noise was about. By this time the pain had Hattie in its giant maw; she was rigid, arched against it, her hands holding the bedhead, her feet scrabbling for purchase on the slippery counterpane. Nanna's face split into a grin.

'Early again, I see! You'll be early at your funeral, you will, my girl!'

Hattie gasped, 'Get Percy – phone work – Gloucester 45—'

'I know the number. Bit too soon to be making a fuss, isn't it? It'll probably be another twelve hours or so. He'll be home by six.'

'Get Percy.'

The old lady, used by now to obeying her daughter-in-law, shambled out again. The pain

447

gradually subsided. If only Doffie were on the phone. Doffie would summon doctors, nurses, an ambulance, and, especially, an anaesthetist.

By the time Percy got home, Hattie had suffered another dozen visits from the pain. Each time she was convinced she could stand no more, yet she was still there. She no longer cared about the baby or about her life. She *wanted* to be early for her own funeral. She wanted to be out of it.

Percy said, 'Well done, sweetheart. I thought it would be soon.'

'Too soon.' Her voice was a thread, she was bathed in sweat. 'Two months too soon, Percy.'

'Don't worry, Hattie.' He was amazed by her evident terror. 'Edmund was two months premature. And Perry was early, too.' He leaned close. 'You've got me to thank for this. Last night . . . wee willie winkie started this one!'

'Get a doctor, Percy.'

'I've already thought of that. He'll be along shortly. He wasn't worried. They're all used to you by now.'

Her heart sank, and as if it knew she was at an all-time low, the pain returned. Hattie screamed, and twisted her body into contortions in her efforts to get away from it. But there was no escape.

Eventually, an ambulance arrived and Percy went to the hospital with her, as frightened as Hattie was herself. The doctor gave her a shot of pethidine, but beneath the drug the pain was still at work, and she whimpered in her half-sleep as her body went into spasms.

The house was on the end of a terrace; large, double-fronted, with a gravelled front which would take two cars. But the drive was empty of cars now. Someone had told Doffie that Reggie now drove an Armstrong Siddeley very like Mr Maybury's, so he was clearly not back yet from his meeting. 'Thank God,' she murmured.

'Why?' Duggie was thoroughly fed up. 'He can't do anything. She's free to leave whenever she wants to. Why you had to come and fetch her beats me.'

Doffie said curtly, 'Do stop going on, Duggie. I've explained to you that Enid is under Reggie's thumb.'

He made a disgruntled sound and switched off the engine. 'Well, hurry up and sort it out. I'm willing to bet half a crown that she won't come with you. I could see this little expedition was going to be a complete waste of time before we set out!' As she got out of the car he added, 'If Reggie turns up, don't expect me to cover for you!'

She flashed him an impatient look and crunched over the gravel towards the bay window which thrust out beside the front door. Then she had a shock, because just inside the window, Enid was sitting in an armchair, apparently asleep. And far from being in her underclothes with weals over her arms and shoulders, she was dressed in an attractive silk frock, dark green covered in penny-sized white spots. An expensive dress; not one that Enid would have bought in a hundred years.

Doffie frowned and tapped on the glass. Enid put a hand to her spectacles as if to hold them on, then stood up to come to the door. When she opened it, Doffie could see that the glasses had been reflecting the sunlight before; Enid's eyes were both black. When she tried to smile, blood trickled from between her lips.

Doffie said, 'Oh dear Lord! What has he done to you?'

Enid was crying, trying desperately not to. She turned and went back into the front room. Doffie followed her. From behind the door, Reggie stepped forward and closed the door behind all three of them.

Doffie gave a small scream of surprise and he laughed. 'Frightened, Doffie?'

'Not a bit.' She forced herself to appear calm. 'Surprised. I thought you were at a meeting.'

'Enid wasn't lying. She knows better than to lie, don't you, sweet? When I gave her her new dress – do you like it, by the by? – I asked her if anyone had called, and though she said no at first, she soon changed her mind. I was delighted to hear you were coming to see us, Doffie. Absolutely delighted. In fact, nothing could have pleased me more. Sit down, my dear. Enid will fetch tea in a moment.' He took her arm and propelled her to another armchair. His strength amazed her; she sat down with a crash.

He ignored Enid, who stood holding on to the back of another chair. He sat down opposite Doffie. Doffie said firmly, 'Enid dear, would you mind going outside and asking Duggie to join us?'

Enid did not move. Reggie smiled again. 'Enid obeys me, Doffie. No one else.' He turned his head slightly. 'Darling, go and make the tea now. Don't come back in until I call you.' He returned to Doffie. 'Strange how things work out, Doffie. When I brought Enid here, I knew something interesting would come of it. But I thought it would be Hattie. Not the delectable Doffie Pettiford. Hattie would have been all right. Anyone with the name Pettiford would have been all right. But you . . .' He stopped smiling. 'Do you remember when Ted brought you to Leadon station house for the first time? Duggie Marsden was in love with you, Ted was in love with you, Will Pettiford soon came to love you . . . so did Hattie. And so did I. The only one who did not love you and never has loved you since then was that old witch Patience Pettiford. She'll be on my side, anyway.'

Doffie made to get up, and Reggie put out a long leg, planted his foot in her stomach and shoved hard. She sat down with a crash.

Her face was red with fury. 'How dare you, Reggie Ryecroft! How dare you speak to me in this way – push me about as if I were some – some –'

'Whore. Say it, Doffie. A whore. That's what you are. Flaunting your body in front of everyone. Like Mitzie did in the old days. Forcing men to fall in love with her and then—'

'You're mad! Completely mad! You're married to a beautiful, intelligent woman—'

'Old enough to be my mother! Well, not quite, perhaps. But too old for me. Always looked down her nose at me—'

'She's been loyal and true all these years! And I suppose you hit her just as you hit Enid! Let me out of here this minute, you monster! When I think of the way you treated Mitzie – Gran's only daughter –'

His face darkened. 'What has she said to you? She's always been mad – a crazy old woman. All

451

her life. If she's been telling you I killed Mitzie Pettiford, I shall sue. For slander.'

'Killed?' Doffie stared, then lunged for the window. Reggie lunged as well. She screamed as they grappled, her voice her only chance. He slammed her against the wall; she was winded; he held her there with one hand while he tore at her clothes. She sank her teeth into his restraining arm. He hit her as hard as he could and she would have fallen to the ground had he not held her up. Then he began systematically to slap her face, so that it went from side to side like a rag doll's. He laughed, enjoying every slap. Then he let her slip to the floor and was astride her in an instant.

It was then that Duggie, summoned by a panic-stricken Enid in her new silk dress, crashed into the room armed with a frying pan in one hand and a rolling pin in the other, and hit Reggie so hard he flew through the air and crashed into the empty fireplace.

The police, summoned by Duggie in a shaky voice – he was already wondering whether he had actually murdered Reggie Ryecroft – found three of them in various stages of shock, the two women needing hospital treatment immediately, the man still clutching his kitchen utensils. And the fourth person, another man, unconscious ... maybe even dead. They summoned an ambulance and asked Duggie to accompany them back to the station. Duggie started to say yet again, 'All I know is ...' And then gave up. Doffie would have to sort it all out later; she usually did. Maybe it would not be such a bad thing if he *had* actually killed Reggie.

* * *

They operated on Hattie at Gloucester Royal Infirmary that evening. The baby was a girl, three and a half pounds. She was still alive when Hattie came round, but no one suggested that she should see her daughter. Percy sat on a chair very close to her bed. He was crying; she had never seen him cry before. All she knew was that the pain had left her and she was not dead.

'What is it, my darling?' she whispered.

Percy grabbed her hand. 'Oh, thank God. I thought you were going to leave me as well, Hattie. Never leave me, darling. I promise I won't touch you again – ever. Just stay with me – be with me—'

'Percy, shut up.' She waited, then said with the little strength she had, 'Tell me what has happened.'

'Oh Hattie – it's my fault – she is terribly malformed. She cannot possibly live. I hope she does not. Oh Hattie, don't leave me—'

'A girl.' Hattie found that her lips could hardly form the words she needed to say. 'A girl. Let me see her.'

He was appalled. 'No, darling. It would be cruel to show you. Just remember her as your little—'

'Shut up, Percy. Get the nurse.'

He obeyed her automatically. She repeated her request and again was fobbed off. She whispered, 'If I don't see my baby – now – I will go and find her myself. Is that understood?'

Eventually they brought the tiny scrap of humanity and placed it in Hattie's hands. She adjusted the blanket expertly and cradled the child, looking into the perfect face that topped the twisted body. Percy was sobbing, but Hattie did not shed a tear.

'Fetch a priest, Percy. Do it quickly, darling. We need to christen her.'

Percy made a choking noise. The Sister, hastily summoned, said, 'This is a normal request, Mr Westbrook. In fact, the hospital chaplain is here at present. I will fetch him.'

So it was that Mitzie Harriet Westbrook was welcomed into the church of Christ, five minutes before her death, which took place in the arms of her mother and in the presence of the Sister who was also her godmother. Two Mitzies from the family, in less than a year.

Hattie had used up all her strength; her stitches were pulling abominably, her head ached and her whole body felt as if it had been beaten. But it was all as nothing compared with the pain. People said you forgot the pain of childbirth, but Hattie knew that this one would visit her over and over again.

She could hear Percy still sobbing. She took one of his hands and tucked it beneath her cheek, and she slept.

Afterwards, Alice and Joe swam again, then clambered back up to the coach and dried each other on the dusty blankets from the bed. Then they dressed. During all this time they had not spoken, but they constantly looked at each other, exchanged smiles, held hands.

At last, Joe spoke. 'What happens now, Alice?'

She drew him to the open door to look across the pool. It was mid-afternoon. She had not asked

Val when he would be home from Worcester. 'We go back, Joe.'

'Could we leave it till tomorrow? I love this place, but I might never come back again.'

'We could, easily. But Val would think I had left him for good.'

'Ah. So you love him after all, Alice?'

She did not answer, but said, 'Besides which, Joe, we haven't brought any food and I am ravenous!'

He heard himself laugh; he had not laughed properly for so long it sounded strange. 'You don't look as if you eat enough to keep a bird alive!'

'I haven't had a good appetite for some time. But I rather think I'm going to start eating like a horse.'

They went on looking at each other; he reached for her hand and she took it and held it loosely.

'There's another reason for leaving soon, Joe. The magic finishes quite quickly. It did for your grandmother. And for my Aunt Mitzie. And for Val and me.'

'Val? You brought Val here? I worry about him, Alice. He is Mr Ryecroft's son, after all.'

'I know. But he came here, and it changed him.' She shook her head. 'He changed before then.' She breathed deeply. 'I have watched Valentine Ryecroft grow into a man, Joe. You and me . . . we were always old, weren't we? People thought we were a couple of children in love. But we were never that.'

She waited for him to laugh again or to ask what she meant, but he did not. After a while he said, 'Do you remember Symonds Yat? My seventeenth birthday party?'

'Of course. Do you remember taking down Reggie's dictation and transcribing it for me?'

'I fell in love with you the moment I saw you looking at me from the top of the stairs.'

'I was the same. And then . . . the Fol-de-Rols.'

'And Cooper's Hill.'

'If I'd been pregnant after Cooper's Hill, would everything have been different?'

'Of course. But I knew you couldn't be.'

'Are you going to be unhappy about today, Joe?'

'No.' He smiled at her. 'And I can see you are not.'

'Does that make us shallow?'

He shook his head slowly, meaning that he did not know. Then he said, 'I've been doing a lot of reading. I've got a place on a teacher-training course in September. The psychology of education is fascinating. There's an American, he writes about children being hurt and terrorized, often by their parents. It goes on, apparently, and we know nothing of it. The thing to do is to lay it to rest and start again. Like a funeral. Something that will enable us to fold away painful memories.'

She thought of Gran's advice and smiled. Then said, 'And this –' She swept a hand around the view. 'This is a kind of funeral?'

'A close to one chapter, perhaps.' He smiled at her. 'We must wait and see.'

They went back inside and tidied the coach as best they could. They hung the damp blankets over the deckchairs, and wondered who would see them like that . . .

Mrs Mearment saw the telegraph boy and followed him to the Pettifords' house. She had

had a feeling she would be sitting with Gran Pettiford tonight.

Ted was appalled at the sight of Doffie and Enid in adjacent beds, bandaged and still. He had gone to the phone box and phoned Percy to ask for a lift to Newport hospital and had been told by an incoherent Nanna that Percy was at his wife's bedside, the baby was dead and maybe Hattie would follow. He felt as if his life was falling apart.

Sister said, 'Keep calm, Mr Pettiford. They are both sedated, not unconscious. Miss Westbrook has lost some teeth as well as suffering from contusions – obviously – and a dislocated shoulder. Your wife's injuries appear to be all to the head and face, although there is bruising on her abdomen—'

'Abdomen?' Ted was even more horrified. 'Was she—'

'She was not raped. No. He might have kicked her.'

'God, when I get my hands on him – the swine – the filthy, rotten—'

'Luckily, your friend and colleague Mr Marsden came upon them before any real damage had been done. He hit Mr Ryecroft quite vigorously.'

Ted had no idea Duggie could swing a punch. 'Where is he now – Mr Marsden?' He had already been told that Reggie was not dead, but was having to be restrained. He assumed in a strait-jacket.

'He is waiting in Sister's office for you to arrive. I will arrange for tea to be sent in.'

'That is good of you. But I must have a word with my wife first.'

457

'She won't be able to hear you.'

'She might. Anyway, I have to do it.'

He knelt by Doffie's bed and looked at the dear face between the bandages. He whispered, 'Doffie. Darling Doff. You are always telling me I don't talk to you. I'll talk my head off if only you'll come back to me. I love you, Doffie. I love your ways, your bravado, your kindness, your energy, your sheer cussedness . . . everything about you. Every little last damned thing about you. I don't know why we quarrel and it doesn't matter. Just get better and stay with me, Doff. Please.'

Was it his imagination or did one eyelid flutter?

He went on whispering for some time. He told her how sorry he was that she was tied to the house with Gran. 'You see, sweetheart, she knew you would give your time to her. She knew that Hattie wouldn't and I couldn't. But you . . . she's been difficult, my love, don't think I don't know that. But she has always known that you would be the one to see her through to the end.'

He paused, holding her hand to his face, kissing each knuckle very gently. He was going to say something about Duggie; to tell her that he understood. But in the end he did not. He laid her hand on the sheet and said, 'I'm going to talk to Sister. Then I'm coming back and I'll be here with you for the rest of the night.'

He went round to Enid's bedside and put a hand on her bandages. Then he made for Sister's office and Duggie Marsden. He had been there half an hour when one of the student nurses, chosen to make and take in the tea, heard wild laughter coming from inside. It made her pause and clutch the metal tray harder against her midriff.

'Something the matter, Nurse?' asked Sister.

'One of them is laughing, Sister,' the student nurse said, her eyes wide. People rarely laughed when Sister was on duty.

They went in together. Duggie Marsden was standing – defensively, it seemed – by the table. Ted was standing on the other side of the table; his head was tipped back and he was laughing loudly.

'Hysteria,' Sister said briefly. Then in a loud voice, 'Sit down please, Mr Pettiford. Nurse, put the tray here. I will pour. Milk? Sugar?'

That started Ted off again. Sister looked at Duggie with raised brows, holding the milk jug just above a cup.

He stammered, 'All I said was that I hit Reggie with a frying pan and followed it up with a whack from a rolling pin!'

Sister said levelly, 'I am asking you whether you like milk in your tea.'

That started Ted off again, but eventually he held up his hand. 'It's all right, Nurse –' The little student's eyes nearly popped out and she glanced apprehensively at Sister. 'It's such a mixture of high drama and farce, I am finding it difficult to take in.' He took the milk jug from her. 'I'll see to the tea. You run along now.'

Sister looked as if she might be going to explode, so the student nurse made a hasty retreat and, after a pent-up moment, Sister followed.

Ted poured tea, still snorting with laughter. Duggie said, 'I thought you'd be mad, Doffie going off with me like that.'

'I was. I thought I might have to hit you.' Ted snorted. 'With a rolling pin!'

'Oh shut up, Ted.'

'All right.' Ted took a breath and let it go in a deep sigh. 'I've known Reggie Ryecroft since he came to Leadon in the Great War. And I realize now that I have never known him. Is he completely crackers?'

'Definitely.' Duggie was thankful to talk to someone who spoke his language. 'What had been going on in that house was nobody's business, I'm telling you.'

'What about down in Deanery Close? Those two kids?'

'They survived because of Dorothy. She took the brunt of his – his sadism. That's what he is, a sadist. A sarcastic, brutal—'

Ted said, 'I've done that. Called him all the names under the sun. I caught a taxi here – I think the driver was scared stiff.'

They drank their tea. There seemed nothing else to say, except one thing, which Ted was finding difficult.

Eventually he managed it. 'Look . . . I don't like what's been going on with you and Doff, but I want to thank you for today. I reckon you saved her life.'

Duggie was silent for a long time, then he said, 'We're all right, aren't we, Ted?'

'We've been friends for years. I suppose we're all right.'

There was another long silence, then Duggie said, 'Have you noticed something?'

'What's that?'

'My feet aren't smelling.'

'Thank God for something then, eh?'

'And Ted – I think you should get a car. And a telephone.'

'Keep your bloody nose out of my business, Duggie.'

'Sorry, Ted.'

'Is there any more tea in the pot?'

Thirty-Four

Alice and Joe returned to Gloucester on the four thirty-five from Leadon Markham. They sat on the side seats, hemmed in by two bicycles and a large collie dog. They had not noticed the weather for some time; now they registered that outside the windows the sky was high and eye-achingly azure; the cows were lying down in the fields, not because they were anticipating rain but because they were full of lush grass and needed to rest.

Joe said wonderingly, 'We're right in the middle of summer.'

'I hope it doesn't get much hotter. Hattie is having another baby soon,' Alice replied.

Joe smiled widely. 'Tell me about her. Tell me about your family. Are you happy? What about your mother? And Mr Pettiford – your father. And what about Toby and Dennis?'

He laughed, but she understood very well. The past had been rid of its poison, and now they could revisit it and enjoy it again and again.

'It's Hattie's third. She is so happy with Percy, it's incredible. But then, marriage is like that, isn't it? Unlikely couples who – who just flow into each other.' He made no comment and she went on,

462

'My parents – they're like that. They often bicker and squabble, but somewhere, somehow, they just – are all right!' She laughed, and so did he.

She told him about Gran having to give up her home and live out at Lypiatt Bottom, and Dad coming back to work in the Control Office again on 'turns'.

'Dennis and Toby are exactly the same. They haven't changed or grown up or anything. But Miss Webster – Helena – is married to Mr Maybury, and Miss Warner has gone to Sidmouth to live with her sister.'

'Who does her work?'

'I did for a time.' Alice stared through the window till her eyes were dazzled with the light. She said, 'I was expecting Val's baby, so we got married and then I lost it.'

He took a breath, controlled it, let it go. 'My dear Alice, I am so sorry.'

'We're living through it. And now . . . I think seeing you again – Val agreeing to us coming here – I think it will be all right.' She turned and looked at him, but could hardly see him for light. 'You asked me if I was happy, Joe. I am. But it's not like our happiness was, intense and total and almost frightening. It's slow-growing, it's so deep I hardly know when or where it started. But I know it's there.' Joe said nothing; she blinked but still could not see him. 'What about you? Are you happy? You said you were married.'

He began to tell her about Louise. He was going to tell her that it was still a marriage of convenience, a ticket to Britain for Louise. But then he didn't. He thought of the small lithe figure moving so neatly around the two rooms in

Newcastle. He said quietly, 'She can make wonderful Yorkshire puddings.'

Alice understood. She touched the back of his hand very gently. 'Oh Joe, I am so glad.'

When the train drew in at Gloucester, Joe made to get out with Alice.

'Stay on board,' she said as she stood up and held the strap. 'Go back to Cheltenham now and finalize all this business with the solicitor. And then find Louise.'

It was a strange thing to say; he knew exactly where Louise would be. But he understood and nodded. They made their farewells without emotion, wishing each other luck for the future. And then, quite suddenly, they hugged each other, then Alice went to the door of the railcar.

Joe stood and watched her walk down the platform towards the ticket barrier. He knew it was unlikely he would ever see her again, and part of him felt a terrible regret. But there was another part – even as she disappeared through the gate – that was looking forwards. September would soon be here and he would at last have a purpose in life. And perhaps by then he would have found Louise.

Alice walked through her small corner of Gloucester very slowly. It was almost six o'clock and people were drifting home. She carried on over the Cross so that she could watch the moving clock in Southgate Street and register time as well as place. Because this was her time. Now. Not the terrible time of being without Joe, agonizing over

464

him, knowing that somewhere, somehow they had gone wrong. Not the time of giving herself to Val, of surrendering to the magic of the Pumpkin Coach . . . that had still something to do with Joe. Not even today, when she and Joe had at last exorcized the past. Now was now. She could almost hear Hester saying in a bewildered voice, 'What are you talking about, Alice? It's obvious that now is . . . *now*!'

She smiled, standing there, watching Father Time with his scythe move creakingly around the clock face. She had a sudden sense of her place in eternity. 'Now', after all, was eternity. Her mind spun with the thought of an eternity of nows. It was infinitely reassuring. She murmured, 'The present is always with us.'

She turned and cut down Westgate Street and into the cathedral precinct, savouring the present with each step, each movement of the summer air on her arms and face. Hester would be home soon and the three of them could come to the cathedral and savour their 'threesomeness'. She smiled again, recognizing that she was being deliberately whimsical. And then the cool dimness of the cathedral nave wrapped around her and she walked very slowly towards the altar, suddenly quite certain that Val would be there.

He was sitting in a pew, staring up at the organ loft, not seeing a thing. He was a non-believer, yet she knew he was praying. She slipped in beside him. He turned his head and looked at her. His eyes were ice-blue, the muscles in his face taut.

He said in a low voice, 'How did you know I was here?'

'I didn't. I just came.'

'You haven't come to see me?'

'I might have done. Yes, I have.'

'You've come to say goodbye.'

'No.' She smiled slightly. 'I think I am here to say hello!'

He said nothing to that; he could have been holding his breath, he was so still.

She took up the questioning. 'Were you praying?'

There was a pause; for a moment she thought he would deny it vehemently. But he said eventually, 'Yes. I was praying that you would come back.'

'And here I am.'

'Yes.'

She leaned against the back of the pew; she picked up his hand and held it between hers almost casually. 'I surrendered myself to the present, Val. When I got off the train and walked along Northgate Street, I had the strangest feeling of – of *emergence*. Coming out of somewhere dark and into the light.'

Normally he would have helped her, tried to understand, pressed her fingers. Now he said nothing at all, just waited.

She went on, feeling her way. 'I watched the clock strike six. I'd come to the surface by then and I was sort of floating. In the present. I walked down Westgate Street, across the Close, into the porch . . . And it was then that I knew you would be here. In the present. Now.'

He whispered, 'Now – yes. And now . . . what happens now?'

'Could we – is it possible we could just love one another, Val?'

His voice was a thread. 'I don't know. I don't know anything, Alice.'

She gripped his hand between hers. 'Have I brought you to this, my dear? You, who know so much.'

'I don't know anything any more,' he repeated.

'You know you love me. You know now that I love you. What more is there?'

He tried to tell her about his father; about her mother; about Hattie and the baby. 'I am tainted with this madness, Alice,' he said in the tiny whisper. 'His blood runs in my veins.'

Alice was appalled. While she and Joe had visited Eden and attained some kind of catharsis, her whole family had been torn apart. She took Val's head on to her shoulder and closed her eyes, trying to hold on to the consolation of living entirely in the present.

She murmured into his ear, 'Listen, my dearest husband. Your soul, your spirit, the real Valentine Ryecroft, is nothing to do with this – this madness. You are able – more than anyone I know – to put yourself into other shoes. To understand people and things right outside your own self. And that is what matters. Maybe you have inherited that from your mother. I do not know. But ultimately it is what counts.' She held his fair head tenderly. 'Val, I love you. I have loved you for a long time and not known it. You are telling me that terrible things have happened . . . I am not saying they do not matter. Of course they do. But together we can do something, help to make them better.'

She felt his free arm creep around her waist and hold her fast.

* * *

Reggie seemed calmer when Dorothy arrived. She sat by his bed with the high cot sides and tried not to look at the restraining webbing that fastened his wrists to the bed frame. He could lift his hands high enough to rub his head, blow his nose, scrub at his eyes like a child, even to take her hand. He did not speak, but his gaze, which had flashed from side to side and so far up to the ceiling that his eyes seemed almost lost inside his head, settled on her face and stayed there for the duration of her visit.

Dorothy kept smiling at him and occasionally she would say something. The staff, hovering close, could not hear the words, but saw that they had a good effect on the patient.

'I knew what you were like, Reggie. That is why I never blamed you. Believe that, please. I was older than you and I thought I could change you. I saw the goodness in you and turned a blind eye to . . . other things.' She looked down at the hand in hers. It was mottled like an old man's, yet he was only fifty-three. She would be sixty next year. Yes, she should have known better.

She leaned closer. 'Poor Enid. Poor Doffie. You knew I loved Doffie as if she were the sister I never had. Was that why you wanted to hurt her?'

His eyes were very close to hers. They seemed colourless; if they were indeed windows to the soul, it would be tempting to conclude he was soulless. And yet . . . She tried to see it all from his angle entirely, excluding everyone else. She imagined him leaving his home in Chalford, where he had been a precious, only child. Going to the station house at Leadon. The sheer charisma of old Will Pettiford and the respect accorded to him by everyone he knew. And the family: the wilful, amoral Mitzie, who attracted him with her very wantonness – and in the end simply disappeared. Ted, younger, better-looking, bringing home someone who was the exact opposite of Mitzie; someone good and kind and funny and beautiful . . . Doffie. Dorothy had never been under any illusion that Reggie had loved her; he had admired her for her intellect and the fact that she was a 'lady'. He had been delighted when she obviously returned the admiration. He could not wait to marry her, set up house, boast about his clever wife. And then, when she turned out to be not in the least like the warm and beautiful Doffie, he had set about making her his – his what? His slave? No, not that. Yet something very like. She had been a virgin, no housewife, she had learned to cook and clean somehow, but he made it clear that she was never very satisfactory in any department. She recalled various rituals designed to teach her how to do her duties and her face warmed, even now, with shame.

And then, painfully, she had produced Val and then Hester, and there were some years of respite. Val had her intellect, Hester had her patrician looks, which unexpectedly turned to beauty. At last, Reggie had done better than the Pettifords. Alice was a pale little thing, not terribly bright.

He justified his insatiable sexual appetite by insisting on trying for a really big family, but Dorothy was well into her forties by then and very much weakened by the births. So he began to punish her.

And then Val went, and Hester too. And Ted was obviously doing very well at work. And there were other things, things that Dorothy would probably never fully understand: something to do with Hattie Pettiford; something to do with work; something to do with Mitzie. And it had all piled up and up and up, until Reggie could take no more.

Dorothy sighed. Perhaps she could begin to understand simply because she had lived with him for so long. She leaned over him further and spoke slowly, trying to sound logical.

'In that case, Reggie dear, it was my fault as well, was it not?' His hands jerked upwards. She straightened quickly, afraid to admit even to herself that he could be reaching for her throat. 'Listen, Reggie. Listen properly, don't think of anything else but what I am saying. I will take your guilt, my dear. You need never think of it again. It has already gone from you and is mine. Do you understand? I am giving you a new start, a new life. As from now – *now*, this very minute, you are innocent again.' She waited, but he gave no indication of having understood. After a while, she leaned towards him again and said, 'Just lie here, clear your mind entirely. The only thing you need to know is that you are my husband and I am responsible for everything that has happened.'

She released his hand with difficulty; at one point she had to prise his thumb loose from her palm. A male nurse who looked like a boxer held Reggie's shackled hands down while she kissed his forehead. She leaned on the cot and smiled.

'Goodbye, Reggie. I will visit whenever you wish. Rest peacefully.'

It was only when she had left the ward that she

realized how close she had come to the RIP – rest in peace – seen on most Victorian tombstones. Poor Reggie. How much easier it would have been for him had he died beneath Duggie Marsden's frying pan. She smiled slightly. She must remember to tell Val and Alice that particular thought. It had a kind of black humour.

During the next week, while Duggie Marsden shuttled between Newport, Gloucester and Lypiatt Bottom, was eventually acknowledged as 'a bit of a bloody hero' by a reluctant Ted and discovered he no longer had any trouble with his feet, while a frantic and grieving Percy drove the old Lanchester between Leckhampton, Cheltenham hospital and Newport, trying to look after his mother, his wife and his sister, Val and Alice moved into the house at Lypiatt and looked after Gran.

In spite of everything that had happened and was still happening, it was a time of great happiness for them. Duggie had given Val compassionate leave, and during the ten days that Doffie spent in hospital with Ted never far from her bedside, they savoured the joy of knowing each other completely. Alice had discovered long ago that Val could be practical – almost house-wifely – in the home. Now she saw how easily he coped with almost any domestic problem that cropped up. He moved the utility rexine three-piece suite to one side of the little-used sitting room and brought down Gran's bed so that she could be part of everyday life again. Between them they carried Gran down. To Alice's surprise, she was delighted with the arrangement.

For a time, Gran was deeply suspicious of Val. Alice tackled her about it as she was making her bed one morning. 'He's not a bit like his father, you know, Gran.' She smoothed the patchwork counterpane so beloved by Gran. 'He's been a victim for so long. You must see that.'

Gran, already drowsy from being washed and combed and 'pickled about', as she put it, said in her new slurred voice, 'I got to think of him as Hattie's brother, not Reggie Ryecroft's son.'

Alice might well have thought this an odd remark at one time. Now nothing struck her as odd. She kissed the top of Gran's head and began the difficult task of levering her back into bed. 'That's right, Gran,' she panted, plumping pillows and trying to ignore the groans of pain as the arthritic body was settled into place.

Alice had spoken to Joe of a different sort of happiness; she had assumed that the intensity she had known with Joe was gone for ever. But during those ten days alone with Val – even with Gran they were alone, maybe in the middle of a crowd they would be alone too – she began to understand that the love she and Val had was growing inexorably into something enormous, breathtaking. She said to him one morning as they were washing up the breakfast things, 'It's silly to be surprised by what is happening to us, Val. After all, it was pretty well perfect that time at the Pumpkin Coach.'

He said, 'Actually, Alice, I am not surprised a bit by what is happening to us. That's probably the reason I was so angry with you when you decided that my ghastly "experiment" was not to be repeated.' He came behind her and nuzzled her neck. 'Sorry, darling. I know you were right to put a stop to it then and there.'

She twisted her head to kiss him. 'It was Joe, you see. I always thought the experiment was for Joe.'

He had never asked her what had happened between her and Joe at the Pumpkin Coach, and he did not ask her now. But as he continued to kiss her, she held her dripping hands well away from their bodies, as if she might be going to take flight at any moment, and whispered, 'You know that Joe and I . . . it's finished. You do know that, don't you?'

He lifted his head and looked at her. Her hair was damp with the steam from the washing up, her eyes so blue he could have drowned in them.

He said, 'All I know is that this is real life, my darling. This is what I wanted and I did not even know it was what I wanted. Thank you.' He kissed her and murmured again, 'Thank you.'

From the sitting room, Gran's voice was raised querulously. 'Alice! I told you I wanted the commode! When are you going to come and put me on the commode? Alice!'

Alice smiled, remembering something from a long time ago.

'Dear Val. You were not my first love, darling. But you are my last.' She waited for him to smile back at her and ask her where on earth she'd got that one. But he did not. He just went on looking into her eyes.

And then it happened. She was looking back at him, waiting for that answering smile, and suddenly she could not look away . . .

* * *

473

Hester heard of all that was happening to her family and felt – not left out, exactly, but somehow isolated. She had had to take part in so many of her father's little displays of power back in Deanery Close, and had been thankful to escape from them. But this was different. Her father was now in an insane asylum and she should be there with the others to begin a new life.

Since that dreadful first-year holiday in Provence, Hester had steadfastly refused to sleep with Richard Tibbolt and it had nearly driven him crazy. Hermione Tibbolt spent more and more time in the Provençal home, where she had installed one of her hungry artist friends. Richard had taken the children out there once and once only. The artist was a woman, and though Richard had always imagined that he was broad-minded, he discovered this was not the case. He told himself he was protecting his children. Meanwhile, in spite of Nanny, he was busy looking after Tobias and Evadne. Life was not easy.

He wanted Hester more than ever. He bombarded her with flowers and presents, all of which she accepted. But if he imagined her acceptance was a sign that she was softening, he was quite wrong. She was a contradictory mixture of innocence and sheer calculation. He should have understood that when she accepted the honeymoon suite for Val and Alice last winter. Even when he installed her in a flat in Clifton, she saw no reason to succumb to his pleadings. He snapped finally and told her he expected something in return for her board and lodging.

She looked at him for a moment, not understanding. Then her beautiful eyes opened wide and she began to laugh. 'You're right – I'm a kept woman, aren't I?' He watched her laughing. She still wore her hair in a thick dark plait; with her patrician features, she was a classical beauty and did not know it. Or did she? He grabbed her and tried to kiss her and they wrestled for a while.

She said, 'Richard, I have made myself clear – I have been honest with you, have I not? If you insist on – on payment, then I will leave here and we need not see each other again. Is that what you want?'

'You know it is not,' he said miserably.

'Well then . . .' She spread her hands.

But when Hester read the letters from home and began to piece together what had happened from Val's vivid account, Dorothy's guarded one and Alice's fervid assurances that she would make Val happy, Hester began to want something more. With her father out of the way, it seemed to her that the Pettifords and the Ryecrofts had crossed the divide and had become one – but not with her. Because she had sent that wretched letter to Alice, she was no longer part of the Pettiford family. Neither Alice nor Val had suggested she should join them to live their dream of being a family. And Uncle Ted – the wonderful Uncle Ted – he did not write. No one sent their love to her. She thought a great deal about it. A common denominator; that was what she needed. A place, an experience they all shared. It must be . . . yes, it was – the Pumpkin Coach.

She telephoned Richard.

'Back before the Great War,' she began, 'one of the directors of the Great Western Railway arranged for this railway coach to be shunted on to one of the colliery lines in the Forest of Dean. It was a sort of love nest. It's always been a love nest, especially for our family. And I was wondering . . . whether you and I could try to find it.'

THE END

FIVE FARTHINGS
by Susan Sallis

Jess Tavener would have said that her life in a Somerset market town, with her husband Matt and their small daughter Lucy, was happy and settled. The recent death of her beloved father casts the only shadow on their domestic tranquillity. Then the discovery of a drawing of her father amongst Matt's belongings, together with another sketch of someone totally unexpected, makes Jess realise that her family and friends have aspects to their past which, as they are gradually revealed, affect all their lives. She is to experience heartbreak and loss before she can begin to reach out to a new, and different, kind of happiness.

Another heartwarming novel from this greatly loved bestselling author, which explores the secrets which lie beneath the seemingly peaceful surface of a small country town.

0 552 15050 9

LYDIA FIELDING
by Susan Sallis

When Lydia celebrated her coming of age, the whole of her Exmoor village celebrated with her. Two men attracted her interest that night: handsome, ambitious Gus Pascoe, who coveted the land her father farmed; and Wesley Peters, brought up as a strict Methodist, whose seemingly upright religious family hid a terrible secret.

Wesley wanted only to protect and cherish Lydia, but when his sister became the scandal of the neighbourhood and was forced to marry Lydia's brother, Alan, a bitterness grew up between the two families which threatened to keep Lydia and Wesley apart forever. In despair Lydia fled to Bristol, where at last she could free herself from the tragedy and heartbreak of her past life.

0 552 15017 7

TIME OF ARRIVAL
by Susan Sallis

It is 1951, and on a fine spring morning the 8.45 from
Bristol to Paddington is preparing to leave. Albert, the
driver, says goodbye to his wife with mixed feelings.
Their seeming inability to have a child has over-
shadowed their happy marriage. Jenny, clumsy but
loveable, longs to make a success of her job in the
restaurant car, but her tendency to get things wrong
soon attracts the interest of Marvin, the steward. The
passengers – some regulars on the line, others making
a rare visit to London – settle down for the journey.
Some talk and get to know each other, some while away
the journey working or sleeping. But as they near their
destination, disaster strikes.

In an instant, lives are changed and everyday concerns
become trivial. In this dramatic new novel, bestselling
author Susan Sallis relates how love and friendship
blossom when strangers are brought together by tragedy.

0552 14903 9

A SELECTED LIST OF FINE NOVELS
AVAILABLE FROM CORGI BOOKS

15034 7	THE ROWAN TREE	*Iris Gower*	£5.99
15066 5	TROUBLE IN PARADISE	*Pip Granger*	£5.99
14537 8	APPLE BLOSSOM TIME	*Kathryn Haig*	£5.99
15033 9	CHANDLERS GREEN	*Ruth Hamilton*	£5.99
14820 2	THE TAVERNERS' PLACE	*Caroline Harvey*	£5.99
15045 2	THOSE IN PERIL	*Margaret Mahyew*	£6.99
15152 1	THE SHADOW CATCHER	*Michelle Paver*	£6.99
15141 6	THE APPLE TREE	*Elvi Rhodes*	£5.99
15017 7	LYDIA FIELDING	*Susan Sallis*	£5.99
12375 7	A SCATTERING OF DAISIES	*Susan Sallis*	£5.99
12579 2	THE DAFFODILS OF NEWENT	*Susan Sallis*	£5.99
12880 5	BLUEBELL WINDOWS	*Susan Sallis*	£5.99
13136 9	ROSEMARY FOR REMEMBRANCE	*Susan Sallis*	£6.99
13756 1	AN ORDINARY WOMAN	*Susan Sallis*	£5.99
13934 3	DAUGHTERS OF THE MOON	*Susan Sallis*	£6.99
13346 9	SUMMER VISITORS	*Susan Sallis*	£5.99
13545 3	BY SUN AND CANDLELIGHT	*Susan Sallis*	£5.99
14162 3	SWEETER THAN WINE	*Susan Sallis*	£4.99
14318 9	WATER UNDER THE BRIDGE	*Susan Sallis*	£5.99
14466 5	TOUCHED BY ANGELS	*Susan Sallis*	£5.99
14549 1	CHOICES	*Susan Sallis*	£5.99
14636 6	COME RAIN OR SHINE	*Susan Sallis*	£5.99
14671 4	THE KEYS TO THE GARDEN	*Susan Sallis*	£5.99
14747 8	THE APPLE BARREL	*Susan Sallis*	£5.99
14867 9	SEA OF DREAMS	*Susan Sallis*	£5.99
14903 9	TIME OF ARRIVAL	*Susan Sallis*	£5.99
15050 9	FIVE FARTHINGS	*Susan Sallis*	£6.99
15138 6	FAMILY FORTUNES	*Mary Jane Staples*	£5.99
15062 2	THE CHILDREN'S HOUR	*Marcia Willett*	£6.99
15032 0	FAR FROM HOME	*Valerie Wood*	£5.99